Blockchain Exploit

By

James Marinero

Blockchain Exploit

Sveta Kovacs is a sociopathic Ukrainian expert in blockchain technology with a Ph.D in cryptography. Her murky hacking past and many online scams have financed her Bitcoin mining operation in Portugal.

Now she has found a way to exploit a weakness in blockchain technology and if she succeeds there are billions of dollars at her disposal.

The new Russian CryptoRuble is threatened and the GRU are on Kovacs's tail. Ex-Royal Marine anti-hero Steve Baldwin is still recovering from the recent loss of his wife, an MI6 officer, and is guarding Kovacs as a favor to an old friend.

An old enemy appears in the mix after MI6 has duped the CIA. But what is the terrorist's role? Is it coincidence?

Geo-politics and international finance are never simple and in the new world of blockchain and cryptocurrencies the pressure points are moving.

Fortunes are locked up in cryptowallets.
Can they be cracked?

Baldwin cannot move with the times, but he can fight back against those who control him and those who threaten him.

Baldwin has the chance to avenge his wife's death, but he is being manipulated by MI6. Again.

Double-dealing multiplies as events move to a climax in Spain.

Who can he trust?

Can he stop another terrorist catastrophe?

Also by James Marinero

Fiction:

Gate of Tears

The Maghreb Trilogy

Sicilian Channel (Book 1)
Sword of Allah (Book 2)
Cause of All Causes (Book 3)

Non Fiction:

Susan's Brother

All are available online for Amazon devices and all e-readers, and in paperback from your local bookstore.

Blockchain Exploit

Published by Wavecrest Publications
3 Murray Street, Llanelli
Carmarthenshire, SA15 1AQ, UK
www.wavecrestpublications.com

First Edition 2021

ISBN-13: 978-0-9956410-8-2
Amazon paperback version

Cover Artwork Credits:
Soldier: Image by Amaynut from Pixabay
Bitcoin CPU: Image by Aaron Olson from Pixabay
Computer code text: Image by xresch from Pixabay
Bitcoin Image on rear cover: Image by Sinisa Maric from Pixabay

Design by projectpdq.com

For Freddie

Who once asked me to explain what cryptocurrency is.

I've tried.

*

Acknowledgments

My thanks to all those writers who over so many years have given me so much pleasure and taught me so much about writing.

And, as always, to Rosy for her sharp editorial eye, valuable criticism, encouragement and support.

Blockchain

Blockchain 'technology' was invented by Satoshi Nakamoto in 2008 for use in the cryptocurrency Bitcoin, as its public transaction ledger. The invention of the blockchain for bitcoin made it the first digital currency to solve the double spending problem without the need of a trusted authority or central server. – Wikipedia

Satoshi Nakamoto is the pseudonym of the elusive inventor whose real identity has never been formally disclosed.

Salus

Salus (Latin: salus, "safety", "salvation", "welfare") was the Roman goddess of safety and well-being of both the individual and the state.

Main Characters & Operations

Svetlana Ponomarenko aliases
Sveta Kovacs
Svetlana Goraya
Borbola Goraya
Clarisse Duval
Clarisse Beauchamp

MI6 Characters
'C' – Henry Brewell
'M' – Emmet Macsen
Joshua Packard – Cyber Terrorism Desk
Caspar Conlon – Global Terrorism Desk
'Mad Hatter' – Steve Baldwin
'Telion' – J C Stone, Case Officer
'Barbary' – John Colville, Senior Case Officer

Other Characters
Boromir - Abu ben-Zhair, aka Ashraf Ibrahim. Terrorist

US Secretary of State for Foreign Affairs – John Scholes
Director of Central Intelligence Agency – James Bartolucci

Prince Khalifa ibn Abu Bakr of Saudi Arabia
Prince Abdallah Yaziz of Morocco
King Abdelhafid of Morocco

MI6 Operations
Operation Pistole
Operation Bilbo
Operation Looking Glass
Operation Elevator

Russian Operations & Agents
'Skopa' – Osprey, an agent in London
Operation 'Stervyatnik' - Vulture

Prologue

It was 2014 and in the only renovated, air-conditioned bunker Svetlana Ponomarkenko turned to the mission commander of the black operation.

"I am ready to proceed, on your command Lieutenant General. The link is ready to be activated."

Lieutenant General Danylo Kravets, head of the Ukrainian Rocket and Artillery Troop 3, looked at the radar displays and target designators. This would at least be some payback for more than 6,500 cyber attacks that the Russians had mounted against the Ukraine, including the losses of huge numbers of Ukrainian D-30 Howitzers as a result of an infected Android app the artillery used for aiming. Revenge would be sweet.

"Master Sergeant, confirm the targets as Foxtrot-One, Two and Three."

"Yes Sir."

Master Sergeant Alexei Hryhoruk moved the trackball and the designators turned red over the Russian Foxtrot CAP as he right-clicked on the targets. Foxtrot 3 was tail-end Charlie of the 3 plane Russian combat air patrol over Donestk in what had been Eastern Ukraine and was now being bitterly fought over. The Russian CAP had strayed – deliberately - into what was still, in international law, Ukrainian airspace. General Kravets turned to the missile controller. "Targets designated Sir."

"How long will the guidance radar be hot for?"

"Until the target is locked on to by the missile's own on-board radar – depending on range three to eight seconds after launch, Lieutenant General. Then the Russians usually move the radar unit immediately, to avoid any anti-radar missiles – not that they would expect any from one of their own fighters."

"Good. Enable the link *now*, Lieutenant."

"Link enabled Sir" Svetlana replied.

The software module that Ukrainian Lieutenant Svetlana Ponomarenko had spent five months developing went live. It opened an encrypted tunnel via a narrow-band microwave link to a fiber optic link. The short fiber optic cable was tapped into the Russian air-defense missile system command and control hub beyond the front line in Donetsk. The tap had been installed by Ukrainian Special Forces just five days previously. It would soon be found by the

Russians, but no matter, its purpose would have been served. That comms tap then utilized the Russians' own microwave link over their integrated air-defense system to the mobile missile unit.

Tension mounted in the secret Ukrainian black ops bunker.

"Software link is live for firing, General."

"Thank you Lieutenant. Master Sergeant, go hot and fire when ready."

*

One

The bar was at the back of the town of Olhaõ on Portugal's Algarve. It was well away from the tourist area on the seafront where Baldwin had left his dinghy padlocked at the dinghy dock in the marina. *Rubaiyat*, his yacht, was safely at anchor in the channel off the island of Culatra a couple of miles away across the narrow channels and salt marshes. Rebuilding was under way on the island – once a very popular tourist destination - following the tsunami which had inundated the low coastal island chain in the Algarve following the Islamist terrorist catastrophe in the Canary Islands.

The ferry services from the outlying islands were just starting to get organized again. The power of the tsunami had not been enough to seriously damage the town of Olhaõ itself - much of the wavetrain's energy having been dissipated on the low islands and marshes which stretched a couple of miles south from the town.

Less than ten miles away the airport, sitting next to the marshes in the town of Faro – which had been inundated - was back in business again as huge tranches of EU money poured in to the region.

Baldwin headed for the bar.

*

Three months earlier he had been miserable in the drizzle as he walked back to the marina in Marina Bay, Gibraltar, passing the security box at the stern of the floating hotel casino named *Sunborn Gibraltar*.

"Steve old mate, where have you been? You look rough as hell."

"Hi Liam. I went away for a spell."

"Anywhere interesting?"

"Not really, just along the Spanish coast."

"So, where is your beautiful lady today then?"

"She's dead."

"Dead?"

"Yes Liam, dead."

"Oh, Christ in Heaven, I'm so sorry, Steve. Are you sure, I mean – oh fuck I don't know what to say."

"There's nothing you can say."

"I didn't know. That's a such bloody shock. How?" The look of pain on Liam's face betrayed his genuine emotion.

“No reason you should have. It was a car accident in Spain. I don’t want to talk about it.”

“When is the funeral, I’d like to send flowers – even attend if I can.”

“It’s all over Liam. Nothing more to do.”

The bit about travel along the Spanish coast was true but not one per cent of the full story. Steve didn’t say that Ellie’s body had been burned to ashes by US Seals in Algeria - burned in a Mercedes belonging to the terrorist who had triggered a tsunami a few weeks before.

“Blimey. The world is going to hell in a handcart. A nuclear bomb in the Canaries, a tsunami in the Atlantic, Israel lining up to attack Iran and now it looks like war in Korea. And now Ellie. Jesus Christ, what a shock. Why didn’t you call me?”

“What for Liam? It wouldn’t change a thing would it? Not a fucking thing. So just can it, right!”

“Hey, steady mate. I’m just trying to help, you know,”

“Yes, sorry, yes, I know you are, but you can’t. No one can help. Things are a bit tough right now.”

“Tell you what, let’s get really tanked tonight. It always helps to talk – remember, I was once a squaddie too.”

“Thanks Liam, but I need to be alone for a while.”

“Fair enough, mate, but drinking alone is not a good idea. God knows, I should know.”

“I’ve had plenty of practice. Anyway, I’ll be moving on soon - I’m going to take *Rubaiyat* round the coast, maybe to Cadiz or up to the Algarve. Spend a few months up that way, sorting myself out. I’ve had enough of Gib, too many bad memories.”

“I don’t know what it’ll be like up there – the Algarve got hit by the tsunami.”

“Did it? I haven’t seen the news for a couple of days.”

“Yeh, along the low lying bits. It washed out Faro airport. They were expecting a major disaster in the US too, but it seems they got off relatively lightly. Fucking terrorists. Can’t predict what’ll be next can you?”

“I guess not.”

“Well, if you need some crew Steve, I’m right here mate. You know I can do it after we sailed her up from Morocco.”

“Yeh. I know you can and thanks again, but I’ve got to get used to handling *Rubaiyat* myself.”

"OK, mate. Well you know where I am – you've got my phone numbers and email address. I'm on WhatsApp too."

"Thanks, Liam I'll see you around."

Baldwin had met Liam a few weeks before when he had arrived in Gibraltar on an assignment – another job that Six had pushed him into. Steve had recognized Liam's tattoos – he had been in the Parachute Regiment. The guy seemed solid enough and had helped him sail his new boat, *Rubaiyat* across from Morocco, with Ellie. The pain of the memory hit him as he turned and headed down the quay to *Rubaiyat.* The sooner he was away from Gib the better it would be all round. Then he'd continue his serious drinking alone.

He felt a vibration in his patch pocket - the smartphone. He pulled it out and looked at it – it could only be Barbary, that bastard from MI6. He dropped the Six phone into the water at the quayside and walked on, but as he approached *Rubaiyat* he could see a man waiting, sitting on a mooring bollard. The man was not dressed as a yachtsman or a tourist, but smart casual in the modern business way, albeit with French cuffs over his wrist. He was pale, so not local he realized. As Steve approached, the man stood up confidently, with an air of self-assurance typical of most military or ex-military personnel. Steve ignored the proffered handshake.

"Steven Baldwin?"

"Who says?"

"I do. You match the description and the picture."

The man held out the picture to Steve who ignored it.

"I've told you guys a million times to fuck off and leave me alone."

"Mr Baldwin, I do not know who you are referring to. I am here on behalf of a London legal firm, Konstanz and Young, to deliver – I have been told – good news. That is all I know. Perhaps you should read this letter before jumping to any conclusions."

He held out a padded envelope. Steve could see that it was addressed to Mr Steven Baldwin.

"Before I read anything, tell me how you found me?"

"Mr Baldwin, my name is David Johnstone. I am a private investigator retained by this legal firm - and others – to locate missing people. Here is my card."

"No-one is missing me" Steve said ignoring the card.

"A poor choice of words in your case then, for which I apologize."

"How did you find me? No-one knows where I am."

"I have my methods Mr Baldwin, which I do not discuss with anyone. Sometimes I have to deliver bad news, sometimes good news and, sometimes, legal writs."

Steve backed away a couple of steps, though he was not expecting any writ. But you never knew, where Six was concerned.

"So how do I know that this is not a writ?"

"Because if it was I can assure you that it would already be in your hands."

Grudgingly, Steve took the envelope and pulled the perforated strip. Inside was another white envelope with a heavy woven texture. It was embossed with a crest and the words 'Konstanz & Young'.

"Mr Baldwin, I will leave you in peace to digest the contents and then return, tomorrow at the same time, when we can discuss any arrangements that have to be made."

Steve looked at him and said nothing as he stepped over the guardrails on to *Rubaiyat* and unlocked the hatch to go below. He knew that the only way he could have been traced was via the internet – and he only ever used that to access his UK bank. Or, someone at Six had leaked his location – the bastards always seemed to know where he was. At least he'd dumped their phone now.

Down below in the cabin, *Rubaiyat* was hot and smelled musty, even though Steve had been away less than a month – most of it drinking his way along the Spanish coast from the US base at Rota, town to town, taxi by taxi, trying to forget Ellie and the terrible events in Algeria and triggered a disaster that had hit hard many of the countries bordering the North Atlantic.

Steve threw the envelope and packet on to the chart table and opened the saloon deck hatches to let the cool morning air blow through. The drizzle had stopped and the sun was breaking out. The clock showed a little after 11 am as he pulled out the bottle of Glenlivet from the drinks cabinet and poured himself a few fingers – a brightener he called it, but the brightness never seemed to last for long these days. Then, he'd need another. There was still ice in the freezer and he added a couple of cubes before sinking half of it in one shot.

Then he sat at the chart table and picked up the white envelope, looked at it and put it down again as he reached for the bottle. Just one more, he thought. And then he stopped.

"Help me Steve, help me" she shouted at him. He tightened the tourniquet and she faded from view as he woke up, soaked with sweat.

The nightmare had returned.

Ellie, bleeding from the wound to her femoral artery, and him trying to slow the blood loss near to the entrance to ben-Zhair's bunker in the hills of Algeria. The only way to avoid the nightmare required a bottle of whisky before sleep and he had known he could not go on in that way. Now the nightmare was with him every night and sometimes even during the day.

He switched on the light and looked at the clock on the bulkhead above his berth in *Rubaiyat.* 03:30. He rolled out of his berth and headed to the galley where he put the kettle to boil.

The white envelope was visible on the chart table and, without reason, he feared what it might contain. He made a cup of tea – black – as he hadn't got round to buying any milk or provisions -and stared at the envelope. He was tired - but not hungover – and the envelope seemed to pulse malevolently in the pre-dawn half-light. 'Get a grip' he told himself and reached for it, wondering where the last eighteen hours had gone.

*

Two

It was 1998, in Kiev, the capital city of the Ukraine. Svetlana Ponomarenko was a quiet, introverted child whose father worked as a school janitor and her mother as a cleaner at the same junior school in the Solomianka *raion* of Kiev in the Ukraine. They were simple folk and expected little of Svetlana, their only child.

Her parents recognized that she was intelligent, and by the age of six had read all the few books (mostly tattered copies of Russian Classical literature left to them by an aunt) in their bleak sixth floor apartment in the filthy block on General Tupikov Street.

Magazines occasionally appeared in the apartment – they had been 'lent' to her she said, though her parents did not believe her and her father's beatings elicited no further information - she kept the secret of her thefts, as she kept many other secrets. Her teachers saw in her a quickness with mental arithmetic and vocabulary at a very early age. She challenged them with penetrating questions typical of a much older child of high intellectual ability. One or two teachers imagined that they saw something darker, hidden from the world most of the time and she was the subject of regular discussion in the teachers' common room.

Her aspirations increased way beyond those of a normal child of her age, as did the interest of her teachers and at the age of seven she was transferred to the Special School 159 in the same *raion* of Kiev. Among the other gifted students in the Special School her intellect continued to blossom and she showed an aptitude for IT – a subject which was just being introduced to the curriculum.

By the age of eight her father's drunken attentions had hardened her both mentally and physically, but in addition she had learned about the power of knowledge to be obtained from books - and the new world of the internet. That knowledge enriched her – both in the way she could physically deal with her contemporaries and in how she understood herself. Svetlana (Sveta to her family) was also marked out by her classmates as too clever by half. Bullying had started at an early age but stopped very quickly when she showed that she could mix it with the roughest of them after almost completely severing one boy's left ear with her teeth.

As she matured further towards her eleventh year her father's drunken interference worsened and her mother, aware of the problem but unable to cope with it, started a downward spiral fueled by the cheapest vodka. There could be few family secrets in a tiny two room apartment.

On the evening of her eleventh birthday, a Wednesday, she was lying on her curtained-off bed when she heard her father come in to the apartment. She glanced at her battered Mickey Mouse alarm clock which had once been her mother's - and illegal at that time as a symbol of American cultural imperialism. 6.30 pm. It was snowing heavily outside and much too cold for her to be out of doors. She put her book to one side. Her father would be drunk by now and her mother would not return from her cleaning job for at least another hour.

"Sveta, I have a birthday present for you, it's a secret."

She knew all about his secrets and his depravity, but she had promised herself her own birthday treat.

Her father pushed the curtain aside and entered her space.

"I will make it very special tonight!"

"Papa, I do not want your birthday present."

"Shut up and get ready, you know what to do." His breath was laden with fumes of vodka mixed with garlic from *kolbasa* sausage, sickening her as she lay on her back. Sveta had rehearsed the moment many times in her mind as she had cried herself asleep after his attentions. She had prepared carefully for this moment. You could learn anything online. She had learned that her father's name – and her own - Ponomarenko, meant 'Priest'. Some joke, she thought, as she prepared herself for pain.

Less than two minutes later the knife went into his back as he straddled her.

She knew exactly where the knife tip should enter and the angle at which it would do the most severe and rapid damage. What she had not planned for was that her dear mother Anya would tell the police that she herself had committed the murder of her husband.

In the circumstances, her mother was given a probationary sentence and stopped drinking. Sveta was given counseling. The counseling had little effect because she hadn't needed it. She had rationalized and dealt with the situation and consequences over many months in advance of the act. She believed that the hatred for her father which she had carefully cultivated and nurtured in the secret place in her mind would make her immune to any emotional or psychological problems. She was wrong.

The effects showed themselves in different ways and her ability to form friendships in school declined. Teachers noticed her increasing social distance from other students but her intellectual development did not appear to have been damaged. She never laughed or joked in school. And she was developing in other ways too. Although not tall compared to her peers, her emerging beauty dominated the classroom, with the boys showing considerable interest – swiftly rebuffed- and the girls showing jealousy – which she soon resolved with fights in the toilets. She seemed to wear an air of mystery like a cloak and the other students learned to keep a healthy distance.

Despite the inability of her mother to provide her with any financial support, she found ways – mostly illegal – to acquire fashionable clothes and all the other accoutrements that teenage girls craved – including a smartphone and a laptop. She had no innate desire for such things but realized that they were tools she could use to improve her future. In an effort to get free airtime and web access for her phone and laptop, she started to hack the network systems. The technology absorbed her completely and enabled her to escape into a world of intellectual challenge.

Sveta's IQ was measured as the highest in the school during every year that she attended, before being given, at the unusually early age of 15, a place in Ukraine's National Technical University to study Information Technology.

By the age of 17 in 2015 she was running a small software company and developed a Ukrainian-specific meld of the Facebook and Twitter Apps. This app was virtually hacker proof and was adopted by the Ukrainian armed forces during the war with the Russian proxy army in the Donetsk and Luhansk *oblasts* as Russia sought to annex the Crimea and protect its access to its Black Sea naval bases.

Conscription caught up with her and she served her year with the Ukrainian Ground Forces. The app had brought her to the notice of a Lieutenant General, Danylo Kravets, who had been tasked with setting up a cyber-warfare unit for the Ground Forces. She went straight into the unit, commissioned as a Second Lieutenant.

By the age of 21 she had a Ph.D. in Cryptography from the world-ranked Technical University, a wide network of useful acquaintances (but no friends), a private side-line in online credit card harvesting, and a lover high in the Ukrainian Ground Forces.

*

Deep under a tor near the village of Upper Hrabivnytsia in the Ukrainian Carpathian Mountains lies a network of tunnels and bunkers. These had formed part of the Ukrainian Árpád defensive line in 1939 but after overrunning them during their invasion during World War 2 the Germans had extended and improved the complex. Sixty years later one bunker had been cleared but other parts were rumored to still hold German booby-traps. Inquisitive eyes stayed well away, the area ringed with dire warnings of uncleared minefields and booby traps.

"Targets designated Sir."

"How long will the guidance radar be hot for?"

"Until the target is locked on to by the missile's own on-board radar – depending on range three to eight seconds after launch, Lieutenant General. Then the Russians usually move the radar unit immediately, to avoid any anti-radar missiles – not that they would expect any from one of their own fighters."

"Good. Enable the link *now*, Lieutenant."

"Link enabled Sir" Svetlana replied.

The software module that Ukrainian Lieutenant Svetlana Ponomarenko had spent five months developing went live. It opened an encrypted tunnel via a narrow-band microwave link to a fiber optic link. The short fiber optic cable was tapped into the Russian air-defense missile system command and control hub beyond the front line in Donetsk. The tap had been installed by Ukrainian Special Forces just five days previously. It would soon be found by the Russians, but no matter, its purpose would have been served. That comms tap then utilized the Russians' own microwave link over their integrated air-defense system to the mobile missile unit.

Tension mounted in the secret Ukrainian black ops bunker.

"Software link is live for firing, General."

"Master Sergeant, go hot and fire when ready."

Beyond the front line in Donetsk there was a coffee round underway. The relaxed vigilance quickly turned to alarm in the missile control vehicle which Svetlana had hacked into. The controllers of the Buk 332 missile battery of the Russian 53rd Anti-Aircraft Rocket Brigade saw their radar light up with one of their own planes targeted. The battery commander looked on in disbelief as he heard the warning alarm from the multiple launch pod. It automatically adjusted its azimuth and elevation to acquire the target and went hot and the lock-on chime sounded clear as a bell in the control vehicle.

Then the alarm sound changed its pitch and warbled. The first of the four Buk 9K/37 missiles (NATO reporting name SA-11 Gadfly) on the TELAR (transport erector launcher and radar) went airborne with an ear-splitting roar. Although obsolete for the key defensive roles within Mother Russia, these Gadflies were still effective against many targets. Two other missiles followed in quick succession.

The first missile acquired and rode the radar beam towards Foxtrot-3, an aging Sukhoi-27 fighter as targeted by Ukrainian Lieutenant General Kravets. Within two seconds the missile's own on-board radar had locked on. The range was less than five miles. The missile issued its IFF – electronic friend or foe - interrogation and the Sukhoi's electronics warfare package squawked back FRIEND – but it was ignored due to another clever bug that Sveta had uploaded into the air-defense system. There was an unfortunate consequence as the pilot managed to evade the missile.

A non-cooperative threat classification system was installed on the missile, relying on analysis of returned radar signals to automatically identify and distinguish civilian aircraft from potential military targets in the absence of an IFF response.

Software isn't provably perfect and it happened that almost directly in the missile's line of sight of Foxtrot-3 at that instant, but 20 miles to the northwest was Japan Airlines Flight JL6818, just outside the Gadfly's nominal operational range – but closing. The missile targeting system acquired the airliner.

The airliner, a Boeing 777-200ER, was on a scheduled passenger flight from Schiphol airport in Amsterdam to Tokyo, via Dubai, with 272 passengers and 15 crew aboard.

Panic was controlled in the missile command vehicle, but it compounded when the self-destruct command had no effect on the missile and the anti-aircraft control team watched the radar for the final few seconds as the missile continued to arrow to the very edge of its nominal range as the airliner continued to get nearer. Then its proximity fuse activated and the explosion severely damaged the starboard engine and its mounting on the airliner. The wing shuddered and warped and with two seconds ripped off the plane.

Within two minutes all aboard were dead as the plane broke up. The millions of pieces of plane - and the bodies - finally fluttered from 33,000 feet to the farmland below.

Svetlana spoke evenly and calmly. "That should not have happened. The IFF should have been over-ridden. Perhaps they changed the codes. I need to do some more work on the software."

"No it should not have happened. Master Sergeant, what did the Russian missile hit?"

"A civilian airliner, sir. It was squawking as Japan Airlines flight JL6818. The other missiles fell to ground."

Kravets smiled grimly. "That was unfortunate. Lieutenant, erase the software and close down all links immediately. Master-Sergeant, erase the audio log from this bunker." Kravets looked around the control room at the three technicians and the Master-Sergeant. "This did not happen. That is an order. Do you all understand?"

They chorused "Yes sir" almost in unison.

General Kravets was astute enough to recognize that the result, although unfortunate, was even better than that which he had planned. He imagined the headlines "Defenseless Civil Airliner Shot down by Russian Missile." The Ukrainian President would be delighted. It would certainly be good for his career.

He turned away, drew his pistol and then swiveled back smoothly on his heels. Svetlana watched with cold detachment and no surprise as the General quickly completed the mission and two bodies hit the floor. There could be no loose ends.

"Come, Sveta, let's get out of here."

A few minutes later, he and Svetlana drove away in his new Humvee as the old bunker entrance and aerial array was destroyed by explosives.

He looked forward to the weekend with Sveta at his riverside *dacha* – and the worldwide newspaper headlines.

*

Three

Abu ben-Zhair had been a customer of Sveta Kovacs, although he didn't know it. In 2016, when his fundraising efforts were in their infancy, he had bought a tranche of credit card data which one of his teams had used to generate some working capital. Ben-Zhair was by now an accomplished terrorist and had masterminded the greatest atrocities of the twenty first century. He doubted that his record could be surpassed but now his focus had moved from the West to the East, with the infidel states of Russia and China clearly in his sights.

Firstly, though, he had to settle the score with the USA. His attack using a nuclear-triggered tsunami had succeeded in many ways but had failed in its most important objective – that of decimating the US East Coast and by extension wrecking the American economy. He wished that he had been the one who had created the Covid-19 pandemic. It surely was not Allah because it seemed that no country was safe from the virus. If not Allah then who was it? The Chinese? Perhaps.

However, ben-Zhair's principal objectives remained unchanged and now that he was believed by the world to be dead his task would be much easier. His revenge on the Satan United States would in one attack pit all the enemies against one another.

Much of Abu ben-Zhair's backing finance came from a Saudi Prince. Wealthy beyond what most people could conceive of, Prince Khalifa ibn Abu Bakr was a very minor member of the Saudi royal family. His closest family were more than usually devout Sunni Muslims of the Wahhabi sect, more observant of Shariah law than was usual in the higher echelons of Saudi society. Most of the Saudi ruling clan were, in common with the rest of the human race – or at least those who professed to being religious - hypocritical when it came to religion. Alcohol was enjoyed in secret, but sexual vices were less the norm among males – after all, the faith permitted polygamy.

The Saudi prince with dollars to burn by the billion was not interested in business. Money had little value in his eyes – other than as a tool to enable him to achieve those things which he thought were important in the world – and those revolved mainly around religion. That included the war against Satan in whatever form he took, whether as the United States, the Shia State of Iran or tyrants such as Assad in Syria. The prince had even provided very discreet support to Osama bin-Laden and the Taliban, and latterly to a range of terrorist organizations which were aligned with the Sunni interpretation of Islam.

The major Western countries knew about Saudi support for Islamist terrorists and that they had provided huge funds to IS in its war against Assad in Syria. The problem was that Saudi buying power in the arms and other lucrative markets was huge. They controlled vast amounts of oil reserves and at a blink they could seriously damage the Western economic model. The West bought the oil, Saudi Arabia spent the petrodollars on arms and consumer goods, on building huge leisure complexes to attract tourists and take more western money. And so the money continued to go round and round, with a small but very useful percentage finding its way to Islamist terrorists. After all, Saudi Arabia was the guardian of Mecca – it had responsibilities to Islam and to the legacy of Muhammad.

And so, the Saudi prince amused himself funding wars and projects which took his fancy. He circumvented the problems of money laundering and funds transfer by making use of the *hawala* whenever he could. To prime the process and prevent the obvious imbalance he had a personal yacht built, as did all Saudi princes. At just over 2,000 tons displacement, this yacht, *Arabian Princess*, was not conspicuously large when compared to those of his cousins, ranking just outside the 20 largest motor yachts in the world. But it was large enough to occasionally transport a ton or two of gold from Saudi Arabia to other countries where gold would percolate out through soukhs and other outlets and so fund his projects. This method was below the radar of the Western security services and impossible to track. But even *hawala* did not have the flexibility of the new cybercurrencies.

Prince Khalifa was not the only such patron of Islamist terrorism in Saudi Arabia, but he was the one who had enabled Abu ben-Zhair to implement a range of earth-shattering atrocities.

Now ben-Zhair was moving from the use of weapons of mass destruction to those of greater subtlety though no lesser effect – cyberweapons – which had the potential to cause economic and civil catastrophe on an enemy. It was a new battlefield. For that he needed to beef up his team, the key members of which had been lost in the attack on his headquarters in Algeria the previous year, an attack from which he'd barely escaped.

Standard cyber-warfare – if there was such a thing as standard – was well developed, the techniques well known and well defended against. The best place to find opportunity was in emergent technologies or paradigms, new applications and software products.

The meeting at a café in Algiers had indeed been a gift from Allah. Nasim Kateb was a brilliant and quietly devout research student when, purely by chance it seemed, they had met in Algiers. During the meeting, which followed a set pattern of his meetings to recruit talented students to join his long-term plan, ben-Zhair had discovered that Kateb's family had been persecuted during the time when France was the colonial power in Algeria – as indeed had ben-Zhair.

Thereafter, ben-Zhair had sponsored Kateb's further education (including a year in Paris as a visiting lecturer), and had also invested in the futures of several similar students he had met. Even if they worked in esoteric areas of the arts and sciences, these were people who impressed him and who he thought could use at some time in the future of the Islamic Caliphate as he envisioned it. At that time ben-Zhair had no conception of Kateb's research subject area of geological sciences. It didn't matter. They shared a very jaundiced view of France and the French, and an enthusiasm for change in Algeria – without being too obvious about it. Kateb was a devout, though not zealous, Muslim.

After earning his doctorate at the University of Algiers, Kateb had published several well-reviewed research papers. Thereafter, one of his responsibilities had been that of talent scout, besides of course his main achievement of conceiving the tsunami that so vary nearly brought the USA to its knees.

Two or three times every year, Nassim Kateb along with several other similar advisors had visited ben-Zhair to spend a few days discussing politics and revolution in the changing, asymmetric world of international terrorism. These interludes had been passed in various farms and old villas and gradually inducted the attendees into a secret way of life, a shared vision and a clear purpose. They also learned how to handle weapons and the basics of unarmed combat. At one special session ben-Zhair had addressed the assembled group. They were sat out in the open under some palm trees at an old farm, near the town of Medea, some 50 miles south of Algiers. It was hot day and the air was dry, the view down the valley one of lush greenery following the spring rains.

"After the first attack, I want to show a pattern of increasing escalation in the power and sophistication of our attacks. We must show the highest levels of technical sophistication, capability, reach and logistical expertise. Only that way will our vision of a Caliphate be feared and respected by world powers. Besides the Great Satan and his running dogs, I include Saudi Arabia and Iran, as well as Russia and China."

Sadly, Kateb was dead, by ben-Zhair's own hand, a true martyr to the cause, but the results of his talent spotting lived on.

As one of his group of experts recommended by Kateb, ben-Zhair had cultivated Abdurrharman Sukarnomutri, latterly a young professor of Web Technology at MIT in Cambridge, Massachusetts. Like all his protégés, he was a devout Muslim in the most extreme sense and ben-Zhair had sponsored the young student through the three years of his Ph.D. at the University of Oxford in England. His doctoral thesis had been on the topic of encryption methods in the .onion deep web more commonly known as *onion-land.*

A true believer, with roots in Indonesia, the largest Muslim country in the world, the young MIT professor had been very helpful in preparing an analysis of opportunities for attacking infidel countries using emerging technologies including novel bio-weapons, cyber-warfare, artificial intelligence and data pollution – the corruption of national and state databases to render countries ungovernable.

The opportunity identified by Sukharnomutri that had particularly attracted ben-Zhair was related to the mathematical corruption of cryptocurrencies. The idea was a way of applying the ransomware extortion model to Bitcoin by corrupting a cryptocurrency mixer (commonly known as a tumbler). These tumblers were available on the deep web and widely used for laundering cryptocurrencies.

This idea had caught ben-Zhair's attention because he had himself been faced with the practical issue of moving large amounts of funding below the radar of currency controls and snooping by governments of all flavors and he knew that even Bitcoin was not completely immune to tracking by Governments. Prince Khalifa abu Bakr had provided the funding for several of his earlier terrorist operations and the use of the Prince's *Arabian Princess* to move gold had been critical to their success, but unwieldy. But now it seemed that there was an opportunity to utilize this new concept of digital, uncontrollable currency to great effect in a way which would create significant damage to all the world's reserve banks and their associated economies.

Prince Khalifa had at first been highly skeptical, but had eventually come round to the idea.

"I have watched the price of this Bitcoin go from $6,000 to $12,000 and back again. It makes no sense, it is too risky."

To which ben-Zhair had replied "What is the price of your oil today, and what was it last year?"

"But oil is different, people want it!"

"And what will be the price of your oil when electricity is generated by hydrogen fusion, and cars are powered by electricity? Will people want your oil then?"

"Oil is finite, its price will go up, it must do."

"Bitcoin is finite, only twenty one million will ever exist. Its price will go up, it must do."

"Only as long as people want it."

"Just like oil."

The discussion had continued on and off in a similar vein for several months as ben-Zhair and the Prince reviewed a range of future projects on the *Arabian Princess*. However, none of the other projects had the scope to hit the economies of the USA, Europe, Russia and China all at once, and all required dangerous technology or infrastructure. Bitcoin computers were available off the shelf and were cheap.

The Prince had reveled in the successes of the Rome atrocity – a radioactive city and a blinded Pope – and that of the tsunami which had devastated islands in the Atlantic and reached into the heart of western Europe. The infidel enemy was on its knees. The Prince would be persuaded.

In Cambridge, Massachusetts, Professor Abdurrharman Sukarnomutri had by now developed a technical plan for the destruction of world economies and ben-Zhair would oversee its physical execution.

The funding required for this project was on a much smaller scale than that for the others so ben-Zhair decided to push ahead anyway with his scheme – much preparatory work could be done with little funding until Prince Khalifa was finally persuaded, as he surely would be.

There were virtual software teams to be assembled and Sukarnomutri was designing software to be built. A server farm would be required, hidden in the dark web, in *onion-land*. It was ironic that *onion-land* more commonly known as TOR, had been developed by the US government and was still part-funded by them. Just as ben-Zhair had used US fusion technology developed by the US to trigger a tsunami against them, so would he use *onion-land* against them. It was Allah's will.

*

Four

Charles Tobin met most people's definition of 'swashbuckling entrepreneur'. After the debacle of his gold extraction project in the Red Sea, Tobin had been captured in Malta by the Serbian assassin and Chinese agent Maruška Pavkovic. He had been brutally tortured before his rescue by agents of MI6, the UK's Secret Intelligence Service.

Tobin was a tough Australian, but the event had left him with deep scars and just one testicle. The huge financial leverage he had utilized for the gold business (and price manipulation scam) had unwound, and he was now down to his last $100 million. He still owned *Auric Adventurer*, his superyacht, but now – God forbid – he'd had to sell his Gulfstream and make use of chartered private jets, shared with tennis players and football stars.

At his home on the Swan River in Perth, he had recuperated quickly from his semi-castration, buoyed up his powerful personality and positive outlook. But even that only stretched so far. By now he had heard all the jokes about men with only one ball – and the only ones who'd been brave enough to make them to his face had been his MI6 interrogators. They hadn't liked him and still kept a watching brief.

He had closed down his enriched seawater refining business in Wales – "Turning Seawater into Gold" as the press had dubbed it - after his Red Sea production platform had been sunk. His plan to extend the gold enrichment technology to extract plutonium from seawater in the Mediterranean had hit a stone wall when the British government threatened him with imprisonment unless he signed over the patents. The scheme wouldn't have worked anyway as the traces of plutonium from French reactors had been far too small for the technology to work.

"Richard?"

"Charles? I can't believe it, after all this time. You've practically disappeared off the face of the earth since your exploits in Malta."

"Not quite, Richard. You've just been avoiding me, I know."

Thompson's laugh was forced and unconvincing. "Hardly, Charles. And what happened to your plutonium extraction project."

"Anyone would think that cleaner seas would be a good thing, although the plutonium was barely at trace levels off the Algerian coast. People did think that it was a good thing for the environment, and so the bastard UK government stole my genetic technology. I had nowhere to go and had to sign the patents over. The Chinese also stole the technology. Anyway I don't have much time to chat. We need to meet, very soon. We can catch up then."

"Sorry Charles, things are a rather busy right now – I'm floating my new business next month and I'm up to my neck in auditors and regulators, as you can imagine."

"Yes I can, Richard. But you need to find the time for me. We go back a long way. I'll make it easy for you – I'll come to England."

Richard Thompson grimaced at the thought. He'd have to meet the man. The reasons for his resignation had never become public – and that's how he wanted it to stay. As did Tobin, but he wasn't prepared to call the man's bluff.

"Can we make it after the float?"

"No. It needs to be much sooner. How about this weekend?"

"Too soon. My diary is full."

"Take Sunday off. Find a way."

Tobin heard the sigh.

"Very well. Lunch on Sunday?" There goes my golf, Thompson thought.

"Perfect. I still have my place outside Winchester. You remember it?"

"Too well, Charles, too well."

"OK, let's say midday on Sunday then."

"I'll be there – on one condition. No female company this time. Just us and the caterers."

Tobin hadn't planned to invite females anyway. In truth, since his mutilation in Malta he'd lost some of his irrepressible confidence in the presence of women. The new silicone implant felt real enough to a woman's hand – or mouth. His knowledge that he was only really firing on one cylinder was affecting his performance in bed, although Viagra did help. But only he knew that and he kept well away from previous girlfriends.

Tobin laughed. "OK Richard, we'll keep it simple. I'll see you on Sunday" The line dropped. No-one ever had the last word on Tobin.

*

Richard Thompson had made his fortune developing and selling derivatives trading software in the City of London before become an MP and eventually a UK Cabinet Minister. He had resigned his post 'to pursue new business challenges' after being caught in a honey trap of Tobin's making. The facts never became public – not even the Prime Minister had known. Sex and drugs - how many careers had they ended - pop stars excepted of course? Tobin had just used the existence of the videos as a lever. Thompson's reputation had been preserved, but the lever was still there.

Thompson's name was well known in London – even worldwide – equity and derivative trading circles, and along with the kudos of his obvious political connections clients came to his door in a steady stream. To all intents and purpose he had run the company, Livengood Futures, but Tobin had held a major stake and had driven the scam forward.

He had picked his clients carefully, following a profile that Tobin had specified. Tobin, in his turn, had been given privileged information about who some of those clients might be. They tended to be very high wealth individuals with a lot of cash to invest. The cash was legitimately accounted for, much of it having come through foreign currency shops, black hotels, pizza outlets, massage parlors, bookmakers and a whole raft of other – mainly cash – businesses. Whether it was the result of genuine trading by these businesses was doubtful, and not questioned.

The end result had, technically, been a successful operation to manipulate the gold futures market. The ultimate outcome came close to war between NATO and China in the so-called 'Gate of Tears' conflict.

The technical success had been to no avail, as the huge political fallout had ended with Tobin losing most of his fortune. Thompson had been left under a cloud having been prosecuted – unsuccessfully – by the Financial Conduct Authority. He had held on to his license by a whisker, but many still thought he was not a fit and proper person to run a financial services company.

*

"It's good to see you again Richard."

"I wish I could say the same Charles."

"Still holding that grudge? I don't know why. You made a bloody good video – in fact I've shown it at a couple of parties."

"Good God Charles…"

"Don't worry mate, I had your face photoshopped for a porn star – you know, the one they call Goliath. Nobody knows it's you, and no one believes it's Goliath either. The dimensions are not the same. But people do ask who the original was."

"Charles, you bastard!"

"Loosen up Richard. The only ones who'd recognize you are your ex-wife and about a hundred and fifty women you've shagged over the years."

"A hundred and fifty – if only!"

"Well that's based on your strike rate when you been at my parties with some extrapolation. I didn't include any blokes in that number."

"There bloody well aren't any! Charles, you've bloody well got to stop this nonsense!"

"Really, I think it's quite fun. Anyway, you really should get that mole on your arse removed – it really is *very* distinctive! Come on let me get you a drink. How about some champagne to celebrate?"

"Champagne is fine though I've nothing to celebrate, yet - the company float is still three months away."

"Right, champagne it is – Cristal in fact – for this special occasion."

Tobin summoned his butler with a wifi call button. "The Cristal - we'll take it out on the terrace."

He turned to Thompson. "Come on Richard, I'll tell you about our new venture" and led the way out to the terrace overlooking the Test Valley. Thompson blanched.

It was a fine spring mid-day with a light south-westerly wind, just warm enough for dining outside. Yellow fields of rapeseed were laid out before them, with the very un-English scent of the flowers strong on the air. "Ah that smell. Reminds me of dirty knickers."

Despite himself, Thompson laughed. "You're really too much Charles. And I'm not getting involved in another of your madcap schemes, no bloody way!"

"But you already are Richard, that's the good part. You're up and running already and I'm offering to back you and save all this hassle of the float on the AIM market. We can go for a full listing on the main market later, if we choose. You'll make much more out of it. And don't talk to me about madcap schemes. Cryptocurrencies are still in their relative infancy and you're in deep."

"I don't want your bloody money Charles, thank you all the same. My company has a good track record and the float is set. If the regulators get a whiff of your name then it'll be a non-starter. You're a seen as a bloody financial pirate and persona non grata in the City, you know that. And anyway, cryptocurrencies have been around for almost fifteen years."

"And the US Dollar for over two hundred years, but before we start fighting about it, you need to hear me out – it's an offer and a plan too good to refuse. And of course it would avoid any issues."

"What issues?"

"Fit and proper directors for a start."

"You can't pull that one on me – videos or not. The rules of an AIM listing are relaxed – and all about 'comply or explain'."

"Maybe, but it would hammer the share price. And after a failure on that scale you would be barred from holding *any* directorships. That's without thinking about your personal reputation, Goliath. I'm sure Rotherstein's wouldn't like the press."

Thompson winced as he imagined the headlines – and they would extend far beyond the Financial Times. Tobin was probably right, Rotherstein's – who were advising on the AIM float – might be a bit sniffy about that kind of exposure. "You surely wouldn't, after all we've been through, all I've done for you?"

"There's no sentiment in business, Richard. So, call my bluff – if that's what you think it is. And don't let's have a pissing contest about who has done what for who. I'll piss higher and further."

Thompson looked into Tobin's eyes. He looked at the hand which held the glass of champagne. He looked at his feet. He knew that Tobin had learned to play poker in the gold mines of Australia and the wilds of the Yukon. He had won games in the World Series in Las Vegas. He was unreadable, he was a master.

But Tobin pressed on. "You know that there's a lot of cost and hassle even with being listed, even on AIM. What is it? Floating costs of six or seven percent of what you'll raise? Many companies de-list from the AIM after finding out the hard way what the real cost is. You could short circuit that with capital from me. Think hard, Richard."

"What's for lunch Charles?"

"Venison, from the estate of course. And the wine is even more special than the champagne. It's a 1900 Chateau Margaux."

"Good God Charles – that *is* special, even for you!"

"Yes, eighteen thousand euros a cork. I have two bottles for lunch. And no ladies to share it with."

Thompson shook his head. Doing business with Tobin was interesting to say the least. But dangerous. "Very well, let me hear your proposition – but I'm making no commitments."

"So, your new venture with Livengood Crypto – Troy, I think you call it - is built on using the cryptocurrency model to speed up one to one equity deals. Is my understanding correct?"

"Correct, more or less. The Ethereum cryptocurrency was designed to enable automated contract execution and settlement. So, I used that model to develop a cryptocurrency which works in the financial markets and speeds up off-exchange contracts."

"Disintermediation?"

"Yes, roughly speaking, though it's not strictly correct to call it a crypto *currency*, but it does rely on blockchain technology. And we do play a part in the transaction, but to a much smaller degree than say a company such as Coinbase would do with a Bitcoin currency purchase or sale. And we've gone beyond the basic cryptocurrency trading model by building in AI."

"Artificial intelligence? That's novel. What does it do? What edge does it give you?"

"That is a trade secret and subject of twenty seven pending patent applications. The value of the IPR is considerable."

"And your programmers have that knowledge? It sounds risky."

"I have several software development teams which work on this, and none of them have the whole picture. They are in different countries – two in the UK, one in the US one in the Ukraine and a couple in India. Of course the bulk of cryptocurrency software is open source code available to anyone via the public Github software repository. Some companies, such as mine, create a custom version with their own proprietary blocks of code. It's called a hard fork in the code."

Tobin nodded. So far, Thompson had not told him much more than he didn't already know from his own research and the launch prospectus of Richard's new company, Livengood Crypto. *AI, though, now that was interesting*. Then, the conversation paused whilst the butler brought in the main course. After Tobin had carved the haunch of venison a rather pretty waitress served the food. Tobin opened the second bottle of Chateau Margaux. The staff withdrew.

"So you liked her arse did you? I saw you peeking. You could spend this afternoon with her if you wanted. She's very obliging – and skilled."

"Charles, let it go will you, it's really becoming very tiresome."

"Okay, back to business then, but you have become boring. Bitcoin – the original cryptocurrency is fully open isn't it? So why would a client trust your software if they can't see all the code and even if it is only for contract execution and not cryptocurrency as you say?"

"That's a really good question, Charles. Don't forget that we trust high street banking software with our money as a matter of course. And all transactions of Bitcoin are recorded in its blockchain which anyone can see."

"But even Bitcoin is open to manipulation and fraud. What about the fifty-one percent attack?"

"To mount a fifty-one percent attack and gain temporary control of the currency would require a monstrous amount of comBuliging power – and that control is of limited use anyway."

"But it happened, didn't it? And the man in the street would *not* consider the resulting double spending possibilities to be of limited use. Nor would I – and that's without taking a short position on Bitcoin futures before an attack. The profit potential is enormous.

We know that a mining pool – what were they called 'ghash.io' wasn't it - exceeded fifty percent of the Bitcoin network's comBuliging power – that was in July 2014 I think, and then there's the thirty four per cent attack too. And that's for Bitcoin – the biggest. The minnows like your company with proprietary code have a serious trust problem to address. And then there's speed of execution – too slow for practical trading. Of course it's all way beyond me."

Oh yeah, thought Thompson as he looked up from his venison, realizing that Tobin had really dug very deeply into the subject - very deeply. "Maybe for day traders, yes, but for other investors no. And don't forget – I'm talking specifically about *speeding up* contract execution. You know, my software could even work in a betting exchange scenario."

"Now there's thought!"

"Anyway, if you think the scenario is that bad then why on earth are you interested in buying in? I'm not interested in any Ponzi schemes like that Bulgarian woman Ignatova pulled off with OneCoin."

"Yes, four billion US they reckon she cleared, but now she's a criminal on the run, shopped by her own brother. No, I'm interested because I have ideas of my own, legal ideas. Interest rates have been zero or even negative for several years now. On top of that we've had the Covid crisis which has massively depressed the global economy. That's why the smart money is expecting a huge increase in inflation as countries try to kick start their economies again."

"Yes, I've heard all that speculation. Could you top up my glass please? This Margaux really is exceptionally good."

Tobin re-checked the wine thermometer and carefully poured. Thompson looked pensive and met Tobin's eyes. Tobin studied the wine in his glass as he swilled it, checking the color and the meniscus. He nodded in satisfaction as he inhaled the bouquet and then washed a large sip around in his mouth, sucking air in to release more bouquet.

"I'm a miner Richard, as you know. I made my first million in the Red Dog mine in the Yukon, refining the gold tailings that that other miners left behind in huge piles. I like the notion of mining in cryptocurrencies. A new twist on mining. I intend to repeat my experience and feed off the piles of others – so to speak. I need a vehicle for that, one that's up and running, like yours. And with people I trust, like you."

Thompson groaned. He'd seen it coming and expected this to be Tobin's approach.

"Or can control."

Tobin shrugged.

"There are no tailings in cryptocurrency, Charles. Bitcoin has been around since 2004, it's old hat. The big money has been made."

"They said that in the Yukon, but I came in behind the groundbreakers and cleaned up handsomely. Today, Richard, the smart money is going into inflation-proof assets. But not oil – that's on a permanent downward trend. The big money is going into the traditional stores of wealth – real estate, art, gold – even wine. The problem is that they are not all fungible – the Mona Lisa is, and always will be the Mona Lisa, traceable and with a public provenance. Any sale – and profit – from her face is very visible. Gold is fungible if you remove the stamping on the bars. Hard cash? The notes are numbered and difficult to move around in large quantities. Transmissable – certainly, but traceable through the banking system. Besides which we're drinking the wine. And I have a superyacht to burn money.

But now we have Cryptocurrencies. Eminently fungible – one bitcoin looks just like another – if you could see one at all – there's no 'hard' form of the currency. Transmissable electronically – or even on paper. The provenance is there in the blockchain – but it's encrypted. Arguably traceable – but unlike a banknote a bitcoin doesn't have a number. And of course, now accepted by mainstream companies such as Paypal and by investors as a value store – just look at the One River hedge fund. They bought a billion US worth of Bitcoin in 2020, when it was below twenty thousand dollars. Within a couple of weeks it hit twenty eight thousand."

Thompson nodded. "There's nothing new to me there at all, Charles. But transactions can be tracked back to source – or at least an email address or IP number. People are getting caught – many of the people who used Silk Road, for example. There are companies out there like Chainalysis selling tracking tools to governments."

"Governments will not be able to police every transaction."

"But they could make cryptos illegal. Or worse still, tax them."

"We both know that will never happen worldwide. They will certainly try – the lack of control over currency frightens the shit out of them. Most countries will create their own, they will have to. You can't ignore a potential upside of five thousand percent in ten years. And anyway, if it's old hat then why are *you* bothering?"

"My ambitions are modest and I need something to do, something that utilizes my skills and excites my intellect. I'm not in it for big bucks."

"No? So you don't really need to float then, do you? Maybe we can satisfy your needs and mine at the same time?"

"Impossible. I'm already locked in with private investors looking for an exit."

"Yes, I heard that there is a big stagging operation underway. Your share price will drop like a stone when they sell off their holdings after the float."

How did he know that about the stagging with still three months to go? Thompson responded quickly. "That's debatable, I'm sure that there's enough interest to take up any slacking in the price. Anyway, most floats get stagged." He sipped his wine and looked at Tobin. "Charles, this is not for publication. I have solved both the trust problem and execution speed with our AI module. It will be announced soon after the float and once the patents are approved. The AI module is in final back-testing now with one of our software teams."

Tobin looked at the label of the 1900 Chateau Margaux as he refilled Thompson's glass. Priceless.

Thompson realized that he'd said too much, much more than he'd intended. The damned man was an expert at uncovering secrets. The problem was that Thompson loved mathematical problems and when he solved on he wanted to show off. That's how he'd become involved with Tobin in the first place and now it seemed that their futures would be permanently entwined.

"I thought that there must be something behind it all. Don't worry, your secret is safe with me." *For now.* "Why don't I just buy them out now at a premium and we skip the float? Then I'll provide additional capital for expansion. We can be much more nimble if we don't get listed."

"It sounds like a complete takeover to me. It will not work." Thompson had parried the first thrust, now he would lunge back. "Anyway Charles, word has it that you're down to your last hundred million."

"Far from it Richard. The pundits don't know what the fuck they're talking about. I've plenty of capital to hand – but it's not something I talk about. Remember that my operations have always been international. I've been in the crypto markets for twelve years now – I got in early in a small way. That's not for publication, anywhere – so be warned.

Thompson looked up quickly, genuinely surprised, as Tobin smiled and nodded and then continued. "Yes twelve years. I got in early and made a bit along the way. When you agree to my investment, I'll sit in the background and you run the show. Of course I would want to provide some strategic input. I've got fifty million US dollars equivalent in Bitcoin ready to plug in to Livengood Crypto. That's at this morning's price. It was only forty seven million last week. Working together we can leverage it to make five hundred million in five years. You carry on with your contract execution breakthrough and have your intellectual stimulation. We can set up a separate division to do other things in cryptos, a hedge fund if you like."

"No way Charles. Our partnership did not work before, and it will not work again."

"But Richard, you seem to forget that you cleaned up handsomely at Livengood Futures, and that it was me who caught the ultimate cold – or so the world thinks. You need to realize that you don't have much choice in this matter. That is unless you are prepared for the Goliath scenario."

Thompson groaned and shook his head at the irrepressibility of Tobin. "We'd never get licensed for a hedge fund operation."

"We wouldn't need to. It would be closed. Internal, ours."

"If that's your plan, then you don't need me. Just set up your own operation."

"But I could use your software expertise."

"What about conflict of interest? I couldn't be offering my execution service and have another division trading on its own account."

"I'm sure we can iron that out somehow. Chinese walls or whatever. After all the bloody banks do it and they've been bending the rules for years." Tobin raised his glass. "To us."

It was almost inevitable. Thompson was wavering.

"Charles, you really must stop calling me Goliath." Tobin clinked glasses with him. "I'll need time to think about this." *'What else has he got up his sleeve?'*

"Then make it quick Richard. It's been a quiet news weekend and the editor of the FT is looking for a good story for tomorrow morning. Goliath would play well, I think. Now then, let's have some pudding shall we, before the cheese? I think that my chef has got some Eton Mess for us."

The venison was sitting heavily in Thompson's stomach. The thought of Eton Mess made it turn over.

"I think I'll pass on that thank you, Charles."

"What? You've already got a bitcoin mining operation underway?"

"Yes, It's been up and running for a couple of years now. It took some doing to find power for the scale of operation that I had in mind. As you probably know, cheap power is the key to it. I got some people to buy in, but only on a limited basis – they buy a monthly subscription, and the price goes up every month as the mining costs increase. The more bitcoin you find, the more expensive it becomes. It's working well but it's now time to change the funding model."

Thompson studied his glass of port. *Tobin was always full of surprises.* "You kept that secret well, Charles."

"Well it's a secret mining consortium. Just like *Bitfury*, except we don't appear in block explorer and hash rate charts. I'll be stopping the subscription arrangement soon."

"What's your consortium called?"

"I'll keep that one up my sleeve for now, Richard. Need to know basis." Tobin winked with exaggeration. "I'll tell you in due course, don't worry."

Thompson shook his head. Tobin was always suckering him.

"Don't look so pissed off Richard. I *will* tell you that it's near Azilal in the Atlas Mountains."

"Morocco?"

"Yes. One of the safest countries in Africa. Depending on whose estimate you go with, it takes anywhere from twenty five thousand to fifty thousand kilowatt hours of electricity to mine one bitcoin using the latest hardware. Morocco has plenty of sun and I've got a big solar spread there, plus wind turbines. And then there's lots of hydroelectricity nearby. I've negotiated a good deal for power with the company that owns a couple of dams. It does help to know one of the Royal Family there, smooths the way y'know. Prince Abdallah Yazid shares my interest in superyachts and horses, although his yacht is a little bigger than my old *Auric Adventurer*. But I'll fix that when you and I are up and running and get to our first hundred million."

Thompson reflected on his time in the Aegean on Tobin's superyacht. *Happy days and friendly ladies*. He could almost smell the sea off Ithaca and realized that the wine was going to his head. Then he remembered the attack and snapped out of his reverie.

Tobin was droning on with his story "Certainly it's possible to mine cryptos at home using a PC, but it's not easy to make much money that way – your average Joe is in a competition against people who have faster, less power hungry hardware in bigger processing farms. People like me."

"I can well believe that, Charles. Although most bitcoin mining farms are in China and they burn coal."

Tobin laughed.

"Yes, the Chinese are into it bigtime. Coal is cheap, but the Chinese are clamoign down on the miners. I've been doing well despite them, and at the moment you could say that I'm a primary miner, though unfortunately I do have to buy their bitcoin mining ASICs."

"How many do you have?"

"I'm using the Bitmain Antminer S9 model ASIC, but I'm not disclosing the exact number of them – for now, but I will tell you that the number is in four figures."

"I'll need to know a lot more if we are to move forward together. We can't have any secrets between us concerning joint operations, can we?"

"All in good time, Richard, all in good time."

"Morocco though. That's a real surprise given that most mining operations are locating in cold places such as Norway or Iceland – or in the case of the Chinese high up on the steppes. The cooling requirements are enormous and there's no cold air in Morocco."

"There's snow in the Atlas Mountains but that's beside the point. I agree that the issue of energy for cooling is a big one, with each of those ASICs using fifteen hundred watts. It's an issue for other miners because the cost of energy is so high – for them. Even so, we use the cool mountain water from the hydroelectric scheme to take away the heat with our heat pumps. No other miner does that – it's a unique solution. Energy for my operation costs next to zero, thanks to my arrangement with Prince Abdallah. He gets a generous share of the *net* profit and in return ensures that the energy company is *very* flexible about pricing for me. It's the way the Arabs work, back scratching without equal."

"So how would all that fit in with me and Livengood Crypto?"

"I'll come to that, but first let me offer you a brandy. I've got something really special for the occasion. Then I'll explain."

*

Five

"It will not work, Dmitri. We sell them our cryptocurrency for cash then we have to wash the cash. Their problem becomes our problem."

"We use agents to do it for us. So, we pass the problem on. Our agents take the cash for our currency and wash it locally, then we give them a big discount."

"And how do we get round the fraud problem?"

"The same old question again. I need to think more about this."

"Obviously!"

Svetlana Ponomarenko and Dmitri Borzov had argued about this problem for months.

"Almost all illicit money starts out as cash, whatever the source, whether it's from a fence, a drugs sale or a jewelry robbery. Cash is untraceable in the main. But it's a big problem in the drugs business since the quantities are so huge – at least as big in volume as the drugs themselves. It's not easy to move cash around and that's where cryptocurrencies win out."

"And they're not traceable."

"Wrong, Dmitri. The cryptocurrencies can be tracked – every transaction detail is in the blockchain. But they are anonymous. Just an address – an encrypted address. And useless unless you have the key. If you have the key you have the money. So, it's very easy to move money. Now the Americans have found a way to link those addresses to IP numbers, but that's easy to get around, we can do that using cryptocurrency mixers to add another layer of encoding. The Islamists use *hawala* for money transfer, but that relies on trust and reciprocal transactions to keep the accounts square. That can be a problem for very large amounts."

He laughed. "I don't think that trust is a good idea. Surely even trust has a price when the amounts are large."

"Perhaps. So, the basic problem is to get the cash into the system in the first place. Locally, criminals use cash businesses such as pizza restaurants or amusement arcades to wash the cash, but on the scale I want to operate we can't do that. We need a global solution."

"A franchise system then?"

"That's maybe not so crazy as it sounds. We certainly want to make it easy for our customers to make large cash deposits. We could operate a bank but then we have to get around the ten thousand dollar reporting limit that most western banks demand."

"Does that apply everywhere?"

"Not in Russia and maybe Nigeria."

"We shouldn't go near the fucking Russians, I hate them."

"Me too, but we could screw their banks."

"Now that's an idea I like."

"Let's reduce it to the simplest scenario. We want our customers to be able to convert our crypto into dollars, and vice versa. So we act as a bank. Then we need branches or agents where the physical cash is traded."

"No. What we need is a means of doing that automatically. If someone wants to trade we provide them with a credit card account for one off use. Or an app on their phone."

"Someone still has to wash the cash, at less than $10,000 per transaction."

"What business will we be in? A one-off scam or a black - *prykhovanyy* - bank?

"Maybe a mix of all of those – especially if I can hack the SWIFT/IBAN protocols that banks use."

"Now that *does* sound like a good idea!"

Five months later they had built a prototype solution using a digital currency exchanger service to convert Bitcoin into an online gaming currency that could later be converted back into hard currency and fed back into the banking system, neatly laundered. Then they started milking the gaming users.

The next step was to eliminate the washing through the online games currency. That took another couple of months to crack. The flow of Bitcoin and other cryptos was now being productionized ready for a big sting.

Meanwhile Dmitri Borzov's HyperSecureSoftware development business grew rapidly with many US and UK companies outsourcing their software development to Eastern European countries in a drastic push to reduce development costs and time to market as the demand for cellphone apps snowballed. But that was only a part of his business. He was also heavily engaged in that part of the internet known as the dark web. The deep web is where we do our online banking – not accessible through Google, and hidden behind high security walls requiring our secure passwords and even fingerprints to access.

No, the dark web is even further concealed behind anonymized routers and even more layers of security, in 'onionland'. It where Silkroad was based, where drugs are bought and sold, where hacking teams sell their services and where guns and even hitmen are available. That was Dmitri's most profitable area of operations. But even there the US government was eventually able to find Silkroad's operator, Ross Ulbricht, capture and jail him.

Dmitri offered several services in the dark web, from specialist hacking to virus construction, credit card scams and malware building, operating under several dozen regularly changing aliases.

*

Six

The intrusion into Livengood Crypto's systems took Sveta and Dmitri several months to plan and execute. During his company's work writing software for Livengood Crypto, Dmitri had hacked his way into Thompson's supposedly secure Slack business communications platform. He was insatiable in his need to know as much about his clients, looking for ideas to steal and software to pirate. He'd managed to infiltrate the Slack chat rooms, private groups and direct messaging used by Livengood Crypto.

He'd shared his findings with Sveta as they were directly related to the major project she had underway with him. She saw great potential where he hadn't and soon convinced him of the opportunity they had if they could widen their access to Livengood's systems.

"I think we should cloak our intrusion into Livengood by widening it within their services provider."

"It's never been done before."

"I doubt that. Most companies keep this stuff quiet when they're hit."

"Maybe so, but it's a tough objective to achieve."

"Well let's take a look at what third party software their services company uses – they'll probably have hundreds of modules in their management system. Maybe we can infiltrate one and use that as a way to get our code in, just like a virus fools a cell and infiltrates the body."

"Okay, I'll start some research. I'll work on network management software – if we can hack that then we'd be able to roam pretty much anywhere and get access to user creds."

"Yes, network management would be a good place to start, and if we can then maybe inject our tools into say a software update from such a third party supplier then we're in."

"In probably more than one company too. It would be like a skeleton key, getting into the software supply chain…"

"…and letting somebody else do the work for us."

"What an idea – a supply chain hack! That could work."

*

Prince Khalifa ibn Abu Bakr of Saudi Arabia enjoyed good relations with his contemporaries in the Moroccan Royal Family.

The relationship had come about because Prince Khalifa had been a pupil at an English public school - Harrow - at the same time as Prince Abdallah Yazid of Morocco. They had formed a firm friendship which had endured from school through their first female fumbles – with non-believers of course – through University, and on into manhood.

Their political views diverged and by 2015 were poles apart, although the Moroccan prince didn't realize it. Prince Khalifa was widely seen to be a moderate but his real views were extreme. It worked better for him that way in pursuit of his beliefs, mixing with the richest business people and royalty, and secretly funding the most extreme Islamists.

Almost every summer Prince Khalifa's motor yacht *Arabian Princess* could be seen at Casablanca or Rabat when he visited Prince Abdallah. Both were wealthy but minor players in their respective countries' royal families with shared frustrations. They often met up with their yachts and families during the summer season at Malaga, Costa Smeralda in Sardinia or in Monaco for the Monaco Formula 1 Grand Prix and the *Chemin de Fer* casino tables. They were often seen together at the races too, including the Cheltenham Festival and at Longchamps for the Prix de l'Arc de Triomphe to watch their thoroughbred horses in action.

At this particular time, one of the names on the crew list of *Arabian Princess* was a man designated as Entertainment Manager. He had been appointed less than a year previously and carried a legitimate Saudi Arabian passport in the name of Ashraf Ibrahim. This year the Moroccan Royal family was in a celebratory mood, having been involved in a high-profile peace process which came about shortly after a flare-up in the war between the Polisario Front and Morocco in the disputed Western Sahara, formerly the Spanish Sahara. The USA had recognized Morocco's claim to sovereignty over the area as part of a wider plan to normalize relations between Israel and several Arab nations. The move caused consternation in many Western governments and had incensed Ashraf Ibrahim. Re-energized, he moved back into circulation from his redoubt – an old Spanish fort - in the Western Sahara.

One spring evening Princes Khalifa and Abdallah were eating dinner in the stateroom aboard *Arabian Princess* in the harbor at Rabat. The winds were light and cooling, rolling down from the heights of the Atlas Mountains and there was very little swell rolling in from the Atlantic – not that it would have disturbed such a ship anyway. After yachts, horses, palaces and women, the discussion had turned to investments. The princes avoided use of the word 'business' as they would avoid bacon sandwiches.

"So, you say you are making twenty thousand dollars a day from mining Bitcoin cryptocurrency?" Prince Khalifa laughed. "And you think that's good? Then Morocco is a much poorer country than I thought. I make that much every minute, and that is just on Wall Street. And that is just five per cent of my investment capital."

"Brother Khalifa, you are fortunate that Allah in His wisdom blessed your country with so much oil whereas we have only sufficient for our internal needs. But now oil demand is falling as the world seeks alternatives and you are practically giving it away. And tell me, what is your risk level on Wall Street? There is talk of another crash, the CLO crash to come. Collateralized Loan Obligations? The banks have moved up from the highest risk poorest people's mortgages and now they're packaging the debt of small and medium companies. Have you heard of that? More of 2008 to come I think with more risky assets re-packaged. At least I run no risk with my operation and I can scale it as I wish within certain limitations. It may only be pocket money to you but to me it is magic, making money out of solving a mathematical problem."

"There are risks with all investments and certainly the future of oil process does not look good, but tell me more about this scheme of yours."

"It's a big warehouse full of highly specialized computers which solve a mathematical equation. When an equation is solved then a Bitcoin is 'mined' as they call it. It's fool proof. It uses a lot of electricity, so basically we convert electricity into untraceable currency. It's called a Bitcoin mining farm. The electricity comes from Allah's wind and Allah's rainfall."

"I prefer gold myself. I can see it, I can touch it. I have a ton of it aboard even now, below our feet."

"And what if *Arabian Princess* sinks?"

"It would still be there and I could recover it."

"And when you take the *Princess* to Antibes, you have to declare the gold."

"In theory, yes, but it's listed as cargo on the ship's manifest. Believe me, I do this often, there's no problem."

"So, when you leave, say France, and arrive in Greece and there is no gold aboard then there is a gap in the record system that the Europeans keep. Where did the gold go?"

"You know how *hawala* works. Some of my investments require me to balance the books with gold."

"So would you declare it as unloaded cargo in France?"

"Definitely not. We unload it at night at sea. Few people know."

"Then there is a trail left by a gap in the records. The Europeans and the Americans see everything with their joined up computer systems. But *I* can go to London and access my bitcoin there, or anywhere in the world. It is in Allah's ether. All I need is access to a computer and a code to withdraw the cryptocurrency. You could do that with *hawala*. There are even ATM machines now which will dispense cash and charge your bitcoin account."

"Yes, I see, perhaps I *should* start to move with the times, or at least learn more about it. Could you recommend anyone to guide me if I decide to do this? I would not want my accountants to know of such a scheme and then my family might find out."

"For you, Brother, I will introduce you to my manager. In fact he's more of a partner really. And, as it happens, he is an expert on gold – he used to own a goldmine. You might have heard of him – Charles Tobin."

"The Australian who tried to extract gold from the Red Sea, off Saudi Arabia, off the coast of my country?"

"That is him, the very same."

"By Allah, I cannot believe it. I have played poker with this man in Monaco. He beat me more than once. But he went broke didn't he?"

Prince Abdallah laughed. "Broke? That is only a rumor. I think a lot of it was hidden from his creditors. Who does know the truth? Only Allah I think. Anyway brother, you are not the best of poker players, even I know that. He is a master. If you wish I will call him and tell him you would like to meet him. I will take you to our site up in the mountains and you can see how it works, although it is technically very complex – even I have difficulty understanding it! But let me warn you now, if you decide to mine bitcoin seriously then you will need your own power station to run the operation. I'm using nearly two percent of Morocco's generating capacity myself."

"That is easy, I have plenty of oil and it costs me next to nothing. Why sell it cheaply when I can use it to mine cryptocurrency?"

"Yes, with prices on an ever downward trend it might well be more profitable to use your oil that way."

"Do you trust this man Tobin?"

"I trust him as far as I would trust a Jew."

*

Charles Tobin flew into Rabat in a private Gulfstream. Sadly, this aircraft was shared in a consortium with tennis players and golfers as he'd had to return his own Learjet to the leasing company. He was not quite fully back on his feet, but this meeting with Prince Abdallah and Prince Khalifa might help.

There was no requirement for immigration clearance as they were pre-cleared'. One of Prince Abdallah's Rolls Royce Phantoms was waiting at the VIP parking of the airport to transfer Tobin the short distance to the Airbus Twin Squirrel helicopter for the 140 mile flight to the Bitcoin mining farm at Azilal. This was the fifth time that Tobin had made this journey and as usual he was disappointed that there was no royal crest on the chopper.

When the Twin Squirrel landed at Prince Abdallah's villa near the facility in Azilal Tobin was further peeved to see a parked helicopter with a royal crest on its side, and then he realized that it was painted above the flag of Saudi Arabia. *Envy will get you nowhere but it will drive you harder*, he thought.

The air was dry and breeze was hot and searing. Tobin was glad that another Rolls Royce Phantom was waiting to transport him the hundred yards or so to the villa.

A day later Charles Tobin had flown back to England and the Princes were enjoying the cool evening air outside the villa.

"He knows a lot about gold, Khalifa, as I told you."

"You did, Abdallah, though he did not want to talk about his project in the Red Sea, in my country's waters."

"No, that is something he avoids."

"Anyway Abdallah, I will admit that you have convinced me about this Bitcoin mining. And there are other coins that can also be mined?"

"Yes, but I would stay with one of the top five, to minimize the risks. There are a lot of thieves out there."

"For sure. I think that I will plan to construct such a scheme, the Family is very keen to diversify as we cannot rely on oil for ever in the Kingdom. We have cheap power, Allah be praised, and we should make a good profit at mining. But for the moment this new project will be my secret. I will have to pretend that it is some other technology site."

"The sooner you start the sooner you can start counting the coins, although you can never see them."

"That is the strangest thing is it not? Just numbers. I must say I have had great difficulty understanding the concept but I have a very good business manager who has explained it. He is excellent at organizing complex projects. I think you might have met him when you were last aboard *Arabian Princess*."

"Yes, I remember him. No Royal blood though."

"No, none at all. He comes from a family in the Maghreb – his father was a politician in the old Algerian Government."

"Can you trust him?"

"Yes. I have prayed and Allah has guided me well. Ashraf has proved himself several times so he will run this new project for me. One day I will be able to tell you more about what we have achieved in the name of Allah. You will be astounded. In the meantime you must visit when my new mining farm is operational."

*

Seven

Julia Claudette Stone – JC to everyone who knew her, and Telion to MI6 - looked at her smartphone and re-read the text confirming the code phrase. She was on a day off from her duties at Saluscent in Olhaõ and had caught the train down to Albufeira in search of new scenery, some shopping and a bit of life. That was the story.

She'd turned down the offer of a drive into the hills with Henri Laporte - she did not mix business with pleasure and anyway despite Henri's rugged physical attraction there was a lurking menace in his eyes, the suggestion that there were two different people in his body. She shivered at the thought despite the warm air blowing in through the train windows.

The town of Olhaõ could not be described as lively, but she'd heard that Albufeira was a hotbed of holidaymakers out for a good time. She had checked the map and knew that the railway station was a long schlepp out of town so she picked up a taxi as she came out of the station.

Josh Packard met her in a noisy bar on the cliffs overlooking the sea. Although early in the season there were plenty of holidaymakers to cover conversation and provide cover. They sat at an outside table, the warm breeze flapping the sun shades and making the sea below them sparkle. After they had completed the security protocol, the meeting lasted only a few minutes – enough for one beer.

"You can pick up the package at the Fedex office. You'll find the instructions have come through on your phone. The unit has been programmed with the precise GPS coordinates based on the drawings and pictures you pulled together. Once you launch it then we'll control it. That was a good piece of work you did, by the way."

"Why do you need me to launch it?"

"I can't go into that now. Just follow the plan, okay?"

Stone looked at him, wondering why she was open to being compromised in this way. She nodded.

"The timing is yours to set within the next three days, and it must be at night, obviously. Give me at least six hours notice so that the control team can be ready."

"Fine. I'm on days at the moment."

"Is there anything new to report on the situation at the site?"

"Just that the team leader is ill. He's been hospitalized and Borthwick is bringing in a replacement."

"Do you know who?"

"Not yet."

"OK, send the name through as soon as you have it."

Josh Packard stood up and smiled. "See you next month. Good luck."

*

With the new Prime Minister the changes had come thick and fast at MI6 headquarters, Vauxhall Cross, as the impact of Brexit was felt and the PM's workload demanded higher levels of staffing and inevitable bureaucratic growth, despite the increasing efficiency of information technology. The threats of IS, ICIM, ISIL, the Taliban and all the others in the Middle Eastern melting pot were now declining and in second place to the Israel/Iran stand-off, North Korean saber-rattling and ever-growing Chinese imperialism – both commercial and military.

'C' once again reported directly to the Foreign Secretary (although there was still a dotted line report to the PM) after the interlude when the Islamic Caliphate in the Maghreb (ICIM) was on the loose with nuclear technology and he reported directly to the PM. The prime mover of ICIM, Abu ben-Zhair, had been killed and his burial in the Atlantic had been announced by the USA. Things had got back to normal, more or less.

In SIS headquarters - VX - a new desk had been created to deal specifically with cyberterrorism threats – it made little sense to spread the expertise across the geographical desks when cyberwarfare knew no geographical boundaries. Head of the desk was Emmet Macsen, at thirty four years of age a mature, experienced head on a young-ish body. Although the old-timers carped about his limited field experience, he had demonstrated the ability to follow elusive targets by an electronic trail across network servers and countries, thorough encrypted gateways – all from a desk, but with a highly skilled team – and GCHQ - behind him. He had also conceived and run a series of offensive cyberwar operations to test the defenses of the UK primary adversaries.

Since 9/11 the focus of MI6 had moved to that of Global Terrorism and reorganization had seen the establishment of a Global Terrorism 'Desk'. 'GT' oversaw those operations, currently under the direction of Caspar Conlon.

The parallel Cyber ('CT') desk focused on threats to the UK from cyber terrorists – who could and did, of course, include hackers.

Terrorism was not all about bombs and knives – it included threats to financial systems and the economy, and to UK infrastructure business in general. CT did not usually require footslogging. At GCHQ Macsen had proven himself an effective manager of cyber teams and displayed a nose for the electronic trail which no-one had bettered. The skills and nose were underpinned with a keen sense of what the intelligence meant and what game was being played. An international chess master at the age of eighteen (and a highly capable hacker on the side), he saw permutations of moves in the cyberworld which could provide a high degree of offensive capability and cloaking. VX was certainly not all about defense. He was the first desk head to have crossed from GCHQ to VX.

It was not without amusement that he was known universally by his colleagues as 'M' – for Macsen, of course, and bearing no resemblance whatever to the character in the James Bond novels.

*

"When did you get in, Josh?"

"I've come straight from Stansted. Bloody Ryanair! Why can't we get decent travel arrangements?"

"It's not a long flight from Faro, so stop moaning. Anyway, is Telion on board?"

"Yes. She's ok to do it this way, M, as long as we keep Borthwick out of it. It used to be so simple, reading emails and listening in to phone calls. Now everyone's encrypted and it's back to square one – physical listening in, like Mata Hari at the keyhole – or pretty close to it, anyway. At least we can get *some* help with technology."

"What did she say about the rest of the team there?"

"A mixed bunch, all ex special-forces of one form or another – and one country or another. She's the only Brit there since the squad leader got hospitalized."

"Yes, a shame that, he was working out okay. He should be back in three months though, before they launch the cryptocurrency."

"There's a new guy coming in she thinks. Another Brit. She doesn't know a lot about him. Ex-Royal Marines she heard. A couple of the team have worked with him before and he's well thought of. Goes back a long way with Borthwick, and worked with Borthwick's 'ScutumEst' security company in Greece. Name of Steven Baldwin, that's with a 'v'."

The auto-scripting audio system picked up the name and Macsen looked at his screen. There was no record of the name on their files – or at least, this set.

"OK, Josh. Looks like we don't have a file on Baldwin."

"I'll open one then."

"I've just done it, code name will be Mad Hatter. Going through to you now." With the permissions that he had set on the file, cross referencing Baldwin's name and code name would be redacted for anyone but himself and Josh – and 'C'. *For now.*

"OK. I'm going to get a shower and a bite first if that's OK. I couldn't face the crap Ryanair were selling. I'll log the full report then."

"Go ahead. Any news on the launch date?"

"Nothing new that Telion's picked up. They keep Borthwick's security team well away from both the software development area and management suite except when they do their daily sweep for bugging gear. She'll install the new hardware tomorrow night. If that pans out then we should be quids-in pretty soon. She *is* worried about their internal cybersecurity team though. They are hot and scan all the storage systems twice a day and swap out equipment on a random basis. There are no direct external web links except from a secure suite underground. The CEO – Ponomarenko - is paranoid about intrusion. Telion thinks that they even have their own private deep web TOR network."

"Telion is doing well if she's got that much already. We need to get her in to that internal development network – and a hook into that external deep web network. There are almost a hundred groups that we know about on the deep web that are working on cryptoscams and Ponomarenko may be one of them."

As Josh Packard left Macsen's office, M closed the audio-scripting app – the transcript as well as the audio recording would be automatically added to the '*Pistole*' operations file. He leaned back in his chair, stretching his arms and thinking about the operation. They kept a worldwide watching brief on more than two thousand leading cryptography students (and their subsequent careers) worldwide. It was a huge task and although largely automated and monitored by AI it was not made any easier by the fact that many students' online presence either disappeared of became bland soon after they graduated, even before if they showed real talent. They were the ones that were most heavily flagged, hardest to track, quickest to go off-grid – and most capable in the cyberwar space.

Routine tracking of companies operating in the cryptocurrency arena had been going on for a couple of years and Ponomarenko's company, Saluscent.com, was on the list. Governments were paranoid about cryptocurrencies – they operated under the radar and could offer almost complete anonymity and money laundering capabilities as well as that most feared of all scenarios – currencies which were beyond the control of governments and central banks. They could in the worst case subvert national economies. Emmet remembered what Josh had said: 'Salus' was the Roman goddess of welfare, health and prosperity. The company's name was surely no random choice.

He was jerked out of his line of thought when an instant message beeped onto his screen:

My office now. 'C'.

'On my way' he acknowledged.

*

Eight

Baldwin head jerked up as he heard a phone ring. He was on deck having just checked the anchor. The sea breeze had kicked in and *Rubaiyat* had swung to face the southwest and the weak incoming tide. There was generally little tide at this spot – the currents flowed in around each end of the island and met just where he was anchored. Some broken cloud marbled the sky but all-in-all it was a fine spring morning and Rubaiyat's anchor was well dug in after a couple of weeks. The trip up from Gibraltar had been straightforward, stopping for the night in the lee of Cape Trafalgar and then an overnight trip through the fleets of squid fishing boats to the Faro river entrance. The soundings in the entrance had changed a bit since the tsunami, but he'd managed to feel his way in slowly on a flood tide.

The phone was a cheap smartphone he'd picked up in Gibraltar, with a pre-pay sim. It was handy for weather forecasts and as a hot spot for his laptop. No–one should have known the number - after all, he'd never used the phone - but inevitably Six had discovered it and he'd told them where to go, in no uncertain terms. Nevertheless someone else had the number, someone besides the unsolicited texts he got from clothing retailers and Algarve bars. The screen showed that the caller was Richard Borthwick – or Dickwick as he was known to Baldwin since their days in the Royal Marines. Steve cursed, knowing that he had not programmed Dickwick's number or anyone else's contact details into the phone – simply because there really was no-one else in his life. But the phone had Borthwick's caller data.

He swiped the phone in anger as much as puzzlement, then heard Dickwick's unmistakable public school accent with just that hint of Yorkshire. Dick was a bluff Yorkshireman, hard as nails, fists like hammers, and a face like a brick that had been broken into pieces and re-assembled badly. Just on six feet tall, and wiry, with an intimidating presence. He had been raised in the Dales, carrying sheep in thigh high snow when only a teenager with God knows what muscle – he didn't seem to have any in his whipcord build. But what a man to have next to you in bar when the locals turned nasty and even the Redcaps thought twice about getting involved. And in worse places too.

Steve knew that Rick had been to Oxford or some fancy college, on his merit, not his father's farming money (or at least, those were the rumors). Then, straight into a commission in the Royal Marines. No wimps made officer in the RM – the officers' physical entry standards were set higher than those of the troopers. Steve had himself exceeded the officer standards in his induction, although he'd never wanted to become an officer, a *Rupert*.

Steve's father had been a fisherman – fishing and farming. Living off what nature provided, he and Dick shared a bond. Not a million miles apart, but nearly.

"Baldy?"

"Dickwick? How the fuck did you get this number?"

"That's a nice way to greet an old mate!"

"Well, that last time we spoke was in a Greek police station after I'd nearly been topped in one of your madcap simple security missions!"

"OK, OK, just simmer down, will you?"

"No, I fucking well will *not* simmer down. You shouldn't have this number, no one has it. If you can find me then others can too."

"So, who are you hiding from?"

"No-one, it's just that…well…you know…"

"Our friends in VX again?"

"No bloody comment."

"Fair enough. We need to talk."

"I'll ask again, how did you find me?"

"I'll tell you, but first we need a secure line. Have you got Signal?"

"No, what's that?"

"An encrypted message app. I assume that even *you* know what an app is."

Baldwin thought back to the 'tutorial' on apps that Ellie had given him. His heart seemed to miss a beat.

"Yeh, I know."

"Well get it installed – you'll find it at an app store. That's as secure as can be in this world. Say half an hour? I'll text you a link."

"Don't wait up for me."

"Come on Baldy, we're old mates, we've been through a lot together. Remember the Yemen?"

"I settled that debt with you in the Ionian."

"Maybe."

"You are the second person to find me this month."

"Really?"

"Yes. "

"So who was the other person?"

"None of your business."

"OK, I know when to shut up. Half an hour then, for old time's sake?"

The line dropped and a text came through. Steve eventually located and installed Signal from the app store then poured himself another scotch. He knew that he couldn't go on as he had in the last month. The drinking had to stop and he had to have a plan and get busy, otherwise he's be dead within a year, the bottle or a bullet. He cursed, remembering that he didn't even have a weapon. He thought about his father and what he would have said. "Get on with it! One foot on front of the other and don't look back." *Easy enough to say, but hard to follow.*

It was different ringtone. Dickwick had waited forty five minutes.

"So, Baldy, you're down in the Algarve?"

"Yes, I'm anchored near Faro. How did you find me?"

"You know I have connections."

"Not good enough. I know you're a cleaner for Six, doing stuff that's even too dirty for them."

"Ouch! That's unfair. Anyway, don't trust phones – though I'm sure this one is OK with this app – but did you check your tablet?"

Steve cursed realizing that he'd forgotten about the sim in his tablet, though he knew he hadn't topped up the account in months. There had just been too much happening – and he's been in hospital after the trouble in Rome. Then Algeria and Ellie's death. The pain coursed through him, tightening his chest.

"OK. Thanks for the pointer."

"Anyway, you do leave a trail that a blind deaf mute could follow – Tunisia, Rome and now I'm starting to hear whispers about Spain. I was really sorry to hear about your loss."

"I don't know what you are talking about." *Where did he get all this information?* It was clear that Dickwick still had deep connections with Six.

"OK, I'll say no more for now. But remember I didn't get you into all that shit."

"So what's this call about? Get to the point because you are running out of time, old mate or not."

"It happens that you're in the right place at the right time."

"Again? That's what you said when I was in Crete."

"Well, there's jobs and there's people. If it wasn't you it would be somebody else – but not half as capable."

"Cut the crap Dick and get to the point."

"Well I guess you need something to occupy your time and maybe some good money would come in handy too."

"You're wrong on both counts there. I have a new boat to sort out and funds are not an issue. I've got a ton of stuff on my plate." *But not enough to keep me off the bottle.*

His mind drifted back to that sleepless night and the white envelope. It carried the crest of Konstanz and Young and he'd opened it three weeks ago in Gibraltar after a sleepless night.

*

During that early morning, he'd sipped the whisky as he slit open the flap of the envelope. It contained a letter. The letterhead was that of Konstanz & Young. Tears began to run down his cheeks as he read the letter, dripping into the whisky glass on the chart table.

Dear Mr Baldwin

The Estate of the late Mrs Ellie Baldwin

I write to inform you that I, William Probyn, as senior partner of Konstanz & Young, am the sole executor of the estate of your wife, Mrs Ellie Baldwin. My firm has acted as legal advisers to the late Mrs Baldwins's family for three generations.

Her Last Will and Testament has been proven. I can tell you that it states that you are the sole beneficiary of her estate. The estate comprises properties, an investment portfolio and other assets. It is not inconsiderable in value.

There is also a Death in Service benefit from her employers and a Government pension payable to you as her surviving spouse.

I would be grateful if you could make an appointment to attend our offices in London where we can discuss the various aspects of Mrs Williams's Last Will & Testament and I can take your instructions in that regard.

If travel to London in the near future is not convenient for you, then I shall be happy to meet you wherever is convenient, although, of course, the costs would be charged against the estate.

Please call me directly on the number below so that we may make arrangements.

Yours sincerely

William Probyn
Senior Partner
Konstanz and Young

Baldwin sat and looked at the letter. He did not understand it. He and Ellie had signed some marriage papers - probably a special license prior to the Algeria assignment as an operational convenience – or so he thought. Barbary had said that it was genuine. But then he would, wouldn't he - or maybe not. It didn't matter at the time.

This letter was in another realm completely. It was surreal. He sat, both impossibly numbed and crying for what might have been.

Less than a week later he'd met with William Probyn in the Rock Hotel in Gibraltar. He recalled that meeting with Ellie in the very same hotel following the *Sword of Allah* catastrophe in Rome He had thought her dead at the time he'd booked into the hotel, just a few weeks ago - a lifetime, in fact. Algeria had followed – and now she was dead.

In a private suite, Probyn handed Steve an expensive looking black leather attaché case and then a key which he removed from his wallet.

"The case contains a copy of Mrs Baldwin's Last Will and Testament, together with other documents which you need to read through. Mrs Baldwin dictated her Will to a notary in Gibraltar just after you were married. It was notarized and sent to through to us in London. It supersedes an earlier will."

That would have been just prior to our departure for Algeria on *HMS Bulwark*, thought Steve. She obviously hadn't held out much hope for the mission. Writing a will had never even occurred to him – he had little to pass on and no-one to pass it on to. Just a wife – newly wed and recently deceased. He couldn't believe his naiveté.

"Can I see the earlier Will?"

"I'm afraid not Mr Baldwin. Mrs Baldwin gave us very specific instructions that it was to be destroyed and replaced with this will. Naturally we followed her instructions, though we did advise her to reconsider given the *very* unusual circumstances at the time of writing. I have to say that the term 'gold digger' came to my mind."

"Now wait a minute, I knew bugger all about her background! She was pretending to be a Greek waitress when I met her." And plenty of other things that she had told him he hadn't believed. Probyn appeared unsurprised.

"Mr Baldwin, I meet all sorts of people and pride myself on my ability to judge character. She was married to you for less than a week and then she dies almost immediately after changing her will. It is natural to be suspicious."

"You bastard! You don't even know how or why she died."

"That is partly true although I have seen a death certificate – there is a copy with the Will by the way - and I'm satisfied that it is genuine. I understand that her cause of death was a skull fracture arising from a car accident. The Foreign Office has confirmed the facts to me. I understand that you held a private funeral for her in Spain. That is somewhat unusual. I do have Mrs Baldwin's interests at heart even though she is deceased. Nevertheless I am happy that the Will reflects her wishes and it is not my place to challenge it. I am satisfied that she was of sound mind when she signed it. I will leave you alone for an hour, Mr Baldwin, whilst you digest the Will and the other documents."

Steve was dry-eyed as he read the will with trembling hands, shaking his head in disbelief.

He did not want a house in the Surrey 'stockbroker belt', an apartment in Notting Hill, a house in Falmouth. He did not want an investment portfolio with a valuation of £8,432,567 (as of 3 days previously). He did not want a share in a racehorse syndicate, nor in various automobiles including a classic 1954 Bentley R Type and a Porsche Carrera Special Edition. Apparently he also now owned an apartment in Athens.

There were many other items but he lost interest half way through the list. The estimated valuation was just shy of £18 million.

The final paragraph of the Will stated that Mrs Ellie Baldwin required that all the assets be held in trust for 1 year after her death, whilst her husband, Steven Baldwin, decided how he wished to utilize or dispose of the assets. During that year income from the assets would be paid to Mr Baldwin on a quarterly basis. She named a firm of accountants who would assist Konstanz & Young in the management of her estate in the interim and provide (should he so wish) tax advice to her husband. Management fees had been agreed in advance and capped.

Another document specified the Death in Service Benefit he would receive from the UK Government - her employers - together with her pension which he would also receive.

He sat there in disbelief. "Good God Ellie, why did you do this?"

At the bottom of the pile of documents, there was a sealed letter. The envelope read: "Personal and Private, to be opened only by Mr Steven Baldwin after the death of Ellie Williams."

It was written in longhand, although in their time together he had seen little of her handwriting to confirm that it was hers. Steve read the very brief letter and although it answered his question he wondered if his torture would ever end:

My Dearest Steve

If you are reading this then I have pre-deceased you, as the lawyers say. We have not known each other very long and I treasure those first days in Crete as I treasure the little time we had together – so much squeezed into less than a year. We could have done so much!

I believe I know what your reaction will be and I do not wish you to make hasty decisions so I have given you a year to give serious consideration to the disposal of my estate – which is now entirely yours. I have no other family – just you. Given more time we might have made it more!

Much of my estate is a hangover from my parents – I have never really had the time to sort it all out. Now, unfortunately or not, I have left you a bit of a shambles.

Live your life, find another woman and move on. That's what I want you to do. Be happy.

Remember I always told you the truth about who I was.

With my deepest love,

Your wife

Ellie

The only pictures he had of Ellie was the secret video she made of the signing of the marriage documents. She really knew the bastards at Six and so she had tucked a small webcam in a corner of the cabin, even recording an amusing introduction. She hadn't told him about it until later, when she was bleeding out in Algeria. Later he'd found the thumb drive she'd hidden at the back of the drawer of nautical charts. After watching it once he'd almost thrown it away in his grief.

She had been as suspicious of her employer as he was, if not more so.

"Baldy, are you still there"

"Yes, sorry Dick, my mind wandered off there."

"Right. OK. Well we all know what it's like to lose a close buddy, maybe you should get some counseling. Memory lane can be on the way to hell."

"Listen Dick, I don't fucking have PTSD. I can handle it. I don't need the job or the money. And Ellie was my *wife*, not just a buddy."

"OK, OK, I'm so sorry – you know that Yorkshiremen can be too blunt at times. You'd be doing me a big favor if you at least hear me out."

"OK then fire away, though you're wasting your time."

Steve put the smartphone on speaker and wandered off to top up his Scotch.

"It's a security job, working for a Ukrainian software entrepreneur, managing our security operation, six guys in two teams – well actually five guys and one woman. Physical security only, no cyber stuff or anything like that. They have their own team for that. It's three months only, prior to the company launching some new software. They're based on an estate near you, in Olhaõ. As I said earlier, right place, right time. The pay is good, a bit more than on that last gig. A thousand US a day, plus keep, and fifty per cent completion bonus."

"That's a lot of money but it's not an issue Dick, I told you that. And if they are Ukrainian, why don't they use a Ukrainian security company?"

"Two reasons. She's Ukrainian and doesn't get on with the Russians. Buligin has SVR people embedded everywhere in the Ukraine and a reputation for knocking off people who cross him - as you may know if you read the news at all. Secondly, she wants non-Russian speakers in her security team as she thinks it gives her more business security in the workplace."

"Wait a minute, did you say 'she'?"

"I did, as in Svetlana Ponomarenko. Not a billionairess but that is sure to happen within a year or two. Google her. Not that you'll find much – she is a very private woman and knows how to stay that way, even in this world."

"Why the change now, what happened to her previous team?"

"Nothing, she's been a client of mine for three years on and off."

"So what's new?"

"My lead guy, Sol Brocking, has a brain tumor. Fortunately it's operable and he'll be back in three months. Hence this call to you."

"So promote one of the others for the time being."

"I would if I could, but some guys can never make officer, no matter how capable as troopers."

"And some guys don't want to be officers."

"Yeh and you're no exception. Why are you giving me so much grief? Look, being busy might help you take your mind off things and would be a really big help to me. I'm in a jam. Come on Baldy, help me out here. I'm on site myself right now but I need to get back to my London office."

"All I can say right now is that I'll think about it. Give me a couple of days and I'll get back to you."

"Can you make it twenty four hours?"

"If you want an answer urgently, you can have one now."

"OK, OK, forty eight hours then. Sorry chum, I can tell that you've been hit pretty badly."

"You don't know the half of it Dick."

"I'm sure I don't – and don't want to either. There's a briefing document on its way to you now. Please hard-delete it once you've read it. And if you need someone to talk to, just call me. As I said I'm on site now, less than ten miles from you."

"OK."

"Forty eight hours then?"

Bakdwin rang off. Self-pity was not in his nature, but he had come close to it over the last couple of months. Moving to the medicine locker in the forward head, he took out another bottle of Glenlivet – the last one - and emptied it into the toilet pan and flushed it away. Then the other open bottle followed. That was the last of the case he'd bought in Gib. He looked at himself in the mirror and cursed - a major clean-up was required if he was going to meet Dickwick. He was surprised that he still cared. *That must be a good sign.*

He made himself a sandwich for lunch and then fell asleep in his bunk, still wrestling with the implications of the will and Dick's call for help. When he woke up it was after 6 pm and he realized that was the first straight four hours sleep he managed in months.

With a cup of tea in hand he climbed the companionway into the cockpit to watch the sunset. Taking a sip of the tea he grimaced – there was no whisky left for this cuppa. Things had to change. Tomorrow would be better, each day an improvement, but by God it was tough. He thought about his father and what had brought him to this place, this time. His own choices, nothing more. – and the ankle which he'd broken on the SBS selection course during the 40 mile Long Drag in the Brecon Beacons.

Baldwin had been born and brought up as an only child in Portsmouth where the family home had been a council flat near Fratton, a mile or so from the docks. Social housing they called it, but Steve's socialization had been tough.

His father Mike made a living at fishing, just, but when the catch was poor then he would come home after a skinful at The Bridge – a pub on East Street hard by the Camber - and give Baldwin's mother a beating. When the catch was good his father, would celebrate with a skinful, then come home and give his mother a beating. Baldy – his nickname by now - started fighting at school on a regular basis (and out of school too for that matter) and this was coming to the attention of the educational psychologists.

By the time he was thirteen, Baldwin had started stepping in-between his parents during their nightly battles and getting a hiding for his trouble, but as he matured and grew he started giving almost as good as he got, and his father became more wary. Nevertheless his parents had split up by the time he was fourteen. He still saw his father occasionally – his father had taught him beach fishing at six years of age, and by the time he was ten years old he had been helping out regularly on the trawler at weekends.

He skipped a day from school occasionally and took his gear down to the beach at Southsea to do some fishing. He watched the ships – tankers, warships, cruise liners and more – entering and leaving the Solent, and his horizons widened as he matured.

He was far from a star pupil in school at the Priory Comprehensive, but he stabilized after his parents split up, and was able enough, though not academic. By the time of his sixteenth birthday his relationship with his father was pretty good, as he knew that his mother was safe; his father had shacked up with another woman down in Southsea, but Baldwin knew nothing else about that side of his father's life.

By now the fighting was in the past – he'd won his reputation.

Then he'd started thinking about joining the forces. Pompey – Portsmouth – was a naval city and had been since even before Henry VIII. So, the Royal Navy appealed to him – some of the lads from school signed up every year, but after a discussion at the recruiting office in the city he wondered if there would be enough action. Yes there was travel, yes there was the sea, but he was unsure. One night in the pub someone had said 'Join the army, see the world and kill people'. He didn't think that was really for him.

He talked to his father about it. His dad sung him a verse, from a Broadway musical, he'd said:

"I joined the Navy to see the world,
And what did I see?
I saw the sea."

"You can see the sea right here in Pompey – and have a lot more fun! And if you come into partnership with me we can buy a bigger trawler. You'll make a good living."

This was stretching a point, the teenager knew. Too often he'd heard his father moaning about EU fishing quotas.

Then one evening over a beer in The Bridge - a pub near the fishing dock - after a good day with the nets, his father suggested he think about the Royal Marines. That seemed to be a good compromise between the land and the sea.

"I've listened to you Steve, and I know you need to get it out of your system", he said, "do a few years, sow your wild oats, and come back to the trawler. We'll buy a new boat when you return and you can take over."

He had been non-committal, but by the end of the week he had taken the first step and committed to the entrance assessment. A visit to the Royal Marines museum across the road from the beach at Southsea had cemented his resolve. Physical sports had never really been his thing, and he had to work himself hard to get up to the fitness levels required to pass his entrance and aptitude testing. Running on the shingle beach in Southsea for an hour twice day worked his stamina up, and he joined a Portsmouth boxing club to gain access to the gym and a trainer, though the weekend work on the trawler had built him a half decent upper body.

He passed his entrance with flying colors, and then worked his way through the batch of tests and trials and completed the 32 week training course as an outstanding candidate. He passed all the timed physical tests at better than the standard required of an officer candidate, which itself was significantly higher than that of a trooper.

A year later, when he returned from a winter survival exercise in Norway, Baldwin heard that his father had been lost overboard from the trawler. Then, within a year, his mother was dead.

He snapped out of his reverie and realized that the sun had set, the sky was red and the lights of Faro were starting to twinkle in the evening haze. He looked around at the other anchored boats as the wake of a passing trawler going down-channel started *Rubaiyat* rolling, their crew preparing their chase boats for a night of squid-netting. He checked that the anchor was properly set and then went below. What would he say to Dick?

A Signal message chimed on his phone half an hour later. It was the briefing document from Dickwick, and brief it was indeed. Steve reckoned that knowing Dick there was a whole lot more behind the scenes than the bare bones he scanned, shaking his head at the name of

Dick's firm – so quickly read as 'Scumtest' but as he'd found out a year ago, it was a play on the Latin for 'shield' and typical of Dick's sense of humor and his Oxford education:

Scutum Est Security Consultants LLC

Client Profile

Client	Saluscent.com
Domicile	Cyprus
Founded	2015
Principal & Owner	Sveta Kovacs, CEO
Reporting Contact	Sergei Gerasimov, COO
Head Office	Nicosia, Cyprus
Other locations	Olhaõ, Portugal (operations) with additional software developers in Kiev, Ukraine.
Principal area of business	Software application development in the currency and IPR asset class spaces.
Contract Status	Active (2016), Contract number 1386

That was it as regards a briefing. Steve didn't bother to read the copy of the client contract which was attached, though he noticed that the 'Cost of Services' section was, unsurprisingly, blank. He put the kettle on to make himself some tea – there was still plenty of good strong Tetleys left over from Gibraltar – and sat down to check his list of boat to-do jobs. The list was one small discipline that he had managed to maintain since leaving Gibraltar – '*Rubaiyat*' was still very new to him and he was still adding to the list faster than he could tick the jobs off.

Then he wondered about weapons. Apart from a good knife he didn't yet have serious kit aboard. Usually he carried a couple of pistols but long weapons were harder to conceal. He hadn't worked out where to site a secure concealed gun cabinet. Many US yachts carried weapons but the previous owner of *Rubaiyat* did not appear to have done so, although Baldwin did yet know every nook and cranny of this vessel. He had bought the yacht 'all standing' from the owner's widow. The yacht had been in Marina Smir in Morocco and the widow in the US. There was still a lot of the previous owner's stuff aboard but most of the personal effects had been cleared out by Ellie. If there were concealed weapons then he had not found them yet.

With his previous boat *'Adèle'* he'd almost got to the end of the jobs list – and that was after two years of sailing round the world following a year's preparation in France and Spain. He hoped that he would not have to put 'Repair bullet holes' on the list this time round.

After drinking his tea he pulled out his new wet suit and snorkel gear. His personal gear was new as he had lost all his possessions when *'Adèle'* had been arrested by the Tunisians. He sighed. New boat, new gear. The hull fouling at this anchorage off Culatra was bad and he wanted to give the yacht's bottom a scrape. Anyway he needed the exercise and a clear head to think about Dick's offer.

What else was he going to do, stay on his boat and get drunk every day? Or was he going to move on to another anchorage and get drunk every day?

Then there was Brazil and Argentina – places which had always been in his mind to visit since he'd asked his father one day what lay at the southwestern end of the English Channel. 'Keep going that way and you'll get to South America' had been the answer. Baldwin had headed that way in *'Adèle'* but lack of wind and ocean current had taken him more to the west, past the Amazon to Trinidad and the Caribbean. Much later, sailing with Ellie in the Mediterranean had given him a different perspective, but now he had no one to share those exotic destinations with. But he did have too much time to think – and drink.

*

Nine

Back in 2014, Lieutenant General Danylo Kravets had been promoted a month after the downing of the Japan Airlines flight. The disaster had caused world-wide outrage. Moscow was on the defensive and blamed the Ukrainian government, saying that there was irrefutable proof that the missile had been stolen from them by Ukrainian Special Forces, but were not prepared to share the details.

Back in Kiev, Svetlana was finalizing her own plans after her year of conscription had ended. The times with Danylo Kravets had been useful but the sex had been unpleasant although necessary for her plan. Danylo had arranged the coming weekend – a few days at his *dacha* while he fished and she watched satellite TV, bored witless with the absence of an internet link of any kind. Although she could work on one of her current software projects she preferred to do that when Danylo was not around. There were no mobile phone connections either, although Danylo always carried a satellite phone for their weekends away at the completely isolated *dacha* on the River Dnieper north of Kiev.

Late that May Thursday morning Danylo picked her up at her apartment on Khreschatyk Street in Kiev and drove to the new marina downtown on the Dnieper River.

It was early May the last of the ice had cleared off the river, but the air still had a winter sharpness. His motor launch was new and modest enough not to raise too many questions – Sveta knew a lot about his background and how he afforded the luxuries in his life, luxuries way beyond his pay grade and not financed by his school teacher parents. Although he had never explained anything to her, they both knew that there was little that her skills could not access in the Ukraine. That made her dangerous to him, so he kept her close. The problem he had was that she did not need to depend on him for money, only the influence and contacts he had – and they were of declining value as each week went by.

He had talked of marriage and children but she had treaded water on the subject, knowing that she'd got as much out of the relationship as she could and that it was time to move on. Danylo was just a step on her ladder and she could see many other steps ahead.

She had much bigger plans than those of his that he had outlined to her. Sveta thought that his horizons were limited, his vision was constrained to further advancement in the military and possible political opportunities beyond that. It was time to for her to move up a step but on her own ladder, not his.

Besides which, she didn't want children and his occasional drunken rages were painful. Whenever Danylo raised the subject of a family she closed her eyes and said "I don't know Dany, I'm not quite ready for that yet." Then she opened the special little box in the corner of her brain and examined the contents – the locked away memories of her father's bestial demands, the horrors of her childhood. The memories and emotions were very private, and their replays very short, but it was enough to solidify her intent and determination to avoid any kind of future for her with Danylo or any other man. She fed her strength with the bad memories. Men were to be used for *her* purposes, and then discarded.

It had been over five years now since she had started making her first real money from the credit card harvesting. As soon as she had her first 50,000 *hryvnia* – about US$2,000 – she had booked the tubal ligation at the Clinic Omega in Budapest. On her return to Kiev it had been a simple matter to bypass the clinic's online security and change the medical record of the procedure to one of a D&C.

Of course she also recognized that Dany's paternalistic wishes were not all genuine - he needed to control her and her knowledge in some way. The end of their shelf life was close, it had to be, it would be. She was sure of that. Fed up of faking orgasms and tired of bruises, she would make the first move.

Danylo's *dacha* was on a small island in the Sorokoshyci Regional Landscape Park about 70 kilometers north of Kiev. They could drive there and use the small rowing boat to cross to the island, but that would take almost a whole day given the long rough tracks through the park. They had to do that in winter, when the snow was not too deep, but now that it was springtime it would take less than two hours in the launch even against the cold northerly wind. And so they butted their way upriver into the choppy brown water, passing strings of barges fussed along by their mother tugs, and arrived at the *dacha* in time for a late lunch. They were well insulated against the cold wind with the best North Face puffa jackets and over-trousers, with walking boots on their feet. During the frequent breaks in the cloud the sun warmed them almost to the point of removing their jackets – and then it disappeared and the chill set in quickly in the wind straight from the Arctic.

At the '*Gourmand – Furshet*' deli in the Atmosphera Mall on Stolychne Shose, Svetlana had bought a couple of food hampers and a pack of delicacies, intending to make this a weekend to remember – at least for her. It had been easy enough to obtain another special ingredient from an old acquaintance at the university – she had plenty of leverage over many of the people she had known there. She was ready.

"Just the two of us again" Danylo had said. "We will do the cooking together. I'll catch a nice big perch or bream."

"You always say that, never catch anything, and I always do all the cooking."

"This time it will be different."

'You bet' thought Sveta.

Danylo had bought the wine and *horilka* – Ukrainian vodka. He preferred the Nemiroff brand and had included a bottle of the wicked type known as *pertsivka* which contained chili peppers.

"Why do you men always need spicy food and drink? I hate the way that spices make my lips tingle."

"Is that why you rarely kiss me on the mouth, because of spice on my lips?"

"That's one reason. The other is that I prefer kissing the other parts. You wouldn't want chili on them would you?"

"In that case I'm glad you don't like spicy food!"

He laughed. She laughed. Their thoughts and emotions were a universe apart – if Svetlana could be described as having any emotions at all. If she had emotions they were in another universe – or locked away in a secret room in her mind.

"I have something very spicy for you Dany, something you will never forget." O*r remember. Special yes, spicy no, but what the hell did it matter?*

"What is it?"

"I'm not telling you, it's a surprise. It's a new line at *Gourmand – Furshet*. Imported."

"I can't wait. Go on tell me."

"No I'm not telling. Don't worry, you'll find out soon enough."

"And I have a big surprise for you."

"What is it?"

"I'm not telling. Don't worry, you'll find out soon enough."

She nodded, laughing at his riposte. God, it was hard pretending to laugh with this man, she thought.

As Danylo brought the launch alongside the rickety wooden dock Svetlana hopped ashore with the lines. Then, whilst Dany got the wood burner started and fired up the generator, Sveta put the vodka in the freezer, the wine in the fridge, and organized lunch. The wind was still too cold for them to eat outside, but the view from the large window was spectacular, straight out west across the river, which was about four miles wide at this point. The river current was still strong at this time of year as the last of the meltwaters and spring rains moved down to the estuary at the port of Ochakiv on the Black Sea.

The afternoon passed quickly and by 6 pm the wind had dropped completely and they were seated on the deck, watching the sun falling westward, Svetlana drinking an expensive Chablis and Danylo with a glass of Nemiroff *pertsivka.* Although the sunsets could be spectacular, they did not move Svetlana. The only thing that made her emotional was locked away in that secret box in a far corner of her brain – and that was unpleasant in the extreme.

"They weren't biting – I think it's the current. Or maybe it's the bait? My father never had any interest in fishing or hunting, so I had no one to learn from."

"It's just as well that I brought some beef. Didn't you ever get a book or look online to see how the experts catch sturgeon?"

"I've watched a ton of YouTube videos and followed all the advice. I don't know what I'm doing wrong."

"Maybe you should go hunting instead. You're good with a gun – I've seen you in action, don't forget."

I don't. She knew too much about him and had a way of reminding him about it. He had to bring her to heel or close the matter finally. They'd been together long enough now for her to make a decision about marriage. Tonight would tell, one way or the other. He took a slug of the *pertsivka,* the ice cold vodka combining with the hot chili peppers to give a mouthful of contrasting hits on his senses. He smiled at her and raised his glass. "How's the Chablis?"

"Wonderful. And the Nemiroff?"

"Literally sensational, as always. Can I top you up?"

"No thanks." She turned away from him and looked to the west. "That's the last of the sun for today. We'd better move inside and if you're ready, I'll go and get the *zakuski* from the oven."

Danylo drained his glass and topped it up. "I'll wait here for a few minutes. Call me when you are ready."

The traditional beef and mushroom stew was a ready meal from the microwave. "It was good, but not as good as my mother's."

"Then complain to *Gourmand – Furshet*, not me. You know I don't cook. My mother never taught me to cook – just as your father never taught you to fish."

"Sveta, you have a certain way of putting me in my place. The meal was wonderful. After all, you light up my life."

Svetlana did a double take. "You never talk like that Dany – are you all right?"

"I couldn't be better, it's a wonderful evening. I'll go and put some music on and get another bottle of Nemiroff. More wine?"

"Yes, there's another bottle in the fridge."

Svetlana retrieved her black Gucci handbag from the side table and located the vial in the zippered pocket near the bottom.

Danylo returned as the sound of John Coltrane's saxophone filled the room.

"One thing my father did teach me was an appreciation of jazz."

"That's decadent music, forbidden under the *communisti.* He could have been sent to a gulag. You are lucky, my father didn't teach me to appreciate anything."

"You don't talk about him much."

"There's not a lot to say. He died when I was eleven. I prefer not to talk about him."

Danylo nodded, recalling the circumstances he'd read about in her file. Stabbed by his wife as he beat her. The daughter too traumatized to talk. Not unusual. The suspicion of the investigating officer was that not everything was as it seemed, but no alternative explanation could be proven and would in any case achieve little.

"Sveta, we've been together now for over a year and grown ever closer. We hold secrets about each other that no one else should know. Our trust is absolute, my love for you unbounded, and I hope that you feel the same way. You know that I want to have a family. Besides, a senior officer in my position needs a wife – and I have never met anyone who could hold a light up to you."

Svetlana guessed where this was going as he reached across and held her hand.

He withdrew his hand and produced a red velvet box from the pocket of his chinos, pushing it across the table to her.

"Svetlana Ponomarenko, will you marry me?"

She opened the box and looked at the ring. A solitaire diamond with emeralds in the mount. Three thousand dollars worth she reckoned.

"Dany, I don't know what to say. It's beautiful." She smiled her best smile as he slipped the ring on to her finger. "I need to think about this, it's such a surprise."

"Sveta, the ring fits. We can do wonderful things together here in the Ukraine. I have a plan to go in to politics and you would be the perfect wife to help me get to the very top. Just think, First Lady."

I'll bet she thought – dig the dirt on the opponents, sow misinformation, fake news, the whole gamut. And all along the way play the part of the tame Ukrainian wife while he had a string of mistresses, just like all the rest. No fucking way was she staying in the Ukraine, no way with him

"Dany, it's such a lot to take in, I need time to think about it."

"I understand. I hoped you'd say yes right away. But sleep on it. I'd like that I can have your answer before we return to Kiev on Monday and return to Kiev as a happy couple with a wonderful future."

"That is fair, I would not want to keep you waiting, *doroha*."

Danylo smiled. "That's the first time you have ever called me darling, I take that as a good sign." In bed she had called him many things, using words that he had specified but 'darling' – never. *What the hell, she thought, it didn't matter now.*

"I've thought about it. The answer is Yes."

He pulled he across and took her there on the table, more gently than he had ever done before. At least, he started to, but then he reverted to type.

*

The General had been reported missing by Svetlana Ponomarenko, who described herself as Kravets's fiancé. She had used his military satellite phone to call the emergency services. In her statement to the military police, she had said that after supper they had walked out on to the dock to look at the stars – at about 9.30 she thought. They had both drunk steadily but not excessively during the evening – she wine and he vodka. She said that they were in good spirits as he had proposed to her and she had accepted. Out on the small wooden dock she had complained of the cold wind and gone back inside while he finished his cigarette.

She told them that she had got ready for bed and waited for him – it was a special night for them – but she fell asleep. She woke about 1 am. and saw that his side of the bed was undisturbed. She thought he might be downstairs but could not find him. She took a flashlight out and checked the dock. She ran back in to the house and used using his military satellite phone – he had left his attaché case open. She did not tell them that she knew the combination to the case. Her statement was accepted without further questioning.

Her call had been taken by the Ground Forces communication center. They had roused the emergency services who logged the call at 01.25 am. An extensive search of the dock area, the dacha and the surrounding woodland had found no trace of the General and a full-scale military search was initiated. Traces of cigarette ash were found on the dock.

There was some concern that the General might have been abducted by rebel forces from Donetsk, but there were no traces on the dock of any struggle, nor signs of any landing on the riverbank nearby.

The body of Colonel General Danylo Kravets was eventually recovered from the Dnieper River on the Wednesday following his abduction. After an extensive search the Politsiya patrol boat found his body lodged against one of the road bridge supports in the city of Kaniv, about 50 kilometres south east of Kiev.

There was post-mortem damage to the body indicative being struck by a propeller with a size typical of that of a tug. The autopsy report was unequivocal – death was due to drowning. The blood alcohol level was more than three times the legal limit for driving a motor vehicle. His blood did not contain any traces of recreational or other drugs. He was fully clothed but as his trouser flies were unzipped it was thought that he had fallen into the river whilst relieving himself.

The dosage of flunitrazepam that Svetlana had used was sub-clinical, just enough to tip the balance but not show up in hair or urine tests – if indeed the medical examiner had bothered to test for Rohypnol. The time that the body had been in the water was an added bonus – the filthy Dnieper was so full of chemicals that any tests would show up almost every chemical known to man – as did the fish.

Pushing the drunken almost senseless Danylo off the dock had been easy. Now no one else knew about her involvement in the downing of the airliner.

She kept the ring.

Two days later, with a new hairstyle and spectacles, she crossed the border into Hungary at Beregsurány. She was now an EU citizen, Sveta Kovacs. The first of her new, genuine Hungarian passports had cost her €10,000 Euros plus a threat to expose a pedophile in the Hungarian Ministry of the Interior. Pedos used the Dark Web, but so too did extortionists. Information was power - and she had plenty. Her spoken English was passable, but her Hungarian non-existent. Her other passports would come once her new face was ready.

With over €500,000 invested in cryptocurrencies, exporting currency was easy, anonymous and secure. She had Google Authenticator on one of her smartphones, her 12 word Bitcoin and Ethereum wallet recovery seeds printed and sewn into the lining of her carry-on case and a Trezor hardware wallet loaded with 15 Bitcoins (worth, on that day, a shade under US$200,000) – the contents of Danylo Kravets's bank accounts which she had emptied.

She headed west, for England, arriving in London two days later after a couple of detours. Under the new UK border rules, her passport was stamped with a 90 day visa and was the first step of her new venture. From a maildrop in Paddington she collected a package containing 3 cellphones.

Paying cash she checked into a cheap and uncheerful hotel in Bayswater Road. She wasn't particular about comfort – she just need a good wifi connection. By the time the streetlights were on she had download a binary from one of her secure servers in the dark web, wiped the ROM on the new Android cell phones and burned the custom Android OS version that Yuri Yegorov in Lvov had developed for her. She then installed her own custom encrypted messaging app.

Yuri had been a student at Lvov University who she had met through an online software forum whilst studying for her undergraduate degree. When she'd been in the armed forces she had recommended him to Danylo Kravets as a potential member of her technical team and Danylo had arranged the posting. Yuri was only alive because he had developed hepatitis and had been discharged from National Service on medical grounds well before the airliner disaster, and without knowledge of the project. Otherwise he might have been dead in the German bunker with one of Danylo's bullets in him.

After she had left the Ukrainian army, Sveta had funded Yuri when he set up a small software development company in Lvov. He and Dmitri Borzov were not aware of each other's link to Sveta as far as she knew, and she kept it strictly that way.

Yuri's company became modestly successful as she steered him towards specific software projects, thriving on the dark web selling limited issue customized Android phones with secure communications software and running IP-hopping servers to support them. It was much like Encrochat although monthly subscriptions were several times that of the $200 Encrochat demanded, and customers were each limited to 10 units and 1 server. Exclusive service, premium prices and low visibility was a safer way to do business. And a better way to keep the law enforcement agencies at bay.

*

Ten

Major Leonid Drozdov came from a distinguished family. His uncle, Yuri Drozdov had been a KGB 'spymaster', running a team of sleepers worldwide – and a team which had assassinated the Afghan President, Hafizullah Amin, in 1979, after which Drozdov had created the elite Vympel special forces (Spetsnaz) unit.

Now, the Drozdov star was in the ascendant again as the young major (who had chosen the GRU and not the KGB's successor, the FSB for his career), headed up the GRU Cyberwarfare Forensic Unit embracing the future and the new digital weaponry. Within 24 hours of the downing of the Japanese airliner over the Ukraine in 2014 his team's investigators had found the optical fiber tap into the Russian air-defense missile system command and control hub in Donetsk. The team also found the remains of a microwave antenna but got no further. The trail was cold.

A month later Major Drozdov sat at his desk in The Aquarium, as the GRU headquarters building is known, just outside Moscow at the Khodinka Airfield. In front of him sat three of his analysts.

"So, what do we have beyond a tap into our anti-aircraft missile command and control network? A month has passed and I have bugger all to report. This does not look good for any of you."

The three analysts looked at one another.

"Come on, one of you say something!" His hand hit the desk, and they jumped as one.

Captain Yuri Sokolov spoke. "Sir, the hard data is very limited, but analysis of soft intelligence suggests a sixty five percent probability that the operation was headed by Ukrainian Lieutenant General Danylo Kravets. However, his death has been reported. He was drowned in a river which runs past his dacha. There are no suspicious circumstances."

"Is that all you have?"

"Sir, we are still investigating, but an agent is reporting that the General was regularly seen in the company of a female lieutenant who acted as his PA. She might have been on one of his teams. We believe her name is Svetlana Ponomarenko. She has a Ph.D. in cryptography. Her doctoral thesis is not available on line. We think that the Ukrainian government has buried it. Second Lieutenant Popov is trying to obtain a copy." Another of the team nodded at this statement. "So far we have been unable to hack into the data around Danylo. We know little beyond what our agents tell us. We could approach the SVR for help, Sir."

"No fucking way. The SVR are not to come anywhere near this. They probably have their own operation anyway. If this gets out I'll have you all court martialed, understood? Keep it off our main system – the bastards are probably tunneling in right now."

They remained silent – his rages were legendary. His anger subsided. "So, it's possible that this General Kravets and this woman could have been responsible for the operation?"

"Highly probable, Sir. We think that she has a history of online frauds and other dark web activities dating back to when she was a student. She has now left the military after a year of service and we cannot trace her." He looked worried, and swallowed hard. "But we are trying, Sir."

"Very well – get back to work and keep me updated. Make sure that Ponomarenko woman is on the digital watchlist."

"Yes Sir."

And there the trail went cold again, for another two years.

And then - "Major, we have a lead on the Ponomarenko woman. You know, that downed Japanese airliner a couple of years ago?"

"How could I forget? A lead you say – a credible lead?"

"Yes, Sir."

"Come to my office immediately."

Major Drozdov put down the phone. He was still a major. having been passed over yet again for promotion in the latest round. He feared that the investigation of the downed airliner had damaged his career. Perhaps there was hope at last, he thought, as Captain Sokolov entered. He wanted to dump this case, but that would look even worse. His uncle had not been a quitter, fighting the Germans all the way into the center of Berlin. No, he would not quit either.

"What have you got?"

"A code signature, Sir."

"What, cryptographic?"

"No, software – at least we believe that it is. You have read the doctoral thesis of the Ponomarenko woman, yes?"

Drozdov nodded. "A long time ago. Too long. Didn't you take six months to get a copy?"

"It was kept in a special archive by the Ukrainian Government, Sir. Encrypted. "

"OK, I've heard your excuses before. But it was a clever piece of work – the thesis, I mean, not your investigation." Clever? That was a fair guess, although he hadn't read it and would not have understood it if he had. "What does that tell us?"

"Sir, many programmers have distinctive styles and ways in which they add comments to the software code that they write and the actual structure of the code itself. Well, the code she developed in that thesis has been syntactically analyzed – not for its logic, but its style. We are using that as a kind of fingerprint." His excitement was obvious.

"I remember. But it hasn't helped any of us has it, Captain?"

"Sir, we monitor all public software code repositories as a matter of course…"

"Yes, we have several operations underway which target them. Tell me something I don't know."

"…and we have found a good match to her style signature in a recent hard fork of Bitcoin code in the GitHub open source code repository."

"What's that?"

"Someone – Ponomarenko we think – creating a specific version of the Bitcoin cryptocurrency code."

"How sure are you that it is her?"

"Sixty to seventy per cent confidence, Sir."

"Right, We need to get that confidence level up to eighty per cent, ASAP, then I can report my success. I'll put extra people on your team. Highest priority. How long will it take?"

"Hard to tell, Sir. I'll need a couple of people from our Deep Data Mining team, plus other resources. We need to get right inside GitHub's archives and then look wider based on what we find."

"You have the rest of the day to email me a brief report, and your specific requirements."

Sokolov looked sick. "Immediately, Sir."

"My persistence is paying off. Keep up the hard work."

"Thank you, Sir." His demeanor didn't improve as he left Drozdov's office. "How long is a fucking piece of string?" he thought.

Inside the office Drozdov sat back in his chair and looked at the picture of his uncle on the wall, in which he was bedecked with medals. He'd famously once declined to join the KGB because his baldness was a distinguishing feature, no good for undercover work. But he'd been persuaded and had become an expert in disguise – even serving undercover in Beijing. Things are not always what they seem, thought the young major. *What is that Ponomarenko woman is up to?*

He went online and checked the Litecoin price – lately he'd started to dabble in cryptocurrency. The only cryptocurrency that the Russian public were allowed to access was the CryptoRuble – or CryptoTrouble as some had dubbed it – which did not offer anonymity - buyers and sellers could be tracked by the government which controlled it to prevent the export of currency. However, some government and military employees could access mainstream cryptos – if they knew how. He was one of the lucky ones.

*

It took a week for the team to hack the databases and backtrack through the trail. They got as far as a server farm in the Ukraine, part of the dark web.

"So Sokolov, it's taken you a week to get to another dead end?"

"We're still trawling, Sir, looking at the other users of this Ukrainian server farm. The accounts are anonymized and we're trying to follow the money, but most users pay with cryptocurrency."

"What about IP addresses and headers?"

"All meta data is anonymized and one-time."

"But we've broken the Onion Ring?"

"Yes Sir, but now we're seeing software defined networks with ad-hoc Rings and one-time peer to peer linkages set up using the cryptocurrency technology – it doesn't have to be used just for money."

"Shit!"

Sokolov was hoping for another rant from his superior, but was disappointed – his guys were running bets on the quickest time it took to get a rant out of the Major.

Drozdov looked thoughtful and not about to rant. He glanced through the partition and could see his team at their desks outside Drozdov's office. Someone would be running a stopwatch, he guessed. It was a bit of fun for him. Nothing was secret in his office.

"What about the other students that this Ponomarenko woman knew? Can we find out who they were, where they work now? Maybe she stays in touch with some of them."

"It's worth a try, Sir, but we'd need to get people on the ground in Kiev,"

"That could take months to set up, but I'll see what I can do. Surely we must have people there already?"

The Major hated the idea of using another arm of the GRU to do the work on the ground, but he couldn't see any alternatives. Unless…

"That will be all for now Sokolov."

*

Eleven

The previous Chief of MI6, 'C', Sir William Gore, had retired immediately after the nuclear-triggered tsunami in the terrorist disaster known as the 'Cause of all Causes'. He hadn't been pushed out – his term was up and he was elevated to the House of Lords where he resolutely refused to speak on matters related to National Security, as was usual. Gore's successor at Vauxhall Cross, Henry Brewell, had been in post just two months as Emmet Macsen entered his office and closed the door.

"Emmet, give me a quick rundown on the 'Pistole' operation that Josh Packard is running."

The rundown took less than five minutes. Sometimes the files did not hold everything, sometimes by accident, omission or even design.

"So, in summary then, Ponomarenko has been steadily creeping up our watch list for a few years."

"Yes, at least we believe it's her, after changing her identity to Sveta Kovacs, with a genuine Hungarian passport. Now she's in the top five hundred – and climbing even more rapidly as the range of warning flags and their salience increases. She's extremely adept at hiding her tracks and so we've had to become more intrusive in our intel gathering. If we knew more today then I'm sure be a lot higher up the list. We've kept the Hungarians in the dark about the passport."

"Could be useful to know there's a back door there."

"Precisely."

"And your gut feel?"

"She's planning something big. These types of people have a trajectory – bigger projects, better concealment and then a big sting. Then, hopefully, a fall."

"And you think that cryptocurrency is her big one?"

"I'm sitting on the fence right now – after all it's no secret that she's launching a new cryptocurrency in a few months."

"Very well. You are on the right track with *Pistole*. You know how paranoid the Government is about these currencies. And not just this government – all the G20 governments, whatever their political color. The Bank of England has been raising warning flags with the Treasury. They did some background work and now it's got to go further and deeper. So, over to us and elevated priority for *Pistole*. It's seen as a threat to national security. We're not sharing this with the Cousins right now given the recent political turmoil over there.

There's no knowing what they will do. A cynic might say that the Government wants to have a handy cryptocurrency to play with, deniably of course."

"I understand, Sir. Is that all?"

"No. I see that the name 'Steven Baldwin' was mentioned in a '*Pistole*' meeting transcript."

"Yes. An ex-Royal Marine possibly being brought in to run the *Scutum Est* physical security team at the Saluscent site. He's not flagged in our files."

"He wouldn't be flagged to you – but it's been flagged to me. He's been involved in previous ops for us. Even I don't have full access. Don't look so surprised – you of all people should know about compartmentalization."

"But surely someone must know?"

"I'm sure they do, and he's probably sitting in the House of Lords right now. That, of course, is speculation and goes no further, understood?"

"Of course, Sir."

"Anyway, given that he has history with us, for us, why don't we try and rope him in to this project? Of course he must not know about our other assets and Telion must not know about him."

"Then Josh Packard can't be his handler. What about Barbary?"

"Not for this job."

"It's getting over-complicated."

"These things always are. You'll have to find someone else to run him."

"How about Borthwick himself, the guy who owns Scutum Est?"

"Leverage is likely to be a problem there – on both counts."

"Don't worry, I'll find something to use. I know that Borthwick is opening a new cybersecurity division in his company though I doubt that he can offer us anything in that area..."

'C' looked at him and watched as the wheels turned.

"…although I guess that is where we need to leave a trail or sow disinformation…yes, yes that could work."

"Good. You can always dangle a few contracts. You'd better get back to it."

"Yes sir."

"And keep the *Pistole* file sanitized for now. Report directly to me about this. In the meantime I'll have lunch with my predecessor and find out what the old fart knows – or will at least tell me."

*

Twelve

"What are you having, Baldy?"

"Black coffee."

"The local way?"

"Just the coffee thanks."

"Fair enough, but I'm going local. Here, read this while I get the coffees."

The *Café do Doca* was in the street that ran along the north side of the commercial dock in Olhaõ, just next to the Chinese bazaar. It was a hot clear morning but the breeze had just started to kick in and ease the temperature as Steve had motored his dinghy through the couple of miles of shallow channels from where *Rubaiyat* was anchored.

Through the window of the bar Baldwin could see the squid fishing boats with their huge arrays of arclights unloading their night's catch at the east wall. There were a few small local yachts and a Portuguese patrol boat on the western wall of the dock. The smell of fish was powerful.

He looked at the folder on Dick's tablet. The first sheet gave a thumbnail portrait of each of the team. He recognized a couple of names from the assignment in the Ionian – Henri Laporte, Aldo Colarusso. The details were bland and said little about their capabilities, although he knew that Dick would have no doubts about their mettle – and Baldwin could personally vouch for Henri's himself. His finger hovered over the name 'J.C. Stone.' Ex-Royal Navy. Now that was unusual – a woman on a team like this. And a Wren too, at that, although technically Wrens were a dead species since 1993 when the Royal Navy had made them extinct, or more properly, merged them into the mainstream Navy. *'Merged' – that was the word and it had caused a few shipboard problems along the way.* He'd known someone called Stone, back in Rome. A guy. Just a coincidence, he thought. Elias Stone, that was it. MIA after the Rome disaster with another guy...Gregory something.

The Saluscent.com briefing sheet was familiar, but this copy of the engagement contract did not have an empty 'Cost of Services' box. Steve whistled quietly as Dick returned to the table with two coffees and a glass of brandy. "Seems there's a few ways to go local – red wine, port or brandy. It's a bit early in the day for port."

Baldwin laughed. "And brandy's not so serious? It's not like you to drink on the job."

"I'm not on shift. Did you read the folder?"

"Yes, but it's what is *not* in there that I want to know about. I can see why this contract means a lot to you. One mill a year? They must have a big operation."

"Not so big and only just profitable. You guys don't come cheap."

Baldwin smiled. *Typical tight Yorkshireman.* "So what's with this Sveta then?"

"A hard business woman, a software techie without match I'm told, and as cold a fish as you're ever likely to meet. Entirely self-made. She spends most of her time writing software and working with her technical team. I've had a few meetings with her, but day to day operations are handled by her Ops Director Sergei Gerasimov. You'll be reporting to him."

"Maybe."

"Yes OK, point made."

"So why such heavy security?"

"As I told you, she's worried about Buligin and the SVR."

"That doesn't wash Dick."

"Look, if it was anyone else I wouldn't say this, so it goes not further, right? And it's only hearsay, OK."

"OK."

"She was originally Ukrainian with the name Svetlana Ponomarenko. The word is that she was involved in hacking a Russian AA missile system that downed a civil airliner in the Ukraine. Russia got the blame."

"Shit, that's a bloody good reason for Moscow to want her – if it's true. But how would you know that?"

"You should know better than to ask. It's probably the strongest reason – if it's true, as you say. Personally, I believe it is. Have you heard of cryptocurrencies like Bitcoin?"

"Only in passing."

"Well, she told me that there are more than five thousand cryptocurrencies or altcoins. Most have died off. I get paid by her in Bitcoins. Even some third world African states have their own – big multinationals too. Anyway, Saluscent is working on new cryptocurrency software. There's huge money to be made and a lot at stake for a lot of competing entrepreneurs. She's turned down some unbelievable offers for her company – and her skills. She sees physical risks as well as cyber threats to her and her company. That's why she lives on site in a small villa at the rear of the estate, actually within the compound we secure. The industry knows that she's the brains and taking her out would clear the runway. So, she has commercial as well as Russian government enemies."

"But still, it sounds thin to me."

"I'm sure that there's a lot more dirty laundry in her closet, but nothing hard my own guys could turn up – looking very discreetly mind you. Even *we* have to do some due diligence. Ponomarenko also built a social network app for the Ukrainian armed forces – hacker proof it seems. It gave her the seedcorn for this venture, which is completely legit as far as I can tell. There was also some very vague talk of a credit card scam. Or three."

"You seem to be very well connected to hear all these rumors."

"I have to be, it's my business. The world is changing Baldy. Just look at the contracts I have. They are changing year by year. The requirements are not as simple as providing bouncers anymore. My people have to have the smarts as well as the beef. I'm opening up a cybersecurity division next month – I found a small specialist consultancy and I've bought my way in. Nobody trusts the big players anymore. Look at Kaspersky…"

"Who's he?"

"Not he. They are A big Russian software company specializing in cyber security software - as recommended by Barclays Bank. You probably use it yourself."

"I've no idea."

"Yes, well anyway, a lot of people think they are close to the Kremlin and the SVR, so their software is under suspicion. Barclays have now dropped it – and it's not allowed on any US Government machines – by law, as signed by Trump."

"It seems obvious in hindsight."

"Too right. Anyway my plate is overflowing and I could really do with you coming on board full-time. What happened to that Master's degree you were doing when we talked last? That was cybersecurity wasn't it?"

"Life got in the way – and I couldn't handle the math anyway, not cut out for academic stuff. I'm not even sure I'll take *this* gig. Especially with this team. I'm not a sexist, but a *WREN*?"

"The WRENs are dead, you know that. JC is an exceptional woman in more ways than one. Believe me she can mix it with the best of them – hand to hand, on the range and even at a Royal dining table. She's been there and done it in some places even *I* hadn't heard of. The last bit's just hearsay though. No names, no pack drill. I also heard that Six were after her but she told them where to go. She's very hot on IT – cybersecurity was her thing in the Navy. Anyway, you'll be impressed." Dick winked.

"So, if she's so good, then why is she working security with you?"

"I'd say it was my charms, but they didn't work. It's because we are the best at what we do. And it's handy to have a cyber specialist in *this* team. You never know what you'll find out."

"What was the client's reaction?"

"They asked why I was using a woman on a physical security team. I said 'why not? If we need to search any female visitors then we can do it without a problem. They bought that."

Dick retrieved his tablet from Baldwin's side of the table and nodded at it, closing the document folder. "You've seen what people will pay, and that's only one contract – I have more than a dozen active right now – and this one is not the biggest by far." Dick stood up. "Come on you can ask her yourself. She'll probably ask you the same question anyway. Their site is only twenty minutes away. Meet the people, see the operation, then decide."

"This is not a '*yes*'. I've got some more questions anyway."

"Come on, you can ask me in the car."

The car was silver, a top of the line Mercedes SUV parked out of the sun at the side of the café and the aircon provided sweet relief as they headed north out of town.

"Why are they here, why Portugal? I haven't been here long but already I've heard a few Russians talking – and not all are working girls."

"Yes, they're here in force and that's a fact, though most of the bad guys are over west towards Albufeira and east around Vilamoura. I guess that this estate was available when she was looking. The Ops Director told me that sun was important – you'll see that they have a few acres of solar panels on site, five acres in fact. They have a subsidiary that does something they call cryptocurrency mining - hundreds of dedicated computers running special software, using a huge amount of power. Seems it's got a lot to do with solving math equations – and money. I always try to check out a potential client's business so I looked into it briefly. Seems the cost of power is a major factor in profitability – hence the solar farm. The rest was way, way beyond me. They use that profit to help fund their other activities."

"I'll need to see the report of the security audit. I take it you reviewed it before signing the contract?"

"Er, no, we didn't actually."

"Jesus, Dick. Why the hell not?"

"Pressure of time and resources, as always."

"So, how do I get a complete picture of what I'd be taking on?"

"Ask JC, she's got a good feel for it."

Steve shook his head. "This sounds like a bit of a shambles."

Dick slowed down sharply and turned in towards the gated entrance. "No, it's not, not at all. You know me."

"Yes, only too well. Sounds like you're making it up as you go along. Typical salesman, all smoke and mirrors."

"Whatever. Anyway, we're here now. Aldo's on the gate duty this morning, though it's all managed from a control room inside the main block. I think that JC is on control this morning."

The fence looked to Steve to be about 3 meters high, two parallel lines of barbed wire 3 meters apart, topped with razor wire. There were camera posts and warning signs at regular intervals.

"Jesus, it's like a prison."

"As I said, she takes security very seriously. There's a lot more that you can't see."

"Look, even I know that Buligin's people don't do full frontal assaults in European countries. The Russians are more subtle these days."

"Yes, now they use cyber attacks. Anyway, the fence sends a message that she's bloody serious."

"And also that she has a lot to protect."

"True enough."

"But now the Russians are into nerve agents – how are we to protect her from that?"

"That's tricky I agree. We provide a barrier and she hardly ever leaves the site. She shuts herself away in the basement and often wears gloves. She's paranoid, OCD."

Dick lowered the window and put his palm on the pad at the steel post outside the gate and then detached the wireless reader from its mount and passed it to Steve.

"It's OK, it's already programmed with your palm. It'll know you."

"But how?"

"You left plenty of prints in Argostoli."

"You bastard!"

Dick chuckled. "Just cleaning up after you, old boy. Just cleaning up. Nearly done now. Open your window."

A small quad-copter flew around as a robo-trolley explosives sniffer checked under the SUV. Then the quad-copter hovered outside the windows.

"It's checking the inside and doing our facial scans." The drone bleeped and Steve looked at it. "There, the hi-res camera just got a retina scan from you. It'll check against a database of known bad guys – those that are on record anyway. AI – artificial intelligence - handles it all."

"Then what's Aldo doing?"

"Controlling the defenses and monitoring cameras. The camera feeds go through a face recognition system and an AI Attitude Recognition system. Whoever designed the Attitude systems thinks that people with ill intent have giveaways in their walk and stance. We don't fully trust the AI yet. That'll be next week."

"Is the team tooled up then?"

"You bet – unofficially, that is."

Baldwin shook his head in disbelief as the heavy double steel gate rolled aside and Dick powered the SUV up the driveway to the parking area, crossing what looked like a cattle grid on the way. "What was that we rattled over?"

"The drawbridge over a modern day tank trap - a big moat around the building. Dry at the moment, but it can be filled within a couple of hours from underground reservoir tanks. That's what we just crossed."

"Bloody hell!"

"Exactly. It's like an iceberg – the building you see above ground is only a tenth of the area of what's below ground – and we think there's a couple of levels down there, though we're not authorized to go below ground. I'll show you the rest of the physical security later. You might think that getting in was easy, but believe me even a tank would not get as far as the front door if an assault was attempted – you can't see half the defenses around this building."

"What the hell is she so afraid of?"

"I really don't know, but it goes well beyond the bounds of normal paranoia – if paranoia can be normal that is."

"And why all the satellite dishes?" Baldwin could see several large antennae – including two maybe twenty feet across – just visible above the roof line.

"I guess she doesn't trust landlines. There are no cables at all coming into this site - not even electricity. Gerasimov told me that they have the fastest satellite bandwidth available – he was talking fifty gigabits – they rent their own satellite from one of the constellation companies. That costs a fortune. Check your phone."

"No signal."

"Yes, all jammed."

"Is that a radar antenna I can see?"

"Possibly. She's nuts about security. Optical cables can be tapped, electricity power cables can be used for snooping. They've got it all covered. They generate all their own power from the solar farm and have the latest battery tech from Tesla to store it. And a huge bank of diesel generators just in case. Even their water is brought in by tanker."

Borthwick's SUV rolled to a stop and he climbed out into the hot afternoon sun. "Come on, time to meet her."

*

After the security scans at the main door, they passed through a body scanner. "Steve, this is J C Stone, everyone calls her JC. JC, I've told you about Steve. He's here to stand in for Sol while he's recuperating."

They nodded to one another as they shook hands with no hint of a smile either way. Dick led Steve to a side room where he opened a steel locker and withdrew a Glock 43 pistol. He didn't bother with a holster, just tucking the weapon into the rear of his trouser waistband.

"Bloody cold in here."

"They keep it that way, just below comfort level. Apparently the machine rooms in the server farm below ground is even colder. Sveta says it keeps people more productive."

Baldwin shook his head. "Fucking Ukrainians", he said quietly, but Borthwick heard him.

"She's our client, Baldy."

"Not mine she isn't."

"OK, that's enough for now." Dick led Baldwin down a long corridor with large rooms off to either side containing cubicles at which staff – most of them apparently very young – were at work. He estimated that there must have been a dozen or so people there.

"Programmers and technicians" Dick said, anticipating his question. "We vet new employees for her. Their cybersecurity team is six strong – they work shifts – and they're in an office next to the main comms room where the satellite feeds are piped, or so I've been told by JC. It's on two levels below ground and it's a no-go area for us – our palm prints will not work there." Borthwick pointed to an elevator. "That's one of the access points. There are others in Sveta's office, Sergei's office and one for the tech people."

"What's down there that's so important?"

"Other than the cybersecurity team and comms suite, Sveta has an office. Beyond that I have no idea, but my guess is back-up computers and stuff like that. Plus of course the server farm. Hundreds of computer servers. All the employees – and that doesn't include us – know that if the alarm sounds then they must evacuate *down* to the lower levels. They have rehearsals which they call fire drills, but it's the strangest set-up I've seen outside the armed forces. It's a bunker mentality."

"Hardly surprising that she wants a strong physical security team then."

"Now you're getting the picture. I get most of it from JC –the WREN."

"This JC seems to know a lot."

"As I said, she's got the smarts."

The first meeting was with the Head of Ops in an office at the end of the corridor. Baldwin was surprised – Gerasimov was young looking with a full head of mostly brown hair – clipped short and shot with grey. He was personable and his questions were brief.

"So Mr. Baldwin, you will be here on temporary assignment. Tell me about your experience leading security teams."

Baldwin glanced at Borthwick and raised an eyebrow. Borthwick spoke immediately.

"Sergei, let's not waste time going over ground which I have covered. Steve and I have served together in several places, including the Middle East. I can vouch for him completely – as I do for all my team."

Gerasimov smiled at the pushback and nodded. "OK, Richard. Sveta will see you now. Until later Mr Baldwin."

"Perhaps, Mr Gerasimov, perhaps."

"What is this 'perhaps' Richard? Is he in our team or not?"

"Just a few last minute details to iron out – including our meeting with Sveta – who might of course reject him."

"I doubt that, she usually goes with my recommendation. Please follow me."

The meeting with Sevta lasted barely two minutes. Her office had no windows – it was in the heart of the building. No chance there for snipers, thought Baldwin, if she's that paranoid. There were no cameras visible to his quick scan.

One wall was covered in large screen displays, eight of them, showing a range of news feeds and market indices. She worked at a large desk – at least two meters long. This had four laptops on it and several tablet PCs. Another wall was all glass and looked out on a huge room stacked with equipment in aisles. Steve could see a robot moving down one aisle and watched it replace some equipment in a rack.

"Impressive, yes?"

"Er, yes, ma'am."

"So, you replace our physical security team leader Mr Baldwin? I see you check my office before checking me – that is not a good sign." Steve looked at the woman, who held his gaze confidently. She was of medium height – five feet four or so – with a hard face more European than Slavic in features. Her red hair – clearly dyed and with purple highlights - was close cut. She wore several gold rings piercing her left ear and there was a gold piercing through her right eyebrow.

She wore a man's lumberjack shirt – so much for cold being productive thought Steve – and denims, with white canvas sneakers on her feet.

Steve nodded. "Yes Ma'am."

"You may call me Sveta."

She stood up from her wheeled chair and offered Steve her hand, which was encased in a blue surgical glove. He took it and shook it. The grip was firm, but as he began to ease his own grip her hand clamped hard on his. Not noticeable to anyone else, she held on for barely milliseconds. His face was immobile as he responded likewise. She smiled and let his hand go.

"I think you will do the job well if you have got this far. Sergei will give you a full briefing. You start now, yes?"

Borthwick spoke. "I just need to do the handover Sveta, and he needs to meet the team, but yes, it should be today."

She turned to Steve. "Is that so, Mr Baldwin?"

"I may need a day or so first to tidy up some personal business…"

"We'll get it sorted today Sveta, don't worry."

"I am not worried Richard." She smiled, but this one was deliberately false. "It is a valuable contract I have with you." The implied threat was obvious. She turned away, sat in her chair and scooted along to the end of her desk.

Gerasimov ushered them out of the office.

"What is this Richard? You told me that you were ready for the handover and now it seems you are not."

"Just a question of semantics, Sergei. Isn't that right Steve?"

Steve nodded.

"Right, I'll take you to meet the team then."

*

Baldwin woke with a start and sat up in his bunk. "Jesus Christ! Flynn Gregory and Elias Stone!" The two faces he knew in Borthwick's team, the faces that had been nagging at him since his return from the meeting at Saluscent. The names were now there in his consciousness, but had been introduced with other names.

He'd noticed recognition in their eyes when he'd met them, but nothing had been said. His own eyes had probably betrayed some hint of recognition – or at least puzzlement - but he had said nothing either.

There was no chance of more sleep now. Steve glanced at the clock and saw that it was just after 02.30. *Rubaiyat* was riding quietly at anchor, with barely a chuckle from the water. He went on deck to take a leak over the side and enjoy the cool early morning air. The moon was setting in a clear sky and he could see a light on a small fishing boat a couple of hundred meters away. He counted quietly as a matter of habit. He was illuminated by four flashes from the powerful sweeping beam of the lighthouse on Cabo Santa Maria less than a mile away. Every seventeen seconds it cycled. He knew that there had been a light of sorts there since Roman times.

Then the kettle began to whistle and as he headed below his memory cleared.

Rome.

That's where he had met Gregory and Stone. They had last been with him at a café as they headed with Ellie to take down Abu ben-Zhair. That operation had failed and both Gregory and Stone had disappeared. That's where he had taken the bang on his head. Concussion. Another flash of memory – it was the Café Abyssinia in Ostia Antica, that was it! The last piece in the jigsaw that was his recollection of those events. Or was it? His next memory was waking up in the hospital in Hertfordshire. And Six had fed him a line and he'd lost his yacht Adèle in Tunisia. And he was still wanted for murder there – another Six setup.

He stirred his instant coffee and headed up to the cockpit, but couldn't enjoy the peace. The thought of Ellie had opened the wounds again and his mind was racing. And then, Gregory and Stone always figured in his conversations with Six during and after his convalescence. Had he seen them? Where were they? What did he know about their disappearance? But Steve had stuck tightly to his story of amnesia. He certainly hadn't been able to remember them.

What the hell was Borthwick up to?

Before he made any commitment to the Saluscent job he needed some answers - answers without Borthwick's usually generous helping of Yorkshire bullshit.

He sat in the cockpit and watched the moon set. The fisherman started his outboard engine and puttered back to the dock at Culatra. Obviously there was not enough in his catch to take to the fish market in Olhaõ or he'd have headed straight up the channel, so maybe he'd bagged just enough to feed his family. Then the big squid boats started coming up the channel in time to unload their catch when the market opened. Steve headed below and fell into his bunk as *Rubaiyat* rolled in their wakes.

*

The distinctive sound of his smartphone woke him. The insistent chiming penetrated the hangover and he was properly groggy, cursing that he had relapsed and was drinking whisky again after finding a bottle he'd hidden in a galley cupboard. Only Borthwick used Signal. Apart from the bastards at Six, nobody else called him anyway. He looked at the clock. 09:00. So, he had actually managed a couple of hours sleep.

"'Morning Baldy. How are you today?"

"I've been better. And before you ask, NO, I haven't got an answer for you about the job. In fact, I want some answers myself."

"OK, at least you haven't turned the gig down. What do you want to know?"

"Two of the lads on your team – are they ex-Six?"

"I don't employ any ex-Six people. You never know where their allegiance lies. My people are all ex Special Forces, more or less. They only follow the money. I prefer it that way. Which guys are you talking about?"

"I think one was called Jim and the other Jules."

Borthwick laughed. "Sounds like a French film I saw once. No, they didn't – or don't - have any involvement with Six to the best of my information – and that is pretty solid. Not Special Forces though. Paras I think they were, but I'd have to check my files. Why do you want to know? Is it a deal breaker?"

"Could be. I want to know exactly what I might be getting into."

"You're one suspicious son of a bitch Baldy."

"It keeps me alive."

"So, what do you say?"

"I'll call you back later this morning. I need to clear my head and think a bit more about your offer."

"Come on Baldy. It's only three months. It's not as if you're signing up for a tour in Camp Bastion. I'll up the pay offer by ten percent."

"It's not about the money, Dick, I told you – I don't need it. The last babysitting gig I did with you nearly got me killed."

"That's the job – and you did a great one there. Saved the client."

Baldwin had saved the same client yet again, later, from a torture cell in Malta – but the client had come out with seriously wounded pride and minus one testicle. But Dickwick didn't know that – or if he did he wasn't letting on.

"Maybe. Give me a couple of hours, or, you can have a NO right now."

The exasperation was plain in Dickwicks voice "OK. Two hours it is." He shook his head and sighed – Gerasimov was expecting Baldwin on site in two hours time. "If it's 'yes' come straight ashore – the client is expecting you this morning. And to sweeten it, make that twenty five percent more on your rate."

"I already told you, money's not important."

"Really? It always was. I know it's not cheap running a yacht. How come you're so flush all of a sudden?"

"That's none if your fucking business!" Baldwin cut the call. The extra money would be handy, despite what he'd said, He still hadn't decided what he should do about Ellie's legacy. He hadn't touched a penny yet although the first quarterly earnings payment of over £40,000 from her estate had come through to his bank account.

It was unlike Borthwick to offer extra money. He was a tight fisted Yorkshireman and obviously under pressure.

But from what – or whom?

Two hours later Borthwick called again.

"Jules and Jim. They resigned, left letters with JC and walked off the job. Didn't show for their shift. Unprofessional to say the least."

"And their history?"

"Paras and it holds up, not that it matters now. I'm flying two more guys in from Belgium today to fill the gap, but I really need you up here now, Baldy. Don't let me down. I'm in deep shit here – Sergei has thrown a major wobbly."

"OK, I'm on my way, just in the dinghy now." Borthwick's sigh of relief was audible even through all the layers of encryption.

"I'll pick you up from the dock in two hours. I really need you to back me up on this, Baldy. The contract could be at risk with these two guys walking out."

"OK, two hours from now, at the dock."

Baldwin thought it strange that just after he met them the paras had walked off the job.

*

Thirteen

Three nights after she had met Josh Packard in the bar at Olhão, Stone drove her Suzuki SUV into the hills behind the Saluscent site. She was about half a kilometer from the outer fence and it was well after midnight when she parked the vehicle under some trees. She doused the lights and grabbed the back pack and night vision googles that had come in a special delivery courier package from Lisbon. She then locked the vehicle – wincing as the central locking chirped loudly in the night, accompanied by the flashing of the indicators. 'That's really fucking stealthy' she thought as she glanced around and headed into the brush, following the trail directions using a mobile app feeding her directions through a earbud.

Ten minutes later the Route Assistant reported that she was in place at her designated waypoint. She could see the floodlights and fence of the Saluscent offices a couple of hundred meters to the south, just below her down a slight hill. She opened the backpack and laid the drone on the ground. She checked the battery status and enabled the payload, then called Packard on her secure phone.

"Telion here. Ready to launch."

"OK, we have it live on our dashboard. Confirm clear of brush and trees for at least thirty feet around."

She quickly scanned the radius, the trees still clear in the IR googles, radiating the heat of the spring day.

"Confirmed."

"Stand back. Launching in five seconds."

She watched as the quadcopter's electric motors spun up and then it ascended with its payload - slowly at first and then headed, climbing more quickly now as it headed towards the company compound. After a few seconds she lost sight of it as its IR masking hid it finally from the sensors in her night-vision goggles.

"Telion, we have a problem. The site is geofenced. We are trying to override it."

"What?"

"Geofenced – identified as a blocked area such as an airport, preventing the drone from intruding. OK, we've now overridden that."

"Oh."

"The drone is reporting no GPS signal. Someone is jamming the GPS signals - US, Russian, Chinese, European, Indian, the lot. The drone is returning to you using its electronic compass."

"I don't see it."

"Wait."

Five minutes went by.

"No sign of the drone."

"OK, we're activating its chime. Listen carefully."

"I don't hear anything."

"You need to find it. We must recover it."

"How? It's dark here. Does it have lights?"

"Wait. I'll get back to you."

JC waited. And waited.

"Telion, are you still there?"

"Yes, it's been over an hour. What's happening?"

"The guys turned on a feature that only the European Galileo GPS network has. We got round the jamming."

"Thanks for letting me know – that's useful information." Her sarcasm was lost on Packard. "It's starting to get light here. I need to move."

"Be patient. The drone has unloaded its package and is on its way back."

Then she heard a slight whirring – luckily there was no breeze – and almost screamed as the drone brushed the top of her head and landed in front of her.

"I have it."

"Good, pack it up and get out of there ASAP. Check your brief for the storage instructions – we don't want the unit getting into the wrong hands. And we might need it later."

"Was it a success?"

"Yes. The drone landed its payload on the roof directly above Kovacs's office. We have confirmation that the payload is secured to the roof. It's drilling through as we speak. The audio probe should be in place in a few minutes. It doesn't need to go directly into the Kovac's office to work."

"Good. I'll head back. Telion out."

Useful intel starting coming through the feed within 24 hours.

"So, what have we got, Josh?"

"We're listening in to the Kovacs woman – at least for some of the time when she's in the upper office. We can't get anything from her basement office yet. Their sweeps are unable to detect the vibration transducer we're using – the metal roof shields it."

"Telion did a good job getting that into place."

"Yes, but thank God we were the ones who built the software for the Galileo GPS satellites."

"Why?"

"Saluscent are jamming all GPS signals around the site – the drone was flummoxed until our guys used a unique Galileo sideband signal to punch through the jamming."

"What's Kovacs so afraid of?"

"We don't know yet. It's obviously either fear of attack or defense of something valuable – maybe both. They have almost military levels of physical and electronic security. The site is like a major data center, built to survive a direct hit by a plane"

"Also it's close to the flight path out of Faro Airport."

"It's surely more than that. We must be missing something."

Macsen nodded as Josh continued "Anyway, so far, all of Kovacs's voice comms have been routine management stuff - the kind of thing you'd expect from a hands-on software entrepreneur. I won't bore you with the full audio translation, but last night she had a conversation with a contact in the Ukraine where she uses a team to develop software – legitimately it would seem. It seems she also uses developers she finds through freelance worksites – we've heard her talking to a couple of people online. We don't have any of her IDs yet on those sites, but once we do we can find out more about the sorts of software jobs she's commissioned. They're probably very discrete pieces of code that will not give anyone a hint of what she's up to. We'd be trying to put a jigsaw together with most of the pieces missing, but it may help refine the picture. The conversation with the Ukrainian guy was via an encrypted messaging app – one we do not know about but with a similar code signature to one used by the Ukrainian armed forces. Just as well that we have audio."

"Do we know more about the Ukrainian angle?"

"A little. She mentioned something to the Ukrainian guy - Dmitri she called him - about an upcoming software release they were working on. Then he said that quote 'the other project would be as good as our 2013 credit card project from which we made ninety million dollars.' Unquote. There *was* such a scam, and five men were convicted in the US – four Ukrainians and one Russian."

"The wrong guys?"

"Could be, the team are still looking into this. They could have been set up. Two questions raise themselves here – One, what's this next scam, and two, is Kovacs her real name? Judging by the way they were talking they go back a long way – maybe even to University."

"So it looks like she really is Ponomarenko - and if ninety million dollars is small change then the next sting will be – well, seriously damaging to someone's pocket – or even a government or govern*ments*."

"Yes, Sir. We're profiling Ukrainian software companies and our people in Kiev are on the case. Also, the angle on the secure voice app may give us some pointers. There's a bit more to it. She went ballistic that he'd mentioned the scam and broken security when she was outside the secure comms suite and said that she would call him back as he wasn't following protocol. She was really ranting at him. Then she cut the conversation."

"That's a tell in itself."

"Exactly. It sounds very military."

"And do we have access to this comms room?"

"Telion says no. Apparently there are at least two levels below ground which she cannot access."

"Can we get hold of any plans of the place?"

"We've tried, but they don't seem to exist on the Portuguese planning system."

"I'll bet that's not a coincidence. And we haven't got any eavesdropping in place below ground level?"

"No Sir."

"Then we'd better organize some. But I don't want to compromise Telion inside the site. We'll need to use our backup man but keep her in the dark about it. Strict separation. Talk to Borthwick and see what he can do. Also, talk to the former Barbary – Stevenson is his name - he will give you a file to give you some leverage. And good work, Josh. Keep me posted."

As Packard left, he turned. "Oh yes, there's one more thing. The fact that they're jamming the all GPS signals - not strongly, but good enough for a couple of miles around her compound. It might affect the planes from Faro. But the Portuguese have not reported any problems, as far as I am aware."

"That's interesting. I'll speak to GCHQ. I wonder what she's afraid of? Whoever or whatever – it must be very heavy."

*

"I've just had an update from GCHQ, Sir. Telion has put a couple of signal monitors is place for them in the vineyards around the compound. The jamming of the GPS signals around the Saluscent site seems to have a range of about a mile and it switches off as planes come into range."

"So Kovacs is not worried about planes, as such, then?"

"That's how it looks, yes."

"Curiouser and curiouser. OK. Let's formalize this. Kovacs now has the codename 'Alice'.

"I'll set it up, Boss."

"And how is GCHQ coming along with penetrating her systems?"

Josh looked at the report on his tablet.

"Very little progress to report. All comms is via satellite and straight out from the satellite ground station through a VPN to dark web anonymizers. GCHQ have intrusion software which they are injecting into the ground station, but my guess is that all the important stuff is too heavily encrypted to crack."

"We can break that."

"Kovacs...erm...Alice has a Ph.D. in cryptography. Even GCHQ may find it's beyond them – or at least will take too long decrypt in a useful timescale."

"Maybe, and with all the Chinese and Iran workload on the GCHQ quantum decryption machines it probably is. Unless this is a matter of serious national security then we might just have to sit it out unless I can jack up the priority. We need to know more about what Alice is planning."

"Telion is sending the drone up again tonight. We're going to use it for infrared filming of the aerial array to see if the techies can come up with some ideas. Even the US satellite picture resolution is not good enough."

"I guess there's no prospect of hacking the satellites she's using?"

"None. We can access the data stream from our hack into the ground station, but there's no way we can decrypt it on any useful timescale – as you said GCHQ's quantum machines have bigger priorities. We can track the data stream so far but then it's lost in the dark web. We can't even make sense of the addressing – but we are at least storing all the data until we get a break."

"But we know where some of it is going. So, what about listening in Kiev?"

"Theoretically possible but it would take months to set up an intercept there – and it's likely to be a mirror image of what we face in Olhaõ. And Alice is the prime target anyway."

"Yes, we'd better forget that for now then. What I'd really like to know is why she left the Ukraine."

"For the sun?"

"Maybe, but I don't believe that for a minute.

"And there's an update from our guys in Kiev. A Dmitri Borzov runs a software development company called 'Hyper Secure Software'. He was at the Kiev Technical Institute at the same time as Ponomarenko. He's actually on our cryptographic specialist watchlist."

"Can we get a voiceprint?"

"Kiev sent us one. It's a match to the guy Ponomarenko was talking to."

"OK, let's give him the codename Dormouse."

*

Josh Packard met Richard Borthwick in an Italian bar off the Nine Elms Road, south of the Thames. It was far enough from the new US embassy to be clear of embassy staffers and handy enough for Vauxhall Cross – and well after the lunch rush.

After they had confirmed identities and Packard had bought a couple of Peronis, they sat at a corner table inside. It was raining hard outside and the April weather was unseasonably cold. Their dripping overcoats were draped over their chairs.

"I was surprised to get a call from Stevenson. He was as cagey as usual. I thought that he would be here himself – we go back a long way."

"Yes, well that was his hope but pressing matters scrubbed his diary, you know how it is. You got his text then?"

"Just in time. I nearly walked out. Just as well that you were carrying that copy of 'Paris Match' or I wouldn't have known you. Anyway, what's this all about?"

"Baldwin, that chap you have leading your team on that job on the Algarve."

Borthwick's eyebrows jumped. "He's a tricky bugger. Doesn't like your lot one bit."

"That's why I'm talking to you."

Borthwick bought another round of Peronis and Packard drilled down to the reason for the meeting, Borthwick became increasingly angry as the conversation progressed.

"I'm not getting involved in this shit. Baldwin and I have served together – and saved each other's lives on occasion. This sort of deal is way beyond the bounds my friendship with him. You or Stevenson need to do this dirty work."

"He'll not meet Stevenson. They have history it seems. I can't say any more – don't know any more, in fact."

"Well, that is a surprise. Stevenson and Baldwin. I can see that they would clash. But then, Baldwin clashes with anyone in authority. Anyway, count me out. I'm already walking on eggshells with him." Borthwick made to rise from his chair.

"Now hang on a bit, just sit down and hear me out. For what it's worth Stevenson's out of the picture."

Borthwick looked hard at him, not believing a word.

"He's been promoted out of the way, though I shouldn't even say that. Now, I'd like to know how the negotiations are going for that armed forces training contract in Qatar. Twenty five million dollars worth, I heard? Plus annual renewals for five years."

Borthwick looked at him, trying to keep his tone level and emotionless, but Packard saw the brief flash of anger in his eyes.

"You seem to be well informed, why am I not surprised? Anyway, I expect them to sign the contract next week."

"You do know that they have asked us – through the Foreign Office of course – about our view of you and your company?"

"I've got nothing to hide. I'd expect you to give me a clean bill of health. It seems you're using a big hammer to crack a small nut here. No wonder Stevenson or whoever you work for sent a gopher – he knew what I would say. I won't be jerked around in this way."

Borthwick stood up, put his raincoat on, then walked out without another word. Packard thought he could see the steam rising off him. The rain had stopped so he turned his phone off and walked back across Wandsworth Bridge to his office in Chelsea. He needed time to think. Despite all his bullshit it had been a lean year so far, and he'd been banking on this Qatari contract signature.

When he got back to his office, there was a message waiting from the Qatari Armed Forces Minister. He called him immediately and it was a brief, uncomfortable conversation. There were some questions about the contract terms and a competing offer from Academi, a major US security contractor, formerly known as Blackwater. They were a formidable competitor and Borthwick had thought that he'd knocked them out of the running for the Qatari contract. He swore – somehow they were still in the frame. Six were meddling, he knew.

It was Stevenson who had originally told him about the Qatari training contract – they were recruiting heavily into their security forces in the ramp up to the 2022 World Cup. He'd had the chance bid on it with UK Government support. Putting J C Stone on the Saluscent team had been the quid pro quo that Six had demanded. Now that Academi was in the running for the Qatar job there was only one way to go. He sighed as he picked up his phone and looked for Stevenson's number. He had 24 hours to save the contract – and a friend to shaft.

An hour later he had booked an Easyjet flight to Faro leaving Gatwick at an unearthly hour the next day. Heathrow and British Airways would have been more comfortable, but time was of the essence.

Unknown to Borthwick, Josh Packard was booked on BA and already on his way to Gatwick. He had several things to attend to in Olhaõ.

*

Fourteen

In the first couple of days on the Saluscent site, Steve went round the facilities with JC. There were several no-go areas for the team, including the basement levels. Steve reviewed the physical layout, control procedures and, as far as he was able, the electronic systems.

After his review, he sat down with JC in the control room and went through his notes with her.

"So, a drone patrols the perimeter?"

"Yes every hour. Sergei has pattern scanning software which analyses it, picking up differences between patrols, or so I've been told. All the sensor data – video, IR – is streamed to a database under Sergei's control."

"More physical security data that we don't have access to?"

JC shrugged, her lips pressed in a tight line as she nodded.

"Right, I'll speak to Borthwick about that and let him sort it out for us. Next point. I'm unhappy about roof access. Just one door locked and controlled from here, but I still see it as a weak point. Let's talk to Sergei ourselves and get it beefed up, with maybe another door in the stairwell. If anybody hits us then more, stronger doors would slow them."

"Bloody hell Steve, are you expecting an attack from the air?"

"Not particularly. In fact I'm not expecting any attacks, but it seems to me like a weak point given strength of the rest of the defenses around this site."

It was over a week before Steve felt that the team had gelled. The two new men were capable and probably overkill – in a manner of speaking – for the job. One was a Spaniard and the other a Belgian. Jose Rodriguez had served in the Spanish armed forces during their brief involvement in Iraq before the Spanish government had changed policy and pulled its forces out. After that he'd gone freelance and gone back to Iraq with Academi nee Blackwater. He seemed solid to Steve although he didn't have much special forces experience. More of Dickwick's bullshit, he thought.

Baldwin had done one-to-one meetings with each of the team, a process that had taken more than a week. He'd taken to using a quiet bar in the Rua Cordeiro, a hundred yards off the main drag where the main church was located. Steve's preference was to meet them individually in the bar and have a wet.

His meetings with Henri Laporte and Aldo Colarusso didn't waste time on background – he'd worked with them before under fire and so they just enjoyed their wets together and reminisced. Steve's story was that after the Ionian fracas he'd returned to his boat in Crete and sailed to Malta just after the cruise liner attack there. Then he'd made a visit to Tunisia on his yacht. That much was true. The nuclear attack in Rome had naturally come up, but Steve only talked about it in general terms, as would any member of the public. He certainly did not mention the fact that he had been ten feet away from the device just a half hour before it detonated less than half a mile from the Vatican.

The other new guy, Pavel Mankowicz was from Chicago and was ex-Delta Force. Steve thought it strange that he had not joined up with Academi or one of the other leading security contractors. His story was that he preferred smaller companies and that someone he'd met in Liège – the Belgian city which had been a hub for mercenaries since the Middle Ages – had mentioned ScutumEst. He'd met Borthwick and signed up.

Mankowicz had stuck religiously to water during their meeting. His story passed muster for Steve, just, although he suspected there was more behind it, maybe a dishonorable discharge. He was clearly avoiding alcohol – at least with Steve.

His one-to-one with JC had raised questions in his mind. She'd chosen white wine to drink, which wasn't unusual in itself. Steve had asked her directly why she'd turned down the chance to join Six.

"How did you know that?"

"My standard test question. You just confirmed it."

"Shit. I guess that proves that I don't have the IQ for it anyway."

"Maybe, or maybe you are just very clever and it's a misdirect."

"No way. I've done enough time for His Majesty. Now I'm working for *me*, and money is important. So, no more Government crap – or pay."

There's always a bit of freelancing especially when money is important. *But was it the truth?*

"Anyway, what's *your* story?"

It was not Baldwin's way to provide his own background. He didn't feel the need – and couldn't be arsed – to prove himself to any of them – the fact the Borthwick had put him in command should have been enough. She was the only one who'd asked him about his story, but it hadn't been a come-on, he was sure of that, and he wouldn't have been interested anyway if had been.

"That's not relevant to this job. I'm asking the questions here."

"This isn't an interview. I've already got the job, remember?"

She looked at him sourly and he reconsidered.

"That was a bit abrupt, sorry. What I can say is that Dick and I go back a long way and he asked me to help him out here, just for three months as you probably know. So, we don't need to go into my background – but I do need to know a bit about each of the team."

"And?"

"So far, so good. Tell me about your weapons and any combat experience."

"Most of it is classified, sorry. But I can tell you about specific weapons experience and the training I went through."

Steve looked at her eyes. What was so interesting about them? "Fine, tell me what you can."

After the meeting with Stone which had gone on longer than he had planned, Baldwin climbed into his dinghy at the dock and headed out into the channel. The moon was in its last quarter and not yet risen. It was a warm, still evening and he was being nagged by mosquitoes as he took the shallow shortcut between the sandbanks. He could see *Rubaiyat's* riding light low above the lights of Culatra with a cloud of other lights further east. The winking of the Cabo Santa Maria lighthouse was clear and the first of the big fishing boats was steaming down the main channel sending a heavy wake breaking along the banks.

J C Stone. The only woman on the team. He'd worked with women – most recently Ellie. The thought brought a stab of pain, but at least the stabs were becoming less frequent. Dick had been right, having something to do and interacting with other people was helpful. He'd learned that women usually had good instincts and that could be useful, but in combat a man's natural instinct was to protect a woman. That could be fatal to both. *But I don't expect combat here.*

So why was there a woman on *this* team? He suspected that Dickwick was doing someone a favor. That bothered him. And then, Stone herself. She hadn't asked the one obvious question that all the others had asked "We're just baby sitting so why such a heavy team for such a simple job?"

There was always more to Dickwick's jobs than met the eye. Anyway, he'd been satisfied that Stone knew what she was talking about, but that didn't mean that she could stay calm under fire – but then no-one expected that to be tested here, on this job. Then he remembered Dickwick's comment about her cybersecurity expertise. Why did that matter?

Steve stopped the outboard motor and drifted slowly on the current, enjoying the peace and lack of distraction as he pondered the situation in the calm evening spoiled only by the attention of mosquitoes.

There had to be more to it given the unprecedented levels of security. What was being protected? People? Technology? Money? It couldn't be money – that would just be in a bank. Technology. That was a possibility – but software would be stored on a cloud server or a data farm off site. People? That was a real possibility. People and technology. Maybe a good sleep would give him some answers in the morning.

He decided to row the last few hundred yards to *Rubaiyat* cursing that he had lost the discipline of exercise since Ellie's death. After a few minutes he shipped the oars as he glided to a stop alongside *Rubaiyat*'s boarding ladder. He'd started sweating after just a couple of hundred strokes and he resolved to get back into shape. That would start with a long run through the dunes on Culatra Island the next morning. Living aboard 2 miles out in the channel and working ashore wasn't a practical proposition. He'd have to find somewhere temporary ashore, at least for some of his shifts. But then, why not put *Rubaiyat* in the marina at Olhaõ? The extra ten percent that Dickwick had promised him should cover that. Then he smiled as he remembered – it was twenty five percent now, not ten. He hadn't been negotiating, he really didn't want the job, but the money eased his worry about what to do with the fortune Ellie had left him. Dick was desperate to have him on the job. Fuck it! Dick could pay the cost of the marina berth. Yes, that would no nicely.

He put the kettle on and took out the last bottle of Glenlivet that had been hidden. He looked at it, his expression one of regret. Then he shook his head and replaced the bottle in the locker. He'd lost count of how many bottles he'd stashed away in odd places, they just kept turning up. Tea it would be, and nothing else tonight.

*

"We're now certain that Sveta Kovacs's her real name is Svetlana Ponomarenko. She was a student at the National Technical University in Kiev. It's all in the folder."

Emmet Macsen opened the folder which was blinking on his desktop.

"I see, a cryptographic specialist. A student photograph, I take it?"

"Yes, but of course it could have been changed. The later one is of the Sveta Kovacs woman – Alice. Sveta is a Hungarian diminutive of Svetlana by the way."

Macsen looked up at him as if he was a fool.

"Sorry Boss, I'm sure that was obvious to you."

"The pictures don't look like they're of the same person."

"I agree. But we're sure of that one of Kovacs, it came from Telion. We already have a file on her - she was tagged when she was engaged for her Ph.D. research in the National Technical University in Kiev – her discipline was cryptography. On the advice of a professor, the Ukrainian Government intervened early during her research and blocked the release of her thesis on the grounds of national security. Nevertheless, GCHQ eventually obtained a copy. I heard that it caused quite a few ripples in Cheltenham. There are hundreds of cross references to her name in the files, almost all of a benign nature. There was no intelligence to suggest involvement in the sale of credit card details on the black web that would tie in with the $90 million scam we overheard – and know about."

"She probably hacked the Interpol files."

"Very likely. Since then her activities seemed to have been legitimate and if she is still being naughty then her trail is well covered.

We've run the picture through the facial analysis software and there's an eighty five per cent match. We think she might have had a nose job done, which would account for the slight difference. She was working with Dmitri Borzov – Dormouse."

"And then Ukraine's proxy war with Russia came along."

"Precisely. Right place, right time, right specialization. Russia mounted a major cyberwarfare offensive against them. Russia copied an Android app developed by an officer in the Ukraine military used to process targeting data for a weapon called the D-30 Howitzer. Then they infected it to feed back the Ukrainian gun positions and hit them."

"Smart stuff." *You don't know the half of it.*

"Yes. Way to go, as the Cousins would say. So, Borzov's company fixed the Android app problem for the army and then the Ukrainian government secure software contracts started to flow. His company is strong, highly profitable and expanding into the Far East using Indian and Singaporean resources, but no involvement with China."

"And I doubt we'll see any either unless he's mad. We've had enough difficulty dumping all the Huawei network gear in our national infrastructure. Thank God we had the sense to keep it out of here."

"OK, we now believe that both Dmitri and Ponomarenko are cryptocurrency 'whales'. By that I mean that they have large Bitcoin or other crypto holdings able to affect marketing pricing with their volumes – if they want to. But that's just an educated guess – the crypto blockchains are no help – they are experts at hiding their tracks. But less than ten Bitcoin addresses hold over thirty percent of the currency."

"So, what are they up to this time?"

"A crypto scam, in the order of billions of dollars. That's what my instinct tells me."

Macsen thought that Josh was doing well with his ideas and deductions but kept pushing. "Who cares? It's only funny money anyway, isn't it?"

They both laughed.

"Those days are long gone, Boss. It's mainstream now, for sure."

"Don't I know it? I'll brief 'C' and I'd better let the Treasury know that something may be in the offing. I'll talk to Langley as well."

*

Fifteen

"Boss, I have Mike Stebbings from GCHQ ready to conference in and explain his proposition."

"Go ahead, let's get started."

"Sir, I'm Mike Stebbings. I head up one of the crypto-virus development teams with responsibility for cryptocurrencies."

Stebbings's face appeared on screen. He was bald-headed with a very big ginger beard and piercing pale blue eyes just visible through pebblestone spectacles which were supported by what can only be described as big sticky-out ears. Few people would have described him as handsome and some would have described him as the archetypal goblin.

"Hello Mike. Emmet Macsen here, head of the CW desk in VX, together with Joshua Packard whom I believe you already know. Our purpose is to make use of the technology – not to engineer it – that's for you guys. Please try to keep your explanation simple for the likes of us."

That was way understated thought Josh – 'M' was up there with the best of them.

"I'll do my best, Sir. Right, what we have heard from the recordings you provided is that this woman, Kovacs, plans to corrupt the accounting that takes place every time there is a cryptocurrency transaction. The accounts are accessible by anyone but are anonymous. Okay?"

"So far so good."

"A typical Bitcoin transaction involves a transfer of Bitcoin value that is publicized to the network and accumulated into blocks. In other words, all Bitcoin transactions are noticeable in the blockchain and can be seen. Two of the main elements in a block are the record of transactions and the Block Header. The Block Header is composed of the hash of the prevailing block and the hash of the prior block and other data. Approximately after every ten minutes, a new block is generated and attached to the blockchain. This is essentially the mining process. This block validates and registers any fresh transactions and this is known as a confirmation of the transaction. Bitcoin mining is done by a node - that's basically a computer with software. There are four types of Bitcoin node on the Bitcoin network. I'll not go into them all right now…"

"Thank God."

"Sorry, I missed that?"

"It's not important, carry on Mike."

"OK...where was I? Ah yes...there are about thirteen thousand 'Full' nodes on the Bitcoin network and the complete Bitcoin blockchain is currently about three hundred and forty gigabytes in size – too big to send back and forth every few minutes – that's why there are other types of node. Anyway, to achieve the validation of your transaction requires use of computing power to solve a non-trivial math problem which is unique to each transaction. Are you still with me?"

"Still awake. Go on." *If he only knew.*

"Good. When your transaction is first recorded, that unique equation is defined using a number known as a 'nonce'. In this context it's obviously not a pedophile, but a thirty two bit number – that's very big. It's a number used just once – hence the word 'nonce'. The number is hashed with data like the value, the time and the Merkle root. The Merkle root is a number used to ensure that the bitcoin data block is complete and undamaged. There are other data items in the hash too, though I'll not go into them now."

"Thank God" Packard uttered and received a scowl from Macsen for his trouble as Stebbings droned on.

"The successful verifier – node - solves your equation and gets a reward – a very small fraction of your bitcoin. That's basically it, but note that validation actually occurs before a block is mined; validation is not the same as consensus. Consensus is reached when the mining nodes agree on the order of transactions, not on what transactions are valid. That's one way in which it's hacker-proof."

"So, what's this 'nonce exploit' mentioned in the audio feed we have?"

"We don't know exactly. We need to get at her code. But what we think is happening is that she has found a way either to solve the equations very quickly – in which case she could control the currency at least for a short time while she 'empties the bank' so to speak, or she might be able to affect the verification process, possibly enabling double spending of your cryptocoin. There may be other possibilities too, but the chances of any of those being possible are vanishingly small. The numbers are just too big, even with the fastest computers and all the time in the world. "

Josh Packard nodded at Emmett who rolled his eyes.

"That seems fairly clear. What can we do about it?"

"What do you *want* to do about it? Stop it? Control it? Steal it? Or just sit back and watch the fun?"

Macsen smiled. "Good question." *This game could be really interesting.*

"At the moment we don't know if she has a general solution or is just targeting one cryptocurrency, perhaps the Monero. The Monero is a good candidate for a large scale scam as it uses an obfuscated public ledger. Secrecy is taken to a new level - anybody can broadcast or send transactions, but no outside observer can tell the source, amount or destination. There are certain things that are almost impossible, though, such as altering the accounts. That's difficult because there are thousands of copies of the ledger. But maybe she *has* found a way. Some cryptos – the group know loosely as *stablecoins* - *may* be easier to attack - for example Tether and Paxos - cryptocurrencies that are backed by dollars, euros and other government currencies. It's easier to buy them as they can be traded directly for your own fiat currencies - with other cryptocurrencies the only way to buy is to first buy Bitcoin, and then exchange the bitcoins to the coins you want.

My guess is that she'll attack a proprietary currency. By that I mean one in which there is a proprietary software code element – a secret ingredient, if you will. Bitcoin – the biggest and best known – is, to all intents and purposes, fully open. None of its code is proprietary. I can give you more detailed options if we can get a look at some of her development code. Then I can refine the options."

"Okay, I think I've got all that. We can't exclude the possibility that she might attack multiple cryptos – maybe at the same time."

"Another thing is that she will need a lot of mining power if she's going to make a real impact in a short time. We don't know how many mining modules she has in that site. My guess is a few thousand maximum. They take space and power, they need cooling. To give you an idea, the Bitmain SanShangLiang industrial park mining complex in China is the largest mining facility in the world. It has 25,000 machines that process two hundred and fifty thousand dollars worth of bitcoins daily. One way to beat that is to pool resources – a so-called mining pool, with operations linked over the internet. It's a common approach, with profit sharing. Of course if she *could annex* other people's resources through some sort of network hack, then God knows what she could achieve."

"There's certainly plenty of food for thought there Mike. Thanks. We are working on several ways of getting access to any proprietary code Saluscent may have. Her company's publicity material on the various social media and specialist cryptocurrency sites indicates that they are launching a cryptocurrency of their own."

"Yes, I know. An ICO – that's an Initial Coin Offering. Some people call it an ACTU – A Chance To Clean Up. It could all be tied in, although that would be very risky as investors – I use the term loosely – have been suspicious of new offerings. But that could be changing. Small caps offer opportunities for much bigger gains."

"Okay, thanks Mike. I'll need to take this up the chain of command. The Treasury may have an interest in this too."

"Fine, Sir. In the meantime I will liaise with Joshua and talk to our intrusion people to see if we can access the target systems at Saluscent."

"I think you mean 'hack' don't you, Mike?"

"Er, yes, Sir, but it's not a word we use round here, as we are legal."

Macsen smiled as the video link dropped. All the best techies in *that* field started out as hackers – and he knew for a fact that Stebbings had started that way.

"Josh, we need to set up a formal team for this – we'll need people from the Treasury and Bank of England. Get me a list of possible names within the hour and I'll talk to 'C'."

Macsen pursed his lips as Josh left, thinking about his own crypto investments. He'd been doing nicely then someone had dumped a load two days ago – probably having a short position on the futures markets. Sell them high and buy them back cheap. He was in it for the long stretch, convinced of the continued growth of digital currencies - but one shouldn't have all one's eggs in the same basket. Especially now.

He left his desk and headed for the washroom. Halfway there he stopped and shouted. "Shit!" Heads raised over partitions and looked at him in surprise as he turned and headed for Josh's cubicle.

"Josh – you mentioned that Russia was going to issue the CryptoRuble."

"Yes, it's imminent, but has been for a couple of years. I think they're close to a decision now. It looks like it will be a CBDC – that's a central bank digital currency, like the Chinese have done with the e-Yuan."

"Given her suspected history with the Russians there's a good chance that she might have that particular currency in her sights. Let Stebbings know and tell him that we think it's a distinct possibility. Don't give him any backstory though."

"Right away, Boss. You could well be right – CBDCs have inbuilt tracking so that the issuing central bank can trace the transaction."

"A back door, you mean?"

"Yes – and where there's a back door then there's a security weakness."

"You mean opportunity."

"Definitely."

*

Sixteen

Baldwin was two weeks into the assignment when Borthwick reappeared. They were in Baldwin's favorite bar – *O Pescador* – on Rua Cordeiro, Olhaõ, a few blocks back from the waterfront tourist drag. By now he was known to most of the staff and the service was quick because he was a good tipper – he had money and hated having to wait for his beer.

Once the beers were on their corner table, Borthwick kicked off.

"So, how's it going Baldy? How's your new team?"

"The guys are gelled now I think, although I'm not sure about Stone. There's something there that niggles at me."

"The fact that she's a woman?"

"No, she's holding back something, I just get that feeling?"

Borthwick laughed. "Your charms not working then?"

"Fuck off Dick."

Borthwick held up his arms in apology. "Sorry, out of order. It's only been, what, six months since you lost your wife?"

"I don't want to talk about it. Four months, actually. And how did you know that she was my wife? Why the fuck are you here Dick?"

"Bad news I'm afraid."

"Lost the contract?"

"Not this one. But another one is in jeopardy. If I don't win it then I'm wiped out."

"That's nothing to do with me. I've helped you whenever I can."

"Yes, you've been the best mate a man could wish for Steve and I hate to ask for more help."

"What is it Dick, you're going to ask anyway – and it must be a big ask if you're calling me Steve again?"

Borthwick outlined the task and as he did so, Steve's face became redder. Borthwick watched the pulse in Steve's forehead strengthen and quicken. Steve's face was grim, his jaw tight.

"No fucking way am I doing that Dick - whatever trouble your business is in. This stinks of Six from top to bottom. I'm not getting involved. I lost my wife because of those bastards."

"I thought you'd say that Steve, although I didn't know about the link to your wife. They've got me over a barrel. I'm so sorry, but I have to do the same to you. I have no choice."

Steve looked up from his beer. He could see the perspiration forming on Dick's face.

"Everyone has choices."

"Not me, not now." Borthwick took a big pull at his brandy.

Steve stood up, turned and left O Pescador. He headed back to *Rubaiyat,* now moored in the town marina. He unlocked the hatch and went below. The last bottle of Glenlivet was still unopened. He sat at the chart table, tore the seal off and took a long pull straight from the bottle. Then he noticed the thick buff envelope on the chart table.

He picked it up and looked at it and then had a bad feeling as he opened it.

The envelope contained a thin cardboard folder and a small packet. The packet appeared to contain several miniscule electronic devices. He put the packet aside and then opened the folder. It held one sheet of paper - a Metropolitan Police charge sheet. It had his name on it with an address 'Of no fixed abode'.

Steven Baldwin was charged with the murder of Ms. Ellie Williams.

He pulled his mobile phone out of his pocket and called Borthwick.

"Come to my boat now. *Rubaiyat*. She's in the town marina near where you picked me up the other week. Don't fuck me about Dick. Get here."

Borthwick looked at Baldwin. He was clearly seething. Uninvited, Dick took a long pull from the Glenlivet mas they sat in the yacht's cockpit.

"Did you break in and deliver this envelope?"

"No way. I've been with you in the bar, you know that."

"Well some fucker did."

"Any signs of a break in?"

"No, clean as a whistle. It's convenient that you'd know when I was off the boat and in your presence, isn't it? So, who did you call, you bastard?"

"No one – I called no one Steve, believe me." This was pure semantics, and he could see that Baldwin was not swallowing it.

"I don't believe you. This was a set-up, just like everything else. I do a mate a favor and look what happens."

Baldwin pushed the charge sheet across the table to Borthwick.

"Steve, I have been told that your wife left a substantial legacy and that you are the beneficiary of her will. The will was dated the day after you were married."

Steve stared hard into Dick's eyes, looking through and beyond them to some other place holding a set of memories deep and painful, far away and yet so near as Borthwick continued.

"They told me that your marriage certificate was bogus and that you were instrumental in your wife's death, that you faked a car accident in Spain to get her money. A file has been prepared for the Spanish police and is currently held in VX. What they do with it depends on what you do next. I'm sure it's bullshit, so please don't shoot the messenger."

Baldwin shook his head. "Dick, you may be a slimy two faced bastard, but I know you wouldn't pull such a stunt unless you were hard up against it. They would have gotten to me somehow. But this is below even their standards."

"You're right. It's a shitty business."

"Well, you can tell them that I have a video of the wedding ceremony where a guy called Stevenson – codename Barbary – gave us the marriage certificate in Gibraltar and assured us it was genuine as we signed it – and the special license. I don't give a shit about the money. For what it's worth her will was prepared by her family lawyer and that too is genuine. There was no car crash. Six set up that story and I agreed. Ellie died from a terrorist bullet and her body was burned by US Seals in Algeria. Ever heard of Abu ben-Zhair aka ABZ? I was there."

Borthwick's face drained of color as the people in the next boat watched the noisy interaction between two Englishmen. They didn't need to speak English to understand what was said, but drama is drama in whatever language.

"Jesus Christ Steve, I'm sorry, but for God's sake keep your voice down!"

"Sorry is not the fucking word and I don't care who hears it. If I ever see Stevenson again I will fucking strangle him then tear his head off and shove it up his arse."

Borthwick climbed off the boat and staggered along the marina pontoon an hour later, his body drunk but his brain in overdrive. *Why on earth was this assignment so important to Six? And why involve Baldy when he had a real axe to grind?*

In the Café do Doca, one of that bars which fronted the marina on the Avenida 5 de Outubro, Josh Packard closed the leather cover of his tablet computer and finished his glass of amontillado – he didn't like the way they served their red wine chilled – and left a 20 Euro note on the table.

He intercepted Borthwick as he looked for a taxi to his hotel.

"I've got a car waiting Richard. Did it all go as planned?"

"Fuck you Packard."

"Come, come, Richard, I'm sure neither of us would enjoy that."

Borthwick and Baldwin had finished the bottle of Glenlivet in less than an hour. Mentally he was far from drunk. Physically, he was fit to drop.

"Get in the car. I'll take you back to your hotel."

Packard headed the rental car through the town and out towards the ring road.

"London is waiting to reply to the Qataris who are becoming very agitated. We need to move fast if we are to save that contract for you. What do you have for me?"

"He has a video of someone called Stevenson aka Barbary delivering the marriage certificate, them signing it and Barbary witnessing it. He also has something he says will prove that his wife was killed in Algeria, that US Seals burned her body and that Six staged the car crash in Spain. He doesn't know what female body they used for that."

"Bullshit."

"I saw the video. His wife Ellie was a real beauty, with brains too, it seems, and well in with you lot. I actually know the Six handler he called Barbary – it is Stevenson in the video."

"And Algeria?"

"He refused to tell me what that was. He did say that it was at the time of the nuclear bomb in the Canary Islands and the tsunami it caused."

"He's bluffing. It's all bollocks."

"Explain the video then."

Packard ignored the request – these details were all news to him. "Listen carefully Borthwick. Baldwin has forty eight hours to deliver a working intrusion at Saluscent, or you can kiss goodbye to your contract."

Borthwick climbed out of the car without another word.

Packard called Macsen's number and briefed him in. Macsen appeared to be surprised by the details about Algeria, but he was clear on the next steps.

"We'll call Baldwin's bluff. Put more pressure on Borthwick. Whatever you do don't go near Baldwin. Let Borthwick do the heavy lifting. I'll talk to Stevenson in the meantime. That video is a real problem, looks like it was really bad tradecraft on his part." 'C' will not bloody like this one bit, Macsen thought – and how much does *he* know anyway? Algeria? What the hell was all that about?

An hour later he had provided an update to 'C' and a rough plan had been devised. The meeting had been heated as Macsen vented about being kept in the dark – 'You and me both' 'C' had replied with little conviction in his voice.

The final statement by 'C' had been unequivocal. "The Algeria incident was classified beyond my level at the time, before I became 'C'- and I hadn't thought such a thing possible. Everything has been erased, it seems. All that remains is in the brain of my predecessor, and that's becoming addled – and, also it would seem, Baldwin's. His Lordship was not a happy man when I met him this morning. You and I and, if what you told me is correct, both Borthwick and Baldwin, are in possession of extremely dangerous information. If Baldwin continues like this then he will have to be removed from the playing field. The sin bin may not be enough to solve the problem – something more drastic might be required. I just don't know why it wasn't done before - he must have had something on 'C' at the time – or worse. We need to be very, very careful. Lord Gore may have friends that even I don't know about. If what Baldwin says is correct then the Cousins know about this and they may have a hidden hand jerking us around."

When Borthwick woke the next morning he scrolled though his messages. There was one short text on his phone which stood out – '*Send this to our man*' accompanied by a link, apparently to a BBC news website. There was no sender's name. He opened the link and swore when he read the brief news story on the page. The headline said it all and was accompanied by Baldwin's picture.

PORTUGUESE POLICE HUNT BRITISH WIFE KILLER IN ALGARVE

International Arrest Warrant Issued for schizophrenic ex-Royal Marine Steven Baldwin

<More>

...

He called Baldwin's phone but there was no reply – he was probably on shift and would not have access to his phone. Borthwick forwarded the link anyway, dressed quickly and headed for his rental car and drove to the Saluscent compound.

"On the way here I realized it's fake news, Baldy – look in detail at the link address. They want you to know how the story will play."

Baldwin clicked on the link and the screen displayed the message 'This story will be available at 12:00 hrs GMT'.

They were seated in Borthwick's rental SUV in the Saluscent visitors' car park and Steve was incandescent.

"I'm going to release the fucking video and see those cunts squirm."

"They've got that covered already – read to the end of the piece. They say that there is a video and it's a fake, part of an elaborate plan to kill your wife and steal her money."

"But I've got Barbary on camera! Thank God Ellie had the sense to install that webcam."

"Don't go down that road Steve. They will find a way around it – that's for certain. They've got me by the balls as well, totally. If we don't do what they say then we're both fucked – possibly terminally."

Baldwin cursed again and hammered his fists against the dashboard of the SUV. Dick waited for his rage subsided. Then he took a deep breath.

"Alright. Let's fucking do it – but I *will* square the account with those bastards, that's for sure."

Borthwick started the car. "I've got to go, Steve. Plane to catch."

*

"Dick, it's me."

"Hi Baldy. Sorry, I don't have much time. I'm in the BA Lounge at Heathrow departures about to board a flight to Qatar. Looks like the contract is going ahead – I'm going to get the signatures thanks to you. Anyway, what can I do for you? I can't really speak here so it'll be mostly yeses and noes."

"OK. It's not going to work."

"What's not going to work."

"This job you dumped on me. The underground levels are impenetrable. I've never seen such security. I talked to JC about it given the background you gave me about her."

"You shouldn't have done that. She may not be secure. Don't involve her."

"Keep your hair on, I'm not fucking stupid. I was careful, tried to prod her enquiring mind seeing as we're responsible for physical security. Anyway, you trust her, you wanted her to dig around."

"To a point, and that's different anyway."

"Whatever. There's no way to get down there covertly without being recorded, caught or trapped. I'm going to need specialist help. The timescale will slip."

"It can't."

"It already has."

"I need to get those contract signatures."

"Well then you'd better get your friends in VX to figure out a solution."

"My gate's closing, I've got to go and board."

"I'll be waiting."

A soon as Borthwick had boarded the plane he headed for the toilets and called Packard, just before takeoff. This was his last chance.

*

"Borthwick's been on the blower, Boss. I don't think Baldwin can do the insertion without specialist help. He'd be discovered within minutes – probably seconds. We could subvert one of Alice's technicians, but that might take weeks."

"And might not prove to be possible at all."

"I know."

"There's a palm print reader but we can work around that. We just don't know what other security they have in place. Telion thinks that there are no RFID tags as she's not picking up signals with her scanner."

"So, what do you recommend, Josh?"

"We dig a fucking big hole and tunnel in, drilling through the walls of the bunker to insert the probes."

Macsen looked at him, clearly not amused.

"Sorry, Sir, just frustration with the situation. We need some sort of diversion to get the techies out of the room. It will have to be a serious diversion as we don't have site drawings of the lower levels. Plus, we'd need a blackout to defeat the cameras. It would all look mighty suspicious."

"Yes, I take your point."

"Alice lives in a villa on site. JC thinks there may be a tunnel, as no-one has seen her leave the compound since Telion joined the team – and that was over three months ago."

"You'll need to confirm that. It may give us a way in but there is still the problem of staying covert."

"I still don't understand why we're running such a complex op against a company in Portugal which is involved in a currency scam – or scams. Surely we just tell Interpol and let the Portuguese sort it out? With respect, Sir, there's a lot you are not telling me."

"There's a lot that 'C' is not telling *me*, Josh, and the pressure is on. You know the score – we've discussed the incident in question. It didn't happen, right. So, let's just follow orders shall we? Maybe that way we can stay in one piece."

"Yes, Sir, but I want it noted that running an agent without complete access to their operational history could compromise the operation."

'M' laughed. "So noted for what that's worth. You need to remember that this isn't a school we're working in. Forget the Queensberry Rules. Put more pressure on Borthwick. Let the shit trickle down."

"It's risky."

"That's life. Now get the shit flowing. We need to know what's going on in that bloody bunker of Alice's."

*

Seventeen

It was past 1 am and Sveta was nearing the end of testing the final software module. Soon she would be able to link and compile the code for burning into the firmware in her BASIC array. The BASIC was a bastardized piece of hardware – a small circuit board of few chips, not the BASIC programming language of old but a Burnable Application Specific Integrated Circuit. A BASIC usually comprised a single chip designed to carry out a specific task.

This was a hybrid design. She had designed the circuit herself and had them produced in Malaysia, not trusting the Chinese although they would have been a much cheaper source. Final assembly had been done by a small company in England. She was the only one who had the full picture. Over the last 3 days the robots had installed the BASICs in the server array on the lowest level below the site. To load all the software up into the ten thousand BASICs in the racks would take only seconds and the software could be updated on the fly.

Using ASICs (such as the AntMiner X3 from the Chinese chip maker Bitmain) to mine Bitcoins was much faster and used much less power than regular computers. Each ASIC is designed to solve the math problem (hash) specific to a given cryptocurrency – the S9 being the latest Bitcoin ASIC in the Bitmain family, with the X3 being the latest ASIC in the design for mining the Monero. Each model was designed to mine a specific cryptocurrency.

Her BASICS – ten thousand of them – were unique and designed to exploit and defeat a feature of the cryptocurrency mining process, cutting out much of the mining work. Beyond that, they were soft-switchable, capable of hopping between mining algorithms – that is, mining different cryptocurrencies, in microseconds as prices fluctuated on the exchanges. But just as importantly, each circuit board consumed only a tenth of that of the AntMiners. Less power meant less cooling requirement. It was a virtuous circle.

There were 10 boards in a vertical tier, 2 tiers per meter, 500 boards each side of 10 aisles, each 25 meters long. The rest of the vast area was shuttered off and contained lithium batteries and switchgear to handle the huge power input from the solar array by day and the generators at night.

She also had access to other miners' sites, although they didn't yet know it.

The key to Sveta's plan revolved around one-time numbers used in the cryptocurrency hashing algorithm. These numbers were known as 'nonces'. She had found a way to exploit several of the hashing algorithms and gain a statistical advantage in validating transactions. That would offer huge short term profits but would soon be apparent to other miners on the network. Then, she would hop to another currency, aiming to hit five in rotation and then start again. 'Rinse and repeat' was a web marketing term – and it was never more applicable than for Sveta Kovacs's strategy.

But that would only be the start. Already her nodes were adding new blocks, tainted blocks, in preparation A twist on the supply chain attack. When another Full node attempted to validate the blocks she had added it would hang for a few seconds. And that would be enough. Node by node she would infiltrate the Bitcoin, Monero and CryptoRuble networks.

Some of the cryptocurrency balances she would transfer to her own accounts, some she would mask so that inspection of the blocks would show them as having been false transactions in the blockchain. But there was much, much more to her plan. In fact, all the details were beyond her – they were being managed at the low level in large part by artificial intelligence.

She would wreck the consensus that blockchain technology relied upon - and smash a few other concepts along the way, including the Merkle Root.

*

The Lincoln limousine drew up at the gate to the huge government complex of Al Qasaira Street in Doha, the capital of Quatar. Borthwick had not slept well and had been further disturbed by the early morning call to prayer from the nearby mosque. That was six hours ago, and now he presented his letter of invitation to one of the guards at the Ministry gates. Borthwick waited with increasing agitation. The outside temperature was 40 C and the inside of the limo a comfortable 20 C, but Borthwick was sweating profusely. The guard returned after ten minutes. He spoke in Arabic and his driver translated.

"He say you not let enter. Come back meeting another day."

Borthwick swore. "That's impossible. That is a letter of invitation from the Minister of State for Defense Affairs. The meeting is today, in half an hour. The date is there on the letter." The driver spoke to the guard and translated, as another guard came out of the guardhouse, weapon ready. Borthwick doubted the quality of the translation.

"He says I must go now. Meeting another day. Minister tell you when."

The driver turned the car.

"Where now, Sir?"

"Back to the fucking Shangri-La Hotel."

Borthwick called the contact number but the Minister was unavailable. The secretary said that he had no date for the meeting, but expected it to be rescheduled within two days.

Back in his hotel room, Borthwick watched the condensation run down the outside of the balcony's sliding doors which faced eastwards across the Diplomatic Quarter to the Persian Gulf.

He'd called Packard, but he'd been stalled and now he had to wait.

It was much too hot to go outside and the aircon was on full – but still he sweated. He looked around his opulent suite. 'Shit or bust' he thought – this might be my last chance to enjoy such luxury. He determined that if he did get the Qatari training contract then he would pad the Scutum Est contract expenses like there was no tomorrow. The Qataris would pay – in spades. He shook his head, knowing that they wouldn't really care. They expected padding of expenses and the officials expected some of the cash to come back to them anyway. They used to have Swiss accounts, but since the Swiss had relaxed their banking rules they were now using Bitcoin. Progress.

Per head of citizens, Qatar was the fifth richest country on earth, with a GDP of $138,000 per capita, or so he'd read in the in-flight magazine. They were probably the biggest grafters per capita too.

For the fourth time he checked that he was connected to the hotel wifi and that the signal was good. He was still jet lagged and desperate for sleep, but knew that would be impossible. He glanced at the room service menu, but had no appetite and threw it down in disgust. He kicked off his loafers, stripped off his clothes and lay on the queen sized bed.

Packard had committed to a response within four hours. Borthwick awoke with a start and glanced at the clock. Packard should have called by now – it was almost four and a half hours. How long had he been asleep?

His mobile chimed and he hastily scrabbled to swipe the answer icon in the right direction. Wrong. He'd cut the call off. He shouted and cursed and then the phone rang again. He gently swiped it and spoke to Packard.

"Richard, go into the bathroom and run the shower."

Borthwick headed into the bathroom.

"We're okay to talk now."

"We have a plan and it will need two people. So you will need to get our two players to work together. We didn't want to do that, but I'm sure you can manage it."

"Who do you mean?"

"The one who's got a murder charge hanging over his head and the one with the saviour's initials. No names please."

"J…Jesus - another one of your lot – I might have guessed as much when you wanted her on the team."

"No comment."

"How the hell do I get my guy on board with that?"

"I'm sure you'll think of a way. Keep us out of it whatever you do."

"He's not fucking stupid, he'll know." But he's half way there already, thought Borthwick.

"Well, it's you he's working for isn't it?"

"He's actually going me a favor. He doesn't need the money. This has all the ingredients of a recipe for disaster."

"There is a big question mark over both his freedom and his wife's estate. You'll persuade him, I'm sure. Your Qatari contract depends on it, make no mistake."

Borthwick shook his head. How in hell's name did Six get the Qataris to muck him about with the contract? Someone somewhere must have a pretty big lever.

"There's a package shipping now to Baldwin with your company name on it. Delivery to his boat, Fedex Priority from Lisbon – it should be with him within twenty four hours. There's a range of devices they can use. There's an encrypted document coming through to your phone in the next half hour. Memorize the details and press the embedded erase button. The plan is sketchy but it should work. You'll have to flesh out the details and options with them, but they will have to be inventive. And flexible."

Borthwick guessed that the package would have originated at the Farm – a Six technical development facility in Hertfordshire – and had probably been sent to Lisbon in the diplomatic baggage, accompanied by a Queen's Messenger.

"Is that all?"

"For now. You need to get on a plane to Faro."

"But I'm in fucking Qatar!"

"First things first, old boy. Get the ducks in line. We're running out of time."

"How much time do I have?"

"Technically you're out of time already, old pal."

Packard cut the connection.

Borthwick swore as he opened the minibar and took out a full bottle of Glenmorangie. By no stretch of the imagination could it be called a minibar - everything was full size and bar was as tall as he was. So much for Islam. He poured four fingers into the cut glass tumbler. Then he added ice from the icemaker. 'Wrong way round' he thought, 'just like this bloody assignment'.

How much time did he have? They were already late, he knew, and Packard was pushing hard. He'd fought hand to hand in Afghanistan, the Yemen and places whose names he hardly knew. He'd seen mates blown to pieces and he'd never suffered PTSD, but these circumstances were shredding his nerves.

His phone chimed again, but he ignored it. The plan could wait – he needed to be sure of his flights. He opened his laptop and went online. He was down to his last credit card. And his Litecoin cryptocurrency.

Almost thirty hours later Borthwick was showing his passport in Faro, exhausted. The quickest way to Faro had been back to London and out again from Gatwick.

He was in no fit state to meet Baldwin – he could hardly string two words together coherently. It had been tough enough persuading him to do the job in the first place. Now this new plan. He'd called Baldwin during the transit from Heathrow to Gatwick – another toilet call. And it had been brief – very brief.

At least Baldwin had confirmed receipt of the package, but he'd gone ballistic when Borthwick had told him that it was a solid plan, but a two man plan. He didn't go into the details of the plan – or the identity of the second person. Baldwin probably assumed that it was he, Borthwick. Baldwin was in for a real surprise.

*

"You look like shit squared, Dick."

They were seated in the saloon on *Rubaiyat*.

"I feel much worse. I'm being jerked around like a fucking puppet on uppers. I'll not mess around. I have been warned in the most serious way possible that the story you told me about the death of your wife is not to be repeated. Ever. They will take you out and they will take me out. I've no doubt about it."

"I don't know why it's such a big secret, Dick. The world knows about the nuclear attack on La Palma and the tsunami that followed."

"For fuck's sake shut up, Steve, they're probably listening in right now."

Baldwin nodded and flipped a finger. "Just in case they're watching as well, Dick. Here, have a wet."

Borthwick looked dubiously at the glass of scotch that Steve held out. "Have you got vodka?"

"There may be some paint thinners knocking around in a locker. Your choice."

Borthwick took the glass. "I seem to be in a permanent hangover."

"Join the club, mate."

"Look Baldy, I've got no time to lose. We have a new plan, but to carry it out you'll need help."

"Is that so?"

"Yes. I'm pairing you up with JC for a bit of spooking at Saluscent."

Baldwin was speechless, his mouth hung open, his color rising. Then he exploded.

"No fucking way! I'm not working with another woman. This job has gone from madness to insanity and now it's beyond certifiable. Jesus, Dick, how do you come up with this shit?"

"Steve, you always say that but hear me out, please. That's an order."

"I thought it would be you. I could live with that."

"You could die with it too. Do I look like I'm in any fit state for an op? I'm corporate man personified now – just look at my waistline. I'd be a liability. I'm living with a non-stop hangover. JC passed our physical with flying colors – you'll have noticed the body she has on her – and that's no joke. She passed our leadership and stress tests too – she makes good decisions under extreme pressure."

"In front of a fucking computer, I bet."

"She passed the failed reserve chute test on a night-time halo jump."

Steve looked at Borthwick.

"Is that so?"

"Yes, outstandingly so. Her solution time was in the top ten percent."

"Sounds like she's an angel – and it's still not on." Baldwin was still wondering what the hell that test was. He'd got his parachute wings way back as every Royal Marine had the option to do, but never Halo - or any kind of reserve chute failure test whatever that was. It sounded terminal. *What happened to the other 90%?*

"Okay, let's put that aside for now and talk about the plan. But first, put the bottle away and find me some paracetamol." Borthwick drained his glass.

The next hour was taken up with the details, looking for all the possible points of failure, the contingencies and the fall-backs, They re-checked the contents of the package. It was labeled 'iPhone earbuds'.

"It makes more sense than the first plan. This is not half-cocked – just three-quarters. Now you just have to persuade JC."

At that moment Borthwick knew that Baldwin was onboard.

"I'm sure she'll fall in with it."

"How do you know?"

"When I took her on she agreed that she'd take on some covert work."

"But this is dangerous – it's much more than snooping in desk drawers."

"Where's the danger?"

"Precisely none. The only danger is to me. I'd lose the Saluscent contract. Don't worry. I know JC. I'll brief her first. You *are* the physical security team anyway. The only danger is friendly fire – and I'm sure you can tell the lads in advance that you are testing out some of the systems and if there are any surprises they should keep their fingers off the triggers."

"Maybe she will not want to work with me."

"Don't worry, I'll sort it. She'll get a bonus. I'm heading back to my hotel now. I'll call her and meet her for breakfast. Then we'll all meet up late morning and walk through the plan, the options and the equipment."

"Dick, I'm really not happy about this."

"Me neither, but I've got to play the hand. They've got us both by the short and curlies. The worst that can happen is that Sveta cans the contract."

"The worst Dick, is that you catch a dose of lead."

Borthwick shrugged and looked appealingly at Baldwin. "We can do this, Baldy."

"We?"

Dickwick shrugged "Well, you know what I mean." As he watched he saw Baldwin move from doubt to commitment - his decision had been made.

"Our shifts work for that plan, but I'll need to juggle things to get the right night.

"It's got to be tomorrow night, it can't wait longer. I fly out tomorrow afternoon, back to Qatar, so I won't be here for the action."

"Why am I not fucking surprised, Dick?"

*

Baldwin arranged that the next day he would be on night shift inside the building – a privilege of rank, he thought glumly. He didn't want to do this, but he was now committed and gave it everything. At least it took his mind off Ellie – and helped Dickwick - as if that was important. The man was in tight with Six, that was for certain.

Stone was on patrol outside with Aldo Colarusso and Henri Laporte was in the security control room. Mankowicz had been given the night off while Baldwin replaced him on internal patrol – he regularly rotated through each of the roles and shifts to give the team some variety – and to get to know their jobs.

Two of the cybersecurity team were signed in on the access control system and were, presumably, in their office below ground. The main - and only - gate was never opened at night.

Badlwin had no idea of the layout below ground and that was the least of his problems. There were cameras and sensors throughout the building, he had no security access to the elevators which led below ground, and there were people in the rooms he had to access. The previous night had been a sleepless one as he relived the nightmare of getting into the new Chinese naval base in the Yemen and planting cameras. Just another nightmare. That had been straightforward by comparison, despite the two mile swim through naval patrols. He had enough material for a different nightmare every night for the rest of his life.

Borthwick had turned the screws on him good and proper and now he was almost beyond caring. But he'd come up with a plan. A risky one, but what did he really have to lose?

JC was in the control room next to what was in fact an armory, although they avoided using the term. She had checked the logbook and apart from the Scutum Est team, there were two of the cybersecurity team in their office below ground, both British – Carl Hoskyns and Dave Lumley.

Only Sveta was exempt from the sign-in process though that mattered little as it seemed she rarely left the site and no-one knew where she went. In fact, no-one on Baldwin's team could recall seeing her leave, ever.

The vibration sensors that Stone had placed on two of the villa windows the night before had picked up some sounds up until about 23:30 hours, and she was assuming that Sveta was at home and now in bed after the sensors went quiet. Getting the sensors on site had not been difficult. Six provide them in small pouches and she just used a slingshot over the fence late one night, then collected them when on patrol. Sometimes the simplest solution are the best.

Baldwin had been impressed by JC's noticing that the sweep team never swept outside the bungalow – and this had given them an edge. That was all a part of the intel package JC had put together for Borthwick during her first month on the job.

Lack of a map of the underground facilities was a major handicap and in the hasty planning she and Baldwin had talked through several possible scenarios. She'd pointed out that if any alarm went off then Sveta was likely to move to the bunker through the tunnel from the villa.

Alarms were the last thing they wanted – but contingencies had been prepared to cover the event – and the alarms were switchable from the control room. But there might be others they didn't know about on the lower levels – where were those controlled? They had studied the equipment and instructions, then selected the components that they thought would suit the detailed plan they had agreed. London had been thorough in the preparations.

The plan required that they work independently, without communications – until they gained access to the underground levels. Timing was critical.

Baldwin waited in the entrance lobby. The security net radio on his belt squawked in his earbud – the volume was down – as Stone did her radio rounds, checking with each of the team, every fifteen minutes as the protocol demanded. He acknowledged her by keying his mike. All security teams had to have radio contact, and this was another chink in the armor that they could exploit even though these units were military grade state of the art frequency hoppers with voice encryption, specified by Sveta herself.

It was just after 01:00 hours. He'd checked that there were no lights in Sveta's ground level office where she seemed to spend so little time – she was rarely seen these days - and then slipped out through a rear personnel door which Stone had unlocked from the control room. The fact that the door was unlocked indicated that Aldo was in the guardpost at the gate. For now. The door opening would be logged, but it was regularly used by the smokers on the team. For good measure Steve carried a packet of Marlboro Lights although he had no intention of smoking. It was unprofessional – and dangerous in more ways than one.

The stealth quadcopter had been pre-positioned in a rented flatbed truck hidden a quarter mile away in the trees. Under guidance from London it flew low over the fence barely visible in the low orange light from the clouds uplit by the town of Olhaõ, then landed next to Steve. He detached the small equipment bag and watched the drone disappear back over the fence as he hid the bag in his uniform windbreaker. He tried not to think about their dependence on the technology – and the criticality of timing. He just hoped that the other delivery would be on time – or at least within the 20 minute window that the plan allowed for.

Every stage of the plan had at best 50% probability – some much less - and when you took 50% of 50% a half dozen times then there was a next to no chance of success…

*

Eighteen

When the Saluscent cyber security team were on night-shift they usually had pizzas delivered at about 1 am. The menus and timings varied, sometimes pizza, sometimes Chinese, sometimes regular Portuguese food. Food was pre-ordered before they started their shift as there were no external comms on site. The lack of telephone lines was in breach of fire, health and a host of other EU regulations. The phone lines had been installed originally and then disconnected at Sveta's direction once the official inspections had been finished. They could be reconnected for the annual fire inspection, though these had never happened as Gerasimov's regular donations to the Firefighters Benevolent Fund had led to all the right boxes being ticked on all the right forms. The site was in permanent communications lockdown, except for the satellite links.

It was just after 01:10 when Aldo called Control. "Pizza for the cyber team. I've checked them, regular pizza. Just having a taster. Good. No weapons, unless you consider chili a threat." Baldwin went to collect them from Aldo at the gatehouse and deliver them to the elevator where Carl would come up to collect them. Chili? That would be the least of their problems.

The smell of the pizzas wafted through the building as Steve walked down the corridor to the elevator. With his back to the camera facing the elevator he opened the top box – chicken piri-piri. Then the other box – tuna. It's just as well that I'm not hungry, he thought. Job done, he closed both boxes carefully, and then the elevator chimed.

"Your pizza delivery Carl. They smell really good – let me know if you have any left over."

Carl nodded. Dressed as the nerd he was, he said nothing, just nodded, no eye contact. He was short and well overweight - he clearly did not need pizza or communication with mere mortals. He took the boxes and the elevator door closed. It would have been so easy for Baldwin to muscle in – and give the game away.

Pizzas, part of the new weight loss regime. It shouldn't take long.

*

In fact it was an hour before Stone got the call on the intercom. It was Dave Lumley – and he sounded bad.

"Control, Dave Lumley in cybersecurity. I need help down here. Get a doctor. Carl has passed out in the toilet and I don't think I can hold out much longer…I think it was the food."

"OK Dave, I'm calling an ambulance now. Help is on its way. Stay calm. You'll need to give us access through the elevator. Technically we're not allowed down there as you know."

Stone winced as she heard a prolonged, agonized groan over the phone.

"I'll try to do that, be quick. Ahhhh…"

"I need to call backups for you and Carl. We can't leave your office unmanned. Try to drink some water."

"Whatever, hurry, please. I'm dying." Another agonized groan.

Hardly, thought Stone, just a very bad case of the squits. *That's what Packard had said they'd get.* Was it the truth? Her face was grim as she keyed the mike.

"Aldo, Control here. Call an ambulance – the guys in cybersecurity are ill. I'm closing Control and going to help. You're backup Control. You'll need to call in the standby shift to cover them."

"I can't let an ambulance in. The gate is locked, outside my control. Remember that there may be a biohazard – you should suit up."

"OK, I can override the ambulance. There, done. Your switches are active."

"Roger that, I'll call the ambulance and then the standby shift. Remember to suit up – we could be under attack."

"You can reach me on the radio, but I'm not sure if it will work below ground. You'd better call Sveta and Sergei too."

"But you can't go down there!"

Stone ignored the comment and ran from the control room to the lobby elevator. NBC warfare suits? She laughed to herself. Attack of the Rotten Tomatoes! Disposable nappies, that's what was needed – if it was just the squits.

Baldwin was waiting in the lobby and listened to Stone's radio exchange with Aldo. Then she came running down the corridor towards him.

"You heard?"

"Yes."

"We have to go down there."

"It's against orders. We have to wait for Sveta."

"Those lads might die if we wait."

"Well I'm not letting the ambulance people go down there."

"Your call - you are the squad leader."

"We should have NBC suits on."

"Yes we should."

Steve ticked off the risks in his head. 100% according to script this far, though he wasn't sure good their acting was for the audio and CCTV. Now it got really tricky. The elevator chimed and the door opened.

Dave was lying on the floor. The stench rolled out.

"Pull him out."

They dragged Dave into the lobby and entered the elevator taking great care where they put their feet.

"Which floor Dave, where do we go to find Carl?"

"Minus one. Cyber Security room. For God's sake get a doctor, I'm dying." He screamed and clutched his abdomen, rolling on the floor. There were other sound effects. And odors.

"There's an ambulance on its way."

They both gagged as the elevator went down, fighting to keep control of the reflexes of their bodies. Stone adjusted the hair grip that Baldwin had passed her, pushing the on switch as she did so and hoping that she'd got the right angle for the embedded camera. They stood awkwardly avoiding puddles as if they were playing Twister. She looked at Baldwin and he nodded imperceptibly as the elevator doors opened.

A long corridor stretched ahead of them for maybe 50 yards. The smell was pervasive.

The doors had only numbers – no functional names. Their eyes were scanning, automatically checking camera positions as surreptitiously as possible. And recording their own video.

"You take the left side, I'll take the right."

"Not necessary Steve – there's a trail."

The trail was both visual and olfactory and she crinkled her nose. Steve noticed and strangely, subconsciously he thought her slightly upturned, freckled nose was pretty.

They followed the trail and entered room 3.

Room 3 was about ten meters along each side and at least five meters high. There was a raised podium inside the door with two desks looking along racks of communications equipment extending floor to ceiling. The desks and podium were splashed with vomit.

One wall was taken up with three massive switch panels marked 'Satellite I/O' and 'Danger High Voltage'. Metal pipes - waveguide feeds - ran up into the suspended ceiling. Below the feeds were the boxes marked Multiplexers and these in turn were fed by cables which were labeled. One of the Multiplexers had a cable feed marked 'SECURE COMMS ROOM 5'.

Their next move had to be carefully finessed. 'Whatever you can, wherever you can'. That was the mission directive about the intrusion devices - 'anything is better than nothing'. And so the plan had to be flexible and rely on quick thinking – and it had to work in front of the CCTV cameras. They had tried to anticipate what they might expect and how they should handle the various possibilities. The additional briefing documents that Dick had provided had helped though they were 'in principle' only – no one knew what they would find.

Baldwin leaned back against the warmth of the multiplexers, a cool downdraft of air sweeping over him from the aircon vent in the ceiling. With one hand behind his back he attached a matchbox sized sticky wifi relay unit behind one of the waveguides on the Room 5 multiplexer.

They looked at one another and Stone inclined her head as she spoke, loudly "Where the hell is Carl?" She walked around the equipment racks and along the podium. The array of control PCs used by the cybersecurity team were all logged out. *No surprises there*. She wouldn't remember everything, but her hairgrip microcam would help. The smell of vomit was rank.

"No sign of him here. We'd better check the other rooms."

They moved along the corridor checking each room in turn. They were all of similar dimensions and linked internally Almost every room was filled with equipment – rack upon rack of processor boards, their lights blinking and robots in attendance, able to move between the interconnected rooms. It was almost a duplicate of what they'd seen on the ground floor above.

They wandered through the rooms at pace noting the cameras and keeping up a chatter about Carl, trying to follow his trail. From room 4 they had to exit into the corridor.

Then they came to room 5.

The door was unlocked and they went in. It was a small room, at the end of the corridor. A door was let into one of the side walls. A few feet away was an elevator door, closed. With a woman's eye Stone thought that the room was rarely cleaned, if ever. At least there was no shit in there, she realized with relief.

One wall was covered with a huge whiteboard, and – surprise - before it stood Sveta. On her desk was an open carton of Marlboro Lights and an overflowing ashtray.

She turned in shock and moved quickly to her desk, a cigarette hanging from the side of her mouth. With her left hand she removed the cigarette from her mouth and stubbed it in the ashtray.

"What are you doing in here? You are not authorized to be here." Baldwin's eyes were on the ashtray as a small pistol appeared in Kovacs's right hand – a Beretta Compact 92 thought Baldwin as he and Stone raised their hands in unison.

He stepped straight in to the breech. "Sveta, there is a medical emergency. The cybersecurity team are seriously ill. You don't need that weapon."

"I will decide that. Ill you say?"

"Yes, we are evacuating them – an ambulance is on its way."

"Nevertheless you should not be down here! And never in this room."

"Maybe, but I am responsible for physical security – and that's everyone on site. We think it could be food poisoning, but if not it may be contagious."

"Are we being attacked? Bio-weapons?"

"I think that's very unlikely Ma'am – we think their pizza was bad."

"Then I had better stay here and…what is that smell?" Sveta's face twisted in disgust. She lowered the pistol slowly.

Stone looked at her shoes and winced. Oops. "We moved Dave, but we are searching the rooms for Carl."

"Well he is not in here! Go and find him. And don't come in here again."

"Ma'am, can I please call the guardhouse and check on the ambulance?" Stone moved towards the desk intercom, her head looking at the whiteboard as Sveta followed her movement. "Not from here. Get out now! We will take this up tomorrow."

It was time enough for Steve to attach the miniscule sticky device under the desk.

Afterwards Baldwin had to admit that Stone had been silky smooth with her distraction. And no cameras. In planning they had assumed that the room was never swept for bugs if no-one was ever allowed in. Such was the arrogance of the supremely clever. It was pure luck, a break that tipped the odds in their favor.

As they turned to leave the room Sveta spoke. "Mr Baldwin, I will take this breach of security up with Mr Borthwick. In the meantime keep me fully informed of the situation."

"Yes Ma'am – the other shift is on its way in to take over the cybersecurity suite. I have called Sergei."

"Good, he will need to rework the rota. Will these people live?"

She's a hard bitch, Steve thought. One to watch. "I don't know – Dave is quite bad. We have to find Carl. Must go."

"And stop fucking calling me Ma'am!"

"Er, yes, Miss…"

He heard Stone's shout from the corridor. "The toilet!"

Of course, Dave had said Carl had collapsed in the toilet. What a dirty job – nerds or not they were innocent and having a tough time of it.

Carl was in a bad way. His pulse was weak and elevated and he was sweating profusely.

"He looks bad."

Baldwin nodded. *So much for Dick's potion, but that had come from...*

"As soon as he's in the ambulance I'm going to bathe in disinfectant. For a long time." She smiled at him.

"We took the tablets so we would be safe from the shits, but the cleaners are going to have a hell of a job." *Yes, there was definitely something about her nose. And her eyes were interesting too.*

It was past 4 am. and Sveta was still working at the problem. The work had been intense over the last few weeks and she barely knew whether it was night or day. The final piece in the puzzle of the CryptoRuble traceability had been there in her mind's eye, tantalizingly close, when those security people had intruded into her secure comms room a couple of hours ago. The chain of thought had been broken and she had been unable to re-link it. She did little of her real work in her ground level office – it was the isolation underground, the lack of distraction – that enabled her to think more clearly. But it was not helping now.

Weeks before, she had hacked in and downloaded the compiled code from the Russian servers. That had taken days of work as the competing intellects figuratively butted heads in cyberspace. Feeling around, liking working a maze with a blindfold with traps and alarms everywhere.

Then reverse-engineering the code had been almost impossible and she'd been unable to locate the sub-routine libraries that were linked in during compile time. They'd been hidden away too deeply. If she'd been able to access the build script then that would have helped but the build environment on the Russian development servers had been empty. That was over two weeks ago and now time was short if she was to have her final offensive module ready in time to coincide with the public release of her own cryptocurrency.

Juggling all her projects was now a major challenge – Sergei only handled the legitimate side of the business, the rest was hidden from him. Both the business and the building were like an iceberg. And this last week Sergei had been complaining about downtime on the mining computers. Installing the BASICs had taken a chunk out of their mining profits and he didn't know why – and never would.

She called Dmitri in Kiev but he was offline and she finally gave up in exasperation.

Draining the last of her glass of water she took one more look at the whiteboard. So close, she thought, so close. Then, she opened the door and headed along the tunnel to the villa, thinking about a glass of wine and a microwave meal. Then, maybe, some sleep.

At least she didn't need to pass the trail that Dave Lumley had left in the corridor.

*

After their shift ended the handovers were done, there was an extensive de-brief with Sergei. An approved cleaning company would be used but Baldwin's night shift would have to supervise the cleaning, so it was almost midday before they could return to their lodgings.

Back at *Rubaiyat* Steve called Borthwick with an update.

"I can't speak Baldy, I'm in the bar. The bastards are still stringing me along. I hope that you've got some good news. How did it go"?

"Well, we got through the night okay. I'm glad I didn't eat the pizza – that stuff we used was really potent. I got a bit worried – I thought one of the guys was going to croak. Everything's in place, although I can't guarantee that it will work. Then we still have phase two tonight."

"That should be a doddle. Did the shipment go?"

"Stone should be doing it now."

"Tell her to hurry it up. This waiting is killing me. How did she do?"

"She's smart and cool, she did well – a quick thinker." And appearing in my dreams too, thought Steve, with guilt, as if he was in some way being disloyal to Ellie. It's that nose, there's something about it. And the eyes. And then there's the way she chuckles. He realized that the list was getting longer by the day.

He snapped back to reality.

"Baldy, are you there?"

"Yes Dick, sorry just a bit tired, that's all."

"Didn't I tell you that she was good?"

"Yes you did. I'm going to get some shut-eye, speak later." Baldwin cut the Signal call.

Meanwhile, back in her hotel room, Stone had downloaded the video file from the camera in her hair grip and securely transmitted it to London via the Signal app.

Phase 2 - the final part of the plan - was relatively simple and was managed remotely, with the stealth drone again at work in the middle of the next night, being used to attach additional relays to the waveguides which emerged on the rooftop to feed the satellite dishes. All Stone had to do was attach the payload to the drone after changing the batteries - the rest was done from a control room in London, but without Baldwin's knowledge. No need for him to know.

A day later the system was fully operational, with the audio feed from Sveta's secure comms room linked by secure off-channel wifi to the relay in the cybersecurity suite on the first underground floor. From there it piggy-backed the satellite waveguide to the roof, where the final solar powered relay broadcast the encrypted feed to a UHF receiver in a room at the nearby Hotel Boa Vista. That hotel had a particularly good internet connection and the room had been let for 3 months to a Ms C Jones – aka J C Stone.

At Saluscent, a service engineer would probably find the rooftop relays one day, but for the moment they would do the job.

*

Baldwin answered the phone. There was no pre-amble as Borthwick gushed.

"Baldy, I've got the contract signed."

"That's good news. And now you owe me big time. Where are you?"

"Still in Doha – R and R for a few days. Anyway you did a great job!"

"I've been getting a lot of flak from Sveta and Sergei."

"To be expected. I'll be there in a couple of days. She wants to re-negotiate the contract and change some personnel."

"That's me out then."

"I doubt that. She's also asked about my cybersecurity division – looking for a systems security audit. It would be a good starter project for my new people."

"That could be awkward. You may have an idea about what's down there but she'll never let your people anywhere near. Besides, JC is already checking out all the cyber security stuff for you and Six isn't she?"

"I've told you, she's not bloody connected with VX."

"Pull the other one Dick."

"I'll ignore that. What we know is nothing we can't overlook when we write the audit report."

"If."

"Yes, if. Nothing's agreed yet. Anyway, we'll have a wet together when I'm there, towards the end of the week."

"Okay, I'm not going anywhere yet."

"Is your boat still in the same place?"

"Yes, in the marina and you're paying the dock fees, on my expenses."

Baldwin pressed 'End Call'.

*

Suddenly, he was wide awake, refreshed, feeling better than he had in months. The dream was fresh in his mind, vivid and explicit although he had never seen or even thought of JC naked. Then he realized that he had an erection and automatically his hand sought it out, to explore it. He had not had an erection for months, not since Ellie…the guilt washed over him like a huge green sea washing over Adèle, the boat on which he and Ellie had sailed together. His erection wilted instantly, but the vision of JC intruded into his consciousness afresh like a white wave and he felt his blood flowing downward. The vision began to fade even as he tried to catch the vision and examine it, and then another wave of memories of Ellie washed over him. It was like there were two competing wavetrains assaulting his emotions.

I have to move on he thought or I will go mad. Yes, JC is attractive, she is smart – and sexy too. But it has been less than six months since Ellie died – and that was my fault. It just doesn't feel right to have these thoughts about JC.

"Jesus Christ Steve, wake up! You didn't put me on that mission, and I alone was responsible for what happened so stop wallowing in your guilt trip. Yes, we loved each other but I'm dead now, so get your bloody act together and move on."

It was Ellie's voice and he could even visualize her saying it. I'm not going mad he thought, it's just inner conflict and Ellie is right. Bloody hell where did I pick up all this mumbo-jumbo?

He glanced at the clock – 05:30. He'd have to move to get to his Saluscent shift by 06:00. Today he was rotated on gatehouse duty.

Back at Saluscent, the situation had stabilized as the two cyber engineers had returned to work after treatment at a private clinic. It had been a particularly unusual and severe case of food poisoning, but fortunately no other staff were affected. It was put down to the pizzas, and all staff were ordered not to order food from 'Gosto de Itália'.

*

Nineteen

Baldwin took the handover from Rodriguez in the gatehouse at 06:00. José handed his weapon to Steve who checked the action and magazine then placed it back on the shelf under the desk. The weapons were legal – just. It was a grey legal area in Portugal and so they were always kept out of sight. José made a note of the change of guard in the log. Then they discussed the log entries for the night. "What's this José, 02:25 Zorro through gate? This log is part of the contract we have with the company. You cannot put stuff like this in it."

José looked at him and then a light appeared to go on in his eyes, and he smiled. "You call it a fox I think. Sorry, Steve, I use the Spanish word zorro. It was a mistake - I was bored. It was a dog fox. But I didn't shoot it. Next time maybe?" José amended the log entry after Steve keyed in the supervisor's password.

Baldwin shook his head and they laughed and José stepped back and took the *en garde* position. "Go on Zorro, go back to your hotel and get some sleep. Pronto." José offered a mock salute and after collecting his backback Baldwin let him out through the personnel gate. Laporte, Mankowicz and the others in the team were already in and Steve listened to Control do the radio check. They're gelling nicely Steve thought, a good bunch on a boring job.

He checked the schedule for the day. It was almost empty – as usual – except for the weekly water delivery, with the tanker scheduled for 11 am. Sergei Gerasimov usually got in just before 7 am. Steve looked forward to the breakfast truck which usually stopped outside the gates at about 7.30 am. as the techies started to arrive. There was also the regular delivery of gas with liquid nitrogen for the cooling system. The pro-forma delivery note also showed acetylene gas, to be stored in a small secure building at the rear. He made a note to ask Gerasimov about it, wondering what acetylene was required for.

The two office staff would not be in until well after 9 am - another tedious morning lay ahead until the food truck stopped by around noon. The hungry staffers would dribble out to select their sandwiches, fruit and yogurt. Sveta saw no need for onsite caterers – she believed that money was the best reward and wanted as few distractions as possible on site. Thank God it's only for three months he thought - unless Dickwick wants more dirty work doing.

There had been an internal inquiry by Gerasimov into the 'night of the pizzas' as it was now called, and the conclusion – assumption really – was that it had been the pizzas. Dickwick had been called in to take a dressing down about breaches of security protocol – and sign the systems security audit contract, much to Baldwin's amazement. That guy had all the luck. That was the only time Sveta had been seen above ground since the pizza incident.

Later that day Borthwick had called the Scutum Est team together in two groups, one before and one after the night shift change. He read them the riot act about the inviolability of the lower levels of the site. He'd issued written warnings to both Baldwin and Stone who accepted them apparently in all seriousness They did not open their warning envelopes until later. The envelopes each included five €200 notes. Steve had no idea whether their intrusion into the lower levels had been a success or not and Dickwick had no update for him when they'd last shared a bottle, but the €1000 was certainly useful, but he just didn't like the smell of it all.

*

The group was seated around a table in a secure conference room in Vauxhall Cross.

Macsen opened the meeting. His pace was brisk.

"I've convened you all here today as I am initiating a formal assignment group. You don't all know each other but I am going to skip the introductions for now to save time. Besides your security tags, you have name and organization badges to be worn only in this building and you will be accompanied at all times. You hand in the badges when you leave. For the record, you have been briefed that you will be searched and scanned every time you enter and leave this building; and you have all agreed to these conditions. You save all signed the Official Secrets Act, some of you for a second time. Nothing you see, hear or otherwise learn in this building is to be repeated outside, not even to your superiors elsewhere.

You are all cleared to Top Secret Level for this assignment, codename AstraNine. The Treasury, Bank of England and GCHQ are represented here. Ms C works in my team and will chair the group." He nodded to a plain but bright-looking thirty-something auburn haired woman sat next to him. She nodded back as he continued…

"This will be the only time that we meet in this building. All future meetings will be virtual from the secure meeting suites in your own buildings. Right, that's the preamble over with. Why are we here? The full implications of what we have discovered are sketchy at best, but could indicate a complex attempt to subvert the international banking system. Mr P here has started analyzing the intel that we have from monitoring the activities of a Cyprus-registered company – 'Saluscent' - in Portugal." Josh nodded as they checked him out. Top Secret or not, names were not being used. "You've all been briefed on the public activities of the company. There is however a lot more we know about its owner, listed in the formal company documents as Sveta Kovacs. We will use her code name Alice in this room. Mr P will now continue the briefing."

"Okay. I will show you extracts of a video shot in the underground levels of the Saluscent compound in Olhaõ. We only managed access to one of the levels and we still don't know what the level below holds. I'll start the clip and provide translation and commentary."

The video started, then paused. "What you see is a whiteboard. The language is Ukrainian and the mathematics – well that language is universal, but beyond me, I'm afraid." There was a titter from one end of table. Josh continued. "Note the date at the top of the board – July 4. There are five 'projects' identified in the boxes on the whiteboard.

1 CCF. Status 100%
2 KBank. Status 95%, customers eight
3 XMR/₽ Status 97%
4 KCoin (Public) Status 95%
5 Swift/IBAN Tee Status 97%

"You can see the arrows that have been drawn to link the boxes. We don't know the meaning of all abbreviations. CCF could be something to do with credit cards – maybe farming – we suspect she has had involvement there in the past, but nothing provable. KBank – well, that one's another puzzle. XMR is the widely accepted abbreviation for the Monero cryptocurrency, but it is conjoined here with the symbol for the Russian rouble, a capital P with a strikethrough. KCoin is what Kovacs is publicly calling her new cryptocurrency, launching on July 4 – that's a regular trading day in Europe and the Far East but not the US. Finally, I'm sure you all know that Swift/IBAN is all about routing of international bank transfers and settlements. We know that there are susceptibilities in that system. For example, in 2016, SWIFT hackers managed to steal $81 Million from the Bangladesh central bank's account in the New York Federal Reserve. They hacked into the SWIFT network using a piece of malware that manipulated activity logs and deleted the fraudulent transactions history. This method has been copycatted across Russia and the Ukraine. We need to bear that in mind.

Now, about those complex math equations you see. Our specialists have looked at them and say that they relate to probability distributions. We do not yet have a final view on the implications of those, but they appear to be linked to analysis of large numbers – thirty two bit numbers with over two trillion digits - which is shown only in its abstract form here. The zeroes that you see are crucial and are generated by a number called a nonce. Dominic from GCHQ will give us a brief explanation." Josh nodded to a smartly-dressed man seated towards the center of the table. He looked as if he was still in sixth form college, but sported a closely trimmed goatee. His approach was lively, confident and authoritative.

"Thanks, er, Mr P. Briefly ladies and gentlemen, I would point out that Ponomarenko – erm – I should say Alice - holds a Ph.D. in cryptography. We believe that she has identified a weakness – known as an 'exploit' - in the use of 'nonces' in cryptocurrency software security technology. Hence the title that you see at the top of the whiteboard in English - 'Nonce Exploit'. Nonce exploits have previously been used in hacking home and business networks where the randomizer is determinative - that is, based on an algorithm. That means if you stop and start your home wifi network then a supposedly random nonce is used. But it's not random under certain conditions. Of course I have simplified that example but in this case with...er, Alice, I would say that she is probably several orders of complexity ahead of that. And wifi software is very primitive, orders of magnitude simpler than that of cryptocurrencies such as Bitcoin." He nodded at Josh, who nodded to Macsen.

"Thank you again Mr P. As I said, the full implications of what we have here are less than sketchy, but *could* indicate a complex attempt to subvert cryptocurrencies. That could also impact mainline fiat currency banking as suggested by the link to the SWIFT IBAN international bank clearance systems. It could be a major threat to the world's reserve currencies. But that's all conjecture. Any threat to currencies causes market instability – and this possible instability could be worse than anything caused by Covid19 or the 2008 sub-prime meltdown.

Some of you already know that those countries whose currencies are considered to be reserve currencies have a secret agreement to work together in the event that concerted illegal attacks on each others' currencies are identified. Please note that the agreement does not include Russia – the Rouble is not a reserve currency. However, as of today Russia is the only G8 country that has its *own* cryptocurrency. Make it G9 and we can add in China as well. Russian banks have a relatively poor track record of being hacked. And you'll note that the whiteboard image shows the CryptoRuble symbol.

In conclusion, Alice might just be designing new banking software, perfectly legally. We have nothing formally actionable here, and we don't at this stage want to involve Portuguese authorities. Notwithstanding, this all smells to high heaven. July 4 is less than three weeks away, so we need to get to the bottom of this *very* quickly.

We have other sources of intelligence and additional information will be funneled through Mr P. He will provide updates as appropriate. Ms C, if you please."

Macsen stood up to leave the room as Harriet Collins started to speak. Josh followed him. "Thank you Sir. Good morning everyone. I hope that we are all clear as to the nature of the potential threat. Our task is to consider all the intelligence and consider what might be the detail behind them. For example, what does 'KBank' refer to? We need to try to get inside Alice's mind and flesh out the assumed plots – and we need to have answers within forty eight hours. Before we start I will cover some more of the admin stuff and team security procedures."

Two hours later and back in his office, Macsen closed the door. "Take a seat Josh. Now, what's the panic?"

"The tech guys are really worried about those video images from the cybersecurity room under Saluscent. Not the whiteboard, but satellite feeds. One was labeled 'QKD Feed'. That could mean quantum key distribution with the result that no observer would have access to the key. The result would be that messages would be unbreakable."

"Just like they said RSA was unbreakable? That got broken."

"Maybe, but they can't break Signal or Proton Mail." Josh looked at his tablet "It's double dutch to me but they're telling me that with current methods anyone can see the public half of the key, and that gives the code breakers a start – they just have to find the other half – the private key. GCHQ is breaking RSA every day with their quantum computers and AES encryption takes more time, but here we're talking many orders of magnitude greater complexity – and time. There isn't even a technology in our dreams that has the potential to crack it. Huawei have pioneered the technology and…"

"Those bloody Chinese again!"

"…yes and one or two banks, including Telefonica, are already trialing it. Now Toshiba and a few other companies have got systems in place. Currently it only works over optical fiber. Our people are saying that it doesn't work over microwave and can't work using current satellite technology. Maximum range is a hundred and twenty kilometers as far as we know. Laser over optical fiber." He shook his head and smiled.

"What?"

"Alice – I just realized it's one of the names used in the quantum key entanglement theory."

"Right – Alice and Bob."

Josh saw Macsen smile and realized that he was well up on the theory – or a god actor, probably both.

"We can't dismiss the possibility that she's got access to QKD equipment at the other end – say in Kiev, or wherever."

"Bob!"

"Yes, in a manner of speaking. But within a hundred kilometers or so – and Kiev is sure as hell a lot further than that."

"What about laser up to a satellite? And down again I suppose?"

"I could see that maybe one of the majors would have it - say the US, Russia, China, India. We certainly wouldn't have it. Would we?"

"Not bloody likely, unless we're using someone else's satellite. But *she* might."

"I did ask. GCHQ said 'no comment' about our efforts. They did say that the Chinese launched a test satellite in 2016. It was called the Mozi project, designed to test that very idea. QKD is only for distribution of the key. It's like the old one time pad. The key is used once only for encrypt/decrypt. But we can't dismiss it, Boss, we need to bottom it out."

"Agreed, but we'll not get away with another physical intrusion on site."

"I have an idea, Sir. Let me explain."

*

Baldwin got the call from Aldo.

"We've got a gap in the log-ins today, Boss. Dave Lumley, one of the cyber guys, didn't show for work. Sergei's been on to the gatehouse asking questions. Apparently he didn't phone in sick and is not on leave. They've got backup coming in, but I thought I'd call you to let you know."

"Good call. Any ideas?"

"He could have been on a bender, or maybe it's still the after effects of the pizza."

"Maybe. They seemed to recover pretty quickly after Sergei offered them a bonus. But it does seem odd. I'll call Sergei now and then head on in though it's outside our remit. Keep me updated." *Remit? How far did physical security responsibility stretch?*

Two hours later Baldwin was at Lumley's apartment in Rua do Caminho de Ferro – Railway Road – in Faro. The block was modern and the air conditioning worked, but it overlooked the single track railway line which ran along the Algarve. Sergei had told him that the company paid the rent so he should go ahead and check the apartment. Sergei's signed and stamped letter of authorization appeared to satisfy the *zelador* – janitor – who after several raps on the door to Lumley's third floor apartment, unlocked it. "Obrigado", Baldwin said, one of less than a dozen words of Portuguese he could call on. The janitor nodded and headed for the elevator, leaving Baldwin alone. He didn't know what to expect, but could feel the warm hardness of the Glock in his rear waistband.

"Dave, it's Steve Baldwin from Saluscent." There was no reply. "Dave it's me." Still no reply. With his pistol at his side he pushed the door firmly so that it swung back hard against the wall, with a bang. No hidden surprise there. He closed the door behind him.

Then there was a shout and three sharp shots. Baldwin pivoted sharply, ducking and bringing his weapon to bear. The man was dressed in black and helmeted, across the room and larger than life.

"Jesus Bloody Christ!"

Baldwin lowered the weapon.

Facing him was a huge wallscreen displaying the sign-out screen of 'Call of Duty: Black Ops 4', in a replay loop. Steve stepped across the room and yanked the power plug from the wall, cursing as his heart rate subsided. "Play Now! my arse. Fucking kids games." Facing the screen was a leather armchair and table with games controllers and an open Styrofoam box containing the remains of a Chinese meal and a couple of empty Sagres beer bottles. Chicken chow mein, thought Steve. The apartment was stylishly furnished but in need of a serious clean-up.

He walked carefully through the sitting area and in to a bedroom – there was no corridor. The bed might have been slept in – it was crumpled but Baldwin doubted that it ever got made up. The floor was littered with clothing.

The kitchen looked out over the railway line along which rumbled a silver-grey three coach passenger unit. He could feel the vibrations through his feet. There was a half-finished bowl of chocolate cereal and a cup of cold black coffee on the small breakfast bar. Beside it was an envelope, addressed to Senhor David Lumley, with a logo at the top with the name 'Clínica Internacional de Olhão'. It had been torn open, but there was no sign of a letter.

The bathroom was clear although there were toothpaste splashes over the mirror and a pile of dirty underwear in the corner. Steve was grateful for the aircon as he looked into the toilet.

There was a second smaller bedroom which held a single bed, and three empty suitcases. A small window looked out onto a daylit shaft across which other similar apartments were visible. A shelf unit was fixed to one wall, loaded with comms equipment and a regular domestic satellite decoder.

Lumley was clearly not there and it didn't look as if he'd fled. There were no obvious signs of violence as far as could be told given the general state of mess.

Baldwin called Sergei to report the all clear and that he was returning to the offices, but Sergei's reaction was incandescent. "Find him immediately. This is a major breach of security for which you…" Baldwin held the phone away from his ear and shouted 'bad signal' as he cut the call.

He called Borthwick.

"Dick, we've got a cybersecurity guy gone missing. It doesn't look as if he's done a runner. I've checked the obvious, but Sergei's going ballistic. I'm only guessing but you should expect a call from Sveta."

"Thanks for the heads-up Baldy. Did you talk to JC?"

"No, she's on a day off and I can't reach her. I've sent texts but no reply. Anyway, I'm heading back to the offices to talk to the other cybersecurity guys."

"Okay. JC's supposed to be reachable twenty four seven, so I don't know what's up there. Do whatever you can while I talk to Sveta. I'll get back to you."

Then it hit Baldwin that maybe this was no coincidence. "Is there anything I should know, Dick, any funny business going on?"

"No, not that I know about. I'll get back to you."

*

"The panic is over, Dick. The guy called in sick, said he was in bed all the time."

"But you went to his place yesterday?"

"Yes. He was definitely not there. It's bloody strange."

Baldwin remembered the envelope in his pocket.

"Okay, keep it under your hat for now. Let Sveta and Sergei deal with it. There's no news at my end. Did you find JC?"

"Yes, she called in – some trouble with the battery on her phone. It's fixed now."

"Good. Got to go – there's another training contract in the offing."

"Before you hang up, I'm eight weeks into this contract, with five to go, so what's the news on Sol Brocking? Was his operation a success?"

"Yes, the operation was a success, more or less, but recuperation is going to take longer than expected, he's lost a bit of movement in one arm. The doctors say he'll need extra physiotherapy. I may need you to hang in there a bit longer, through July at least. You'll get a bigger bonus."

"Fuck that, Dick. Three months was the agreement."

"Sorry Baldy, I've got a plane to catch, we'll talk about this later. Stick with it, you're doing a great job. I just hope that this sign-up is easier than that bloody Qatari show."

"But Dick…"

Too late, the line had dropped.

*

"It's definitely quantum key distribution Boss."

"You're sure?"

"Absolutely. However we haven't seen any sign of kit. The only commercial gear has relatively short range and has to use continuous fiber optic. It can't work over satellite links."

"As far as we know."

"That's right. It has to have a clean comms channel to preserve the polarization of the signal. Transmitting through the atmosphere on the way up to a satellite would destroy the content, the key."

"Okay, enough tech, I believe you. Alice has been working on software and now we know that this chap Lumley and his colleagues have been testing it for weeks as she provides new releases. They are working to a target date of 4 July."

"That confirms the date then?"

"Yes, it's on a Friday this year."

"A good day to break into a bank. Both a Friday and US Independence Day. A long weekend for nefarious work."

"Exactly. But the rest of the world will still trade on that day."

"Yes, that's interesting.

"Any problems with Lumley's interrogation?"

"No. The letter about a follow up to the food poisoning did the trick. Once he opened it he was out within a few minutes. The lads drove him round in the ambulance for a couple of hours while the drugs worked and we grilled him. He knew about the QKD stuff – but only in outline. He just followed the test scripts that he was given. He'll not remember a thing but he will have a very sore head."

"That was a good idea of yours. Tell Harriet that July the fourth is looking stronger as a key date, but nothing about quantum key distribution."

"By the way, I've heard from Borthwick. He said that Baldwin knows about the disappearance of Lumley, but that's all."

"Keep it that way. Baldwin is a major problem and too clever by half. It should blow over once that cyber guy is back at work. Today?"

"Probably tomorrow."

"Good enough. Now that we know that it's definitely QKD then I'd better update 'C'."

*

The evening was warm and sultry with a light northerly breeze bringing the scent of sagebrush and a hint of ripening vines down from the hills behind Olhão. They were in the bar in the Rua Cordeiro. It was a Friday night and the day shift was winding down, with Steve buying.

Henri was talking to a smartly dressed Portuguese woman at the bar, taking a chance while her man was in the washroom. Trouble there, Steve thought. He nodded when Mankowicz held up an empty beer bottle and JC did the same. They were alone at last. Baldwin looked at JC, studying her nose. "What's wrong – is there a zit there?"

Steve reddened as he met her eyes. "No, no, not at all".

"I'm glad to hear it" she said with a laugh.

"How did your day off go – what did you do?" he said, suddenly embarrassed.

"Nothing much, a bit of shopping and of course trying to get my phone battery sorted."

Just then Mancowicz returned with the beers as some shouting started at the bar. Henri held his hands up palm forward and backed away from a Portuguese man who was very agitated. Baldwin quickly crossed to the bar before Henri had created enough space to sucker the guy completely and hospitalize him. Stepping into the gap he dragged Henri back to the table.

"Get a hold of yourself Henri. You know the rules."

"Sorry Steve. I didn't know she was with somebody."

"Crap. You've been eyeing her up all evening."

Henri shrugged. "Has anyone got a pencil?"

JC opened her purse and after rummaging she passed an eyeliner pencil to Henri. "Will that do?"

"Magnifique, merci." He took a table napkin and wrote a number on it. "In case I forget." He passed the eye pencil back to JC.

"What's that Henri?"

"Her phone number."

"You bloody Frenchmen are all the same."

"Well, it makes the world go around, no, JC? Maybe I can have yours too?"

"I don't mix business and pleasure, and you're not my type anyway, you're much too ugly. So piss off."

Henri shrugged. Baldwin thought Stone could kill with that smile as he eased his chair away from the table. "Let's be serious for the moment, before we get too far into the beers. We had a right royal row this week at the client because one of their staff went AWOL, on top of all that crap with the bad pizzas."

There was laughter around the table. "It's not funny! It doesn't look good whether it's our fault or not. It's not really our responsibility I know, but I want you all on your toes at all times. They pay a lot of money for the best service. So, sharpen up! "

Baldwin stood and turned, speaking quietly.

"By the way has anyone heard anything about a hospital follow up for one of the guys who had the food poisoning?" He watched. They all looked at him and shook their heads. All except Stone. She looked at the table as she shook her head and finally looked back at Baldwin and met his eyes.

"Enjoy your beers guys, the tab is still running at the bar, sorry I can't stay any longer." *I need to think about JC and what she's up to.*

As he walked back to his boat his mind was in a state of confusion and disappointment. It had only been a suspicion but now he felt almost certain that Stone had been involved in the mystery of Lumley's very brief disappearance.

Did it matter? Not as far as the job went, but the suspicion of a lie had rocked him and he'd had enough hurt from women to last a lifetime. *Is it my imagination?*

*

Twenty

The man sat down on the park bench and took out a book to read. It was in English, a novel by Frank Herbert about a deadly disease manufactured to kill women only. It was his habit to stop at the bench two or three days a week. If it rained he would go to the bandstand and read in there. One chapter per visit, that was his routine. Sometimes he would have paper cup of coffee with him, bought from the stall near the park entrance about twenty yards away.

Today the air was cool, so he was a wearing dull-green waxed cotton jacket with a scarf. His head was bare, with just the beginnings of a bald patch in the midst of brown hair kept at medium length. He wore gold rimmed spectacles. Light brown twill trousers were accompanied by dark socks and well-polished plain brown Oxford shoes.

By this time of the morning the joggers had all showered and gone to work and the children were in school. To the rear of the bench was a short expanse of grass and some shrubbery, with an iron railing fence separating the park from the footpath and roadway and a row of shops on the other side. Nothing remarkable, but a keen observer might have surmised from the straightness of his back that there may have been some military experience in his background. They might have also observed that his deep-set eyes were never still – sometimes reading, but most of the time scanning the park in front of him, the paths, the people, the nannies with pushchairs. Unobtrusively.

He'd noticed the small fresh chalk mark on the side of the bench before he sat down to read. When he'd finished his chapter he stood up and put the book in the copious left hand pocket of his jacket. He stooped to retie his shoelace and rubbed against the chalk mark, scuffing it. Then he set off, with his empty coffee cup, following his usual route through Battersea Park. He cut across the wet grass and slowed near a litter bin. He dropped the coffee cup in and set off again along a path through a small copse.

Satisfied that he was unobserved, he fished around under the dead leaves and retrieved the small package from inside the cleft in the old oak tree. It slipped into the right hand pocket of his jacket, alongside the small pistol.

He hadn't met this particular agent in several months. The agent didn't need hand holding, encouragement or ideological reinforcement. Threats and manipulation were not necessary. He requested only money. The packages came regularly and he didn't know what they contained. He was never asked to task the agent to obtain information about a specific topic, but he had been told that all the information came from a high level and was of sterling quality.

Back in his apartment he opened the package to expose an SD card. It was not his job to know what was on the card, only to act as a conduit. The old ways are still the best, he thought. After making a copy onto the PC and then on to another card using his PC he repackaged both cards – one in a Fedex envelope and the other in a UPS envelope. Each went to a different address, then another, but each would arrive at the same desk in a suburb of Moscow in a few days time. He made a third copy and put it in his pocket.

Then, finally he checked that his PC – this machine was never connected to the internet and had no wifi - was clean, using the specialized hard drive scrubbing software with which he had been provided. The note in the package he'd retrieved from the dead letter drop was computer printed and just said 'I want 3 months payment for this or there will be no more.' He would mention this in his weekly report to Moscow. In return he would be provided with a string of alphanumeric characters which he would pass to the agent. The new currency, apparently. He didn't understand it and wouldn't try. He preferred US dollars himself, but his mole didn't and never had.

He could always steal a few hundred off the top of a pile of hard cash if he was so inclined but even that would catch him out. With the new-fangled cryptocurrency he couldn't steal anything, or at least, he hadn't yet figured out how to do so. He did know – and certainly his superiors also knew - that such an agent had no loyalty and could be selling the information multiple times. Despite intensive research they had been unable to find any vices of his agent except a liking for money, digital money. The only controlling lever they had was exposure of his treachery to the government. These days even being caught in a homosexual sting was no guarantee of leverage as many openly gay people worked for MI6, unless of course there was a foreign agent involved. Perhaps it was time for a reminder. He would talk to his superior.

He double checked the locked door of his apartment and the precautions he had taken to detect intrusion, then took the elevator down.

As he drove into town to despatch the packages, he marveled at the efficiency of these American courier companies. Things were so much simpler these days. Not all the old ways were the best.

On the way back he stopped at the Big Yellow self-storage compound and locked away the SD card in his personal box, along with the pistol. Till his next appointment in a week plus a day plus an hour, until the pattern was reset in seven weeks time.

*

The complex of buildings in Yasenevo, southwest Moscow, was the headquarters of the SVR, Russia's Foreign Intelligence Service.

At his desk on the fifth floor of the older Y-shaped building, Vladimir Novikov watched the replay of the video. Novikov's great uncle Sacha had been the Chief Marshal of Aviation for the Soviet Air Force during Russia's involvement in the Second World War. Military tradition ran strongly in his family, at least it had since the Revolution.

The agent, code name 'Skopa' – Osprey – was one of his English tier 3 moles providing high grade intelligence from the heart of SIS in London. Skopa was expensive to run, with an outrageous demand for money accompanying this latest video.

Was it worth it? Novikov had no idea as he was unable to assess the value of this particular clip – he didn't speak Ukrainian and his mathematics was poor. However he did understand the English words 'satellite' and comms room. He called the head of his analysis team and requested urgent translation and analysis. Skopa had never disappointed him, but there was always a first time.

An hour later the translation was on his screen, with a preliminary analysis. The video tags provided time, date and location, but the analysts were unable to throw any more light on the implications beyond its links to cryptocurrency and a company called Saluscent in Portugal. There was a brief explanation about Swift/IBAN, BTC and Kcoin. An overview of the company's operations and personnel accompanied the analysis, but work continued. He noted that security services were provided by ScutumEst, a British company with possible links to MI6. But what was really worrying was the reference to the Rouble.

This could be big, he thought. He put in a request to his superior for a pan-agency search. These searches were run by a small, high-power agency – the Central Information Bureau - which Buligin had created to span the information silos across the Russian government, particularly the security services. This was an ambitious 'big data' project, bigger than anything anywhere else in the world. Ex-KGB/FSB himself, the President had recognized the unwillingness of agencies to share information – a major weakness in every government. Run by a former FSB crony, General Vadim Mikhailov, the CIB over-rode information turf wars from the top down. It also gave the President unparalleled access to *all* the important data in Russia. One weakness was that much of the information was still held in paper files – some going back to the times of Tsar Nicholas. But progress was being made and the older Cold War files from the 1950's had already been digitized. World War 2 would be the next tranche and then on back to the Revolution.

Less than hour later the call came from the General to discuss the request and the reasoning.

Anything to do with cryptocurrencies was now of high priority – the CryptoRuble launch was just months away and the President was determined to make a big hit with it. The rouble might not be an international reserve currency, but the President had every intention to make the CryptoRuble the digital equivalent. Russia was hurting from international sanctions, the imposition of which relied heavily on US control of international banking. Buligin hoped that the CryptoRuble would help undermine the effectiveness of the sanctions, just as Venezuela was doing with the Petro.

The General authorized Novikov's search request. Immediately, Novikov set up a parametric search file on the SVR intelligence database – a vast databank that hoovered up all intelligence reports, SVR signals intercepts and the international press and media, as well as data from other countries, particularly the US, UK and China – at least where it could gain access. It was more easily able to delve into the terabytes of data held by the FSB and the GRU.

Within an hour the search was underway at the Russian Central Information Bureau, using state of the art American computers and AI. The searches ignored file tags as file owners were notorious for mis-tagging files in order to hide data. The CIB had access to all the key information silos in Russia – even those which were the most closely guarded in the vast bureaucracy. They also had electronic tunnels into the big data in many of the former Soviet Socialist Republics. Many, but not all.

Novikov was just clearing the last of his emails when the first search results notification came through. His search tags had matched to a current GRU case file owned by a Major Leonid Drozdov of the Cyberforensics Directorate. He shut his office door and lit a cigarette while he reviewed the file. Drozdov had done a good job, without doubt. His eyes opened wide as he saw that Drozdov had been researching the downing of the Japanese airliner several years previously. There was still no proven link to Ukraine on file. However, Novikov held his own suspicions based on low grade intelligence from a source within the Ukrainian special forces, nothing more than idle talk picked up in a bar that had found its way back to him a year previously.

He lit another Winston and sat back in his heavily padded leather chair to consider his approach. It would have to be based on power as there was sure to be a battle for control over this case, but then it always *was* about power, he reflected, truth was irrelevant. He called the General and explained the search findings. And so the case escalated up the chain of command. Svetlana Ponomarenko's name went hot at several large and important desks in Moscow.

But there was a shorter route too. At the CIB, Vadim Mikhailov had reviewed the day's search requests. The search requests that came across his desk were all high priority by their very nature and the results were occasionally interesting – almost as interesting as the list of *who* was asking for *what* searches. He picked out what he considered the top 3 and sent them directly to the President, as he did at the end of every day. Then he called his driver to take him home to his apartment off the Novy Arbat.

Two days later the power battle was over. A mission team was being formed. Operation Stervyatnik (Vulture) would be run by the SVR, with additional cyberforensics input by the GRU. Nobody thought that it was a practical mission structure, but that was what had been mandated at the very highest level. Maybe some sort of set up was in play. Such was life in Russia, today, as it had always been.

With the disarray in NATO following the helpful US administration policies of an inept US President, the Russian President felt increasingly confident about his stance over the Ukraine, Belarus and even the Baltic states. Nevertheless, 'Vulture' would have to be deniable.

*

Twenty One

It was the Tuesday morning after another heavy lunch in Winchester with Tobin; Thompson sat with heartburn in the meeting room of his City office ready for a video meeting. On the train into town that morning he'd logged into the Slack system to check on the progress of the final integration testing of the new software. Some problems had come to light on the overnight run, although they were not described in the messaging history. Unable to talk on the train, he'd messaged his head of Software Development. The response had been terse. '*We need to talk 10am?*'.

Livengood Futures kept a small office suite on City Road close to the Square Mile, near to banks and investors, considerably scaled down since the gold market debacle a couple of years earlier. Livengood no longer had the kudos of the EC1 postcode on its letterhead, but EC2 meant that the rent was slightly lower, although still painful.

Most of Livengood's staff were based in his software development headquarters near Reading. The teams there were Technical, Integration and Testing, and a fledgling Support department. They were the operational core of the company.

The Winnersh Triangle near Reading was part of what was known as the Silicon Corridor, near to the M4 motorway and major mainline railway into central London – and close to Heathrow Airport. More importantly, the area held a rich seam of software talent within easy commuting range - and poaching range. Thompson looked around the plush meeting room and out on to the summer greenery of Finsbury Square. Come lunchtime the park would be full of finance professionals grabbing a sandwich and some summer sun. The room was used for client presentations but with the emphasis of the business moving towards retail online brokerage it was rarely used these days. He was lost in thought, still wondering what Tobin had planned, his coffee now cold, when his screen chimed and announced that Aaron was joining the meeting.

Livengood's Head of Software Development, Aaron Robinson, joined the meeting – or one-to-one as it was today.

"Hi Richard."

"Hi Aaron. I don't have much time so make it brief." Thompson preferred face to face meetings but these were relatively rare these days. The next best thing to being able to look into a person's eyes and judge their body language was a video meeting – but even that was a poor substitute. Still, he expected no such problems with Aaron.

This morning however, his initial impression was quite to the contrary. Robinson looked really worried.

"The good news is that the final integration test has reported no errors."

"That's good then, but it's not what I saw in the team's discussion on Teamview this morning."

"Yes, the integration tests completed properly – but the integrated binary set is bigger in total than expected – not hugely so, but not what we've expected based on previous tests. It's not really bad news, just that something doesn't feel right. Sharon is running the release code through a code analyzer now. We can't nail it down to one component. We're also running the release code through the user test packs, but as you know, that's a big job even using the bots."

"What's your gut feeling about this, Aaron?"

"My gut tells me that we should be looking closely at the crypto components. Maybe there's a versioning issue with the code and the Kiev guys uploaded an older version. I don't think it's the AI modules or the other modules. And the AI knowledgebase is clean – I'm sure of that. Or, it could be that something in the Exchange interfaces has been changed without our knowledge, but that's a long shot. The interface XML specs are tightly controlled. We're talking to the Exchanges now, to check."

"Mmm, yes, an interface problem is a very long shot. But be careful with the Exchanges, we don't want to make them nervous at all. Anyway, the City would be screaming by now if there was an issue. We'd know all about it. Your gut feel is probably right, though you'll have to check everything anyway. Twice."

Thompson had kept a very strict separation between his development teams even though inhibiting collaboration was not good practice for software development. But there was just too much money at stake. Aaron was the only person authorized to speak to each of the four development teams, and was one of the very few people at Livengood who had almost the complete picture, incentivized by a share ownership plan. It was almost like a spy network, with cells and cutouts. Such stratagems were essential with software that processed billions of dollars. But it did cause problems and extend timescales and error counts – and brought surprises.

"And the source for the other modules is up to date?"

Thompson watched as Robinson looked at a list and pressed some keys at his end. “I’m sharing it with you now. Looks like the Crypto Manager module is the one exception.”

The list appeared on screen and Thompson could see a green tick against each of the modules, confirming that the source code version and test pack version matched the compiled binary code for each of the modules System Core, Exchange Interfaces, Customer API, Price Manager, AI, AI database, System Management Suite, Security, Intrusion Detection & tracking, Sales History, Payments API, Paypal API, Stripe API, Presentation and Web Manager. And the interfaces to the Bitcoin and Monero networks.

CryptoManager had a red cross in the tickbox.

“OK, your gut feel could well be right. I’ll try to get hold of Kiev myself, now and kick their arses. In the meantime keep me posted.”

*

Twenty Two

"Caspar? My office, now."

A few minutes later Caspar Conlon closed the door of Henry Brewell's office. Viking genes via Northern Ireland gave Conlon a goblin-like appearance which was so distinctive that he could never serve in an undercover capacity. Brewell thought that he bore a distinct likeness to Stebbings of GCHQ. Perhaps they both had Eric the Red as ancestor. However, Conlon's brain and instincts were of the highest caliber for running the Global Terrorism Desk. His genes provided him with all the aggressive approach of a Viking on the rampage. Accordingly he was not the best of man-managers and the wits in his team called him T-One – terrorist number one – behind his back of course. Despite what some perceived as the negative aspects of his management style, he got results in battles which were usually the result of surprise attacks, often the political and departmental sort.

"What is it Sir?"

"I've just been to a meeting with my predecessor, Sir William Gore, or should I say Lord Gore of …damn…where was it? Anyway, there's a big problem come to light. Do you remember that stuff about ben-Zhair and Algeria?"

"You told me to forget it."

"I did indeed."

"And I did."

"Good. Well, this is for your ears only, some more for you to forget. Less than five – six – people know the truth and even now I'm probably getting only half the story. Not even the PM at the time knew, the current one certainly doesn't. The fact is that before you took on the GT Desk an agent of ours – an off-the-books agent I might add - personally captured Abu ben-Zhair, you know, ABZ, the Algerian who almost sank the East Coast of the US in a tsunami."

"No one forgets ben-Zhair. One of our guys, Barbary, was running the agent, name of…"

'C' put up his hand. "Don't say it. Current codename Mad Hatter. ABZ was, and I quote the press release 'captured in the Mediterranean region and died in US custody on a flight from Europe to the US. He was buried at sea in the North Atlantic' end quote. We know that his body was dumped in a weighted shroud out of the rear ramp of a C130 at wave height, somewhere between Spain and Andrews Air Force Base. That was public knowledge, announced by the US State

Department, except of course for the plane details. Anyway, Lord Gore – my predecessor - is quite certain that ABZ is still alive. The US was completely fooled and apparently we have incontrovertible evidence, supported by DNA."

"Shit. But, but...surely the Cousins did a DNA test – that's routine these days, even in-mission, they'd have done on the plane. They did it with bin Laden in Pakistan years ago."

"But what do they compare it with?"

"A proven DNA sample."

Brewell nodded. "You know we were running the show until the very last moment when the handover took place. Mad Hatter had found a sample of ABZ's hair and passed it to Barbary. That much we know. As you know, Barbary brought the sample back and we told the US that the DNA matched. A couple of weeks later we discovered the mismatch. What only 'C', now Lord Gore, knew was that the hair showed a DNA match with a flesh sample from *another* mission where ABZ was injured in a firefight when we nearly nabbed him. Easy enough to fiddle in the DNA datafile we sent to the US as proof that the man on the plane was ABZ. So, the man on the US plane was *not* ABZ. He was a substitute, a good look-alike at the right place and time – enough to fool Mad Hatter who had a picture on his phone to match against - and to fool the US – who didn't have an original DNA sample of ABZ."

"But that means…"

'C' held his hand up "It means that it is buried."

"So why has this come up now? Surely we just sit on it. The US will keep it quiet for sure."

"The point is that the US still does not know and if we tell them now then you can imagine what that will do for trans-Atlantic relations."

"A fucking disaster...er...Sir."

"Precisely. Gore was glad to get it off his chest. I've never seen him so worried, practically crapping his pants. It was all down to him. It's a fucking red hot potato and now *I'm* holding it. It's come up now because the guys at GCHQ had a hit with their latest facial recognition software. They were testing it across major European airports. Bugger Brexit, we're hacking all the cameras across Europe, even beyond but don't quote me on that. It's a huge operation arising from weaknesses in security cooperation and data access now that we're outside the European fence. But that's all beside the point. As you know, a man by the name of Ashraf Ibrahim landed in Madrid Barajas Airport two days ago on a genuine Saudi passport, flown in from Rabat on a scheduled flight. The facial scan was a good match to the picture that Mad Hatter had on his phone in Algeria. GCHQ don't know who they picked up, just that the image was flagged for reference to me specifically."

Conlon was nodding like a donkey, but realized that 'C' wanted to play pass the potato and was probably rehearsing his story for later replay to another, more senior audience.

Brewell continued "It's is in our databases under a pseudonym. That's why I asked you to track him without knowing why myself – until my meeting with Gore today. Your desk did well to pick up the guy's tracks but too late. So, I'm telling you now that the guy was Abu ben-Zhair, ABZ."

They looked at one another.

"Un-fucking-believable!"

"But true, it seems. You know that the rental car tradecraft was good, suspiciously so, but not good enough. I have here the results of the DNA test from the dandruff Barbary's man found in the rental car."

Conlon looked at 'C' "I can guess."

"Yes. The same as our sample from way back. Ben-Zhair. Hence the megaflap."

"Hell's bells."

"Ringing loud and clear. And it's not just the US reaction that might be an issue if this got out, it's fear of what ABZ might have planned next. His bloody Caliphate has set off two nuclear explosions already, and that's public knowledge, as was the US attack on the Iranian nuclear facilities in retaliation. God knows what's he got planned next as the failure of the tsunami – if you can call it failure – must be really irking him. And we're not telling our political masters yet so HMG is caught in the jaws of a huge trap and they don't even know it. I'm bloody glad it's not my decision. Damned if they do and damned if they don't. Some people are even suggesting that he was behind the spread of Covid-19 and you have to wonder if it really is all wild talk. So, it's all hands to the pumps here without us being able to tell the crew why there's a hole in the bloody ship. A cliché but sums up the situation quite nicely."

"So, you want a plan, and quickly?"

"Yes, I'd like to hear your ideas first, ideas that do not include the obvious, like find the guy. You already have people on that now and GCHQ has been told to get on it for real, it's no longer a test of the new software. We need to be creative. I've been given two hours to come up with an outline plan before I brief the PM and Foreign Secretary, so you have one hour." He looked at his watch. "Come back at two thirty and present your plan. No pressure, right?" 'C' tapped his screen. "This operation will be called 'Bilbo', as in …."

"…Lord of the Rings."

"Precisely. I'll transfer some more people in, you'll need to brief a new team and re-prioritize. Your teams are not to know it's ben-Zhair, not a sniff, is that clear."

"Ultra non plus"

"Precisely."

"And what if anyone notices the resemblance between the Barajas airport images and those the US published?"

"Tell them it's a coincidence, we all know that ben-Zhair is dead, don't we?"

They smiled and nodded to one another as Conlon stood up. This was what the job was about – a hunt, surging adrenaline, high stakes.

'C' turned back to his laptop and scrolled down.

The Looking Glass and Bilbo operations were just the tip of his threats iceberg for the day. He started to prepare for the meeting with the PM and Foreign Secretary at Downing Street in two hours time. That was likely to be a very difficult meeting as he pushed the policy decisions upstairs. That's what politicians were paid for. At least he could blame his predecessor.

*

It was the protocol for emergency contact.

Another London park, the next on the list. There was no doubt about it. He'd checked for a sign as a matter of course and although he'd told them he was finished with them, checking had become second nature over the last couple of years. Even now with the ultimate in message encryption they still did not trust technology. It was probably just as well - hardware intrusions were always possible. Who *really* knew what was inside their mobile phone? Chinese chips were everywhere. He could just ignore the sign and carry on with life as normal, but there would never be normality again unless he wanted to go and live in Buligin's crime ridden and corrupt oligarchy – and that would hardly be normality. Or, he could just disappear with a new identity – he had several ready. And of course he could use his Bitcoins almost everywhere. Even Nigeria, but that country would never be on his travel itinerary. Over the years he'd tracked down many people who'd thought that they could go off grid with a new identity, but they were eventually found. How long would *he* have? Five years maximum? He would be found for sure. Disappearing completely for thirty years or so was certainly a pipe dream. The first five would be the hardest.

It was a sure bet that his paymasters would want him to remain in post as long as possible. He was in it for the money, he was not driven by ideology in the way that Philby had been and he derived no intellectual pleasure from fooling his masters or betraying his colleagues as if they were playing chess. Betrayal is what it was, there was no denying that. Betrayal for money.

God knows how I manage to keep it a secret.

In reality he managed his habit as Sherlock Holmes had managed his - regular doses, with no escalation. He'd got through the original MI6 positive vetting with no problems, and the regular follow ups were also without problem. After all, how long had Philby got away with it? Decades. The huge increase in recruitment at MI5, MI6 and GCHQ since 9/11 from which he had benefited did suggest that standards might have fallen both in vetting and candidate selection. He certainly hadn't had to successfully complete a Times Crossword within 20 minutes to pass the entrance tests.

Gambling addiction was different to drugs, he really believed, at least for some of the time. If it was managed properly then his life could continue as normal. He managed his habit well, and now that he had real responsibility he was getting a buzz from his work and the *other thing*, a buzz that offset the other craving at least some of the time. He put the keys in the locks, entered and deactivated his alarm system, then checked for intrusion as was his norm. All was well with his tell-tales - no intrusion, he was sure.

His apartment was actually his sister's apartment, one of several which she owned. Annabelle was a clever girl whose own 'habit' was property development. The fifth floor unit was on the South Bank, a short distance from Waterloo Bridge and although she was his sister she certainly did him no favors when it came to the rental rate. The rent was almost extortionate but as she had pointed out many times – that was the market, if you don't like it then move elsewhere. He had no wife or children - no partner and his life was fairly bleak except for his career and his habit - and his betrayal. He was straight and obviously wedded to his career, settling for the occasional one night stand to keep his hormones balanced – the online stuff wasn't half as satisfying. He 'hadn't found the right girl yet' as he told the vetters.

After pouring himself a gin and tonic he put on 'Dark Side of the Moon' and settled down in his armchair looking out through the full height windows across Thames to the lights of the City. From his attaché case he took a burner phone and set out to prepare a report. When he met his handler the following morning he would use the phone's NFC functionality to pass over the report. It would be encrypted and he'd extract a painfully high price for the key. He could of course just give them the phone. He laughed. It would be thrown back at him. Then he'd drop it into the river and buy a replacement. He idly wondered about all the secrets Old Man Thames was keeping, some, no doubt, just below his balcony.

*

The meeting with the PM and Foreign Secretary had been difficult to say the least. The threat to the special relationship with the USA had been frighteningly clear – the UK could not in these post-Brexit days afford to piss off the USA in any way, shape or form. 'C' got the distinct impression that his predecessor, Lord Gore of Hook, was to be called in for a severe dressing down. But what could they do? Take away his life peerage? That was unlikely. On reflection, Brewell thought that his predecessor had done the right thing. *God alone knows what else he buried. I certainly hope I don't find out.*

Never present a problem without at least a couple of solutions was the maxim and Macsen's suggestion had been accepted, although presented of course as Brewell's own idea. Limited disclosure, blame the scientists. It might damage the confidence of the US but that would be manageable.

'C' closed the door to his office and opened the direct line to the Director of the CIA, Jim Bartolucci. The CIA Director was currently unavailable according to his aide, but would certainly be able to return the call within the hour, perhaps. Lunch would have to wait so Brewell poured himself a cup of coffee and checked his latest alerts; there was nothing that the respective Heads of Desks couldn't handle at the moment. He was just picturing Lord Gore being shouted at in the PM's office when the call signal came from Langley. Yes, getting the hair dryer treatment, that's what his team Man Utd used to say about being lambasted by their manager, Alex Ferguson. Even that might be better than being handbagged by Margaret Thatcher had been for his predecessors.

"Good morning Henry."

"It's late afternoon here Jim." The opening exchange rarely varied, but today humble pie was on the menu. "I'll get right to the point. We have a major problem here. There's been an audit at one of our government labs that tests DNA and some methodological irregularities have been discovered. The person concerned has now been fired but that's beside the point."

"What problem?"

"It's about Abu ben-Zhair. The DNA profile we sent you was not the right one. The lab screwed up. We think ABZ is still alive."

A chuckle was clearly audible through the heavy encryption, no nuance lost. "I already know that Henry. I wondered when you'd get round to telling me."

"You know?"

"Sure. We never buried anyone at sea. The guy you handed over is buried in the desert in Arizona or someplace, I forget where. It's best that way - and I didn't tell you that. He coughed up a load on the way. A quick result was what the President wanted. Political expediency, election year, ratings and all that. So a quick result is what he got – after all truth is the first casualty of war. Didn't work though, he lost the election as you know. Anyways, we're still looking for the real ABZ and we believe he'll think he's safe and maybe get a little careless. And of course we're wondering what he'll do next, if he hasn't already done something, like initiate Covid."

"Jesus, Jim, why didn't you tell me this before?"

Bartolucci chuckled. "Never got round to it I guess. You sure you only just found out about the DNA problem?"

"Hand on heart James, just yesterday I swear. The PM is going to call the President."

"I think he should. When I get a chance I'll send you an update on what we learned from ABZ's stand-in. Gotta go now anyway, if there's nothing else?"

"Thanks Jim, that's quite enough for now."

"Oh before I forget, we'd really appreciate an *accurate* DNA profile of ABZ when you guys can get round sorting out your lab procedures – and we'd really appreciate you actually sharing any intel you *do* pick up about him."

Bartolucci was chuckling as the line dropped.

Brewell kicked the leg of his desk and swore. Bartolucci had known all along and had just let Gore's rope get longer and longer. And now he, Brewell was on it. HMG had been played. The bastard.

Try explaining that to the PM.

He called the Foreign Secretary's direct line. He had no intention of doing the dotted line report again today - his hair was dry enough already and the Foreign Secretary could get the treatment instead.

Now Brewell would have to review much of the all recent interchanges with Langley in a new light. *Thank the Lord Gore.*

*

Twenty Three

Yuri Grigorovich and Boris Ivanov had flown into Madrid from Moscow. At Madrid's Barajas airport they met with Galina Petrovka and Irina Gryaznova, apparently their girlfriends. After a three hour wait, they connected with a flight to Faro in Portugal, arriving late-morning. The Portuguese immigration officer saw a lot of Russian passports. In her view there were far too many Russians in her country. Criminals and prostitutes, that's what they were. She scanned them and no flags were raised – the proper documentation had been supplied to the Portuguese Embassy in Moscow with the visa application and the visas showed up on his screen. Then she carefully checked each of their tourist visas against the details on screen and finally waved them through with a 30 day stamp. Then she picked up the phone to the *Alfandega* – Customs – desk and told them that she thought the Russians were behaving strangely. She'd had a bad day and didn't like Russians. After a tiring half hour with the Customs the four left the terminal and collected a Europcar rental 4 x 4 and headed for Olhaõ to check into their hotel.

Then they did what tourists do and headed for the bar and the pool. Once the girls were set up by the pool, Yuri and Boris headed off to the warehouse on the industrial estate off the Rua Calouste Gulbenkian to the east of the town. The camper van had already been driven down from Lisbon and was ready. The driver gave them the keys without a word and left on foot for the railway station, following instructions from Google.

Yuri drove the camper, followed by Boris in the SUV. Further east along the Rua Gulbenkian they turned into the National camping park and bought a two week ticket. They chose a quiet plot sheltered behind a stand of Mediterranean pines and then carefully checked through all the gear in the camper which had been stowed by the GRU Resident at the Russian Embassy in Lisbon. After transferring some of the equipment to sports bags they re-packed the rest under the floor of the van, set the alarm and left in the SUV. On the drive back to the hotel they passed by the Saluscent site with Yuri holding his mobile phone against the corner of the window in video recording mode. The GRU mission planners had thought it strange that there were no images in Google Streetview when there were images of other buildings in the vicinity. Saluscent appeared to be blurred out in the Google data, just as Google blurred faces and car registration tags.

Yuri and Boris joked about the girls and about the beer – there would be none of either for at least two weeks – or ever. This Zaslon advanced reconnaissance team of four had worked together before and this would be no holiday. It was strictly professional, as always, and they maintained the highest standards.

The elite Special Operations Group called *Zaslon* had formerly been known as the Russian special services regiment Vympel, one of the wide range of Russian special forces – collectively known as *spetsnaz*. The mere existence of *Zaslon* within the SVR (the Russian Foreign Intelligence Service) is denied by Russian authorities. The group is assigned to execute very special operations outside Russian territory. Operating deep undercover, the 500 or so highly experienced operatives speak several languages and have extensive operational experience gained while serving in diverse secret units of the Russian military machine.

The four Russian holidaymakers went out for dinner that evening and then on to the camper van. There, Boris recounted the briefing that he and Yuri had received in Moscow. They reviewed the latest update which had come in by satellite via the rooftop dish antenna, a common accessory on camper vans. But not all camper van people watch satellite TV.

There were no fresh satellite images in the feed. The mission commander, Major Valeri Kuznetsov, had been unable to get a Russian intel satellite re-tasked so they would have to rely on the US – and on Google.

The night's objective was to get the hides identified and prepared. Another drive-by in the opposite direction past the Saluscent site had given them images of the scrub across the road from frontage and an idea of where they might position the hides. The rear of the site was more difficult and would be recce'd the following day. The other sides of the huge square Saluscent estate were dotted with private villas. Google satellite images showed the huge solar farm and that could provide them with cover, but they had no intention of breaking fence security at this time. Approaches to the hides would have to be across country and they would remain outside the company's perimeter. That did not apply to their drone however and they planned to do a night-time overflight to gather more data. Their objectives for this phase of their mission were relatively simple, but the objectives for the next phase were still being discussed in Moscow, and the details would depend on the team's findings.

*

As the reconnaissance progressed, the data was fed back directly back to mission control, with 24 hour live camera footage and long rang microphones installed and controlled from the hides. Technology was all very well and good, but the human element was still essential in reconnaissance and this mission was no exception.

Over the next week the team built up a detailed picture of the site, the security team and staff – at least to the extent that was possible. Shift changes and procedures were observed and logged. Moscow fleshed out some of the details about the Scutum Est operation and personnel, but the files were sparse and the company's cybersecurity was effective, and would require a lot of currently unavailable resources to be cracked.

They were intrigued by the use of drones by Saluscent to scan the perimeter and the plan would have to deal with that problem.

"So what do you think about their security, Yuri Grigorovich?"

"Professional and well run, but no match for our boys, Boris Ivanov."

Boris looked across the table in the camper. Galina Petrovka was a short plain Russian girl with a hint of Slav in her dark eyes. But at the pool, men did not look at her face – her body was in superb shape as befitted the punishing physical regime she – and the team – followed.

"Galina?"

"I agree with Yuri Grigorovich, but I do not understand why they do not have dogs."

"Yes, an interesting observation. Irina?"

"There are several possible entry methods, but it is true that the lack of dogs is a puzzle. We may be missing something." Irina Gryaznova was thin faced with a dour expression as befitted someone born in the aluminium smelting town of Novokuznetsk in western Siberia. Joining the army had transformed her life – and her tall body. Totally focused and ruthless – as were the others - she also had the highest IQ on the team.

"We have received orders to reposition the cameras. We will do that tonight. Tomorrow night we deploy the drone. Yuri, Galina – you will move the camper van during the day. Here."

They looked at the screen as he pointed to the map and the required position, not knowing that someone else had recently used the very same position for launching a drone.

"After take-off it will be controlled from *missiya* HQ. This van will be the relay station, using the satellite link. We wait and then recover it. Understood?"

They all nodded.

Later that night, outside Moscow, Major Kuznetsov and his planners studied the live infrared feed from the drone as it checked the roof and aerial array at Saluscent from close range. The drone's position was overlaid on a wallscreen which displayed a blurred satellite image of the Saluscent compound. They didn't know whether Google itself, or an outside agent, had blurred it, but outline zoning plans had been hacked from the Olhaõ municipal development authorities and overlaid onto the image. However, there were no detailed plans to be found on file. There appeared to be a gap in the records.

The Russian drone controllers had suffered the same GPS signals blackout as the British, and had overcome it in almost the same way, using an alternative military signal set available from the Russian Glonass GPS satellite network.

The controllers increased the altitude of the drone and scanned the grounds in infrared, out of the ground level line of sight of the guards, and avoiding Saluscent's own drone patrols

"What is that?" Kuznetsov pointed to a large stripe which ran all the way around the Saluscent compound.

"Sir, the infrared is showing a temperature gradient. We have nothing on our optical cameras from the recce team. It could be a big trench or duct - at least three meters wide. It might be covered over."

"We need to find out more about that. Continue."

The controller directed the drone onward. It checked Svetlana's bungalow and then the acres of solar panels.

"Propulsion battery malfunction, Sir. It's going down. It cannot do an RTH."

"What's that?"

"Return to home, Sir – to the Zaslon team in this case."

Kuznetsov swore as he looked at the blinking drone position, still over the solar panel array and headed towards the double fence on its return route. The motion of the quadcopter slowed and then stopped, but the blinking continued.

The controller spoke again. "Zero altitude Sir, and no motor power - it's on the ground or a panel. Shall I destroy it Sir?"

"Yes, destroy it. Use the acid pack – we don't want to draw attention to it with an explosion. Fucking Chinese batteries, I bet."

He knew that whichever method was used would not result in complete obliteration, but acid was almost silent and there was a chance that the traces might not be discovered for some time – at least long enough for the mission to be completed. But it didn't work out like that.

*

It was the late the following morning when Baldwin was called to Gerasimov's office, urgently. He'd been unable to sleep after his night shift and cursed as he cleaned his hands – changing oil filters was one of his pet hates – then locked *Rubaiyat* and headed out of town for the Saluscent site in one of the hire cars the team used.

"Mr Baldwin, we have made a strange discovery and we need you to explain it, as you are responsible for physical security here. Come with me."

They left the building through one of the rear doors and walked around a bank of six huge generators and reached the maintenance area. They took a golf cart. Gerasimov drove and headed out into the solar farm.

"The autonomous power supply management system detected a shortfall in supply from Avenue Six this morning. It dispatched a maintenance robot to check. The robot located a grid cable failure which it could not repair, and notified our chief engineer – who is on vacation. I am his stand-in. Yes, you may look surprised, but electrical engineering was my bachelor's degree course."

"But we are not responsible for power supplies, Mr Gerasimov."

"Agreed, but you are responsible for protecting our physical assets against intrusion and sabotage."

"To a point, yes, but we cannot protect against cruise missiles."

"Wait and see, Mr Baldwin, we are almost there."

Baldwin saw the sign for Avenue 6 as Sergei turned down the wide aisle between the rows of panels. The solar panels loomed on each side of them as the golf cart approached what looked like a darker patch of the closely trimmed grass. The cart stopped and they got out.

There was a hole in the ground about eighteen inches across. From it radiated four arms, each with the remains of a quadcopter rotor. They could see a slight vapor rising into the morning air.

"I should not need to tell you what it is. It appears that the main body has been dissolved by acid and it is that acid which seems to have leached down into the ground and severed a power cable – which is how we discovered the problem. Sveta is extremely concerned and is calling Mr Borthwick right now. You look shocked Mr Baldwin. What do you have to say?"

What the hell is going on here, Baldwin wondered, is JC running an op – or worse, is there another player in the game?

"Sergei, I need to photograph the scene – I can do that with my phone right now." He pulled his smartphone put of his pocket just as it started to chime. He looked at Sergei. "It's my boss, I need to take this." Sergei nodded but made no move.

"Yes I'm at the site now, about to take some photographs. It's definitely a drone – the working theory is that it's been self-destructed with acid."

"We need to protect against this Baldy."

"Listen Dick, short of throwing a net over the site there's nothing we can do."

"These things navigate by GPS. I told Sveta that we'd sort out a GPS jammer and she said that they already have one deployed. So, she thinks this drone must have been military grade gear."

"She has a GPS jammer here? What the hell's going on Dick?"

"Buggered if I know. She's going ballistic and has requested more people so I'm doubling the team size for a few weeks. You stay in charge."

"Surely we're not expected to guard against aerial attacks – that would be ridiculous?"

"Er…the contract is not specific on that, it just mentions physical security."

"Hell's bells Dick! We need to talk. "

"Not now. I'll come out in a couple of days. Hold it together for me Baldy, I'm relying on you. In the meantime, we go to condition Red Two. This is not about cyber – it's physical and it's right in our court, like it or not. So, brief the team. But first, collect the bits of that drone and some soil samples and ship them to our lab pronto – I'll text you the details. I've told Sveta that we'll have answers within forty eight hours. Remember Red Two – you know what that means."

Yeh, fill the fucking moat for a start. We're in a civilized country with gun laws – and shitty prisons. And we don't have anti-aircraft defenses.

"Right Dick, I'll send pictures through in the next few minutes and I'll get the samples sorted pronto." *And then I'll set up a meeting with JC…*

*

"How much further forward are we, Josh?"

"Not a lot, Sir. The audio feed from the bunker is good, but she doesn't give much away in plain voice with Dmitri – it's all about software code details and test results – useless without more context. The keyboard audio analyzer is useless as she uses a touch screen. We should have had a camera installed there."

"We're lucky to have what we have. No more ideas on what's on the level below?"

"No, it's still all surmise – Telion thinks it's a huge battery bank which the solar farm charges. There's a bit more on the analysis front too, r.e. the power consumption. We've looked again at the drone footage of the aircon and the solar farm to judge the heat extraction levels.

With about two and a half acres of solar panels they are generating about one megawatt of power at peak sunshine. She has generators installed as well to cover the night and cloudy days. Telion also says they have diesel fuel delivered every week, ten thousand liters at a time. It all adds up to a reasonably sized cryptocurrency mining operation."

"Turning electricity into money you mean?"

"Yes, but on nothing like the scale of the big US or Chinese operators."

"And that's just part of the operation?"

"Yes, you saw the whiteboard. We're trying to identify which of the miners she is. There's got to be more – Bitcoin mining demands ever increasing resources, by design, to stay profitable until it hits the limit of coins. That's why new coins are attractive – the mining is cheaper."

"But the price of the other coins is lower."

Josh looked at Emmett Macsen, realizing that the man was already up to speed – and letting him know. Josh nodded.

"Can we find out how much money she's making?"

"Not really, Sir. The miners use handles – such as…wait a minute…I have an idea…sorry, got to go."

Josh turned and hurried from Macsen's office.

Back at his cubicle, Josh opened up the translated transcript of the audio from Sveta's secure basement room. The number 666 had stuck in his mind, and he did a quick text search. There it was, *dannylow six six six screech,* in one of her conversations with Dmitri two days ago. The translator had added the comment *[English? spelling?]* One mention in three days of transcripts. He realized that 'screech' meant exclamation mark. She had gone ballistic when Dmitri had mentioned the words dannylow666!

Josh knew that there was a way to track down miners – at least their handles – as these were recorded in the blockchain every time a crypto coin was mined and validated after which a small reward was paid to the miner.

It was just a hunch, but he set to work, assuming that it was the Monero cryptocurrency. It would be a slow job, but solvable by computer. He called one of his team and they downloaded the Monero blockchain – it was still under 50 Gigabytes in size. The problem was in the spelling – what should it be?

He set a search program to work on the Ponomarenko file, looking for a homophone match for 'dannylow'. Less than five minutes later a flag chimed up on the toolbar of his workstation.

'Homophone match found – *Danylo* – 3 occurrences'

Josh clicked the first bookmark.

'Known associate Lieutenant Colonel Danylo Kravets, Ukrainian Armed Forces.'

He clicked the link and read the brief bio, finishing with date and cause of death. Then he checked the other bookmarks. Yes, it made sense. For such a clever woman she seemed to do some stupid things.

He called Sian Davies to his desk. She was the team's resident blockchain expert.

"Sian, we need to find all the transactions on cryptocurrencies for a miner known as *danylo666k*. Can we do it?"

"It's going to take a while, maybe a couple of days. As a matter of course GCHQ does a complete download of all the leading blockchains every day or when there's a major price movement – anything with a market cap of over a billion US dollars. The Bank of England likes it that way."

"Good. Start with Bitcoin then work through the others in order of market cap, say the top six. I need an approximate valuation of the coins mined, at current US dollar prices – and anything else you can dig up. Also, I want to know every altcoin that particular miner is active on."

"That might take longer – there are more than fifteen hundred altcoins"

"You'd better get started right away then, hadn't you?"

"Okay. Thankfully we can do most of that on automatic pilot."

*

Twenty Four

"It's out of our hands now Sokholov."

"Why Sir?"

"We are cyber forensics specialists, so they say we can't run a physical intrusion operation. The whole operation has been hijacked by the SVR." The tone of his voice was one that suggested he had eaten something very unpleasant. He was on the edge of a rant.

"Really?"

"Do you think I invented that for fucking fun, Sokholov? And don't forget 'Sir'!" The rant was live.

"No Sir, of course not, Sir. It's just that the SVR, well they don't have our profile."

"Fucking profile, what use is that? The Chief of the General Staff has been overruled by Buligin!"

"You don't know that for sure – er… Sir." Sokholov hoped that the stop-watch was running. He looked through the glass of the door. Yes, it was in play.

"It's the only thing that could have done it. We will be going in behind the special forces advance guard to do the forensics with some SVR people. We will be leaving for Portugal in three days time – you and I, with another team. So, prepare your traveling gear. We will be mustering for in depth briefing, starting this afternoon. We will be traveling undercover as tourists. Do not provide any explanation to your team – I will arrange cover for you while we are away. And you can expect the SVR people to be hostile to our presence."

"At last the Chief of Staff got us on the team, Sir."

"He probably had to give his right bollock for that!"

The excitement was obvious in Sokolov's eyes as he snapped a "Yes Sir" with a smart salute and turned out of Drozdov's office.

He looked at his team. They had done well - the work had been painstaking and slow, but they had got as far as Dmitri Borzov and the link with Ponomarenko – or Kovacs as she now called herself.

Drozdov didn't rant, not really. He started to do a fist pump but thought better of it. *Yes! Bugger the bet, I'm going to Portugal on a mission!*

*

The briefing was dynamic and lasted two days. 'What if' was the most frequent question, with the plan being shaped by the team as they dug deeper, finding flaws and eliminating them, identifying contingencies and fallbacks.

The eight members of the SVR Zaslon team were experts in these operations with wide international operational experience. All except Drozhdov and Sokholov of the GRU. They kept in the background until the ingress and egress stages of the plan had been thoroughly analyzed and refined. They were seen by the others as passengers and unwelcome.

Halfway through the second day, Major Yegor Ramazonov summarised the plan.

"So far, we have covered the logistics, the ingress and egress to the site, focused on the simple objective of gaining access and getting away cleanly, with a time on site limited to one hour maximum – and that includes time for our esteemed colleagues from the GRU forensics team to do their work. We have covered the physical defenses and the level of opposition we expect.

"Major Drozhdov, all you and your colleague have to do is turn up at the gate and we will open it for you. Then, when your work is completed you may return the way you came, as tourists on a cheap flight."

There was laughter from the Zaslon team, but Drozhdov was not amused, and it showed. "We will be there on time. Just make sure that we have access."

"You will have access as planned, and at the time required. Now, please explain to us what is so important that my men have to get you in there – and out – safely."

"I am not authorized to release that information to you or the team. It is not necessary for you to know" *And even if I knew it myself I wouldn't tell you, he thought.* "Your team are just there to do the dirty work. We are the specialists." Sokholov, seated next to him, stared straight ahead, trying to suppress a smile. Drozhdov went up a notch in his estimation.

It was Ramazanov's turn to look annoyed.

*

Twenty Five

The evening of the 30th June didn't quite turn out as Stone had expected, although she hadn't really known what to expect. "Meet me for a drink?" That's all Baldwin had said, more an order than a request. She'd agreed and he'd called round to her hotel and picked her up. Then they'd headed over towards Faro and stopped at a roadside bar. The chat in the car on the way had been banal to say the least, with Baldwin seeming to be on edge, though for someone who said he didn't do small talk he'd managed pretty well. But something was clearly bothering him. She'd heard from Laporte about Baldwin's trip in the golf cart with Gerasimov but Baldwin had said nothing to the team and had so far refused to answer questions about it.

The bar was filling up with passing motorists on their way home from work dropping in for a quick one and the setting was far from romantic – not that she had romance in mind. But recently there had been a few occasions when she'd caught Baldwin off guard looking at her and he'd blushed and turned away. Stone asked for white wine and Steve ordered a beer. He did not look happy.

"So JC, tell me what the hell is going on. Are you running another op for Six that I don't know about?"

She looked askance at him. His tone was aggressive and his body language awkward and unsettled.

Steve slid the envelope onto the table. "I think that this belongs to you."

"What's that?"

"I think you left it in Lumley's apartment when you had battery trouble with your phone. I was there. Lumley wasn't, although he'd called in sick." He watched her reaction as she realized that her face had given her away. "Don't deny it. Just tell me about it."

"I can't Steve. I'm under orders."

"Aren't we all? I'm so disappointed in you JC – you can't work for two bosses, so make up your mind. I'm responsible for protecting a client, its staff and my team – including even you. I've experienced the low down dirty way that VX can operate, first hand and many times, so I can understand if you are not a volunteer."

"But I am."

"Fair enough, I was too – once, and that was enough. Look, if there's anything that impacts our security then I need to know about it, or you're off the job. So, what's it to be?"

"I can't say anything."

"OK, I'll take a wild guess about what happened."

Baldwin outlined his sketchy guess.

Stone nodded. "That's more or less what happened, Steve, although I can't go into the details of what Lumley said – or the questions asked of him."

"But it was as a result of our intrusion into the comms room?"

"No. The cybersecurity room."

"You saw something?"

"You did too. That's it. I've said too much already. Are you satisfied?"

"No. I want to know the rest."

"More? I bet there is. Steve, you tell me what's going on! Your trip in the buggy with Sergei. You need to be straight with me and with the team!"

"Keep your bloody voice down!"

"Something's bugging you and I don't want you taking it out on me. We went to Red Two today with more people being added to the team, all regular staff sent home on indefinite leave and we've been given no reason, no explanation. You ask me out for a drink and lay in to me, *why* I don't know. For what it's worth I'm not running another op for Six and if I was I wouldn't tell you, unless I'd been ordered to. That is, beyond what you already guessed. Which for the record I do not fucking confirm."

Baldwin looked hard at her trying to judge whether she was a first rate liar or genuinely ignorant of the events in the solar farm.

"Sergei found a crashed drone in the solar farm this morning. Self-destructed, we think with acid. Only the rotors left." He watched as her eyes widened in surprise.

"Yes. The rotors were shielded…"

"Stealth design, anti-radar?"

"…yes, I think so, although I didn't share my suspicions with Sergei."

"I launched a drone here a couple of times for Six about ten days ago. It installed bugging gear on the roof. That led to operation poison pizza."

"Shit. So that's it. Now it's all starting to make sense.. But why didn't you let on?"

"You know as well as I do, Steve. Need to know."

"I need to know where your loyalties lie, JC. Six or the team."

"You swore an oath when you joined the marines. I swore an oath when I joined the Navy."

"It's not that simple and you know it."

"That's what guides me, though. King and country before Borthwick."

"God, what a fucking mess."

Stone shrugged. "I suppose it could be Six, but they'd surely tell me and involve you as well, as they did last week. Unless they have other people on the ground here. But I really know nothing about that crashed drone."

"I've sent the rotors and soil samples to Borthwick. We'll have some feedback in a couple of days. I didn't see the drone we used last week – it was dark. You say it's not yours?"

"I can't say for sure."

Baldwin looked in to her eyes and for a few moments he was lost. He recovered his composure quickly, but Stone had not missed the moment.

"JC, those bastards *cannot* be trusted. But if it's not ours, then whose? And why? What's so fucking special about this place?"

"The drone we used is in storage in a lock-up in case we need it again. We can go there and you can look at it if you like."

"Thanks but I wouldn't be able to tell the difference."

"Perhaps we should share our knowledge?"

"I can tell you what I like, but you're the one restricted by Six, not me. Here, I've got some pictures here on my phone. Look. Is there any similarity?"

"Four rotors is pretty standard, but I can't really tell from that picture – there's not much left is there? But ours was matt black. The bits you saw look grey to me."

"Yes the rotor shields were definitely grey. Though that's not conclusive about origin."

"By the way, the Saluscent site is geofenced."

"What's that?"

"A technical set up with special beacons which prevents drones entering. It's way beyond what most geofencing is. This is a hard fence."

"So whoever sent that drone in was able to override that?"

"Yes, it must have been military grade." *Just as we had.*

Baldwin looked at her – that nose intrigued him even more – and it was then he realized that he believed her story. Across the table she could see that he'd made some sort of decision, his shoulders seemed to be set differently and she felt that the tension between them had eased. His chin fascinated her, and she idly wondered how much difficulty he had shaving the cleft. And his brown eyes reminded her of a pet spaniel she'd had as a child. Sam, yes that was his name. Steve's were full of profound sadness, unlike Sam who had been a bundle of fun until…she put the thought out her mind.

They both seemed to be lost in their own thoughts. Then their eyes met and after an embarrassing few seconds his words brought her back to reality.

"Uhh…we're at Red Two, JC, so we'd better come up with some ideas, fast. Come on, drink up – we'd better and get back – I've got some team scheduling to sort out, and the dogs arrive tomorrow."

"Dogs?"

"Yes. Dobermans, silent killers. They're coming in from the Scutum Est kennels in Germany with two handlers. "

"This is getting very serious Steve."

"Too right it is. I didn't sign up for this."

Baldwin dropped a few euros on the table and they left the bar.

Back in the rental car, JC spoke first. "OK, Red Two. How long will it be this way?"

"I guess until Borthwick or Sveta tells me differently. We'll need to run through the Red Two protocol checklist when we are back on site tomorrow."

"If the site is under surveillance then we should do a sweep of the perimeter, maybe out to a couple of hundred meters."

"They – whoever it is - will *have* to assume that we found the drone. They will have cleared up and pulled out."

"We have to check anyway if only to keep us on our toes. That was no toy shop drone, for sure. I mean, who puts acid in a drone to self destruct? We have to check and the sooner the better. It'll be too obvious in the day and I don't want to wait another twenty four hours in case it rains." Baldwin looked at the sky. "We're at new moon and that's just set – ideal conditions. I'll drop you at the site – you can fill in for Aldo. Here, you'd better drive while I call him."

"So you're telling the security team the real story then?"

"Only about the mystery drone - I've got to drop the pretense of a Red Two drill, it doesn't wash now that the office staff and developers have been sent home. Just us and cyber security now, plus Sergei – and maybe Sveta although we haven't seen her since pizza night. It's time to get real, though what we're up against I've no idea." He speed dialed. "Aldo, it's Steve. Get some kit together for a night reconnaissance, assumed hostile and elite. Just you and me. Stone will stand in for you. We'll be there in about half an hour."

*

Yuri and Galina got the text ordering an immediate return to base at the camper van. Most of the brushover work had been done the night before, once they knew that the drone was down. They checked and stowed the equipment then notified Moscow. After setting the alarm and booby trap incendiary, they headed back to the hotel to pack. The camper would stay for the next team, but they would be cutting short their holiday and heading to Moscow to brief the mission planners.

*

It was just getting light when Steve and Aldo returned through the gate, carrying their gear in sports bags. Stone checked them in as they wiped off their black facepaint. "Well?"

"Nothing at all. We carried out a sweep of all the brush, but it's not easy in the dark. If anyone was there then they are the best – or we just missed the traces. So, we have only the downed drone to go on. The rest of the team should be arriving this afternoon and maybe by then we'll have some feedback from Borthwick. I'm heading back to my boat to clean up then I'll be back by oh-seven-hundred to brief Sergei."

"Don't forget to wash your face before you go come back. You've still got some black patches." She smiled as she touched a patch in the cleft of his chin and then one on his left ear. "Here, and here."

"Yes Ma'am."

Steve dropped Aldo off at his hotel and headed for *Rubaiyat.* As he unlocked the hatch his phone chimed. It was Borthwick.

"How's it going there?"

"Quietly right now. We just did a sweep around the site to check for surveillance with a two hundred meter perimeter – including a couple of villas. Nothing found."

"So they're either good or imaginary – or they were further out. But that drone was real, I can tell you. Not one of Six's – they are adamant that they are not running an op. I sent them a few bits, but in the meantime my lab tells me that the paint is an anti-radar coating and that the rotor design is similar to a couple of drones downed in Syria."

"Shit! So it's Russian then, though I guess it could be the US?"

"Looks like it's Russian. As far as I can tell the Cousins are not in on this act."

"Sveta's giving me a hard time. Says that it was luck the drone crashed and if it hadn't we'd wouldn't even know that someone was mounting an operation."

"She's got a point."

"Yes, well I told her that we knew she had radar and that we should have access to it. She said that it's an automatic warning system. Then I asked her why it hadn't worked. She said that it was fully operational but no threat had been detected. You know what that means."

"Heavy tech, very heavy."

"Yes, so she's now given us access to the radar feed."

"We're finding something new every day. It's not good. At least we'll have the dogs here soon."

"When I told her she asked why they weren't there already. She denies that there are any other physical defense systems that we don't know about. Shit, I've got to take another call. Call you back. Don't go anywhere."

Baldwin put the kettle on and was stripping off ready to shower when the phone rang again.

"Yes Dick?"

"I'll not tell you who that was but this is bloody serious. London are going apeshit about the Russian drone. At least we know now that there's another player on the ground."

"Unless it's a misdirect."

"What do you mean 'misdirect'?"

"Maybe the Cousins are using a captured drone – or any Russian proxy state could be involved for that matter."

"Six are betting it's Russian."

"Well, I'm keeping an open mind. For someone who has absolutely nothing to do with Six you are remarkably well connected. I'm so glad there's only two weeks left on my contract. I'm sick of the bastards."

"Don't start piss-taking now Baldy, it's not the time. And it's more than two weeks."

"We'll see about that. So, what are the orders? I'll be briefing Sergei in half an hour. What do I tell him – that we'll sit around and wait for something to happen? I'm sure that will impress him."

The sarcasm was not lost on Borthwick. "You're on the spot. What would you recommend?"

"Don't look at me Dick – I'm at the bottom of the shit stream. I need to know what's *really* going on before I can come up with a plan. So, tell me, what do your London friends say?"

"Bugger all. They're just very worried."

"And what does Sveta say we're protecting?"

"Intellectual property and advanced software."

"Which is protected by her own cyberteam. Surely the software is in the Cloud somewhere. So why us?" There was silence. "Well Dick, as you've gone quiet, I'm going to tell Sergei that I'll only speak to him if Sveta is there. Then, I'm going to tell them both that the drone was Russian and that if we are protecting a tangible physical asset then we need to know what it is – and where in the building it is, otherwise we walk off the job. Agreed."

"Do it. We need to rattle their cage. The contract specifies that we must have access to all details of current physical security to enable us to do our job. Otherwise they are frustrating our ability to satisfy our contractual obligations. I'll call Sveta later and remind her that Red status doubles the contract rates – but you handle the withdrawal threat directly with Sergei. A two pronged attack."

"You and your bloody contracts! Still, I'm glad to hear that my daily rate will be doubling for Red Two status."

"It doesn't quite work like that, Steve."

"What a surprise! And why not give London the same story about us withdrawing – see what that does to them. You should be OK now that the Qatar training contract has been inked. They can't hold that over you."

"Good idea Steve, and worth a try" *But they've still got plenty of other ammunition to use on me.*

"And before you go, what about kit for the new guys? They should be arriving this afternoon."

"The truck is on its way, should be crossing the border from Spain in a couple of hours. It will go to the warehouse to unload. It's on schedule."

"Fine, and don't forget the dogfood."

"We keep them hungry, Steve….oh shit, very funny"…but Baldwin had already cut the call.

*

"Not here? Mister Gerasimov, I am responsible for the physical security of this site and the people here. Sveta has not checked out."

"She doesn't need to, you know that."

"But none of my team has logged her going out through the gate."

Sergei shrugged. "So?"

"Are you saying that there is another way out of here?"

"I am not saying anything. I only have facts – which I share."

"And the radar – we've only just been told about that fact."

"Some facts I am not permitted to share with you."

"Listen, if there is another way in and out of this site then I need to put guards on it. So how does she come and go?"

Another shrug.

"This could be dangerous for her. We will have dogs in the compound from tonight – they could kill her."

"They will not be a problem. Anyway, you will use friend-scent sprays. Give me an aerosol can and I will pass it on to her."

"I will, but there *must* be a tunnel, that's obvious, so that she can come and go without notice. Where is the entrance, where does it come out? For Christ's sake Sergei, there may be Russian special forces – spetsnaz - out there, you've got to tell me!"

"I do not know Mr Baldwin."

Baldwin wondered why even the threat of the Russian Spetsnaz did not seem to faze Gerasimov.

"I have a conference call with her scheduled for ten am. You can speak to her then."

"Where is she?"

"I don't know. She doesn't account to me for her movements."

"Well, here's a heads-up for you, Sergei. Unless you start sharing all the physical security details with me, then I'm taking my team off site as from oh-eight-hundred tomorrow."

"Don't threaten me. You will be in breach of our contract."

"No. You're already in breach – you are deliberately frustrating our contract execution. And that comes direct from Mr Borthwick!"

"I will take this up with Sveta and I am sure that she will speak directly to Mr Borthwick about it."

"I thought you said she couldn't be contacted."

"I did. I also said I had a call arranged."

"That will not change anything."

"Mr Borthwick is usually very amenable to our requests."

I bet he fucking is, whenever money's concerned. Anywhere, anytime, anyhow, just like a whore.

Baldwin was just turning in for the night when Borthwick's call came.

"So how did it go?"

"You first. What did Sveta tell you?"

"I couldn't reach her directly."

"That figures. She's off site and no-one knows where. Sergei and I did a conference call with her. Apparently she comes and goes at whim, she must have a tunnel or a bloody invisibility cloak. Sergei denies all knowledge of one – a tunnel, that is. I said that we were withdrawing our services tomorrow as from oh eight hundred unless they stopped frustrating the contract. I told her that I wanted full access to all physical details of the site including plans and architects drawings."

"How did she take it?"

"Calmly. She said that she would be in touch with you and that she would be back in a couple of days. In the interim she would be out of reach. This all stinks to high heaven, Dick."

"It's making me uncomfortable too. She needs to agree reasonable grounds for me to go to Red, otherwise I can't bill the extra costs."

"And profit no doubt! I'm pulling the team out tomorrow."

"No, you're not. Let's wait until I have a discussion with her. Besides, there are other fish to fry."

"Such as?"

"We need to keep JC there."

"Why?"

"I can't tell you that right now."

"It's fucking Six again isn't it? She's been launching drones for them. Fuck knows what they are up to. Bloody hell Dick, we may be putting our lives on the line here and we don't know why. Russian fucking drones flying about and all I have is hunting guns and a pack of hounds. And all you can talk about is your fucking contract. And don't say 'do or die' to me, we're volunteers, remember." Or almost all are, he thought, as the bitter memory of his supposedly fake marriage surfaced again.

"You have all the people, all the gear you asked for. Tell me what else you need."

"A bloody crystal ball, a good reason and access to all the security systems. And some Stingers."

"No can do, sorry, and you should follow orders and not keep asking 'why'. Anyway, I'll see if I can find out any more from my London friends."

"And get me all the deep background you can on Sergei. For an ops director of a software company he seems to be much too relaxed in the circumstances. He didn't bat an eyelid when I mentioned spetsnaz to him. And one more thing – I think we should go to condition Red One or we should get the Portuguese army in."

"Imminent threat of attack? We can't support that with intel."

"Yes we can, anyone with half a brain can see that Sveta's seriously paranoid. All these defenses, all this tech, a bbunker mentality. Why? For some software? Are you blind Dick? There's much more to this."

"Maybe. Anyway, the contract does not cover Red One."

"Bugger the contract. I'll feel happier if we have all the team on site twenty four seven, locked down for at least for a week or so. Or get us out of here completely. It's not only about protecting the client now – it's about force strength for self-protection."

"And who's going to pay for that?"

"I'm sure you'll figure it out Dick."

"How will we billet them and feed them? It's not straightforward, Baldy. Tell you what, you come up with a plan and if it holds water I'll talk to Sveta."

"If you can get hold of her. And I'm not paid to do planning."

"We can sort that out.

"You're stretching our friendship too far Dick. All this coming and going of our team, with new people coming in – surely the local police must have noticed? We don't want any trouble from the local rozzers."

"Don't worry. Sveta's got that under control. Sergei liaises with the mayor about new hi-tech jobs for locals, sponsoring a course in the local college. Plus they are building a new pavilion – read drinking club – for the local police sports team. Sveta is the mysterious, secretive local entrepreneur. She pays a lot for her privacy and they give her plenty of slack."

"But the locals must wonder about all these obviously hard guys around town – I had to pull one of our guys out of a punch-up the other night."

"If I hear officially about any trouble between any of our guys and the locals then he – or she – is pulled off the job immediately and loses the month's pay to boot. Who was it? Henri, thinking with his dick again?"

"It came to nothing. No names, no pack drill, Dick. I can handle it."

"Be sure you do. I don't want anyone rocking the boat."

"The fucking boat is going to sink big time if we do get attacked. This isn't central Africa. Red One or Out. And frankly, I'd vote for out."

"As you said Baldy, this isn't central Africa. Do you really think the Ruskies would mount an attack? I bloody don't."

"What about terrorists?"

"Why would they do that?"

"Money makes the world go around, and she's mining it here isn't she?"

*

Sveta was in Paris Charles de Gaulle airport waiting for her return connection to Portugal when she took the call from Sergei. Baldwin was conferenced in and provided an update about the supposedly Russian drone. The call was short and mostly one way. Say nothing, hear everything as the Chinese proverb went, but she was in an airport lounge anyway.

'So, the wolves are gathering' she thought, and wondered how they had got on the trail as she walked towards the boarding gate.

And Baldwin had finally deduced that she had a tunnel. "What tunnel?" she'd said, but she knew that he didn't believe her. He'd never find the entrance anyway – it was hidden in the garage of another villa she owned, on a large plot adjoining the double fence round the site. Sergei had probably guessed months ago – in principle at least, but he would have no idea about the villa. All the construction had been done before he joined the payroll, an easy dig through the soft sandstone when the villa was being re-modeled. It had been money well spent even though the contractor had commented on it being a strange shape for a wine cellar. Then again, he was used to strange requests from the wealthy villa owners in the area, Sir Cliff Richard included. Wine cellars, wet rooms, dungeons – he'd built them all. He'd built a very profitable business on discretion and satisfying the strange requests of the super-rich.

Three months later the Saluscent site development – including the small villa within the grounds - was started by a different contractor. Sveta was *very* precise about the position of the utility room and the small wine cellar underneath the small villa on the site. A few months after completion, with help, she'd easily breached through the two meters of soft sandstone into the tunnel, finally connecting the two villas herself, much to her satisfaction. The itinerant who'd helped her for the day had later fallen off a cliff, drunken senseless, according to the local news.

Buckling her seat belt in the first class cabin, she smiled at the memory. Yes, things were still going to plan – more or less - although she might need to take out some extra insurance against Buligin.

*

Twenty Six

It was mid-morning when Baldwin had made the introductions and briefed the enlarged team. One of the new guys had been delayed in a car crash in Frankfurt and there were now twenty people in the team plus himself. The teams were asymmetric, with heavier presence between 2 am and daybreak, when any attack was most likely.

There was some surprise when Baldwin explained that they were guarding software. The guys could see that he did not believe it himself and he didn't feel like trying too hard to convince them. No-one really thought that an attack was likely, but Baldwin was nervous.

"Software, what the hell Steve?" Mancowicz voiced the thoughts of most of the team. "We all know that software gets stolen over the internet or wifi or something. It sounds like crap to me."

"Nevertheless we take it seriously. Your life could depend on it."

After the schedule, transport and accommodation arrangements had been made, Baldwin detailed Henri to visit the warehouse and check the shipment of kit, which would be brought to the site later that day. Most of it was legal and licensed to *Scutum Est* for armed security purposes. Some of it was not. The briefing over, Baldwin called Stone to one side.

"Meet me for a drink?"

"Will it be as romantic as last time?" She raised her eyebrows as she smiled.

"It's business, but we need to do it off site." Steve saw the disappointment in her face and ignored the dig. "Let's do it at lunchtime if it's not interfering with your plans. It will not keep until tonight and it'll be our last chance before Red One."

"Lunchtime is fine."

It was not an alcoholic lunch – alcohol was forbidden at any time during Condition Red – so they drank water with their grilled fresh sardines at the Café do Doca.

"In the briefing paper I read when I started this gig, you'd said that there were two levels underground. How did you figure that out?"

"Just by looking at the elevators. You went down in one, you saw the buttons."

He nodded. "And you have no idea what's down there?"

"Batteries I suppose. And the server farm. They have a lot of them according to the power control panels I've seen, but I've never seen batteries above ground, anywhere."

"That sounds reasonable."

"Why the question?"

"I'm just wondering what the hell it is we're supposed to be guarding."

"Me too – I don't think anyone on the team believes that it's software."

"Whatever it is, this assignment could get ugly."

"It's all in a day's work."

They looked at each other in silence, a comfortable silence, until Steve became conscious of it. "I think Sveta's off site."

"Really? That's unusual. What makes you think that?"

"Borthwick had a call from her, says it sounded like she was in an airport. Said he was keeping me in the loop."

"When did she go?"

"I don't know, though I'm sure Sergei does – but maybe not how."

Baldwin explained his tunnel theory – and his growing discomfort with Sergei. "So, give the tunnel idea some thought."

"Okay, but here's something else to ponder. If we were doing surveillance then surely we'd want to monitor the main – the only – gate closely, just to see the comings and goings?"

"Okay, so? We spent most time of all checking the area with a good line of sight to the gate. Nothing."

"What about looking the other way? We have gate cameras – may they have picked up something passing."

"Good thinking. Let's get the recording checked – go back say five days. You just volunteered."

She groaned. All that video to review. Then her face lit up.

"What about our own security drones?"

"The one that checks vehicles?"

"No, the others - one does a patrol of the perimeter every hour."

"Ah yes, of course", Baldwin agreed realizing he'd forgotten all about that.

"Well, you know they do a pre-programmed patrol at thirty meters altitude right around the perimeter. Visual and infrared. It only takes a half hour or so. All the output goes directly to a database under Sergei's control."

"Who reviews the output?"

"They have AI pattern scanning software which analyses it, picking up differences between patrols, or so I've been told. More physical security data that we don't have access to."

"Agreed. But anything of interest to us would be beyond the perimeter."

"It's very likely the cameras would be wide angle."

"What about the GPS jamming they use?"

"Maybe they turn off the jamming during the patrol. I'll see what I can find out."

"Okay, I'll ask Sergei about the data, although I'm sure he would have told us if there was something. One more thing, I'm setting up a Tiger team to look urgently at our security from the standpoint of an assaulting force. Ingress and egress scenarios. I want you to lead it."

"Why me?"

"Because you've got a wider perspective, you know stuff that we can't let on to the team. You will be able to widen their thinking without giving anything away."

"I suppose that makes sense. But what's the target? No-one believes that it's software."

"That's the sixty four thousand dollar question, isn't it? I suppose it could be Sveta herself. She wears gloves, works in a bunker and doesn't go out at all it seems. She may not sign the access log but the gate guards make a note when she leaves that way – and there's been nothing for over three months."

"How much time have I got?"

"Ongoing – get the guys to think about it, but give me your initial ideas within twenty four hours."

"That's asking a hell of a lot. Tell you what, I'll stick a brush up my arse and sweep the floor while I'm doing all the other stuff."

Baldwin smiled. "Now there's a thought." And he dodged as she tried to slap his face – with the hint of a smile. "I'm sure you can do it – you've been here a couple of months now with your eyes wide open, or so Dick has told me."

She rolled her eyes. "Anything else you want to dump on me while we're at it?"

"How about another drink?"

"No thanks, I need to get back – I've got much too much work on my plate, thank you, Boss, and the clock is running. And we're not supposed to be here anyway, are we?"

She stood up and headed for the car. Steve drained his glass, dropped ten euros on the table and followed, cursing his gaucheness and her barbed comment. Why was he riding her so hard? Was it a result of his own guilt over Ellie?

*

Back at her desk in her workroom under the Saluscent compound, Sveta checked her inboxes and Slack workroom for the latest test results. The final passes had been successful barring one glitch with Dmitri's test pack. She checked the test script and spotted the flaw. After repairing it she re-ran the test pack herself and by 6 pm. she had satisfied herself that the software was ready. She ran the compile script in the pre-release environment and checked the output files and log.

They were clean and the software was ready to burn.

She checked the install script then moved the compiled code into the release area. It was now just after midnight.

The release checklist was long and she worked her way through it, looking at the clock as she completed the final item.

She entered the command to trigger the install script. It was almost an hour later that the script terminated.

She checked the output file.

No errors.

10,000 copies of the software had been loaded – burned – into the BASICs.

She was ready and walked out of the room to the cyber security suite. She could have just called, but needed to stretch her legs.

"All OK guys? I need to upload some software and need 100% bandwidth."

"Yes, we're good. Satellite is at 100% throughput, ground station is fully operational. No threats detected."

"That's great."

She turned and walked back to her office and checked the Salus launch script, and then re-checked it. And then she checked it again. It had been close, but she was ready.

She opened a screen and located the cloud services web portal. She logged into the company's area and navigated to the development system. The credentials screen came up and she took a deep breath. There was no room for error now or she would be locked out. Sveta entered Tombo997 as the user ID, then the password EzKGaL84yZuRgZR.

She was in. *Thank you Dmitri.* Dmitri had worked hard to obtain the credentials for the broker's systems and through the user accounts they'd investigated she'd read through emails and discovered a link to a secret Bitcoin mining consortium based in Morocco. That was proving to be invaluable as she had piggybacked on their mining ID for the current project. That would sow even more confusion over the coming days.

She reviewed the scripts package once again then uploaded it, unpacked it and invoked the master control script.

The counter was timing down steadily, another script checking the comms channels and validating the servers' readiness. All her cryptomining had been suspended for the last six hours in preparation for this moment – and she had been nearly a year in assembling the software. Dmitri had played his part well.

Then the script paused.

'Server malfunction'
'Auto repair underway'
'Awaiting repair before continuing'
'Seconds to fix: 360'

She held her breath, as the seconds counted down, looking through the window onto the huge server farm on the floor below as a service robot moved out from its parking bay and headed down an aisle. It stopped and four arms went to work to replace the module.

The count stopped.

'Module replaced'

She watched, holding her breath as the service robot returned to its bay. The Salus Launch script rolled on down the screen

'Replacement Module Hardware test underway'
'Replacement Module Hardware test completed, Issues: 0'
'Replacement Module Loading software and burning'
'Replacement Module Software load completed CRC check 100%'
'Bringing replacement module online'
'Pre-launch tests complete. No of issues found: 1 (fixed)'
'Resuming software execution script'
'Time to initiation: 1h 10m 21s'

The countdown continued.

Everything was ready. Salus was now on autopilot.

In just over an hour the US markets would be closing for Independence Day.

She put in a Signal call to Dmitri in Kiev.

"Hi Dmitri. There was a problem with the test pack. It's going to take a few days to sort out. We'll have to delay the launch."

"I can't believe it. What was wrong?"

"I'm still investigating, but we'll miss the fourth of July" she lied to him. "I don't want you to do anything more. I'm going to audit all your work. We cannot take a chance with this. It has to work a hundred percent first time. I'll call you when I have the answer."

She cut the call.

Dmitri didn't yet know that his access to all Saluscent systems had just been revoked and his files erased. Using embedded software breadcrumb markers she was actively tracking down 'secret' copies that he'd made. He hadn't had the complete set of modules and anyway the key ones were under her direct control. She probably would not find them all, but it didn't really matter now. She'd also found several interesting scams that Dmitri had been running with his company, mostly small time, but there was one which she'd picked out as worth pursuing, something that would give her pleasure.

You could find anything on the web these days, if you knew how. CaaS - 'Crime-as-a-Service' was an established concept and hitmen were relatively easy to find on the dark web although references were obviously hard to come by. And, of course, there were legal agencies such as the FBI and Interpol which used impostors to flush out those with criminal intent. One had to be careful, and she was.

Twenty four hours ago she had given a kill order to a man in Frankfurt who was at that moment *en route* to Kiev. Now she sent a Signal message to confirm the hit order. It would indeed be Independence Day for Dmitri – he'd be free of all earthly shackles. She felt sad that timings did not allow her to carry out the task herself; with no strong feelings either way about Dmitri, it was just that she'd missed the thrill of a close kill since that man in Bucharest. Not even Gerasimov's death had been a thrill. Quickly and efficiently dispatched, his body hidden in a cupboard in her office. In a few hours it would go atmospheric.

She shook her head ruefully as she looked at the screen. How different her life might have been if her father had not abused her. Five – or was it six – men might still have been alive? She was losing count. Anyway, there would soon be one more.

Blockchain Exploit

*

Twenty Seven

"Airbridge three one seven, you are cleared to land, runway two eight."

The pilot nodded to his co-pilot who responded "Cleared to land runway two-eight, Airbridge three one seven."

The Antonov AN-32 variant cargo plane lined up for final approach into Faro airport, its undercarriage lowering as it passed the outer marker beacon. It was just after midnight and the airport had just officially closed operations. However, the plane had declared an emergency fifteen minutes earlier. A warning light indicated a fuel pressure problem with the starboard engine and the plane was unable to reach any other alternative airport on its remaining fuel.

The co-pilot flicked the intercom switch. "Five minutes."

"*Pyat' minut, priznannyy*" came the reply from the cargo bay, acknowledging the advisory.

The plane, flying under the name of the Russian cargo fleet 'Airbridge', bucked as the pilot kept it on the glide path in the fresh and gusty north east wind. The landing gear locked lights were on green. All was ready.

"Faro control, Airbridge three one seven. We have a landing gear warning light showing. It may only be a problem with the lights. Request go-around and visual check by control tower if possible."

"Airbridge three one seven you are cleared for go-around. No other traffic. Will attempt visual, but may be too dark for us to see undercarriage. Faro control."

The pilot pulled back on the control yoke as the co-pilot pushed the throttles forward. The twin 5,100 hp Ivchenko AI-20 turboprop engines responded as the plane leveled off, passed the control tower and started a steep full power climb.

"Airbridge three one seven, your gear is down, repeat your gear is down."

"Gear is down. Thank you. Climbing to approach level and continuing go-around. Airbridge three one seven."

The Captain Grigor Ostopenko turned to his co-pilot and nodded. Olhaõ was quickly approaching ahead of them. Senior Lieutenant Valeri Netrebov flicked the intercom. "Ramp opening enabled, one minute, height two thousand feet. Wish them good luck from us."

In the loading bay the loadmaster heard the co-pilot over his headset and saw the light come on as he opened ramp and locked it.

The Spetsnaz team were on their feet and ready to run as they buddy-checked their weapons and gear. They watched the large screen display over the ramp. In low-light mode to preserve their night sight, it showed their position approaching the jump off point – and their target – on a moving map. At the side a panel of numbers displayed their height, ground speed and wind information, with just seconds to go.

This was to be a high-precision jump in the dark and with a fresh, gusty wind. They had done it before many times during practice for the mission in the past two weeks, but that did not make it any easier. Everything was being trusted to technology, and they were right on the bleeding edge. The loadmaster watched the screen and then the green light came on. “Go!”

Major Ramazanov was first out following by his team, two at a time. Their ram-air parachute wings quickly deployed in a strictly programmed sequence. The units above each trooper’s head operated the control-lines using a real-time data feed from the plane to keep each man on a trajectory to the target – and away from his companions in the dark. In their helmet displays a small display showed their relative position to the target and each other. It had taken a lot of training to build the confidence in them to ignore the hand control lines and to trust to the technology. They glided at thirty knots towards the target, the lights of Olhaõ fading away behind them. This was arguably the riskiest part of the mission – and they would be down well before the Antonov completed its ‘emergency’ landing at Faro.

The nine black wings started to circle, losing height and bleeding off ground speed, the programmed descent keeping Ramazanov at the head of the rank. Positioning was controlled by individual GPS and computer. They could see the floodlit Saluscent compound clear below them as they neared the final glide path. Ramazanov saw confirmation on screen as the short range jammer went active. Down below, Saluscent’s patrol drone went into automatic return-to-home mode.

*

Major Drozhdov and his team were in a campervan parked up a few hundred meters down the road from the Saluscent gate. They could not see the black clad Spetsnaz now just less than a thousand feet away, black in the sky like vultures circling as they descended on their prey in the warm darkness. Dropping in the invisibility cone above the 48” rotating radar antenna on the top of the flat Saluscent roof, they were as stealthy as Russian high technology and Spetsnaz skills could deliver.

The data stream from the Antonov lined up the Spetsnaz team for their final approach – and the moment when they would pass through the useless radar beam, each man fighting the urge to override the automated control system in the gusts of wind. The radar would present no problem as the radar's signal processors were unable to filter out the jamming signals from the Antonov. The team were coming in 2 seconds apart, with about 50 meters of roof on which to land into the wind. The control system required almost inch perfect accuracy.

"Faro Control, Airbridge three one seven. Request one more circuit for systems re-check before landing."

"Airbridge three one seven, cleared for one more circuit."

In the rear of the Antonov, the loadmaster had raised the ramp and watched the datascreen as the controllers strapped in the console chairs monitored the glide paths of the Vulture team.

They waited – the next twenty seconds were critical as the wind over the landing zone was unpredictable. Could the automatic chute control systems respond quickly enough? Surprise would be vital for the Vultures, crash landings could be fatal.

Drozhdov heard a breathless Major Ramazonov in his earbud. "Vulture one safely down."

He looked at his watch and nodded to Sokolov and the others inside the camper van.

"Check your weapons."

"Checked, Sir."

"Right, let's go."

They checked their backpacks and helmets, switching on their headcams. Their packs included toolsets, high speed terabit hard drives, assorted cables, adapters, a compact satellite uplink set and other devices. This kind of mission was unusual for the deskbound Russian military cyber experts, so the mission prep had involved several intense days of improving their fitness, refreshing their weapons skills and tactical awareness – and a lot of work on interface cables, hard drives and ripping software. However, the driver was regular spetsnaz - as was the other man in the front passenger seat and the two in the rear. 24 hours ago they had been tourists from Romania.

*

Twenty Eight

The shift change had just been completed. Rodriguez was on gate duty along with de Clerc, a squat, pug nosed South African, one of the new additions to the team. Stone was in the control room having just completed the handover from Baldwin. There were two teams of two on ground patrol and a roving perimeter patrol outside the compound fence. Additionally, two of the team were on internal patrol. The off-shift teams were in the process of bunking down in the six rented motor homes which Borthwick had arranged – and which unknown to him, had been registered on the latest Russian satellite passes over the previous two days.

Up on the roof, less than a hundred feet from Stone in the control room below, Ramazanov swore as he watched the last of his team come in to land on the roof. There was some illumination in the backscatter from the floodlights. Then the wind gusted slightly and the spetsnaz trooper hit the edge of the roof with a thud and was dragged before the nylon wing could be killed. Ramazanov could barely make out the shape of the mast which carried the radar antenna but he could see that it was now wrapped in a black shroud of ram-air parachute nylon twisting as the antenna revolved. It took only seconds more and then finally stalled the radar unit's drive motor with a tortured metallic groan.

*

Stone was seated at the control console when the master screen popped up a warning message. She was relaxed and still thought that Baldwin was being paranoid. Then the console flashed a warning.

'Warning – Patrol Drone guidance failure RTH'.

That was quickly followed by

'Warning – Radar Data Feed Failure'.

Two systems failures at the same time. *That's no fucking coincidence.*

She keyed the radio alarm button and counted to five.

Baldwin heard the radio warning through his earbud as he was finishing his mug of tea.

"Baldwin here, what's up?"

"Radar down and drone failure. Not sure if it's coincidence."

"That's no fucking coincidence. Go Red One NOW. I'm on my way."

At Red Two the off-team were on already on 5 minute readiness at night and within ten seconds Baldwin had put out the lights on the Hymer camper van at the rear of the office and pulled on his Type-3 vest with its ceramic chicken plate over the heart. He checked his weapon and eased himself out through the door as he listened to Stone's brief update on the open channel. His eyes were still adjusting to the dark as he molded himself to the ground, remembering something from his training way back, something Chinese about 'flowing like water'.

The plan provided for three muster points around the building perimeter. It would be at least a couple of minutes before the rest of the off-shift was in gear – hopefully they would not all be asleep yet, he prayed.

What was the threat?

*

Ramazanov spoke through his throat mike. "You know what to do. Go!" Four of the team raced for the rooftop access door. The other three ran to the edge of the roof and started uncoiling ropes, looping them round the aircon units. They were over the edge in seconds.

The Major watched as the injured trooper stabbed a syringe of morphine into the thigh muscle of his broken leg and nodded.

"We'll be back, Gennady. You can help with the extraction and give us cover if we need it."

The trooper nodded grimly and turned his head, avoiding Ramazanov's eyes. It was a bad break, he knew – and he knew what the standing orders were for such an event on such a mission. He didn't believe Ramazanov and he didn't feel the silenced bullet from the Grach 443 pistol enter the back of his neck. There was a shout and Ramazanov turned and ran for cover as the rooftop door blew.

*

Stone hit the silent alarm button on the radio unit. “Going to level Red One, all units acknowledge.” It seemed extreme, but that’s was the protocol they had established. Still, there was that downed Russian drone.

“Control, Fox One, let me in through the back door now.”

The door opened and Baldwin slipped in locking it behind him and running for the control room.

Rodriguez shut off the guardhouse lights as de Clerc gathered the weapons and night vision googles, handing one set to Rodriguez.

They ran low out of the guardhouse and over the steel grid. “Inside inner perimeter” Rodriguez whispered into his mike. There was a clang as the steel grid dropped into the trench behind them.

“Control here. Gate defenses activated, Raising fence and retracting drawbridge now. Underground levels access locked down, elevators disabled. Lights out. Dogs loose.” The eight Doberman Pinschers ran out of their opened kennel in response to the silent whistle as Rodriguez and de Clerc ran towards their muster point in the entrance vestibule. The dogs now had total access to the open ground of the compound.

De Clerc turned to Rodriguez, whispering in his guttural Africaans accent “I hope those fecking dogs recognize our SnIFF scent.”

“It won’t matter once we’re inside. Keep moving.” Just then a dark shape hurtled out of the night at Rodriguez and swerved silently past him at the last moment.

“You see, it works. They get a refresher of our friendly scent every day.”

“Groete aan God!” De Clerc slipped his combat knife back into its sheath.

“Nothing on camera feeds” Stone said to the team. “Acknowledge”.

Eighteen lights illuminated on her control screen as the coded signals came back – all the team were active and inside the boundary of the moat - she could see their RFID markers at the muster points on her screen map. Except for the Rover team - they were still outside the compound, a couple of hundred meters away on the public road, still at the eastern corner of the compound, on the flank as planned. She checked that the electrified razor wire fence was locked in position at the outer edge of the empty moat. Her IR cameras showed the dogs running free. Satisfied, she keyed the mike. “Full lockdown.”

Baldwin's voice came in over the radio. "Fox One to Control. What's happening?"

"No other alarms. I don't know what we're up against – if anything. No, wait. The outer roof access door tamper alarm has just activated."

He swore. "Shit! The roof. Fox Team three covers the roof access stairwell." He cursed again, remembering his words to Borthwick. The new inner steel door had only just been installed.

"Control, Fox One. What's the latest?"

They felt a sharp tremor and heard a muffled thump.

"Sounds like they've blown the first door."

"Fox Two, Control, status?"

"I'm covering the bottom door, sounds like they're working on it from the other side."

"Badger one, Control. Status?"

"Nothing here to report."

"Badger one, Fox One. Stay sharp."

"Hang on, they're coming over the edge of the roof. At least three of them."

"All teams, Fox One. Lethal fire authorized."

He heard a burst of machine gun fire, couldn't recognize the weapon, but the sound was smooth as a sewing machine, suppressed but amplified through the site's sound monitors and fed to his earbud.

"Control, call the police, tell them we're being attacked by terrorists." *That's a start, but fuck all use.* He heard another burst of gunfire and knew it now for the MP5s they'd brought in from the warehouse the day before. Barely unpacked, certainly not tested. No suppressors. *Dick and his fucking budget.*

He recognized the next bursts as suppressed Uzis and then heard the crump of a grenade or maybe a door being blown.

He swore - this was way beyond what they had signed up for.

"Control, Fox One. I'm going to help Fox Two and Three at the stairs."

"What about the cybersecurity guys downstairs – and Sveta?"

"We're not allowed down there, remember. Anyway the elevators are locked off. Shit shit shit."

"There's another option Steve." She reached for masks on the wall.

"Yes! All teams, Fox One, prepare for gas. Acknowledge." *I can't fucking believe this.*

There were now multiple faint bursts of firing both inside and outside the building as he slipped the mask on. It sounded as if the attackers weapons were suppressed. Too long, it was all taking too long. The acknowledgments came in and Stone ticked them off. “No response from Fox Two and Three.” She looked at him and he nodded. She lifted the flap and hit the gas switch on the wall.

The aircon units howled as the extractor fans spun up to three times normal speed pumping the air out and sucking in 100% carbon dioxide from the tanks. Non-toxic, used in the fire extinguisher system, but suffocating when oxygen was not present in sufficient quantities. The team’s special masks carried five minutes supply of compressed air. The were thousands of liters of CO2 in the tanks, but did the oppos have masks? Maybe Kovacs had got some things right.

*

Major Ramazanov had reached the edge of the roof just as Stone switched off the compound floodlights. His night vision goggles adjusted automatically to boost the images as he scanned the front of the compound and saw Rodriguez and de Clerc run into the building beneath him, too quickly for him to snap off a shot. Then he saw the hot shapes of the dogs running free and cursed. “*Sooskin* - Dogs in compound - son of a bitch” he advised his squad. “Lots of them.”

Just as Drozhdov’s driver started the camper van rolling they heard the warning about dogs come over the radio. Drozdov cursed. “The briefing said that there were no dogs!”

“*Der’mo byvayet*” said the lead trooper in the front passenger seat. “Shit happens, we deal with it. Fasten your seat belts.” His foot was flat to the floor. They’d expected to get a manual shift camper, but none had been available, and the automatic transmission was sluggish picking up.

*

Baldwin sprinted from the control room towards the roof access stairway and as he turned a corner he heard stuttering burst of fire – and then the bursts stopped.

There was a pile of bodies ahead of him. One of them raised his weapon and let rip but the aim was wild and went high as Steve fired two shots with his Browning Hi-Power. The loud report was in sharp contrast to the suppressed machine pistol. He checked the bodies and found Fox Two and Fox Three. Davis and Lipsky, dead. He quickly checked the four other bodies. They wore black combat gear like his but with obvious differences in weapons and body armor. Mostly head shots and thigh or groin shots. Three were dead, the fourth was unconscious. Without thought he crouched down and shot him in the head.

Bump, bump, bump.

He saw the grenade drop off the last step on to the floor, two meters away from him. These guys obviously didn't care about friendly fire.

With a surge of adrenaline he twisted the twitching body in front of him. A split second is all it took as the grenade's shrapnel shredded the dead trooper and spanged off the steel door. Another Spetsnaz trooper came down the stairs firing, but Baldwin had rolled to the side and swung his legs forward, taking the Russian sergeant's legs from under him. Baldwin's roll continued and he got a shot into the Russian's left side. The Hi-Power was the .40 caliber version and enough to knock over a trooper in body armor. But this shot had been lucky and gone through the bicep and into the unprotected area under the armpit. The bullet took pieces of rib into the Russian's heart. He sighed and died.

The new steel door to the stairway was twisted and hanging off one hinge after the explosive charge had blown it open. Baldwin stood up to the side of the stairwell behind what remained of the door and fired three round the corner and up the stairs. There was no return fire.

He could still hear sporadic firing from outside the building and ran back towards the control room, slipping a fresh magazine into his pistol.

*

Ramazanov checked the time in his helmet HUD - time was running out fast and this was going wrong very quickly. The plan allowed 20 minutes at most to get to the data – whatever it was and destroy the underground installation. He keyed his beacon with the egress code. The recovery chopper would be with them in 15 minutes.

Suddenly, the roof aircon units started to whine then he heard firing in the stairwell followed by a grenade explosion. Then there was more firing from the guys who had abseiled to the ground outside the office block and were trying to deal with dogs. The Dobermans were buying time for Baldwin's teams to regroup.

Tapping his throat mike he heard four clicks in response. Heavy resistance. And dogs. Time lost, and the advantage of surprise was slipping away fast.

He ran towards the blown roof door just as three shots sounded. He paused and peered down. There was the smell of cordite and blood. He stepped cautiously down the stairs. By the time he had reached the lower blown door his chest began to feel tight and he could see a fire alarm light flashing. His breathing became more labored and he looked around. Not teargas – he was used to direct exposure and had trained with it, knew it, knew the taste. His legs gave way as he turned back towards the bottom of the stairs.

"Control, Rover One, we see a campervan moving quickly along the road."

"Fox One here. Rover team - what's your status?"

"We're spread in the brush cover across the road from the gate, about twenty five meters apart."

"OK, let's wait until they're at the gate. They may not be hostiles and drive past. If they turn for the gate then the moat will stop them and you will be in their rear."

"I hope this fucking radio is encrypted!"

Baldwin wondered about that too. Borthwick might have tried to shaft the client on the equipment. After all, it was a low-risk deployment wasn't it?

"JC, you stay here for one minute if your oxygen lasts. Count it down then re-set the drawbridge, we'll need to cross it. We're relying on you."

Then the firing outside started again and Baldwin headed for the front door to support the rest of his team.

*

Twenty Nine

The *Admiral Makarov* had cleared the harbor at Sevastopol in the Crimea on the Thursday morning and set course southwest at full speed, about 30 knots. That evening and 250 miles later, with special permission from the Turkish government the Russian frigate worked her way through the fifteen miles of the busy Bosphorus which splits Istanbul and separates Europe from the near-East. She crossed the Sea of Marmara and ploughed onward through the Dardanelles, entering the Aegean Sea just after dawn the next morning, with almost 2,000 miles to travel to her objective. She was the third in the Admiral Grigorovich class, less than five years old and one of Russia's most effective fighting ships.

Overhead, she was being tracked by US AWACS planes operating with the US Sixth Fleet in the Eastern Mediterranean and her voyage and speed had raised a few eyebrows at the Sixth Fleet headquarters at Capodichino in Naples. They were not aware of any planned exercises and there was no accompanying flotilla. And she was in a hurry. The decision was taken that she would not be assigned a specific tracking aircraft and that monitoring would rely solely on the Naval NOSS satellite constellation.

Sixty hours later the frigate cleared the Straits of Gibraltar and emerged into international waters, with Cape Trafalgar to the north in the early evening when the Airbridge Antonov with its Spetsnaz team was still en route to the Algarve. The ship's course was now set 290 degrees, directly for the traffic separation scheme which controlled shipping rounding Cape St Vincent at the south-western tip of Portugal. She maintained her speed at 30 knots. The Cape was 160 miles away and a major turning point for shipping traveling between the Mediterranean and northwest Europe – and for Russian warships transiting between the Murmansk, the Baltic ports and the Black Sea.

On the aft deck, the shuttered hangar doors rolled up and the Kamov Ka-27 transport helicopter (NATO code name Helix) was maneuvered out and strapped down securely before the service crew carried out their pre-flight checks. Ugly and compact, this civilian version of the heli had been loaded on at Sevastopol specifically for this mission, replacing the standard anti-submarine Ka-27pl variant that the ship usually carried. The twin co-axial rotor design of the Kamov Ka helos eliminated the need for a tail rotor structure, reducing weight and landing area size – and that would be critical for this mission. Whilst deniability was important if things went wrong, so was the importance of recovery if things went well. That is why a stealth pack had been hooked into the avionics.

By midnight the Admiral Makarov was more than half way to Cape St Vincent, just as the Airbridge Antonov AN-2 was requesting an emergency landing at Faro airport.

The recovery beacon signal came in just before 01:00 hours. The flight crew wound up the turbojets and the heli lifted off in full stealth mode, setting course due north for the flight of 30 miles into Portuguese territory.

*

The Rover team could see the firefight in the compound close to the office block and watched as the camper van accelerated along the road. Stingers and steel posts had elevated out of the ground in the approach to the gate. But then there was a series of explosions and three fence posts collapsed. The camper van went through the weakened fence at more than 40 miles an hour, the electric fence arcing and shorting out. Momentum carrying it another 20 yards with the remains of the fence hanging trailing from the front. The front and side doors opened and black clad shapes dived out, rolling and firing.

"Fox One, Rover One, fence breached, somebody must have prepared the fucking way in. Engaging now. "

After less than a minute's exchange of fire there was silence at the camper van and then two of the left flank Rover team made their way across, with covering fire from their right flank. Firing erupted again and the Rover team was down to two men.

"Rover One, Fox One. Status."
" We need support, Boss, two down."
"Fox One, Badger One. I'm on my own. Need support.
"Weasel One, Fox One. Status."
"Weasel One, Fox One, do you read?"
"Weasel Come in." No response.
"Any Weasels, come in." Silence.
"All squads, Evac plan A. Now.
Stone hit the drawbridge button.
"Rover team, we're on our way out. Don't shoot us."

*

"*Grebanyy ad*! Where the fuck are our team? They are supposed to cover our entry!"

"I guess they didn't get here yet, Major. We'll cover you, head for the offices." The two Spetsnaz troopers alternately reloaded and laid down heavy fire to cover the cyber team as they ran up the road towards the office block – and the moat. They arrived at the moat as the drawbridge locked into position.

"A trap?"

"I don't think so. Get across."

At the offices the firing had stopped. They headed for the entrance. And met Baldwin.

"Control, Rover Two. I'm on my own and need ammo. Two hostiles still engaging me, and at least two headed for the offices. Got to go."

Stone's count got to 60 seconds and she flipped a switch on the control panel re-setting the drawbridge. She silenced the banshee fire alarm. For a moment there was silence. Then there was a distinctive thwumping sound from the south.

Sprinting out from the office she saw de Clerc and Rodriguez, both dead. Baldwin was crouched behind a pillar and taking fire from the right flank. She picked up de Clerc's weapon, checked it, then found another magazine on his body and slammed it in, easing her way forward to Baldwin's side. The fire from the right flank was now high so that the other two Russians could complete their approach, firing as they ran, having crossed the drawbridge.

Baldwin got off two shots as he pushed Stone to the ground. She rolled and came up firing with de Clerc's weapon. They were hampered by lack of night vision goggles and her shots were off target but then there were screams as they heard growling and more shouting ahead, then more shots and screams. Then silence again.

Then thwumping, louder.

"That chopper's coming in from the sea I think, it's very close now. Come on, let's move. We need to get across the moat."

"Steve, look."

Behind them flames were licking up through the windows of the office block.

"Well at least the fire extinguishers are on. Move. We need to stay away from the drawbridge – we don't know what's down there."

The bullet missed Stone and took a chip out of the concrete pillar. Baldwin turned to the sound. Ramazanov was crawling towards them from inside the building. His gun clicked on empty. Baldwin's short burst punched through the Major's composite helmet.

Just inside the fence the spetsnaz troopers turned and zig-zagged quickly across the compound from the camper van, confident that they had cleared the opposition outside the gate. One of them, the landing master, ran into the center of the grassy area and checked around with a laser ranger. Clear to at least 25 meters perimeter, no obstructions above ground. He pulled the tab on the infrared flare and placed it on the grass.

"Vulture command, we have no comms here at all. No response from any of our team."

But Vulture mission command already knew it was a bust. They knew from the vitals of each of the team and the IR headcams, from the data transmitted to the mission control room in the bowels of the frigate *Admiral Makarov* thirty miles offshore. Abort meant abort. The recovery chopper would be destroyed at sea, before it reached the *Makarov*. But first the two remaining troopers had to be recovered.

*

Thirty

Sveta heard the klaxon and saw the red light flashing. She looked over at the Site Status screen and saw the Drone and Radar error messages and below that the words CODE RED ONE flashing. Warning messages continued to scroll down,

She cursed and turned to hit the master systems switch for the software development systems. Everything on those systems had been encrypted and backed up on to the cloud, her own personal cloud. She started the erase procedure for her local software development environments.

The server farm was still operational and she saw the Salus System Status Screen showed 100% activity from the BASIC arrays. A counter showed the number of CryptoRubles transferred from their owners into a range of over a thousand accounts she held across the top 50 cryptocurrencies. The numbers were increasing steadily as she watched. And then as the numbers reached the $9 million trigger on each account they steadied as another software component kicked in and started to transfer those funds into a further set of cryptocurrency addresses – all of which were validated and quickly confirmed on the fly thanks to the piece of software Dmitri had pirated from a London client. It was called Troy and optimized performance using an AI plugin conveniently available from that same client – and further optimized by Sveta. She watched the operation in progress.

She and Dmitri had even pirated the client's system and bandwidth and it was performing admirably. As fast as the crypto was coming in from the target accounts, it was going out, cascading exponentially through multiple sets of accounts. The crypto networks were being flooded with new blockchains for consensus verification. It was a combination of DDoS – distributed denial of service – and a supply chain attack via the distributed blocks. Only a specific set of servers were able to validate transactions and, with the help of Troy, those servers in Morocco were working flat-out.

Sveta smiled at the thought actually earning currency for validating her own theft transactions. The cascade was huge. There were upwards of 100,000 recipient accounts which her software bots had opened and controlled – and she owned. Even if the tracking companies could follow her footsteps it would take years to unravel. And it would be years too late.

There were backups elsewhere for everything - even the mining servers. But not for the BASICs. They were unique. She checked the screen again. Yes, the numbers at the first level of her recipient accounts were heading down towards zero. The lower levels of the cascade would continue for a few hours yet. More than 25% of the funds were being converted from cryptocurrency into US Dollars, Swiss Francs, Euros and Sterling and then being transferred into a range of accounts in the Cayman Islands, Jersey, Lichenstein and Switzerland. The funds were being routed through Bitcoin mixers which Sveta and Dmitri had built some years before when engaged on their Dark Web credit card scams. These mixers made tracking of the bitcoin transactions even more complex by 'fogging' the blockchain. *Thanks Dmitri, thanks Livengood, but I was the one who hacked the IBAN banking protocols. Such a plan, it will be talked about for years. Suck that, Ignatova.*

Another screen showed the times in the key trading cities of the world. NYSE had just closed and would be shut for Independence Day, although after-market trading was still under way.

Just then she felt a shudder and heard a dull thump.

The Site Sensors Status screen message said 'Shock Detected, 0.5 Richter'.

She spun the locking wheel on the elevator access door, then started securing the systems below ground. The first stages of siphoning of the cryptocurrencies were almost complete and the BASICs had almost finished their job. They were unique, but their task was over. The rest of the work would be handled elsewhere.

She gathered her pistol and personal items into a sports bag. At her console she saw a string of messages on the control room log. Then she saw

'*CO2 gas flood enabled*'

That indicated major problems above ground, but she'd guessed that anyway. No fire warning, no problem. The subterranean levels used a separate set of air conditioners and coolers for the hundreds of kilowatts of heat that were put out by the server farm. 'Better by design' - wasn't that some company's advertising strapline she wondered? She was safe. For now.

'*Satellite uplink failure*'

Close, but not close enough. It had to be the Russians. But how? Sergei? She wondered for seconds then shook her head - it was time to go, She wiped clean the whiteboard, realizing that some clever CSI types could probably recover some of her recent scribblings, but surely not from incineration – it would be too little too late. Sergei's body was in a cupboard, and in a few hours it would be transformed.

Sveta didn't think about saying her goodbyes to the cybersecurity guys in the suite next door. They wouldn't be gassed anyway. But they did know about the QKD - if only at this end. She shrugged and ran for the tunnel, clamping closed the tunnel entrance door behind her.

*

In the cockpit of the Kamov Ka-27, the pilot could see the image of the infrared flare quite clearly on his display. There was no sign of any gunfire and the landing area was clearly lit by the burning offices. He could see two human shapes at the landing perimeter, waiting. Mission command had told him to retrieve the two survivors, but he was nervous because this was a civilian Kamov Ka, and therefore unarmored. The light from the wildly burning building was being suppressed by the night vision system, and he could just make out a trench-like shape just crossing the edge of the landing area. It did not have the thermal signature of the approach driveway which he could see clearly. He would have to be well clear of that, whatever it was. Yes, the thermal signature suggested water. A river? And there were the dogs – their thermal signatures were clear and moving. There were other immobile thermal images scattered around. Not quite hot enough to be alive and human.

Baldwin could see the Kamov Ka staring to descend. He turned to Stone.

"Put a fresh mag in. Now."

She clipped in the last magazine from de Clerc's vest.

"Now give it to me. We've got one chance. I want you to sprint for the moat as those two guys board the chopper. As fast as you can – and get down in the water."

The Kamov Ka was by now 20 meters off the ground and flaring as it slowed to a hover.

"No. I'll hang on to my weapon. I'm sticking with *you*."

Baldwin could see that it was pointless, there was not time for argument.

"Right, we run now, at that chopper and empty our weapons as we reach the moat. I don't think it's a military version. Aim for the hull, the main body, and then jump into the moat and stay down as long as you can. Go Go Go."

She nodded and they upped and sprinted together, straight towards the moat, straight towards the helicopter. Baldwin used his teeth to pull the pin out of a Chinese grenade as they ran, wondering about its fuse time and Borthwick's budget focus. The remaining two spetsnaz troopers were on the same side of the moat as Baldwin and Stone, but intent on watching the Kamov Ka land. Then one of the Spetsnaz noticed them. He shouted at his companion as he brought his weapon to bear.

It took only seconds. The trooper's aim was good, but Baldwin stumbled and the grenade dropped out of his hand and rolled forward across the grass, slowing almost to a stop as it reached the moat, just two paces ahead of him.

The loadmaster on the Kamov Ka was waving frantically as the chopper hovered over the edge of the moat. The troopers ran for it and jumped for the chopper's lowered netting just as Baldwin's count got to four seconds. The grenade toppled into the water of the moat and a gout of water erupted immediately. The loadmaster fired a burst as Stone let loose with her MP5, but her run stopped almost completely and she staggered, then fell into the moat. Baldwin had recovered himself and opened up with his Hi-Power.

The range was a little over 30 meters and the noise of the turbines was deafening as his weapon finally clicked on empty and he jumped for the moat. The wounded loadmaster fell out of the open doorway and dangled by his safety line as the chopper's engines screamed up to full power and the pilot hauled on the collective to climb. The spetsnaz troopers ignored the dangling loadmaster and laid down fire towards Baldwin. Too late. He was underwater, frantically searching for Stone.

Then three dark shapes hurtled out of nowhere and set about the troopers, snarling and tearing at them as the Kamov Ka lifted away.

The 40 caliber Hi-Power packed a heavy punch.

A civilian helo.

One bullet.

That's all it had taken, Baldwin's last bullet drilling through the alloy skin in just the right place, the distorted slug of lead still carrying enough momentum to sever the electrical control harness of the helicopter's cyclic and collective fly-by-wire circuits which controlled the rotors' pitch and angle. The cabling would normally run in armored casing in a military helo, but this was the civilian version. Tough for some, lucky for others.

The pilot was frantically pulling on the collective and preparing for an auto-rotate – freewheel – to the ground. But he knew that the chopper didn't yet have enough height and time to build the aerodynamic lift – and its flight attitude was nose down, literally out of control. It veered towards the edge of the moat.

Baldwin and Stone didn't see the Kamov Ka spiral like a drunken ballerina and then pitch into the ground to the side of the moat. But they felt the explosion and saw the flash through the water.

Across the road, Rover Two groaned. "Result" was the last word he uttered as the sirens of the emergency services grew ever louder. But it was too late – he bled out as two dark wet figures ran past the wrecked camper van and crossed the road into the brush.

*

Thirty One

The short run through the tunnel had made her breathless and she still could not believe that the site was under attack. She passed under the modest villa which she lived in when on site, then continued through the tunnel under the boundary of the Saluscent compound. Less than 20 meters further on she emerged into the wine cellar under the villa which fronted the main road past the compound.

'Alice' was leaving the rabbit warren.

Surrounded by empty wine racks, Sveta opened the cupboard in the wine cellar. She removed the back panel to expose the safe mounted in the recess which had been cut into the rock, and then dialed in the combination using the old fashioned twist knob. Although the odds of this safe being discovered were very long, she didn't trust electronic combination locks. She opened the door to reveal another much smaller safe, welded in. Then she took the gold chain from around her neck and used the key it held to unlock the door to the inner safe.

She reached in and pulled out another Beretta Compact 92 and a box of ammunition and laid them on the table next to the cupboard. They were followed by ten bundles of US $100 bills which she placed in her backpack, along with a purse containing a set of personal documentation including passports, drivers' licenses and credit cards. Finally she added one of the two new unused Honor smartphones. She was almost ready to go. All that remained in the safe was that most precious of items – the keys to her fortunes – five little metallic boxes.

She smiled. Those fools were working hard to protect the software and secure comms link in the Saluscent offices, but that was all a blind. Everyone – including those stupid Russians – thought that the value was in the contents of the building – whether software, gold or whatever they could imagine. The fact that it was highly secure and heavily guarded meant that it must contain something of huge value, mustn't it?

No way.

The value they sought was in those five small metal boxes in the safe in front of her, here in the second villa. Credit card sized, each of the four Cryptosteel 'Mix' hard wallets held two seed phrases for her main currency accounts. Eight accounts in total, adding up to over $4.5 billion when she had last looked at the screen before leaving her subterranean workroom. And even those accounts were peanuts compared to what was now being transferred into her tax haven accounts.

There would be a lot of angry people out there in the currency world – angrier and poorer after her efforts. The online forums would be buzzing with the scandal and the multicurrency cryptoheist would make headlines on the main news channels. That was all about what she held in four of the Cryptosteel wallets. But most of all, the anger would be in Moscow.

Sveta now held a large portion of the world stock of CryptoRubles in an account accessible only by the seed phrase held in the fifth Cryptosteel wallet. Or had held, to be more accurate. She opened it and emptied the contents, the ninety six stainless steel letters falling in a sparkling chain to the floor.

The contents of the other four boxes followed on to the floor. The accounts would be empty within a couple of hours, the currency moved to other accounts and the transactions on the blockchain verified in record time by her software.

She was leaving – and taking her secret with her.

Sveta Kovacs climbed up the steps from the wine cellar and moved into the garage. She left the villa in the plain white Seat Leon and headed east, towards Spain. She could pass through any security check in the world carrying the equivalent of US$110 billion and no one would detect it.

Five lines from Shakespeare was all it took, five lines from five plays – with some rearrangement. Easy enough to remember, but almost impossible to be broken by computer. Her seed phrases gave her access to her crypto accounts. They were as secure as she and her memory were. In most countries of the world – at least those which she was interested in enjoying - she could buy a smartphone anywhere, connect to the internet anywhere, access her money anywhere. With access to a range of established online identities. She relished the challenge ahead.

Later that day she left the rental car at the Europcar compound in Seville Airport. As she boarded the flight using a new passport, she reflected that it might have been wiser to have blocked off the tunnels and hidden the traces of her escape. No matter, she realized that she thrived on the idea that she had left a trail, however thin, to taunt the Russians who would surely be hunting her. It was exciting, and the excitement stimulated her intellectually and physically. She was on a real 'high' as she settled into her seat.

*

Thompson took the call from Aaron Robinson, Head of Software Development.

"Hi Richard. I've been trying to get hold of the guys in Kiev but they seem to be offline and have been since after midnight. Their Slack service is down and I can't get through on the mobile phone either."

"Have you tried the landline?"

"We haven't got any of those any more here at the Triangle. Old tech, remember?"

Thompson grimaced. "Of course. I need to know how the latest code problem might impact the go live date for our beta users. We're already two weeks late. The release is very public and I need to manage the news. We don't want more egg on our faces. Keep this tight, Aaron."

"Only the Test Manager and myself know about the problem. Sharon knows the score, she knows which side her bread is buttered, she'll keep it tight, don't worry. And the error logs are clean, as I said."

Bread, butter? Keep it tight? Thompson almost laughed. *Aaron's shagging her. Not a good situation, but hard to prevent in teams under pressure.*

"OK Richard, but you know what they say – if it passes all the tests, then it's fit for purpose."

"But if our test set is incomplete?"

"Well, I agree it's not a pass if you see the size of the binary as a test in itself. Maybe it's nothing. I'll double check all the integration test logs."

"One more thing - is the source code from Kiev up to date?"

"Hang on, I'll check. Sometimes they just send us the compiled binaries for us to link and test – they may be one or two increments behind with the source. Depends how pressed we are to meet a test milestone. It's been pretty hectic lately."

"You're supposed to download the code from the shared repository then compile and link it in Reading."

"Yes, well not sure if we did this time."

"Then you'd better be fucking sure. Check, now, then call me back."

Thompson stood up and paced around the room. There were clear procedures to be followed.

Ten minutes later his laptop chimed.

"We're good, Richard, all as it should be. We have the code, it was properly compiled and linked here."

Thompson closed the meeting and cursed. He had spent many months researching the companies he had engaged to build the software components and now used eight companies in a range of countries all around the world with the exceptions of Russia and China. The company he used in the Ukraine was one of the foremost in the field of cryptocurrency. They were not cheap.

Its owner, Dmitri Borzov, held a Ph.D. in cryptography and had built a successful business in the sector, boasting development of at least fifty of the upwards of 6000 cryptocurrencies in use in the world in 2019. They had met several times, both in London and in Kiev when Thompson was doing due diligence – and on one memorable occasion in Frankfurt when the development deal was signed. He tried the phone number again, and checked Slack, without success. Then he tried the private cellphone number he'd been given almost a year before. "If all else fails, Richard, you'll get me on this special number, day or night. Remember - it's only for emergencies - the only other person who has it is my wife."

'I bet you tell that to all your clients, just like I do' Thompson had thought at the time, but he'd never had cause to use it.

The number went straight to voicemail.

Thompson sighed. It didn't feel right, but these snags did occasionally occur. As Aaron had pointed out, if it passed *all* the tests then it was fit for purpose.

He called Dmitri's number again.

Voicemail.

He turned to his laptop and sent a critical priority message to Dmitri over the Slack system. 'MOST URGENT Call me as soon as you get this.'

He sent a similar text over the cellphone to the 'special' number. *Special number my arse. It might not be important but I pay this bugger to be available.*

It was so close to the release date now and his stress level was increasing by the hour – and with each snag. And now this. He raged.

Ching! His laptop chimed and he looked at the Slack screen – a message from Myroslava Evaschuk, Dmitri's Head of Development.

'Can you talk now?'

He clicked on the video call and her face came into view. She was sobbing, her makeup was streaked and she was red eyed, but he hardly noticed – he was almost seeing red mist himself.

"Where's Dmitri? I can't reach him. He's not returning calls. It's not good enough. I pay you people a lot of money. You should be available."

"Er…good morning Mr. Thompson. Sorry. Police here. No contact allowed until now. Er…I have ver bad news. Dmitri dead, he killed last night." She broke into another burst of sobbing.

"Good God Myra. Dead? I can't believe it."

"DA, Dmitri uh uh uh he dead."

"Jesus, that's a shock. Hell. I need to think. U hmm… so who's managing the business now? Who do I talk to about software problems? We haven't been able to contact you. We're getting close to the Troy release date here."

"Not sure who in charge today. I run software. Maybe General Manager, Kuzma Zelensky. I try to find out." By now she was crying continuously and even Thompson was starting to blub as he watched.

"OK, I've met Kuzma a couple of times. Can you bring him in to this call?"

"Kuzma on holiday. I think visit family in Donetsk."

"Jesus Christ Myra. What a bloody mess. Does he know about Dmitri?"

"Cannot contact him. Cellphone problem."

Thompson cursed under his breath, raging at Myra would achieve nothing.

"Have the police arrested anyone?"

"Not yet, they interview us now. Formality they say."

"What happened?"

"Not sure, Kiev TV news channels says robbed outside apartment. Police not tell us anything, only that Dmitri dead. Dead, Dmitri I no believe it."

"OK, until I hear otherwise – hopefully from Kuzma within a couple of hours - I'm holding you responsible for your company's work for us.

"I can help with software, nothing else. Maybe I go home."

"Can you give me Kuzma's cellphone number."

"You do not have? If not I cannot do. Not allowed. Company policy – he have to give you mobile number himself. I text him and tell him to phone you."

"You'd better make it quick or I'll cancel the contract."

"I can help with software, not contract. Is there a problem at the moment?"

"Yes, a very big problem. You need to speak to Aaron. Now!"

"Yes I will do that now. Then I go home."

"Make bloody well sure you do speak to Aaron now!"

"Sure. I speak him now. Then I go home."

"And I want Kuzma's cellphone number. Straight away!"

He cut the call and headed to his office. It wasn't midday yet and his digestion had barely recovered from his lunch with Tobin two days before. He pulled the bottle out of his desk drawer and poured a shot of Glenlivet into a mug of cold coffee. Then he gave Aaron the news about Dmitri.

Half an hour later Aaron came back on line.

"I've spoken to Myra. Boy, she was in a state, but I think I got sense out of her. It's falling apart over there. Anyway, everything seems to be OK with the Troy software. However, it seems that they cannot process some work because only Dmitri has – er… had – the password to a system source file. It was work he'd done himself."

"But we have the source anyway."

"Not entirely. The code to those routines appears to be scrambled. It got past our code inspection."

"Fucking hell!"

"Er…yes. Sharon says that…"

"Fuck what Sharon says, this is down to you Aaron, one way or another. How the hell can we build the binaries if the code is scrambled?"

"Looks like there's a special compiler directive in there. We don't know how it works – and neither does Myra. She thinks it needs a password from Dmitri to be included in the source code. One off. Each time. He puts a password in and the source compiles fine. Never the same password. We can see them, two fifty six bit. Strong."

"And what does Dmitri's password protected sourcefile do?"

"We're not sure."

"Christ Almighty Aaron, what the fuck is going on there! We're about to go live with a groundbreaking financials system and there's *secret* code in there that we don't fucking know about?"

"It looks that way. I'm going to get the guys to remove the file from the build script. We'll then rebuild the code and re-test. Maybe it will work."

"The chances against that are bloody astronomical."

"Maybe, but there's one more thing Simon has just discovered. I think he should explain it himself. I'm going to bring him in on the call if that's OK."

"Yes, bring him in. It had better be fucking good news."

'Simon Mablethorpe joining meeting now' the voice announced and Livengood's Head of Technical Infrastructure joined the meeting.

"Good morning Richard, Aaron. We've got a big issue here. I'll get right to it. There was an alert at four am this morning from our services provider Titanium – a bandwidth exception."

"But we're using hardly any. Anyway the warnings levels are set at five terabytes a week. We'll not come anywhere near that for months yet."

"We used it in just four hours last night."

"Five terabytes in four hours – that's bloody enormous. How on earth have we used that much?"

"I checked with Titanium Web Services. They've just told us they've been hacked. A supply chain hack á la SolarWinds – that massive US Government intrusion by Russia. Titanium are not saying much yet – reading between the lines other companies were hacked too. It might have been going on for months. However our logs are normal with no undue usage until early this morning. The National Cybersecurity Center at GCHQ has been notified. Titanium believes the signs are that is was not the Russian Cozy Bear hackers AST29 – an SVR group - but someone else, possibly Turla, an FSB group who it is believed assisted with Trump's election in 2016. Kaspersky were the first to float the idea."

"Kaspersky? The Russian cybersafety outfit? That's fucking rich!"

"Yes, it certainly sounds odd, but that's what they said about the SolarWinds hack."

"Have we lost anything?"

"I don't think so but it's early days in the investigation. I'm afraid it gets worse, much worse. The system logs are showing that last night there was activity in our Development and Software Release environments. And worse, in our prototype Live environment. Code from the Release Test system was migrated into the Live Environment area and opened up. As you know the Live Environment is not in use yet – it's ring-fenced until the day before Troy goes live. Or should I say it *was* ringfenced. It was opened to the world for about four hours early this morning. There are no Troy transaction logs for that period – they *might* have been created and then removed, we don't know yet. *But*, I am pretty sure the Troy system was operational in *some* fashion because there are network traffic logs which show considerable volumes of traffic, approaching several terabytes over that period and some Troy static data has been changed. But everything is secure now."

"Secure? How can you be sure? Simon, you fucking designed that infrastructure setup, how could we suffer such an intrusion? You guys are telling me that the new system worked, but we don't know who used it and for what? They've been able to go anywhere they like in our system? That's a bloody disaster. If this gets out Troy is dead in the water before we start."

"It seems that they could go anywhere in other Titanium customer systems too."

"That's no bloody comfort to me. I don't give a shit about other Titanium customers."

"It may not be so bad. We don't think they stole the code. It looks like they just wanted to use it." He paused, took a deep breath and said "I checked the access logs and there were no password changes, no new users, the only user who logged in, just before midnight, was tombo997. The user has full access privileges to the dev, test, release and live areas. So it looks like they used genuine credentials. The user is still logged in. I...I er...I believe that's one of your user names, Richard."

"Jesus Simon, tombo997 *is* one of my UIDs! How the hell could they have got hold of it? Even the correct password?"

"It looks like it yes, as I said no new passwords created on that account for over six months. They must have been phishing."

"I am *very* bloody careful about my creds. No way have I been phished. You say they wanted to just *use it!* Some bloody consolation that is! So, all transactions could be traced back to us – to me! I don't fucking believe it. That's fucking great then. So whatever happened points to us. What did they do?"

"I just don't know. There are no obvious tracks that our scans detect. Titanium have got a cyber forensics company in now. The company's called CID – Cyber Intrusion Detectives. I need you to authorize them to look at our systems. We need to know that it can't happen again."

"You're certainly bloody right about that. No-one but we three is to know about this. I want you to see that CID are nailed down tight on non-disclosure. No press stories or leaks at all. Do what needs to be done but make sure that there's no physical connection of our Development and Production systems to the outside world until I say so. Get on it now. I'm going to raise hell with Titanium." *And book a flight to Antarctica.*

"I've already locked down our dev, test, release and production environments and given the teams a story about router problems."

"Then keep it that way. Until further notice. Disconnect from Titanium."

"It's not that easy Richard. All our web connections go through them. I've isolated us as much as I can."

"Find a fucking way. You've got two hours or you can go find another bloody job!"

Thompson closed the call and looked out through his office window. He fiddled with his laptop trying to find an online news channel for Kiev, but they all wanted him to subscribe. He swore. It wasn't the money, it was the hassle and time, the fact that they'd been hacked right open, the software used, God knows what for. *Stupid question.* He checked the IT news channels and discovered that TheRegister.com website was already reporting rumors of an intrusion at Titanium Web Services.

It was now approaching lunchtime and the girls in the park were lying down with their yogurt and fruit juice, taking their tops off and catching some sun. London hummed around them, under them and over them, a money machine in top gear. Behind the scenes there was IT chaos.

He opened the bottle of whisky. *What a bloody morning!* He took a sip and then put down the glass. Un-fucking-believable. *What the…*

He hit the call button. "Aaron, Richard here. I want you to talk to Simon – no one else not even Sharon – this has to be kept tight – and discuss with him the possibility that this morning's events were linked."

"Dmitri you mean, and the intrusion?"

"No, not Dmitri's death specifically, but the fact that he might have some embedded code in Troy that we didn't know about, and that there was an intrusion via Titanium. That compiler directive is a big worry. Is there a linkage? If Dmitri hadn't been murdered we wouldn't have known about the code would we? Maybe we just got lucky. *If you can call it luck.*"

*

Thirty Two

Four hours after the downing of the helicopter Baldwin and Stone were seated in the saloon of *Rubaiyat*. The end of the bottle was in sight.

The boat was sitting quietly at anchor just inside the entrance to the Faro Channel, a few miles from Olhão. They had gone aboard her in the marina, almost dry after their hike down from the Saluscent compound. At the dock, they had cast off the lines within ten minutes and caught the last of the tide down channel as the dawn was breaking behind them.

"That was some fucking night. Evac Plan A. Great. Every man for himself. Some fucking leader I am. We didn't even know what we were protecting."

"Maybe it was a 'who'?"

"Sveta? Could be I suppose, she seemed to be the brains behind the show."

"Look Steve, we did what we could. There was no one left to save."

"Sveta? The cyber guys? We don't know for sure. There might still have been someone alive there. Fifteen good guys we know about." He swallowed the last of the whisky. "You can sleep in one of the forward cabins."

"I doubt I'll sleep – my brain is really wired. And my chest hurts."

"Doesn't seem like anything's broken anyway. You're lucky. Straight-on impact – that vest saved your life. At least Borthwick didn't skimp on the costs there."

Stone half-smiled, half-grimaced. "It's hurting like fuck but I think the pain killers are kicking in now – and the whisky helps. Do you want to check my chest again?"

Baldwin looked at her, bra-less under a T shirt, and shook his head. "If there's no sharp pain when you breathe deeply then your ribs are probably okay. That was a military load that hit you, got to have been. You were very lucky."

He'd hauled her out of the moat half-conscious and half-drowned. Then he'd half carried, half dragged her out of the compound and across the road. His father had taught him to never do things by half, but tonight had certainly been an exception.

When they had found cover in the scrub he'd pulled her vest off and lifted her T shirt. He'd had to cut off her bra to check her chest for damage. Women on the front line certainly complicated matters, he'd realized as he'd held a pocket torch in his mouth and examined the bruising. The chicken plate had done its work, spreading the impact trauma of the bullet and the bruising was light and generalized. Absentmindedly he realized that her rib cage was well protected by flesh. Then he'd left her for a few minutes to check the others of the Fox team. All were dead – they'd been up against top notch operatives. He was sure they had been Russians. By the time he'd returned from checking the others Stone was more cogent and there were no signs of shock. As the first emergency services vehicles came up the road they were tabbing away through the scrub.

By the time they had reached the town they'd cast off their obvious outer military gear, dumping it in the brush along the way. Then they just looked as if they'd been out on hard night's clubbing. Choosing the narrow dark side streets through the old part of the town they made their way to Stone's apartment for her to collect her passport and some clothes – and her laptop, she insisted. Then they'd headed for the marina.

He checked his watch in the dim light of the cabin, then rummaged in a galley locker. "Here, get this energy bar down you. There's more if you need them. Get some rest even if you can't sleep, and think about our options because we'll need to decide pretty quickly what we do next. I'm going to check the anchor."

He went up on deck as the false dawn lightened the sky. The northeast breeze had fallen away and the morning air was dry and cool. *She's a fucking tough woman.* The tide had turned and *Rubaiyat* was comfortable, the anchor secure. Above the hills behind Olhão the previous strong white glow from the emergency service floodlights was now barely invisible in the pre-dawn, but there was a steady stream of flashing red lights in evidence in the sky – choppers, he thought.

He headed back to the cockpit and lay down, his mind racing and his body aching.

Four miles away from Baldwin, as the crow flies, a computer program had switched a relay. The lower levels of the Saluscent site were by now a few inches deep with water from the fire hoses that had found its way down the elevator shafts, and the fire on the upper levels was out.

The rescue teams searching the lower levels noticed a slight garlic-like smell and put it down to a bad choice of breakfast – they'd had their food delivered to the site as the search continued.

Jorghino Salazar was seated in the Rescue Coordination Center, a trailer just outside the Saluscent site perimeter. He had only been in post a couple of months after the previous Fire Chief had retired and he was still in the process of visiting all the major industrial sites in the area, carrying out a personal check of their Fire Safety & Evacuation Procedures. Tonight had been his first visit to the Saluscent site, a week earlier than planned – and for the wrong reason.

His three search and rescue teams were spread through the lower levels when the fire brigade's portable gas monitors started wailing.

'*Gás explosivo*' flashed in red against all six gas detector IDs on the panel in front of him.

He touched his throat mike, fighting hard to stay calm.

'Todas unidades. todas unidades, este é o controlo. Código nove, código nove. Gás explosivo, evacuar imediatamente, evacuar imediatamente!'

Each of the 20 beige colored G2 cylinders was approximately 1.5 meters high and had contained 10,200 liters of acetylene gas under a pressure of about 15 atmospheres. The gas is not always stable and its combustion temperature with oxygen is 3,100 degrees C. The cylinders were stored in a temperature-controlled secure store behind the now burned-out main building. They were still cool, still viable.

The electrical relay and its control system on the lower floors had, like all the other equipment, survived the ground and upper floor fire. It did as it had been programmed to do and had opened a set of valves. Gas had flowed.

Baldwin felt the shock wave and a second or so later the rumble of the explosion. He jumped up in the cockpit and looked to the north east.

Stone ran up from her berth, shouting. "What the hell was that? A plane?"

Baldwin shook his head and pointed. "No. It looks like the Saluscent site."

They both stared at the cloud of debris, dust, body parts and 10,000 bitcoin mining machines raining down four miles away from their anchorage.

The acetylene gas that had flooded the lower levels of the Saluscent site was enough to leave a huge crater and another 33 dead when it erupted.

"Jesus!"

"You said it. Come on JC, we've got to get moving. Get ready for seat your clothes on!"

They could have left the estuary that morning and headed for Magazon, just over the Portugal/Spain border and less than forty miles away, mixed in with the outgoing trawlers, but it might have raised suspicion. The seventy or so miles across the bay to Chipiona in Spain on the Guadalquivir estuary, or further on to Rota, made more sense, getting offshore and away from the authorities. His mind drifted. Rota had bad memories for him – the US base there was where he had been exfiltrated to from Algeria by US Seals team that had burnt his dead wife's body.

There's going to be a fucking storm about this. Just wait till I get hold of Dickwick.

His phone rang down below. He ignored it but then Stone appeared at the hatchway holding it. "I thought you were asleep. Looks like it's Borthwick."

He took the phone and accepted the call.

"Baldy is that you?"

"Yes it fucking well is. You've just missed the fireworks. And this is what a phone sounds like as I throw it overboard."

"Steve, wait, we need to …"

The phone splashed into the sea about ten meters from the boat.

"Fuck you Borthwick."

Stone looked at him.

"Move it, JC! Now!"

Back in her cabin she picked up her Six phone and turned it off. She'd lost her ScutumEst phone along the way – she thought it might be in one of the pockets of her discarded flak vest, now in the scrub somewhere between the Saluscent compound and the dock at Olhão. Along with her bra. She tried to smile, but it wouldn't come.

*

"Josh, what's the latest on the situation in Olhão? I've got to brief 'C' about it over breakfast."

"OK so far, Boss."

"And we don't have any direct reports yet?"

"Only one source in the Portuguese National Guard and we've heard nothing yet. We've closed off all the contact numbers and email addresses, comms apps and so on – they've all been sanitized. We're clean."

"Good."

"The FO have been informed by the Portuguese that two British nationals are requesting consular access. They were rescued before the place blew up. What do we want to do?"

"Tell them to drag their feet, cite staff illness or something. We need to let things cool down for a couple of days."

"Their names are Lumley and Hoskyns."

"Are you sure?"

Josh looked at Macsen with a 'do I look that stupid' expression on his face.

"It seems that they were found on a lower floor, locked in. Our sources say they were unarmed. Cyber security guys, nerds. They were the only survivors. Their names are already on file as staff in Telion's reports going way back."

"And what about Telion and the guy we roped in?"

"No word as yet, but we do know that all the dead are male – no woman. So far. It's still early days though."

"So at least we know that Telion is not on site – or they haven't found her body yet."

"It looks that way. Her Six phone is returning 'number unobtainable.' However her phone is active and tracking puts it on the water near Olhão. So maybe she's on a boat. The phone reported her vital signs within the last hour. She's under considerable stress."

"Stress or duress?"

"We can't tell from the limited data."

"That's something at least, but don't wake up the phone yet."

"Boss, I've been trying to get hold of Borthwick, and he's finally come through. He says that Mad Hatter is alive – he spoke to him a couple of hours ago but got cut off. Some sort of problem with his comms. He thinks it's a problem at Mad Hatter's end."

"Can we get a fix on the phone?"

"No, it's dead as a dodo. We've run down Borthwick's call history and his last call to Mad Hatter's phone gave us a fix within five miles of Olhão. GCHQ couldn't pin it down to a smaller radius, there are not enough phone masts there to triangulate."

"What about Telion?"

"Waiting for your go-ahead to activate her phone. We're still getting the satellite tracking signal, it hasn't moved."

In London it was just after 7 am. They had been in the office since the reports of the Saluscent attack had started coming in, quickly followed by information about a huge crypto-heist.

"OK, let's wake her up."

Josh picked up the red cellphone and dialed Telion's number, followed by #!932Telion to remotely switch on her Six phone – whatever she did to it.

A sleepy female voice answered "I'm here but I can't talk."

All the security was handled by the phone, her vital signs confirmed, voiceprint good, fingerprint recognition good. No duress keywords.

"We need a full report of the last twenty four hours."

"I've got no access to secure mail."

"Then send us an audio report. You've got the software on your phone. It will be quicker than typing on a smartphone."

"I know. I'm on a boat with Mad Hatter, I'll have to see if I can charge the phone here. It's down to two percent."

"Fuck."

"Sorry, what was that? I missed it."

Josh looked at M. "A glitch I think."

The phone beeped and the line dropped.

"So much for technology."

The red cellphone chimed in Josh's hand.

"SMS. She's found a charger and will send a report through ASAP."

"OK. We need to work out what they do next, and that doesn't include staying on a sailing holiday in Portugal. It's a fucking war-zone."

Half an hour later Stone's audio report came through and was auto transcribed. It included a brief report about a suspected explosion at Saluscent.

They started watching the live footage that was just coming in from the news channel vans parked near the Saluscent site. There were replays of the gas explosion across six viewing panels on the wall.

"That was some bloody bang, Boss."

"Gas they say. I don't believe that. A bit of a mess really. Still, our assets seem to be okay. We need to get them out of the area."

"Yes, but isn't it risky for them to try get away on that boat?"

"Mad Hatter seemed to think it was do-able when they discussed it, though he told Telion that there's camera and radar surveillance at the entrance to the Olhão channel."

"The harbor entrance?"

"Yes."

"Maybe GCHQ can take the system offline for a few hours. How long will they need?"

"Search me, I'm a desk jockey not a bloody sailor. Sorry, Boss. I don't know how fast they'll go."

"They'll certainly need to go twelve miles out into international waters."

"But what if the locals have got patrol boats there?"

"I'm sure they have, though maybe we can help with that too, maybe lay a false trail. Bring up a map on the screen. Let's look."

"Spain?"

"That could be a problem, they'd still be in EU territory. In the circumstances the patrol boats will not give a shit about twelve miles. Gibraltar or Morocco may be possibilities, though it looks like they'd have to sail through Spanish waters to get to Gib. I don't know the form but they might need documents to get into Morocco whereas we could fix things with Gib."

"Surely this will only be a problem if the Portuguese suspect them? The local rozzers may not realize that they got away. There are a lot of burned bodies to identify spread all over the countryside. That will take a few days at least I reckon."

"Yes, but all male – no female."

"If the locals know about a female. OK. We need to get hold of the Embassy in Lisbon and tell them to make sure those guys – Lumley and Hoskyns was it – keep their mouths shut if they want our help. Then get hold of GCHQ and see if they can do something about that harbor entrance surveillance. Just ask the question for now – get them prepped. And get back to Telion. She and Mad Hatter need to talk it through – we'll need to know how fast the boat can go. And get the latest from our sources there, what the Portuguese suspect, if anything. And make sure Borthwick is fully onside with us and not talking to the locals at all."

"What about Barbary?"

"Where is he?"

"He should be leaving for Faro about now."

"Ryanair?"

Josh nodded as 'M' rolled his eyes and looked up at the ceiling.

"OK. We've got a few hours to think about how to deploy him. Meanwhile, I'll think about how we lay a false trail for Telion and Mad Hatter, just in case the hounds start baying. In fact, I'll start now. It'll be good to get my hands dirty for a change."

"What's the latest statement by the Portuguese say?"

"They're putting it out as a drug-related business war between Russians and Ukrainians in the Algarve using mercenaries. And a gas explosion. All foreigners, no Portuguese. They say they found a secret underground computer site which was laundering cryptocurrency drug money."

"Not so far from the truth then?"

"Close enough to work for now I think. One more thing. Our source is saying that the police found discarded equipment and clothing nearby. They think two people got away."

"Shit! So they know then."

"They may suspect something yes. But what?"

"OK, keep me posted."

"Anything else Boss?"

Macsen missed the sarcasm. "Yes, check on what they might need for Morocco – papers and so on. I'll check the map."

Josh sighed, sorry he'd asked. Macsen was close to the ragged edge. Why? This was a big terrorist incident, certainly, but not earth shattering. Maybe there *was* more to it.

Josh stood up and walked back to his cubicle, suddenly smiling at the thought of 'M' in hacking mode and 'getting his hands dirty'.

*

Thirty Three

The Russian government had not chosen to go public about a theft – all they had said was that there were technical issues with the CryptoRuble and that trading had been suspended for a short time. Of course, with cryptocurrencies like Bitcoin it was not possible to suspend trading – that was inherent in the concept, but the Russian CryptoRuble, like almost all cryptos issued by governments, could be subverted by the issuing government. They simply inserted a blocking transaction into the blockchain, drawing a line under the transactions until they chose to restart the currency. It caused huge problems as the currency became unusable whilst blocked. Or so they believed.

*

"I've got to join another meeting of the 'AstraNine' team. The finance people are wetting their pants with all the excitement."

"OK, let me know how it goes – it'll be quicker than waiting for Harriet's meeting minutes on TeamPlayer."

As Josh left his office, Macsen wondered about his own Bitcoin account. It seemed that the smaller holders such as himself had not been targeted, The thefts had been only from the major holders. Thank God for small mercies, he thought. He'd have to slip out for a sandwich and check his account later. But the currency was now really unstable.

*

She had just walked through the Green customs channel in Heathrow Terminal 5 and out to the Arrivals area when she saw the rolling news flash on the BBC news channel displayed on the wall screens.

"Suspected Terrorist Attack in Algarve. More than 30 dead."

People in Arrivals stopped to watch - as did Svetlana Goraya. The screen showed helicopter shots of the Saluscent site surrounded by Portuguese army, police, ambulance and fire brigade vehicles. There was what appeared to be a huge hole in the landscape. Svetlana turned and headed towards the Ladies facilities – a change of appearance was definitely next on the schedule.

*

"Josh, is there any more on the incident itself, beyond what we can see on the news websites? Is Barbary there on the ground yet?"

"He's out of the airport and mobile now. We still haven't been able to get our hands on the full list of casualties. The latest count is around thirty dead including the people on the downed chopper. Many will remain unnamed that's for sure. Our sources are telling me that the chopper was a Russian job, a Kamov Ka-27, civilian version. The model has been sold to many countries, East and West. That confirms what Mad Hatter told Telion – he said he thought it was a Kamov. The Portuguese have no flight plan on record and the chopper was not detected by their flight controllers."

"A black ops job then?"

Josh nodded. "It looks that way, yes. So far the Portuguese are releasing very little information, even to Interpol and NATO. All we know is coming from our source in Portuguese Intelligence, SIRP, and that's not much. This *could* have been state-sponsored, engineered for deniability. So, first stop Russia. I floated a line to one of our friendly journos and she's asked the Russian Embassy for comment. The Russians are denying all knowledge, saying that all their aircraft are accounted for. However we do know that a plane landed in Faro after midnight, a Russian commercial cargo flight. It had declared an emergency. On top of that we know that a Russian warship, the Admiral Markarov was passing through the area, about thirty miles offshore at that time. The plane left Faro as soon as the airport opened at oh five hundred. That's a lot of coincidences."

"OK, then let's look at the flight tracking data."

"I already did that. GCHQ are trying to get me the history from one of the commercial flight trackers, but there seems to be some sort of data problem."

"Sanitized?"

"Could be. If that's so then that's nation-state level stuff and not terrorism."

"Langley may have info but don't go through them yet, we don't want them to know we have a more than normal interest in the situation. That heli had to have come from somewhere too. Keep at it. Right, next item. What do we have on the crypto situation?"

"Harriet's got the AstraNine people on line now, a meeting just about to start. Do you want to join it?"

"Yes. Audio only though – I look like hell right now."

"Ok, Boss. We're joining the meeting *now*."

The briefing from the Bank of England had just started.

"Cryptocurrency prices are down around twenty percent since the announcement of the theft, but they appear to have bottomed in the last hour or so. It would seem that there are still plenty of buyers out there. There has been no impact on the pound and equities appear to be stable following a slight dip of less than five points which we tie to the announcement.

The Russian Central Bank has said that CryptoRuble trading has been suspended for twenty four hours, citing technical problems with computer hardware. Further, they stated that there has not been any cyber attack and that all currency was accounted for."

There was the sound of muted laughter.

"If I may go on, our Bank's technical department believe that there has been a thirty percent reduction in CryptoRuble liquidity in twenty four hours to midnight last, with most of it being removed within a period of one to two hours after about two am GMT. The loss of liquidity is estimated to equate to about eighty billion US dollars at the then prevailing rate. Overall cryptocurrency liquidity appears to have fallen, after allowing for ongoing mining activities. Other cryptos have lost liquidity to the tune of about thirty billion US dollars. So, we have a sum of about one hundred and ten billion US dollars which is unaccounted for. That's all I have to say for now, madam chairman."

"How can CryptoRuble liquidity fall? It doesn't make sense. Where has it all gone?"

"We're working on that. It will take time to decipher, but we will get there, eventually – and probably too late. Our working assumption is that the CryptoRubles have gone into other cryptocurrencies, some maybe secret and possibly tradeable on the dark web. There are several thousand public cryptos – that will take a lot of checking."

"Thank you. Our team *here* is seeing funds flowing across cryptos very quickly – transactions are being verified in microseconds. It's very unusual because there should be consensus for verification. There appear to be a huge number of accounts involved, some sort of cascade process. It looks as if the crypto consensus mechanisms have been subverted."

In Vauxhall Cross, Macsen checked the mute button and turned to Josh. "That's enough of that for now. We need to think about the

Saluscent crypto launch that their website and blog talks about. I wonder what's going to happen to that – or has already happened?"

"I'll bring it up at the end of the meeting, but I can't see it happening at all. Who would buy in to that?"

"OK. I'll leave that to you. I need to get some air, maybe go for a run to clear my head."

*

Apart from his eyes, Macsen looked refreshed after his run and a shower.

"Alice is missing, as is Gerasimov. We're hearing that the locals got to the lower levels under the compound and found a tunnel which links an office with two villas – one inside the grounds and one outside. All via a wine cellar. And no sign of Alice there either. They found an open safe and what looked like metal confetti on the floor. Then there was the explosion. There's bugger all left underground. Completely barbequed. All the hardware was blown to bits. The Portuguese police and Rescue services lost half a dozen guys."

"Jesus, that's good intel. Can we get one of ours in there?"

"Bloody hard to do that. Barbary is close by and says the area is crawling with security. He's got his Press Pass out but it's not washing. The SIRP has got it locked down tight as a ducks arse."

"OK, let's speak to Telion again. We need to sort them out."

Josh turned to the speaker phone and called.

A female voice said *'Secure satellite link active*. Macsen looked at Josh and raised his eyebrows. Josh shrugged.

JC picked up. "I can talk."

Josh spoke. "Where are you? You weren't to move without orders."

"I'm not the skipper. We're about ten miles offshore I think. The skipper thought we should get out while we could."

"And you were not stopped?"

"We were intercepted at the harbor entrance. The skipper already knew some of the guys on the GNR boat – that's the National Republican Guard – apparently he'd been drinking with them in Olhão a few times. I stayed below, out of sight. He asked them what all the noise had been about last night. Bloody cool he was."

"And what did they say?"

"Suspected Russian drug war, Chechens trying to muscle in, they think. They didn't know a whole lot – they'd been at sea overnight and were on their way back to the dock."

"He told them he was heading across to Chipiona in Spain and from there we might head up the river to Seville. They seemed to be happy with that."

"Well for now you're best out of it. What's the speed of the boat you're on?"

"Six or seven knots – that's nautical miles per hour. But it depends on the weather and sea state."

"As slow as that?"

"Yes. What's happened to Alice?"

"She's running, we think. The Portuguese found her escape route – a tunnel under the compound. Then the whole lot blew up."

"Just as I suspected then."

"Yes. What's Mad Hatter's real plan?"

"I think to get as far away from you people and Borthwick as he can."

"Well, that certainly fits his profile. We may want you to go to Gib. He will not like it. You'll need to work on him."

"We agreed to get offshore first and then decide. It's about another sixty miles to Chipiona."

"Work on him, get yourselves to Gib."

"Why?"

"Just follow orders when they are given, OK?"

"Copy that. Are you done with me?"

"For now."

Stone cut the call.

"Who was that – your bosses in Six?"

"Yes. They want us to go to Gib."

"Why?"

"They wouldn't say."

"I bet they want to get their hands on me and shut me up. Easier to do in Gib. – it's almost part of the UK."

"You don't really think that do you?"

"Yes I bloody well do. If you knew that half of what those bastards have done to me your hair would fall out. Oh fuck, big trouble."

Baldwin pointed over the starboard quarter to the west. There was a large gray patrol boat in sight.

"She's going full chat, doing about twenty knots I reckon, heading this way. Five miles I reckon so we've got fifteen minutes, twenty tops. This could be big trouble." As they watched the vessel's shape became more distinct and they could see her bow waves arcing out on either side. Baldwin opened a cockpit locker. “Here, get these fishing lines over the side. I’ll put the VHF radio on.”

A westerly swell of about a couple of meters height was running. “If they’re going to board us they’ll send a RIB. They will not attempt to come alongside with this swell running – at least I bloody well hope not.”

The patrol boat looked to be about 40 meters long as it slowed down about a hundred meters off their starboard side. They could see Alfândega emblazoned on the side of the hull.

The VHF radio crackled into life on channel 16.

“*Rubaiyat, Rubaiyat, Rubaiyat,* this is Alfândega Portuguěs, Alfândega Portuguěs, Portuguese Customs Service”.

“Alfândega Portuguěs, this is *Rubaiyat*” Baldwin replied.

“Good day Capitão. We would like to come aboard to inspect your documents. Please stop your vessel immediately”.

“You are welcome to come aboard but I do not want to heave-to in this high sea. I will maintain course and speed if you agree”. *Two miles to the twelve mile limit but it might as well be two hundred.*

“That is acceptable. Maintain course and speed and we will send a RIB across.”

“Acknowledged, *Rubaiyat* standing by on sixteen.”

Stone could see a RIB being launched down a ramp off the stern of the patrol vessel. Six black clad figures were aboard, four carrying long weapons.

“JC, leave the talking to me. These guys do not mess about. I’ll need your passport. We’re on our way to Chipiona if you get asked. Keep it vague.”

“Do you think I’m stupid Steve?”

“Not at all. It’s just that we can’t be too careful.”

“Christ Almighty, after all we’ve just been through you come up with a statement like that?” She shook her head in dismay.

The RIB approached then on the leeward side and three men climbed nimbly aboard, working with the roll of the vessels. The fourth man slipped and groaned as his knee hit the gunwhale hard as the RIB pinned him against *Rubaiyat*. A colleague hauled him aboard over the lifeline, soaked to the waist. He was not amused.

Two men stayed on deck in the scuppers under the mainsail while two men moved aft.

“Good afternoon, Capitão. Alfândega Portuguěs, Portuguese Customs Service.”

"Good afternoon." Baldwin was tempted to ask them for ID as he would usually have done, but this was certainly not a good time to be bolshie.

The badge on the officer's uniform read 'Cabroso'. He held out his hand. "Your passports please."

Baldwin passed them to the officer. "What was your last port?"

"Faro." *Near enough.*

"And your next port."

"Chipiona." *Maybe.*

"Why are you going to Chipiona?"

"For the Andalusian sherry." Baldwin smiled his best smile.

"But we have good wine here, Portugal is famous for its port, yes?"

"Yes, for sure, but have drunk much port. The sherry comes next. We plan to move on from Chipiona up the river to Seville, maybe to see a bullfight."

"Ah, but the Spanish, they kill their bulls, in Portugal the bulls live to fight another day. Does your lady really want to see bulls killed?"

He looked at Stone and she smiled broadly. "Not really, but it will be an experience. I do think the beef is better in Portugal." She smiled again and the customs officer was softening. "And I enjoy dancing. I would love to learn the flamenco."

The officer flicked the pages of her passport. "I am sure you would dance very well, Miss Stone. Very well. Capitão, I would like to see your ship's papers please. This boat is registered in Gibraltar, yes?" He pointed at the ensign at the stern of *Rubaiyat.*

"Yes. I bought her six months ago in Gibraltar. When I entered Spain I obtained a temporary import exemption for the EU, it's in the folder. Here." Steve handed over a folder with the ship's documents. "It should all be in order."

"Hmm, yes I see. You still have some time left. Do you mind if we look round your ship?"

"Go ahead."

The officer nodded to his companion - 'Espindolo' on his badge - who headed below, struggling in the confined space with his weapon.

"JC, please show the officer around." *I hope he doesn't look under the cabin sole. Never did have time to stow the SIGs in the holding tank.*

"You have heard about the serious trouble in Olhão last night, Capitao?"

"Yes we heard something on the local English news. A drug war wasn't it?"

"So they say. Many dead. What is your occupation Mr Baldwin?"

"I'm retired. I was in the British army until I broke my leg and was discharged." *Exaggerate.* "I have been sailing for several years since. My wife died last year." *The truth hurts.*

The officer raised his eyebrows and inclined his head as if to say 'You don't hang about' and turned his head to look down below where Stone was giving the guided tour.

Cheeky bastard. "Miss Stone and I are just friends. I need crew."

"Of course, Capitaõ."

Stone emerged from the hatch followed by the customs rummager who nodded to Cardoso.

"It seems that everything is in order Capitão. I wish you and Miss Stone a pleasant voyage to Chipiona. Miss Stone, I hope you enjoy the dancing, if not the bullfighting."

Cardoso waved and the RIB which had been standing by pulled alongside. The men clambered aboard, safely this time, and the RIB accelerated away to the patrol boat. Baldwin waved but nobody saw him.

"That went surprisingly well. Those buggers are not usually known for being sociable. They'd never get into the jollies with boat handling skills like that. And we didn't get fined, not like we'd done anything wrong anyway."

"Not fined? What about the bottle of whiskey that guy Espindolo took."

"What do you mean? There's no whisky aboard, I drunk it all. Or we did. We finished the last of it this morning."

"There were six bottles in a locker under the forward bunk."

"Shit. I'd forgotten all about those." *I really have been out of it.*

"They probably thought we were running the stuff. Anyway, the guy looked at me and I looked at him and shrugged. So he stuffed a bottle inside his uniform fatigues."

"The bastard."

"I thought it was better that way. I didn't want to give him a bloody blow job." She laughed and Baldwin cracked, releasing the palpable tension of the previous eighteen hours.

They watched as the RIB was hauled back aboard the patrol vessel which then accelerated away north eastwards in the direction of Vilamoura.

"OK a change of plan. We're heading for Gibraltar."

"I thought you told them Chipiona."

"I did. Then I changed the plan, the skipper's privilege. Why, do you want bullfighting and flamenco?"

"I can pass on the bullfighting, but some dancing would be good. I need some serious R&R." She looked at him with a half-smile and raised eyebrows.

Strange, I never noticed her eyebrows before.

"I don't dance."

"What, a sailor who doesn't do the hornpipe?"

He almost laughed. "Get bloody serious JC!"

"I would do given half a chance." She jiggled her shoulders at him.

Baldwin swallowed hard. "As I said, change of plan. That should make your bosses in Six happy."

"Are we cleared to leave the EU then?"

"No, but bugger that right now, I hate bureaucracy. Thank fuck they didn't look under the floorboards as well."

"Why?"

"It's better that you don't know. If we get stopped again we can say we're going to La Linea, that's Spain – EU – right next to Gib."

"How long will it take to get there?"

"It all depends on the weather in the Strait – the wind is funneled through, either with you or against you, there's no in between. But either way there's no strong wind expected over the next couple of days, so let's say twenty four hours, max. Why are you asking - have you got a dancing date?"

"No but I do have an employer and I'm still officially working."

"For who – Borthwick or Six?"

"Both."

"Two salaries is good."

"Yeh, while it lasted, but I think it'll be down to one now. Anyway, I'll let Six know, if you don't mind."

"Could I stop you?"

"You could try…" She smiled, a smile full of warmth. The eyes, the nose, her freckles in the sun and now the eyebrows. "But I'd fight back."

Did she just wink at me? Jesus Baldwin, you're losing it.

And then the memory of Ellie hit him, like a kick in the stomach. He and Ellie had found and bought this boat together. Could anyone ever replace her?

He headed for the chart table. "Our new course is one two zero degrees by compass, Cape Trafalgar eighty five miles. Your watch."

"Aye aye, Sir" she laughed as she altered course on the autopilot and started to trim the sheets. Baldwin felt his heart leap again. The sooner the torture was over the better he'd be.

*

Thirty Four

"GCHQ has dug into the passenger databases of all airports and ferry ports within eight hours drive of Olhão and found a match to Kovacs's biometrics with a woman going through Seville airport to Heathrow two days ago. The e-passport was in the name of Svetlana Goraya, a Hungarian national. Hand baggage only. There was a BA ticket in her name – a return from Heathrow through Nassau to the Cayman Islands, but she didn't show for the flight."

Macsen scratched his chin. There was two days of growth there and his eyes were red-rimmed and bloodshot.

"We're feeding all the camera data through the facial recognition analyzers now. Hopefully we can pick up the taxi or train she used from Heathrow. It will be a slow process to track her down and we'll always be days behind. We're monitoring ATMs in case she uses credit cards."

"She's much too smart to get caught that way. Better get an all ports watch set up just to cover all the bases. You never know, she might try to slip out on a ferry or even the Eurostar - if she wants to get out."

"But she'll want new documentation before she goes anywhere?"

"Maybe. At least we have some of her biometrics – and her fingerprints under the new visa rules."

"GCHQ have added them to the checklist – they'll be scanning all image feeds from the Passport Office and DVLA."

Macsen scratched his chin again, subconsciously realizing he'd have to get a new electric razor to keep in the office. "Don't you think it's curious that she always uses the same given name – or variant of it – Sveta, Svetlana, Sveta? It's not good tradecraft."

"Yes but it's a good precaution against getting caught out unexpectedly. If she *is* an amateur then her tradecraft is relatively good."

"Agreed, but I really doubt she's been formally trained for intelligence work, which would put her outside the Ukrainian FISU or SBU. We'll have to go with what we've got and not try second guessing her. The biometrics is all we can work with for now. I've got to admire her – stuffing Buligin like that. And the other currencies too. I wish she worked for us."

This time the bench was on Hampstead Heath and it was the first face to face meet for a few months. They had both been in the park for over half an hour, each ensuring that they were clean. The jogger sat on the bench at precisely 11.06 am. and took out a bottle of water, watching as the other man on the bench fed a biscuit to his highland terrier. In fact, the terrier belonged to a neighbor and he occasionally offered to walk it. The dog was a useful prop. “Good boy, Scottie.”

The jogger opened the water bottle. “I had a dog once. It died. I’ll never have another.” He took a slow drink as the older man spoke, both satisfied with the protocol.

“Anything more that you can get on the Hungarian Kovacs woman would be well rewarded – very well rewarded. The situation is unprecedented and my orders come from the very top.”

The jogger screwed the top back on his water bottle and grinned as he replaced it in his bag. “I’m surprised you have any money left to pay me with - I hope that they are not paying your salary in CryptoRubles.”

“Do not joke about this. You know that we have huge resources. Much of what you have heard is unfounded rumor, put about by American speculators.”

“Okay. I can tell you that she is in this country.”

“We know that already. You think that we cannot hack the Portuguese systems? We need more than that.”

“No, you do not need anything more from me if you are so bloody clever. There isn’t any more, we’ve lost her. I’ve given you top grade intel now for over two years. This is the last time that we meet face to face. It’s too dangerous” The jogger stood up. “I must finish my run.”

“Wait, do not be so hasty. It is not in either of our interests to part on bad terms. Sit down, let’s discuss this further.”

“Why should I?” The jogger sat down again and stretched out his right leg. He began rubbing the calf muscle and flexing his foot.

“Your habit, that’s why we should talk.”

“My habit? I’m clean, you bloody well know that. I don’t do drugs and we are regularly tested.” *Jesus, how the hell did they find out?*

“Your habit, requires money. You were a walk-in remember, we did not recruit you – you volunteered information in return for money. Of course we are not so stupid as you might think, we do not believe everything you tell us – the possibility that you are a double agent is very real to us. We very much doubt that you have a retirement fund and plan to buy a villa in the sun when you retire. We have paid you a lot of Bitcoin over the last couple of years.”

“You know that the stuff I have given you is pure gold.”

"Some of it may be accurate. We do know that you need money. So, think about what I have said and go finish your run. We will maintain the meeting schedule. Or else..."

*

As they spoke Svetlana Goraya stepped off the Eurostar on to the platform in Paris. This was Sveta's last passport – for the moment. As long as she was in Europe she would not have to cross any borders and risk a biometric check that might show her to be someone with the name Sveta or Svetlana. She didn't like to use a different given name but she knew it was the smart thing to do. She had Covid vaccination certificates to match each of her passports and other documentation, and hacking the vaccination databases had been relatively simple, so she was safe digitally. But if she *was* tested, it would be apparent that she had no antibodies for the illness as she'd never got round to actually being vaccinated. So she definitely *was not* safe biologically.

From Paris CDG she took a cab and headed into the city center where she was treating herself to a week at the George V hotel. Everything she needed to do could be done from a phone, tablet or laptop – except for the shopping of course. A new identity would mean a new wardrobe. Of course.

The appointment at the exclusive Clinique Limassol on the Avenue De Lowendal in the 15th Arrondissement was still five days away. Once the bandages were finally off ten days after that then her new face would be good enough to fool the best of face recognition software. There was plenty of open-source facial recognition software available, but Sveta had found it easier to hack into Facebook and take a copy of their software and she looked forward to testing it on herself – the word on the street was that it used AI. A database to test-scan her new face against would not be a problem – she had downloaded a few hundred profile pictures of 'friends' from the hacked Instagram account of a pop star. With social media histories already set up on Facebook and Instagram for her new identities, all she needed was a profile photo, and she'd have one in a couple of weeks after the op. She didn't expect Buligin's FSB to be able to track her, but they would surely try.

To pass the time she loaded a copy of The Complete Works of Shakespeare, translated into Russian, from a thumb drive. A tattered version had been on that bookshelf in her childhood home in Kiev.

She had treasured the book then and she still treasured the words, for the words hid her treasure. Learning and reciting two of the plays had been a way of mental escape during the years of her father's attentions.

From 'Romeo and Juliet' she had drawn the conclusion that love was a pointless and wasted emotion – as the reality of her early family life had demonstrated only too well. 'Julius Caesar' had taught her that there were few limits to what people would do to gain power. Her approach to life was based on these simple lessons from Shakespeare.

Just five days to fill with shopping, dining out, some theater and her Kindle. Maybe there would be time to find a new friend – or two. She smiled – 'Gay Paris' had a different meaning these days.

*

Macsen had been called upstairs to meet with 'C', Henry Brewell, in a secure meeting room.

"Take a seat Emmet. As you know, the economy is up the swannee after Covid and the Government is desperate to sort out the situation. The fact is that the business base for tax raising has declined so dramatically that the we are looking at tax rises that are so big that public order could be threatened. The scenario is really very bleak. The UK could be reduced to the sort of economy that East Germany had in the sixties. That's public speculation of course, of which I am sure you are aware. The problem is that some people in government are starting to believe it themselves.

"So, the AstraNine project team will be morphed into AstraTen this afternoon. More senior representatives will be co-opted. You – not Josh Packard – will sit on it. Harriet will provide continuity in the chair. This is a very delicate situation and I am concerned about the possibility of leaks given the wider representation. I will personally ensure that each member re-signs the OSA in my presence. And I'm starting now with you. The Cabinet Secretary actually made *me* re-sign the Official Secrets Act not two hours ago, as if *he* is party to the most secret workings of the State. Yes, you may well look surprised." Brewell pushed a piece of paper across his desk and handed a pen to Macsen. "I have to make the point. So sign. Now." Macsen signed the OSA. "Now, the rationale for AstraTen is not to go beyond you, no lower down the food chain. Just get your team to follow orders."

'C' continued. "Right, this is Ultra. I've just come from a meeting with the PM, the Chancellor and the Governor of the Bank of England at Downing Street. As you know the Treasury have a team of people –

not really agents in our sense – engaged on a variety of projects to protect Sterling, prevent fraud and illegal currency manipulation and that sort of thing. Well, it seems that some bright spark over there has suggested that there may be an opportunity to prop up the economy with some – even all - of the cryptocurrency that's been nabbed by our dear Alice. The thinking advanced further and now the idea is to er ...'get hold' of Alice and offer her an immunity deal if she cooperates and helps us...how shall I put it...helps us er...*control* the cryptocurrency that she has magicked away. Hence this meeting. You don't look surprised."

"Not really, Sir. I can see that it would be very tempting to the Bank of England and Treasury wonks, although I'm surprised they would consider such a step which could be construed as illegal."

"Let's not get into the legality. We just follow orders here."

"That's the Nazi defense, Sir."

'C' looked witheringly at him. "We're not exterminating people here, so I'll ignore that comment. Now, there's more. You know that many countries have already created their own digital currencies – including obviously Russia, China, Venezuela among others. The UK has been dithering, for want of a better word. If we create our own digital currency then we can, fairly easily I'm told, introduce Alice's little treasure chest into the equation. Of course I couldn't possibly suggest that we would make use of her techniques for further economic benefit but some people may indeed argue that corner in the future."

"I can see the logic of that."

"Good. So, *we have* to get hold of Alice and bring her to a sanctuary, a safe haven in our warren shall we say, where she will be available for negotiation. Of course I am sure that there will be other parties involved in such a search and it could get messy given what happened in Portugal. The operational details of finding and relocating Alice will not be a matter for the AstraTen team – those will be our secrets under the name of *Operation Looking Glass*. Resources will not be an issue. GCHQ have already been told at the highest level that operation *Looking Glass* is Ultra and only prioritized behind protecting the Queen. The operation will be compartmentalized to your team and GCHQ."

"What about North Korea?"

"A good question. There's no doubt that North Korea is heavily into bitcoin so that they can use it to evade sanctions. As you yourself told me some time ago you thought that they were involved in operations to steal Bitcoin. Looking Glass might enable us to …er… treat them with some of their own medicine. The irony would be quite delicious. Any more questions?"

"Not at the moment, Sir."

"Then get to it. Find her and bring her in."

*

"*Looking Glass?* A new operation? But why are we using all these resources to chase Alice? She's nothing to us. I don't understand why we got involved in the first place."

"You're forgetting the basics of your training Josh. An 'agent' only asks Who? What? When? Where? and never asks Why? You still have an operational cover – and don't forget those nice holiday trips you had to the Algarve."

'M' smiled as Josh remained po-faced. "Bloody Ryanair."

"I'll humor you, just this once. Simple economics."

"Economics?"

"Wasn't that your discipline at Oxford?"

"Well, yes, but…but…are you saying that HMG wants to get its own hands on the hundred and ten billion that's gone adrift?"

"I didn't say that, but it would be difficult, to say the least."

"To fix the economic mess following Covid?"

"I didn't say that, although it would hardly be enough would it?"

"It would be a good start though."

"If you say so."

"But the Government would have to show it in the accounts somehow."

"Would they?"

"How could they hide it?"

"I'm sure a good accountant could find a solution to that. Or a cryptocurrency specialist. But I forgot – you're an economist not an accountant or a cryptocurrency specialist. Neither am I so let's just park that one shall we? Right, I've listened to enough of your speculation for one day – and that's all it is, just speculation, but make sure you don't speculate with anyone else. We need to find Alice – Ponomarenko, Kovacs - or whatever she's calling herself today. That would just be the start. Then we extract her – to where rather depends on where we find her. And we need to find her before the Moscow crowd do." Macsen smiled again. "So, what have you got for me this morning besides more pointless speculation?"

"Okay, we've got a probable image match to her at the Heathrow taxi rank, Terminal Five. She was wearing a hat pulled low over her eyes, and sunglasses. We're pretty sure that it's her, though she didn't come through the e-passport machines. Apparently they were not working again. We've also ID'd the cab she used."

"I thought she was going to straight through for the Cayman Islands?" Realization dawned on him. "Portugal blew up into more than she expected and then she changed her plans."

"It looks that way. The news broke on the BBC at about the time she landed. She wasn't using Uber, so we've got no mobile phone signature to pick up. We've traced and spoken to the cab driver. We are lucky he remembered her. She asked him to take her to the nearest computer store, which was at Harmondsworth."

"Was there a camera in the cab?"

"Yes, and audio, but she knew and worked the system with a newspaper and iPlayer. We haven't got much to go on.

"How far behind her are we?"

"More than two days now, at least. There was a problem with the camera data network."

"Shit! So much for face recognition technology. It's bugger all use when the network goes down."

Josh nodded. "At least we've got the data from the PC World store and some camera footage. A cash payment for a tablet PC – not an iPad, a Samsung Galaxy."

"Android then? So, she's properly tooled up. I bet she's got a custom kernel loaded by now."

"Very probably. GCHQ reviewed the security camera data at Seville airport and she didn't have a tablet or laptop when security scanned her hand baggage, but there was a phone in the tray."

"She's probably got anything she needs on a thumb drive."

"Or tucked away somewhere in the cloud – or out on the dark web."

"Where did she go after PC World?"

"We don't know. She must have taken a different cab. There are no street cameras in the retail park."

"OK, then let's get back to basics. Get hold of our Head of Station in Budapest and find out if he – or she – has a line on who could be supplying the seemingly genuine Hungarian passports that Alice has been using."

As Josh left the office Macsen logged on and opened a new file area and set up the team members for Looking Glass, then scanned his mailbox. There was a low level alert for him. He was surprised as the low level stuff should be handled by one of Josh's team. A team at the Treasury monitored past transgressors of UK currency laws and one of the team had enquired on the name 'Tobin'. The enquiry had been logged by GCHQ. The name was flagged in the system at Vauxhall Cross. He tried to locate the file on Tobin but discovered that he required 'C's authorization to do so. 'C' provided it immediately without comment.

Macsen opened the extensive file and whistled as he scanned it, remembering some of the press stories from when he'd been a junior officer in Six. *A big player.* Tobin – tagged with the code name 'Midas' - had been quiet for a couple of years since he'd tried to manipulate gold futures with his madcap biotech method for extracting gold from seawater, which apparently worked. Some of the file was restricted access – even now for Josh. After being kidnapped in Malta a Six operation had freed him, not quite dead, but with one testicle removed. He was one tough Aussie, also holding a British passport. Baldwin had been involved in the rescue according to the file. *Baldwin again? The bugger gets everywhere. But why am I being alerted?*

He dialed the Treasury extension number on the alert.

"Somerville here. What can I do for you?"

"I'm responding to an alert I received about a Charles Tobin. Why are you enquiring about him?"

"Who are you? What department?"

"I can't tell you that, but I have your alert, so I *am* authorized to discuss this. So get on with it, I don't have time for bloody games or email ping pong."

"Okay, sorry, understood. I'm just checking now. Ah, here we are. Network analysis – who meets who, just metadata from phone calls, people who have been of interest to us. Our friends in Cheltenham let us know."

"So Tobin was of interest to you. So what?"

"He's been calling someone also of interest. Richard Thompson, ex Cabinet Minister."

"Get to the bloody point man!"

"That's it. We didn't see anything in it, after all they are old friends it says here. Only one office is to be alerted if they intersect, must be you then. Venn diagrams and all that. The alert directive is a couple of years old. You've got a nonsensical email address. Where are you anyway?"

"None of your fucking business." Macsen cut the call. Unfortunately with modern technology there was no way one could literally slam down the phone. *More's the pity.* Then it hit him – ex Cabinet Minister. Thompson. His fingers danced over the keyboard. Wikipedia provided more recent information - former President of the Board of Trade, resigned for family reasons and to pursue other interests. *Hidden scandal?* Trading software expert. Thompson was about to float a company. Livengood Crypto. Rapid settlement systems using novel cryptocurrency technology. Disintermediated trades. *Did it mean anything*?

Macsen checked the time at the bottom of the screen and decided he had to get back to *Looking Glass* operations, he'd wasted too much time already.

*

Thirty Five

Macsen had put the matter of Tobin, Thompson and Alice onto the back burner in his brain, expecting some insight to come overnight. However a new alert triggered a quick re-appraisal. The monitoring of Tobin – a virtual electronic tag which their latest AI system, fondly known as Baskerville, now maintained – showed that Tobin had cleared passport control in Southampton and flown by private jet with a flight plan filed for Rabat, Morocco. *What's he up to now?* 'M' requested that Baskerville check on the airport movements at Rabat within a two hour time frame of Tobin's arrival. The response came twenty minutes later. He scanned the movements list without enlightenment, and headed for the water cooler. It sometimes worked. His brain tried to join the dots. Rabat? Where had that come up recently? He took his paper cup of water back to his desk and re-activated his laptop, cursing as the water on his finger screwed the print recognition. After drying everything he logged in to find another alert. He gulped his water and closed his laptop, then headed for 'C' floor and the secure meeting room.

"You both know each other of course?"

Macsen and Conlon nodded at one another.

"For the record, this meeting is Ultra, understood?" They nodded. "Out loud if you please."

"Understood, Sir" in duplicate.

"You both have Ultra operations running. Baskerville thinks that there may be some overlap and alerted me. Please keep your contributions here to a summaries of recent activity that may be pertinent so we avoid any cross-mission pollution, for the moment. Emmet, please update us on the alert you received in the last hour."

"A person, code name Midas, of interest to the Looking Glass operation has flown to Rabat. I don't yet know the significance, but awaiting further data imminently."

"Thank you. I'm clearing you in to operation Bilbo, need to know only. Caspar, please tell us why Rabat is of significance."

"Operation Bilbo has been trying to locate a black - priority one - terrorism target, code name *Boromir*. We've located him and back checking by GCHQ has shown that he is listed on the Morocco immigration database as a senior crew member on a superyacht called *Arabian Princess*. A so-called 'Entertainment Manager.' The vessel is owned by Prince Khalifa ibn Abu Bakr, a very minor player in the

Saudi Royal Family. The vessel is currently in Rabat and *Boromir* flew from there to Madrid Barajas on a scheduled flight three days ago. The GCHQ facial recognition system identified him."

"Thank you Caspar. So is there a linkage? Baskerville didn't seem to think so ten minutes ago when I asked. What do you gentlemen think?"

"More information might help clarify it. I'm waiting for some aircraft movement data from Rabat, trying to pick up my target's tail." Macsen look at Conlon, eyebrows raised as if to say 'What are you betting'?

"I don't believe in coincidences like that."

The tablet in front of 'C' pinged. "There we go, it's just come through this minute, and it seems that Baskerville has more data. Linkage confidence is now 90%. So much for artificial intelligence – but we already knew that didn't we? You can't always beat gut feel. Baskerville reports a helicopter from the *Arabian Princess* filed a flight plan from the yacht to Azilal, Morocco. Baskerville has linked it to the results of your enquiry Emmet, another flight plan for a helicopter owned by Prince Abdallah Yazid of Morocco from Rabat to Azilal, within fifteen minutes of Midas arriving in Rabat."

"Can we get airport video footage, say from the control tower?"

"I'm sure we can. Baskerville has already beaten us to it. And here it is. I'll put it up on your screens."

They watched the clip as Midas – Tobin – disembarked from the Gulfstream with a carry-on and laptop case, looked around briefly and then climbed into a Rolls Royce which drove a couple of hundred meters to a Twin Squirrel. Within three minutes the helicopter was airborne.

"It's all right for some isn't it?"

"Yes Caspar, the question is whether he's dirty."

"I reviewed his file yesterday, Sir. He's a sharp operator all right and has taken HMG for a right royal ride over the years. On the edge and probably over it once or twice, but I don't put him down as a terrorist. He's got his fingers in several pies but his current interest seems to be cryptos. He has ties to a UK company known as Livengood Crypto."

"Livengood? I recognize that name."

"Yes, run by Richard Thompson, ex-Cabinet Minister a few years back. He and Tobin got into some dodgy stuff in the gold market, biotech and market manipulation. There were some questions as to why Thompson resigned but no-one got to the bottom of it."

"Biotech? Anything to do with pharma or viruses? Jim Bartolucci at Langley mentioned Covid and ABZ in the same sentence."

"Not as far as we know. Tobin – erm..Midas - used the biotech for the extraction of gold from sea water. Made it work too, it seems."

"Ah yes, I remember now, sounded like science fiction. HMG now holds the patents I believe, there was some sort of settlement with HMRC. So you think he's clean then, no involvement with Bilbo?"

"I wouldn't bet the farm on it, Sir."

"And you, Caspar, what's your instinct tell you?"

"We hang in there, see what develops."

Ping – the unmistakable sound of Baskerville. Initially the designers had programmed a *woof woof* sound to indicate arrival of an alert, but that was soon ditched as being a sound too far.

"Ah, Baskerville again. The helis are located at a villa owned by Prince Abdallah Yaziz. I'm pulling up Google Earth images now, sharing with you." They looked at the images on their screens. There was a large building nearby which looked like a large warehouse, and with a several hectares of solar panels, and wind turbines.

"That looks like a cryptocurrency mining farm to me, and Midas is there. Look, I can see power lines coming in. Or going out."

"You could be right, Macsen. Baskerville reports internet linkage with data transport profiles typical of a crypto-mining farm." 'C' looked at Emmet. "The question is, where do we go from here?"

Conlon perked up "Keep up the tracking of Boromir, get Head of Station in Rabat to find out more about *Arabian Princess* and develop a source aboard her."

"But we don't know if Boromir will return there, and it takes time to develop sources, He'd be a fool if he did."

"We have to cover the bases, Sir. We could get GCHQ onto elint for the ship – phones, satcoms and so on."

"Phone decrypt time is expensive and there's huge demand for it. Satcomms are still problematical, but I'll talk to the Director. Emmet, your thoughts?"

"More of the same Sir. Track and trace. Monitor Livengood Crypto. Bugger!"

"What?"

"I'd forgotten. Baskerville saw a tie up between Livengood and Alice. And you know Alice goes back a long way and now has access to almost unlimited funds."

"And was it terrorism or an act of war in the Ukraine when that airliner was downed, if indeed it was her?"

"We may never know, but it's certainly a pointer."

"I'll put a low-confidence bias linkage into Baskerville and see what he comes up with. And I'll score him eight on the latest find."

"Him?"

"Well, it's not a her for sure. The latest brain upgrade is working wonders" They all laughed - Baskerville had recently received an AI upgrade and had now acquired an identity of its own, at least in their eyes.

Way back in the early days of the web there had been a search engine which was known as Jeeves. 'Ask Jeeves' was a frequent irritant to web users and its use declined as Google grew to dominate the online search space. The idea was taken up within GCHQ and 'Baskerville, the data hound' was born. The name was also a dig at 'Holmes' the system the police used for major investigations – 'Home Office Large Major Enquiry System' – certainly a tortured acronym.

Baskerville was designed to sniff out data linkages across disparate data sources from websites to satellite feeds and images, media organizations, blogs, existing secret file content, DVLA data, traffic camera feeds, interrogation transcripts, social security, even tax investigations – and, of course, social media – Baskerville's ambit eventually included NHS and patient medical records.

With very few exceptions there was no data in the UK that avoided its keen nose. This rapid growth had come about after 9/11 and, with the latest extension of self-learning AI, its reach and capability were increasing exponentially. And UK data was not the only food it thrived on. Baskerville searched the world of data for linkages – and new connections to breach.

This was way beyond 'big data' held in a local database. Access to the Deep and Dark webs was no problem either and Baskerville's territory was unlimited. The world was literally its database, but it was an ever increasing challenge as Russia, China, North Korea, Iran and others sought to re-define the internet – the so-called splinternet – to control what their citizens had access to, to influence their thinking and keep them away from dangerous western influences with robust defenses. Even there, Baskerville was finding ways through and chasing rabbits down warrens.

Users fed in plain lists of topics, names, places – whatever – and Baskerville hounded out linkages. When a user got results they simply fed a score back in, 0 to 10, indicating the usefulness of the links found. Thus Baskerville knew when it had performed well and could learn to be even better. And build its knowledgebase.

There was concern that AI systems such as Baskerville could become sentient and then the worst of science fiction would become reality. No lesser person than Stephen Hawking had said as much.

*

It was just after noon and *Rubaiyat* was close-reaching in a wind just north of east blowing at 12-15 knots. She was averaging about 8.7 knots, almost as fast as her maximum hull speed. There was little sea and only the occasional fishing boat to avoid.

"I'll take over now, JC. Go and catch up on your sleep for a few hours. It will be a busy night off the Cape and through the Strait. The latest forecast looks okay with a weak front coming through and the wind turning westerly. That will make the Strait easier."

"Thanks, I think I'll laze on deck and get some sun if that's alright with you?"

"Sure, go ahead."

"You probably know mister know-it-all, but there's a trawler about eight miles ahead on the port bow. He's making about five knots north east the last time I checked. And the AIS also shows a ferry heading for Huelva, but he's well past and clear astern. The wheel is yours skipper."

"Thanks, JC, but I've already seen her. Go and get your head down."

"What did you just say to me?"

"Get your head…oh shit. Sorry, you know what I mean!" Steve felt his face coloring.

JC laughed and he saw her eyebrows dance. "Is it okay to take a couple of cushions on deck, skipper?"

"Go ahead. The aft deck is best, there'll be less spray there."

"Thanks. I'm going below to change first. Can I get you anything while I'm down below?"

"No thanks."

Baldwin looked around the horizon, checking. He couldn't yet see the trawler, but the ferry was just visible, on its way back from the Canaries. He eased the mainsheet a little and checked the speed. *Rubaiyat* was giving him another ¼ knot, and he was well pleased with her sailing performance – the first time he'd sailed her on a long reach in a quiet sea. He bent to ease the genoa sheet. *Rubaiyat* was holding a steady course under autopilot.

"Steve, what do you think?"

He turned around and saw JC in a bikini bottom, just.

"Do you think the bruising is clearing."

"Uh, um, yes, it does look better."

"It's still quite tender, here." She took his hand and placed it just between her breasts.

Rubaiyat lurched as the wake of the ferry finally reached them and they fell together on to the port cockpit seat. "Fuck!"

"Sorry, JC, but you should know better than to distract the helmsman!" Baldwin scrambled to regain his footing. "Are you OK?"

"I'm fine. Here, I need some sun-tan lotion on my back." JC handed Steve the bottle, raising her eyebrows with a pleading, amused look on her face. Then she turned in the cockpit and bending over put her hands on the seat, her legs apart to brace herself against *Rubaiyat's* gentle motion in the sea.

Baldwin looked down at the bikini bottom stretched tautly across her buttocks and could see beads of perspiration in the tiny soft golden hairs at the base of her spine. He swallowed.

At that moment *Rubaiyat* crested a slightly large wave and he almost lost his balance, stopped only by the pressure of his hips against her buttocks as his right hand found a sheet winch and halted his further falling.

"Oops" she giggled "That was close." One of her hands reached round her bottom but Baldwin had recovered and stepped back.

He flipped the top of the bottle of lotion, then squirted some of the white fluid on to Stone's shoulders. As he rubbed he was trying to focus on the memory of Ellie, to focus on anything but the taut body under his hands as he realized he was hard.

"That's lovely, Skipper. Just a bit harder if you don't mind."

"There, just about done."

"No, not quite."

JC deftly judged the roll of *Rubaiyat* and with both hands pulled her bikini tight into her cleft, before re-bracing herself as *Rubaiyat* steadied.

"Just my cheeks left to do, and then my front."

"You'll have to do your bloody front yourself. I'm done here."

"Spoilsport! Now, can I do anything for you?"

"Yes, get me a beer from the fridge."

"Are you sure? Maybe a massage to relieve some tension?"

"The beer will do that. Stop bloody teasing me."

"I'm not teasing you. You are an attractive and clever man. What has a girl got to do?"

"Get my bloody beer."

"Okay. I'll get your bloody beer." JC stood up and kicked off her bikini briefs then bent down to pick them up. Nothing was left to Steve's imagination. She stepped over to the companionway, headed for the galley. "I just love the sun, the sea and fresh air, don't you?"

Baldwin tore his eyes away as JC stepped backwards down the companionway steps, her breast gently swaying with each step.

She looked up at him. "I don't know what you're so bloody afraid of, Steve. It's obvious that you're not impotent."

He glanced down at the obvious bulge in his shorts and turned away, embarrassed, saying "We have a tough night ahead getting around Cape Trafalgar and through the Strait. I don't want any distractions."

"Tell that to the fucking marines." she shouted. He sighed, torn between the memory of a woman he had loved deeply, and a woman who he fancied like hell. It would be a long night with entanglement to avoid.

With the shallow banks off Cape Trafalgar less than 20 miles ahead, they watched the sun go down, cold beers and potato chips to hand, the tension of the afternoon forgotten for the moment. JC was wearing her bikini briefs again, topped off by a T shirt, Steve in canvas shorts.

"I'll need to do something about the weapons before we reach Gib."

"What are we carrying?"

"Just couple of SIG 226s. Plus a hundred rounds of 9mm parabellum."

"Where do you normally keep them?"

"On my previous boat they were kept in drums of old oil."

"Can you do that again?"

"I haven't got any old oil – or new oil for that matter. We left in a hurry, if you remember. Maybe I'll put them in the holding tank – well parceled of course."

"What's the holding tank?"

"It's where the shit from the heads goes when we're in harbor or in a pristine anchorage. I empty it then when we're at sea, through a valve in the hull."

"Ugh, that's really gross."

"That it is, for sure. I didn't have one on the previous boat, hence the oil drums, but it should work. I doubt that the Gib Customs will bring a dog aboard, but you never know. Some can detect gun oil as well as drugs. I think I'll stow the weapons before supper, if you'll cook."

"With pleasure. Anything else we need to worry about?"

"Not really unless you're hiding something."

"You saw all I've got this afternoon."

"Leave it off, please, JC."

"Sorry. Umm…right, tell me about tonight."

"Well, the Banco Trafalgar as it's called has fish farms on it. We could cut through the inside but there may be very heavy tuna nets set off the harbor of Barbate, southeast of Cape Trafalgar. The nets are big and strong – some of the tuna can weigh almost half a ton and the nets are heavy enough to disable a small ship. Although the tuna season is over by now, the nets may still be set and I don't want to take a chance in the dark. So we'll go around the outside of the fish farms and keep well away from the nets. Also, the Spanish coastguard have set up an exclusion zone in the area because of Orca attacks on yachts. It only applies to yachts up to fifteen meters long. We're longer, but I don't want the coastguard checking up on us at night."

"Orca attacks?"

"Yes, I'm not kidding. They've been smashing into yachts' rudders in this area, disabling them. And up off western Portugal as well. Nobody knows why."

"They're fighting back against something, are they?"

"Maybe. They're smart animals. Anyway, the wind is starting to fall already so we may well have to use the engine through the Strait. I don't want to arrive in Gib before daybreak anyway."

"What about ships?"

"There will be plenty of those. We'll move across to the southern - Morocco - side of the Strait where the shipping will be heading east, but we'll be near the coast and outside of the traffic scheme. After midnight we'll meet ferries crossing ahead of us on the routes from Tarifa to Tangier and from Algeciras to Ceuta, but there shouldn't be many that late."

"That sounds like a good plan. Did you know I got the STCW watchkeeping certificate when I was in the Navy?"

"Well, that's a great surprise. I thought you were cybersecurity."

"I transferred into cyber when they finally recognized my talents."

"I didn't know that was possible. Still, I'll sleep easier tonight."

"To tell the truth, I only did the simulator stuff, so don't ask to see a piece of paper. I hacked into the simulator software."

"There goes my sleep."

"Not at all. I used to sail cross-channel with my Dad when a teenager, not that long ago. A bit of local racing too. My mum didn't like boats."

"I did wonder where you learned to trim sails. I thought that there must have been something nautical in your background, besides the Navy."

"So, you will be able to sleep. You need it - I doubt you've slept more than three hours in the last couple of days."

Baldwin stood up. "You're right. You get supper sorted and then take the watch from twenty hundred. I'll come on at midnight after catching up on my sleep. Right now I'm going to move those weapons from the bilge to the holding tank, if I can find some heavy rubber gloves."

*

Baldwin looked at the clock. 02:00. He was dog tired and the coffee at the midnight change of watch had not helped much. He was now on his second much stronger mug.

They had passed Tarifa on the Spanish coast just after midnight and the latest forecast had been for light winds with a slack pressure gradient through the Strait, so he'd change plans and opted to stick to the inshore traffic zone on the north, Spanish side of the Strait. The sky was clear and the moon was in its first quarter, over their stern and sinking to the west. The engine was on, helped the mainsail and genoa filled by a cool katabatic breeze from the south, the air rolling down from Djebel Musa, the southern pillar of Hercules and the highest peak in the Rif range of Morocco. The land on the Spanish side of the Strait was much lower and relatively flatter.

The tidal currents were tricky here and Baldwin checked the tidal atlas frequently, adjusting the course to make the best of them. The currents could reverse direction in less than a hundred meters, but it was too dark to see the boundary. The powerful light of Tarifa was illuminating the sails with its 3 flashes every 10 seconds. Baldwin looked again at the tidal atlas, fighting to keep his eyes open. Then he was gone, snapped awake again a few seconds later by a voice.

"Ellie, is that you?" There was no reply. He shook his head and reached for the mug of cold coffee. Hallucinations were not uncommon for tired sailors on night watches, he knew. This seemed so real. Then he thought he heard the voice again.

"Steve, don't be an idiot. We may not be together but I want you to live a life of happiness and fun. I said so in my letter. We had some

great times but now you need to move on. Go with the flow and let me go."

"Jesus Christ!" Baldwin stood up and headed down the companionway. He retrieved a bottle of whisky after some rummaging in the forepeak. How many more were there?

"What's going on?" A stark naked and bleary eyed JC stood in her cabin doorway and looked at him, then looked at the bottle in his hand. She rubbed her eyes again.

"Erm…just checking the stores so I know what alcohol to declare when we get to Gib. Go back to sleep, you need it."

"I'm wide awake now, thanks."

"Sorry, I didn't mean to disturb you."

"You didn't, I'm a light sleeper. If you don't mind I'll get some fresh air, it's a bit stuffy down here. After all I've never sailed through the Strait before. Would you like some coffee?"

"Yes, why not?" Baldwin looked at the bottle in his hand and sheepishly moved back into the forecabin to replace it in the locker. "Okay, two bottles of scotch to declare. *I think.* I'd better get back on deck. There are usually a few fishing boats along this stretch at night." As he turned he looked her up and down, delighting in the view of her body, hills lit by moonlight through the deck hatch above them and mysterious dark valleys where the moon was not shining, the echo of Ellie's words in his mind. *Go with the flow.* He fought back. "By the way, it's quite cool on deck, you'd do well to put some warm clothes on." A small cloud passed over the moon and the cabin suddenly darkened to blackness.

"Okay, I'll be with you once the kettle has boiled. I *will* be warmly dressed." Then the cloud passed and the moonlight through the hatch re-illuminated her body. She smiled at him.

He thought the smile beautiful, generous and warm as his body stirred. "Erm...good, it will be daybreak in a couple of hours and it should be a bright clear sunrise." He was wide awake now.

"I'm looking forward to it." She smiled again.

Steve moved forward and kissed her briefly, gently on the lips. Her arms reached out to him but he quickly moved sideways and away, heading through the saloon for the cockpit, struggling with the awkward erection in his shorts pushing to get out, the whisky forgotten.

Jesus, one step at a time. Now it's her arse. Bloody hell.

*

Thirty Six

The Baskerville alert sounded simultaneously on Conlon's and Brewell's desktops. No time for face to face, every second was vital as they opened a TeamPlayer call with each other.

"You saw the alert Caspar?"

"I'm on it Sir. I've got a three-team heading for Battersea Heliport right now, just leaving their desks. I'll brief them when they're in the air and when I know what your instructions are."

"Make sure this is tight. I don't want the DGSE in Paris to know about this at all, not a whiff. We may need to organize some other backup for them. I'm bringing in Paris Head of Station on this call now. Jeremy are you there?"

"Yes, but I'll call back in a few minutes when I can talk safely, I'm on my way to a reception at the Brazilian Embassy."

"As soon as you can Jeremy. Now, Caspar. I'm not totally clear on this alert. Is it good?"

"Should be, but I'd really like 'M's input on this."

"Okay, I'm forwarding the alert to him now. Bringing him in on this call. It's your operation and target Caspar, your meeting. I'll do policy and authorization."

"Yes Sir,"

"Macsen joining."

"Emmet, you see the Baskerville sniff?"

"Just digesting it Caspar."

"We need an explanation, quickly."

"Jeremy Jones joining."

"Jeremy, 'C', you're cleared for this Ultra."

Jones acknowledged with an instant message.

"Go ahead Emmet."

"Baskerville's used a zero day exploit in the Telegram secure messaging app, well actually it's a feature but I don't know how long…"

"Get on with it man!"

"Okay, Baskerville's triangulated a location for ABZ, erm...Boromir. It appears to show that the target is just outside Paris, in a hotel. We have the address."

"Baskerville shows ninety percent confidence, what do you think?"

"Using the People Nearby feature of Telegram messaging can help triangulate a mobile phone. It's a loophole that Telegram haven't closed yet. I'd go with Baskerville's confidence level but it's strange that the target would have that feature enabled." *Shit, how in hell is Baskerville able to emulate a mobile phone in Paris?*"

"But how would it know the target's phone number?"

"I'm just checking the clue history. Yes, yes, I see. Baskerville's got a list of all the mobile phones used on a ship called *Arabian Princess* in the port of Rabat – that's over the last ten days. GCHQ has been monitoring and back digging all those phones since getting the details. One phone from the ship was used once in Madrid Barajas on the day that Boromir was there. Now it has been used again – or at least detected – at that hotel. Baskerville found it and triangulated through the Telegram app."

"Do we know where the call went and what the conversation or data was?"

"We have the encrypted call, but just as at Barajas we cannot break it. The call metadata is garbage."

"Garbage? How can that be?"

"It was piggypacked through a phone number with an encrypted target phone number, easy enough to do."

'C' broke in. "Okay, I believe that Boromir is being somewhat careless, the world thinks he's dead and he's a bit relaxed about it. Caspar, what's the three-team status?"

"Just taking off now, Sir. They'll have to clear in through French Immigration and Customs, two hours tops. Cover story is ready."

Caspar regained control of the meeting. "Jeremy, as you might have gathered, we've got a team en-route to France, I will give you the details shortly. While they are in-air I want you to get all the data on the hotel, usual mission prep. I'll want them suitably equipped for a covert take-down of Boromir and probable cleanup but only after positive ID. We'll use Accident Scenario. Let's not hurry this too much, but let's be sure and play it safe before going wet. The ideal scenario would be a snatch and hold while we check the DNA. At last we've got a good passport photo from the Madrid airport and I'll send it on to you along with the DNA profiles for checking. Any questions?"

"That's clear"

"Policy clearance Sir?"

"Good enough for now."

Their screens chimed.

It was another Baskerville alert.

OPERATION STATUS CHANGE
Alert Ref: Bilbo-210118/2

Operation Bilbo
Target Boromir Location Tracking
Target Location Success, Confidence: 80%
Latest data age: 3 hours
Rationale:

1. *Boromir confirmed guest at Hotel Grand Grenouille, Sannois, Paris;*
2. *Passport number match to Madrid Barajas Airport immigration system, name of Ashraf Ibrahim*
3. *Location method: Cellphone triangulation (transient), cellphone no longer operational*

Warnings
#001: 5% probability target impersonation
#002: 15% probability Image ref Mad_Hatter001≠Passport ref Madrid Barajas+Hotel Grand Grenouille

Notes
Hotel register records target vehicle registration number
<click for details>

End of Alert

The excitement in 'C's voice was palpable. "That's good enough for me. Get moving people!"

TeamPlayer chimed on his laptop.

"Brewell leaving meeting."

'C' headed back to his office. The evening was warm and the Embankment rich with tourists. London was starting to get back on its feet after the pandemic. The song 'Waterloo Sunset' came to mind and he didn't know why.

He called the Foreign Secretary after pouring himself a brandy. The tone that greeted him was distinctly frosty and unseasonal.

"Hello Brewell. I won't say it's good to hear from you. I've just come from Downing Street. The PM was far from pleased with the latest news. It's not doing his blood pressure any good. He has enough on his plate with Brexit fall-out and the Covid economic crisis. He wants to keep Washington sweet. I hope that you're not calling to give me more bad bloody news."

"No, Foreign Secretary. I'm calling for your guidance. As you know the Bilbo operation is highly classified. We're on very thin ground and I need your advice. This conversation can't go to your Permanent Secretary and will be non-attributable."

"But you'll have a recording."

"Not if you instruct me otherwise."

"Let's play it by ear then."

"Very well. We know where the Bilbo target is located. I've a team en-route now. We have a number of options – you probably don't want to know them all."

"Where is the target?"

"France."

"Then stay the hell away at all costs. We don't want to rattle the French cage in any way now just after Brexit – we've still got a huge negotiating agenda. Turn the Bilbo target over to them."

"Sir, if I might point out, the French know sweet FA about the Bilbo situation. It would not really be a good idea to tell them. Washington would be totally pissed off and there would be a massive loss of public face."

"If the public ever find out."

"Would you trust the French on this?"

"Hmm, you have a point. Then what do you have in mind?"

The team will not like this.

*

"Stand down? Sir, we have a team on the ground, fully mobilized and ready for the take-down."

"Nevertheless, stand them down. Put them in a hotel for the night. We'll keep them on hand just in case. Another firm will be employed for the job."

"Not the Cousins? But Sir, we've got this nailed."

"It's not my decision Caspar. Keep them well clear of any action. This comes from the highest authority. The other firm will be advised of the location only. I want our people back at their desks within twenty four hours."

"Yes Sir."

Brewell's call to Jim Bartolucci had resulted in a rapid reaction and a CIA team was being assembled in Paris with additional resources flying in from London and Berlin. He'd provided Langley with the passport details and hotel address, citing a tip off.

'C' had already canceled his evening plan to see 'La Boheme' at Covent Garden. The tickets were priceless and his wife would be feeding him cold tongue for weeks. She'd called a friend who would accompany her and 'C' hadn't asked who the friend was, didn't want to know. He was just on the way down to his armored limo when his smartphone beeped. Baskerville Alert. Nothing more, per the protocol. He turned back to the elevator and headed for his office.

He fired up his laptop, logged in and opened the alert.

OPERATION STATUS CHANGE
Alert Ref: Bilbo-210118/3

Operation Bilbo
Target Boromir Location Tracking
Target Location Change
Latest data age: 6 hours
New location: Unknown
Confidence: 90%

Rationale:
1. *Boromir no longer confirmed guest at Hotel Grand Grenouille, Sannois, Paris*
2. *Passport number match to Madrid Barajas Airport immigration system, name of Ashraf Ibrahim*
3. *Location method: Cellphone triangulation (transient), cellphone no longer operational*
4. *Hotel checkout confirmed in register system*
5. *Hotel bill settled by Visa Card*

<click for details>

Warnings
Existing
#001: 5% probability target impersonation
#002: 15% probability Image ref Mad_Hatter001≠Passport ref Madrid Barajas+Hotel Grand Grenouille
New: None

Notes
Hotel register records target vehicle registration number

<click for details>

End of Alert

"Fuck!"

Caspar came through on TeamPlayer.

"I'm mobilizing the team to try and pick up the trail, Sir."

"Hold on that Caspar, I need to make a call. I will get back to you in about fifteen minutes."

Brewell dialed Bartolucci and after a few minutes run-around he got through.

"Jim, we have intel that the target in France has moved."

"You'll need to speak to the Mission Commander on that, hang on, Henry, I'll bring her on to this call. No names, no video."

"Okay. Is she in France?"

"No, she's running the op from here. Here she is, joining now. I'll leave you two to it. Speak later, bye."

And just like that Bartolucci was gone. 'C' was peeved.

'Good evening."

"Good evening Ma'am."

Her response was sharp and clearly brooked no nonsense.

"It's Ms., Ms. Jones to you, for now, will do just fine."

Great start. 'C' placed the accent as Southern, the Carolinas maybe, an accent he had become familiar with during an assignment in Norfolk, Virginia. *Sweet memories of southern belles, but not this one - steel knickers no doubt - or something else.*

"Well – Ms. Jones - the target of your op has moved."

"If you mean the French op, I know. He checked out a half hour ago before our guys could get there. They're snarled up in traffic. We couldn't use a chopper for obvious reasons and we don't want the French in on this, no way. So close. We'll still finesse our way into the hotel and try to recover DNA for confirmation while we try to pick up his trail from here."

"I have a team who may be nearer, is there anything we can do to assist?"

"Yeh, tell me who the source was for the location."

"Sorry, I'm not able to do that right now, it was a tip-off." *As if I'd tell you everything.* "But I can give you the registration of the vehicle he's using."

She sneered "We got that already from the hotel register system, thank you. We're trying to pick him up through the French traffic cameras and other data."

"Anything else I can help with?"

"Yeh, tell your people to stay the hell away or they'll get hurt."

'C' was nettled. "Is that a threat?"

"Not at all, why should it be, we're allies remember? Neither of us want collateral damage do we?"

"Of course we don't."

"Then I'll end the call. I'll call you if I need anything, but that's very unlikely to happen. Have a nice day."

The call dropped.

A hard bitch, but let's see if she can get results, running her op from an office in DC, backed up by the DIA, NSA, a constellation of satellites and whatever else. But we have Baskerville.

"Caspar."

"Sir."

"Stand the team down on Boromir as instructed. The Cousins have now got this one. We'll keep Baskerville active on the operation and add the CIA into Baskerville's parameters on Boromir. Let's see what he comes up with."

"Boromir is unlikely to head back to the *Arabian Princess*, is he?"

"Perhaps. It really depends on whether he was spooked at the hotel, after all we don't know why he was there. But he *has* been getting careless. Anyway, keep the details very tight – the Cousins think we had a tip-off. They are not aware of the trail we've been following."

24 hours later the trail was still dead.

"Emmett, how's the situation with Alice?"

"Cold, Sir, but Baskerville is still working on the clinic research. But I do have some thoughts on *Looking Glass* and Boromir."

"Go ahead."

"Well, he was using Telegram, according to Baskerville, and the phone number was presumably that of a one-off burner phone. So, if he uses Telegram on another new burner phone then he'd have to install the app. We could tell Baskerville to sniff out the Telegram installs from the GooglePlay and iTunes stores and see if there's a close triangulation to Paris in the last, say forty eight hours."

"Can Baskerville do that?"

"There's one way to find out, but it is a long shot. We don't even know if Baskerville can access the app stores for app download history."

"Okay, I'll discuss it with Caspar. It's his op and if he's agreeable then we'll try it. You have enough on your plate."

"Speak of the devil!" Their screens pinged simultaneously.

But it was Alice that was back on the radar now.

*

OPERATION STATUS CHANGE
Alert Ref: Looking Glass /210108/3

Operation Looking Glass
Target Alice Location Search
Latest data age: 3 days

Target Image Match Confidence: 95%

Search Basis Image_Alice210603.bmp source: Telion, Saluscent, confirmed UK passport control Heathrow Airport 05 Jul. Hungarian passport, name Svetlana Goraya

Rationale:
1. *Image match confidence 95%, 47/50 comparison points*
2. *5% probability mismatch due to eye color*

Details
1. *Location: Private filing system, laptop <Click for detail>*
2. *Organisation/Image holder: Clinique Limassol, Avenue de Lowendal, 15th Arrondissement, Paris, France*
3. *Patient name: Clarisse Duval*

Warnings
New: Eye color mismatch

Notes
Located Image attached.
Additional images in same folder attached.

End of Alert

"Bingo!"

"Not so quickly Sir. The matched image is almost perfect, but the post-op images I'm just opening are well…"

"…of ... oh Fuck! Vladimir Putin!"

"Well, at least we know she was there, Sir. I'll see if we can retrieve the rest of the clinic's image data. We could get the DGSI to talk to the surgeons in the clinic. Maybe they have paper copies."

"No way, that would really let the cat out of the bag. We're to tread very carefully with the French, very carefully!"

"Understood, Sir."

"Get on to the data, see if there's anything that our forensic data guys can unravel from the folder, deleted images and so on.

Meanwhile I'll talk to Caspar about Boromir and ask him to call you about your suggestion."

*

It was almost a week after the massive cryptoheist, and Conlon was sitting across the table from 'C'. The pressure on the Bilbo and Looking Glass operations was piling up as progress was painstakingly slow.

"Sir, I'm bothered that Boromir has gone back to the *Arabian Princess*. He may be careless but he's not stupid. I'm wondering whether there isn't something deeper. He's left no trail for us to follow the money but his funding has to come from somewhere. The more extreme Saudis are sympathetic and known for funding terrorism."

"On the scale of nuclear bombs, his last attacks, I would doubt it, Caspar. It would be too big a chance to take. The Saudis couldn't afford to piss off the US like that."

"Well, they were implicated in 9/11. That started a whole series of wars."

"Yes but there was no concrete proof, other than the fact that OBL came from a very wealthy Saudi family. It may be worth looking into but God knows how we'd find out. We haven't got many good sources in Riyadh. The West – and the rest - have been trying for twenty years and we still don't have half the story."

"And then they chopped up Khashoggi in their embassy in Turkey. They're really stretching things since MBS started running the show there."

"Mohamed bin Salman is a bright guy, I think he knows where the limits are, but he pushed it with Khashoggi. He was really at the edge there. But to go beyond that – I think not."

"Perhaps there isn't Saudi government involvement with ABZ. Maybe it's a private operation. Could Prince Khalifa be a funding source for ABZ?"

"Hmm…yes, that's certainly possible. He's probably got a couple of billion dollars to spare – we can check on that. That would be a good reason for ABZ to return if Khalifa's the honeypot. Either way, he must be feeling very confident. How do propose we proceed, Caspar?"

"I'll talk to Head of Station Riyadh. There are no whispers in the files but maybe it's because Khalifa just plays the rich playboy as a cover, and everyone buys the story. His yacht certainly gets about.

That could be useful for moving money or materiel. And we just found out that he's set up a huge bitcoin mining farm in the desert."

"That's interesting but it seems everyone is getting in on the act. It's probably just a coincidence, but start digging. Leave HOS Riyadh to me – if there's any mileage in your notion then it's worth me having a word myself."

*

'C' looked across the circular meeting table in his office. "I've read the reports, Emmet, but I want you to tell me the latest from AstraTen yourself."

Macsen returned his gaze steadily "Well, the initial excitement has fallen off and now we are working to identify strategy options for how we'll play it if and when we get hold of Alice. The Treasury wants cryptocash to ease borrowing and lower the post-Brexit and Covid tax hikes, the Foreign Office want to use it for political leverage, the Bank wants stability in the currency markets above all else. So, they're all arguing and preparing papers. Wonking all over the place – except that they have to do the actual wonking themselves and can't use their departmental wonks to do it for them because this is Ultra."

"That must be fun to see them do some real wonk for a change."

"It's bloody tedious. The draft papers send me to sleep."

"What do you think we should do? The PM's asked me directly and that pissed off the Foreign Secretary who is now dumping shit on me."

"In my book it's leverage that matters to us, security leverage, though how we can use the situation for that I don't yet know."

"I agree. We have to rise above ministerial short-sightedness. What if we could control the big bundle of CryptoRubles which we think she holds? What do you think we could we do with that?"

"I think that the Russian government is quite capable of just blocking it all off, a one hundred percent devaluation. What's a few hundred billion in their view. They would shrug and move on. The country's sitting on huge natural resources wealth. Long-term it's nothing to them."

"But they need capital and expertise to realize those natural resources. They do need foreign currency – even the USSR recognized that."

"Yes, sure, but the Soviets just borrowed from the West with no intention of paying it back, believing that Communism would win out and repayment would not be necessary. But times have changed."

"Yes, but Russian foreign debt is about three point five trillion USD, the UK's is about two trillion – excluding our lavish pensions of course."

Macsen looked at 'C', surprise in his eyes.

"Yes, I've been reading the draft papers."

"I fell asleep before I got that far, Sir. As to crypto, we don't really know how they've implemented track and trace in their design. We'd need to find their blocking mechanism – there has to be one if they are to retain control – or at least a back door into individual accounts. But if we can really suborn the CryptoRuble and shut off their control we could print their money for them to all intents and purposes. That's what makes me think they'd just shut it down at the first sign of trouble."

"Like they did immediately after Alice's raid. But that shut down was only for five days. Maybe you should float it with AstraTen and see what they think. But do it subtly. We don't develop currency policy here in VX."

"But we'll give it a go, Sir."

'C' smiled. "No we will not."

*

Thirty Seven

It was a fine Mediterranean morning. A high pressure area was the weather norm for August and the day was no exception – hot, with little wind. Tobin had breakfast laid before him on the aft deck area outside his master suite on *Auric Adventurer*. She was moored alongside the quay in Port Vauban, Antibes.

He had been drinking his coffee while admiring the local talent passing on the quay – although many of them were Russians, he knew. He checked his Bitcoin account and swore, checked again, swore again. By the time he had called his system manager his breakfast of Eggs Benedict had congealed in front of him. He speed dialed his cellphone.

"Richard?"

"Good morning Charles."

"No it's not a good fucking morning. We have a big problem."

"How did you know?" *Impossible, no way could he know about the intrusion.*

"Know what?"

"You called, so you tell me."

"My Morocco mining operation has been fucking compromised good and proper. Two fucking weeks of mining proceeds have been diverted into another Bitcoin account. My guys have tried to shut down operations until the problem is sorted, but we can't stop it mining."

"What do you mean can't stop it?"

"We've been hacked, passwords changed. *My* systems management people are fucking *locked out.*"

"Good God, that's unbelievable!" *Now that's a big bloody coincidence given what happened to us on 4th July*. "Your guys should be able to cut the power to close it down."

"They're working on that right now, but the system is designed to be resilient."

"That's a bitch of a situation, Charles, but there's nothing I can do from here. It's your bat and your ball. You kept the project secret from me, except that it exists at all."

"The problem is, Richard, that the hack originated from Livengood Crypto. My guys say it's in the log. The user was someone called tombo997. Got in on the fourth of July."

"Impossible Charles, bloody impossible! No-one here has access to your system. And anyway we're not on line yet. Besides which the user is on your system, not Livengood Crypto. Our systems are not connected." *I hope he swallows that one.*

"It seems that we were connected for a few hours. I'm holding you responsible. That's four dollars a day lost profit for each of my ASICs, well over ten thousand of them."

"You have as many as that? We're not responsible here for *your* system security. And if you say that our systems were connected then you're wrong, you must have been spoofed – or it's an inside job. You say it's in the system logs but if your guys can't access the system then they can't read the logs."

"Look Richard, I'm not getting into a technical pissing contest here. My people say that our logs are copied and emailed out every ten minutes as a precaution. The evidence is clearly there. I'm putting you on notice for at least fifty thousand dollars a day for two weeks – and still counting until the system is shut down – and then there will be loss of profit until it's back up again."

"As I said, you must have been spoofed. If your guys are so hot on the logs then how come it's taken them two weeks to find out about this problem? Surely you're monitoring your bitcoin account on a daily basis?" But it was too late, Tobin had cut the call. Thompson was worried - less so about the money, which would be dreadfully painful if proven. That was surely impossible – he knew *he* hadn't been anywhere near Tobin's mining farm. But he was more concerned that it could have been a result of the Titanium intrusion, more about what else had gone on, where else had the hackers roamed, leaving *his* fingerprints? And then there was the question as to why Tobin didn't know for two whole weeks.

At the other end of the now ended call Tobin was pondering the situation. He didn't really believe that Thompson was responsible for the hack, although there was certainly circumstantial evidence of it. He *did* know that most people were capable of theft on a grand scale if under enough pressure – and if they thought they could get away with it. He'd walked the line himself, even crossed it and buried a few bodies in his time.

And then there was the puzzle about how the theft had been going on for two weeks without his people realizing. He checked the bitcoin account – and other cryptos - twice a day without fail and everything had seemed normal until that morning.

His partner Prince Abdallah could be a problem. Could he keep the bad news away from him? On the other hand, he could tell him they'd been hacked and exaggerate the profit loss a bit, yes, quite a bit. Just as he'd done with Richard, *More than ten thousand ASICs? If only…*

There was a lucrative charter coming up for the *Adventurer* starting the following week, so he decided to head back to London immediately and face down Thompson.

*

"My account was emptied. One thousand five hundred and thirty seven bitcoins disappeared overnight. That's over forty five million dollars, two months of mining at yesterday's price. I have built the biggest mining farm in the world – bigger than anything in China and it has all gone. An investment of nearly a hundred million dollars. Tell me Abu ben-Zhair, what in Allah's name has happened?"

"We are still investigating, Your Highness."

"I have just spoken to Prince Yaziz in Morocco. He still has his Bitcoins. I didn't tell him about my loss. No-one must know."

"If you believe him. Would he really admit to the loss? He would be as embarrassed as you are."

"Perhaps. But I do not think he would lie to me."

The money involved was less than peanuts in the grand scheme of Saudi Arabian royal wealth, but for Prince Khalifa it was a matter of prestige, something he did not normally care much about, apparently. Until now.

"Your Highness, there have been many thefts overnight around the world. Not only Bitcoin but other major coins and also Russian CryptoRubles."

"I don't care about them. This project now has high visibility in the Family. It does not look good – and I look like a fool. Especially as Prince Abdallah has not been stolen from."

"Naturally, I understand Your Highness's concern, but I do think it very likely that Prince Abdallah has also been stolen from."

"This needs to be resolved – and quickly. I will not be made out to be a fool. Go, find a solution or the *Saker* project will be canceled."

Ben-Zhair backed out of the Prince's office in the desert palace. He was raging – they were so close to the launch of the *Saker* – Falcon - project to attack the Russian and Chinese major cryptocurrencies with ransomware – and leave a trail which would lead to the CIA. He had no doubt that the Prince's Bitcoins were lost – the frantic Telegram message exchange with the professor in Massachusetts was clear enough - a worldwide attack on cryptocurrencies had taken place. *Saker* would still proceed. Whether the Prince permitted it or not didn't matter – Sukhanomutri and ben-Zhair had contrived a way to maintain control from the outset.

What is the answer? This scheme is only a cover for Saker anyway. A few more weeks is all we need. But now, it seems that the Russians have lost their CryptoRubles. You can't steal something that's already been stolen. Or maybe you can?

*

There was a new alert in Macsen's inbox.

It was from the National Cyber Security Center, part of GCHQ, and marked Secret. A cloud systems data center had been subject to an intrusion two days previously during the hours of midnight to 0400. It listed the companies affected by the intrusion. The backup data center had also been hit. The list was not public but companies were required by law to report intrusions – though not all did so. Macsen quickly scanned the list then acknowledged the alert and closed his inbox. He headed for the coffee machine and waited for a long black to finish pouring, wondering about the next tasks on *Looking Glass*. Then he turned and ran back to his office and opened the NCSC alert again, his coffee forgotten.

Yes. Livengood Crypto had been one of the companies subject to an intrusion. He opened a TeamPlayer screen and added the name Livengood Crypto into the Looking Glass file. It was just another piece of data that would be included in the delving that the tireless Baskerville system carried out, constantly trawling websites, news feeds, blogs and social media seeking links between disparate data items in an operations file. It could also be linked in to cross reference against mobile phone conversation decrypts held by GCHQ but that would require 'C' to prioritize and authorize access to the GCHQ resources. *That wasn't warranted, yet.*

It was half an hour later when Macsen's screen popped up an alert from Baskerville – the sniffer was working.

'ENTITY LINKAGE ALERT'

New linkages found: Charles Tobin (Midas), Livengood Crypto, Titanium Web Services, NCSC, HyperSecureSoftware (Kiev), Dmitri Borzov (Dormouse), Svetlana Ponomarenko (Alice).

<u>Click</u> *for linkage diagram.*

Macsen clicked for the linkage diagram, looked the graphic and drilled through the hyperlinks. He read a thread of news stories, some chatter on Twitter and other social media about the intrusion at Titanium. He felt a growing level of excitement as he read, but didn't know quite what it all meant. Then he came to the last item, a press report from the Kiev Star newspaper - Dmitri Borzov had died during a mugging.

He'd been told that the next upgrade to Baskerville would include more detailed inferential reasoning breakdown. Half the time they didn't understand how Baskerville's AI made the data connections. Until then, he and his team would have to try to figure it out for themselves. It was like being in a driverless car and made him nervous.

Sitting back in his chair and staring at the blank wall – pictures were a distraction from clear thought - he felt sure that they were well on the trail, but it was petering out with the death of Dormouse. The golden rule was 'follow the money'. That would take forever, if ever, with cryptocurrency. But it was also possible to follow software. Software left its own kinds of trails, trails that could be brushed over but never totally erased obce they'd been exposed to a network. There was always software sniffing, imaging, and there were bots snapshotting, copying, preserving for posterity, leaving their own trails of snail slime. Certainty of security was almost impossible.

The US maybe had the tech and resources to follow the crypto-trail and they were probably working on it at that very moment. The US Treasury would be just as concerned about a major crypto theft as the UK, or France, Germany, Japan or Russia. And the rest too. Langley was being as quiet with Six as Six were with them about the subject of the 'cryptoheist' as the media were calling it. Most governments would see the theft as an opportunity as well as a threat. He hit the call button. "Josh, get back in here now."

"We need to talk to Tobin and find out what he's up to. Let's put the frighteners on him. Hang on, yes, Baskerville says last known location Winchester, his estate. Get the local rozzers to request he visit the local nick to help them with their enquiries. As it's on home turf we'll have to get Five to do the work, gently, but you sit in remotely. I'll clear it with 'C' now".

"What are we looking for, 'M'?"

"It's a fishing expedition, I'll forward you the Baskerville alert . We can throw in the downing of an airliner – that might get his attention to start, then there's plenty of other stuff in the alert. Tobin's a tough cookie and he'll have to be leaned on pretty hard I think. Anyone who's stood up to losing a bollock under interrogation by a terrorist will be made of stern stuff."

"Okay, I'll get on it now."

"And the same again with Richard Thompson. He might prove to be more pliable. Same angle. Try the various items and see what gets a reaction. We'll feed the interview videos to Baskerville – let's see how he works real-time.

*

Thirty Eight

"Yes Emmet, what now?"

"We've just heard back from Head of Station Budapest."

"About time, what's she got for us?"

"She thinks they've identified the guy who's selling Hungarian passports. He's high up in the Ministry of the Interior, an associate of the Prime Minister. It seems there's quite a racket going on. It revolves around the Citizenship by Investment scheme."

"Many countries have schemes like that, Malta and Cyprus for example, even New Zealand. Put money in and get citizenship."

"Yes, but HOS says this scheme is being bent way out of shape and is easy to exploit with a bit of graft in the right places – high up places like *very* close to the Hungarian Prime Minister."

"Can we leverage the situation?"

"HOS is working on it. Meanwhile GCHQ have been digging into the Hungarian passport system now and starting with the root of Sveta Kovacs looking for matching images across passports. It will take time, but so far they have found a good match with the name Borbala Goraya."

"Goraya you said? That sounds familiar."

"Yes – a Svetlana Goraya flew into Heathrow from Seville the day after the fracas in Portugal. We're fairly sure that was Kovacs aka Ponomarenko. Alice."

"It's got to be her, Emmet. Amateur tradecraft."

"What a trail she leaves…"

"When first she sets out to deceive."

'C' could hear the excitement in Macsen's voice. "And?"

"Baskerville has found a Eurostar ticket in that name from London to Paris on the seventh of July."

"She should have been picked up on a facial scan at the Eurostar passport gate. How did she get through?"

"A technical problem it seems. All the e-gates were down and the passengers were being processed manually."

"The gates. Again. It's a recurring theme when she's traveling. And why were the gates down?"

"I'm waiting to hear back from the Home Office on that."

"Were they hacked and disabled?"

"Maybe. But if they were, is the Home Office likely to admit that?"

"They have to, at least internally, they couldn't cover that up. So we're now only what, two weeks behind her when we were two days behind. We've got to think ahead."

"I have been. I've just requested that you authorize a search on European plastic surgery clinics, starting in Paris. It's a long shot, but worth turning Baskerville loose on I think."

"I'm reading the request now. But talk me through it."

"Okay. I'm basing this on the possibility that she might wish to change her appearance enough to fool the technology. That means plastic surgery. This search would not focus on police or government image databases, not on social media. Instead it will scan all known private hospital and clinic databases that Baskerville can access. Clinics tended to store images of the work they performed on patients. I'm not especially interested in breast enhancement or penis enlargement pictures, just facial features adjustments."

'C' laughed. "That *is* a bloody long shot." as Macsen continued. "This is obviously a highly sensitive arena notwithstanding the fact that it's France and we've been told to tread very carefully. *But* it is in the private sector, not government."

Security procedures varied widely and in some cases images were not held centrally by a clinic but on a surgeon's personal laptop. Macsen was betting on the hope that the target had undergone facial surgery. The search protocol had only recently been established and the standing list of clinics was growing steadily, along with the list of access credentials that Baskerville had been able to sniff out.

"Do you think Baskerville can do it?"

"Well, we have the latest deep-learning upgrade, let's try it, at low priority. It could take a week or longer – if – at all – to get a hit. The earlier version never once came back with a successful search in more than a dozen searches spanning six months of operation. We'll keep it localized to Paris and perhaps widen it if there's no hit there."

"Very well, I'm authorizing it now. You can initiate the Baskerville search. Paris arrondissements only for the moment. But she could go anywhere, except London. Switzerland is also noted for its clinics. We might try that later. It's a bloody long shot though."

*

Thirty Nine

Over a period of seven days Olivier Henry-Tessier at the Paris clinic had performed three operations to adjust several of the critical dimensions of Sveta's face, namely mouth-size, the philtrum, eye-separation, face-proportion and nose dimensions. He'd also made some adjustments to her ears. She knew that among all biometric systems, facial recognition had the highest false acceptance and rejection rates. Nevertheless, that was what was used for mass screening of the crowds at airports and ferry terminals – even in the street - so that was what she had to deal with. More demanding were the increasingly prevalent e-passports which compared passport pictures from the passport application database with images taken under tightly controlled conditions at the e-gate.

She'd learned enough to be confident that the changes to her face would be sufficient to defeat the latest software – her chin would be lengthened slightly with an insert of fat, her eye separation adjusted and her brows raised. And that was just the start. The latest facial scanning devices assessed 80 critical dimensions and computed ratios. The latest research was even assessing a subject's walking gait, but that was a few years from implementation.

Henry-Tessier's fee of three hundred thousand Euros was eye-watering and seemingly disproportionate, but of little consequence when set against her assets – and the risks she would face without the changes. Life would be so much simpler. The clinic was well used to treating the most high profile of clients from politicians' wives to captains of industry, no non-medical questions were asked and the highest level of discretion was assured.

"Mademoiselle Duval, I am happy with progress and I am now ready to remove the final bandages from your face. I will not be putting fresh dressings on. Are you happy for me to do so?"

"Yes, go ahead, I'm ready."

"I have to tell you that there will be some bruising and discoloration, and that there will still be some butterfly wound closures which will in place for a few more days. I would advise that you wait a couple of days before looking at yourself in a mirror. The discoloration will disappear within a week or so. And afterwards I will have to remove the dressings from those places from where I have removed some tissue for the work on you face. Do you understand?"

"Yes, I understand, but I will want to see myself in a mirror today."

"As you wish."

Henry-Tessier carefully removed the dressings and examined his handiwork, as he had twice every day since the final operation. The wounds were healing well without an inflammation.

"Ah, *trés bon,* excellent. I am sure you will be very pleased with the result." Of course, some patients were never pleased and kept coming back for another tuck, stretch or adjustment. *C'est la vie*. It was good for the pension plan and the repairs to the roof of his chateau near Limoges. "Here is the camera."

Mlle. Duval – Sveta – gasped when she saw her face. The chin, her eyes, her brows – although they had been shaved – and her ears. Most of all the mouth with puffy lips and the swollen chin beneath. There was extensive cruising. Who was she looking at? "It is really strange looking at a face which I know is mine but do not recognize."

"Most patients have a degree of surprise at first. Some of the changes you required were quite radical, but simple enough to carry out."

"My lips look very puffy."

"Yes, there is still some swelling, but that will disappear the over the next few days."

Sveta opened the gallery on her mobile phone and checked the images she had agreed with Henry-Tessier several weeks before when he had modeled her new look on his computer system. She moved the streaming camera around from side to side, up and down. As she did it, her software computed the ratios and a graph showed the percentage changes.

"That is interesting software you have there, M'amselle. I would like to be able to use it here in my hospital."

"I developed it myself but it's still a prototype. I will send you a copy when I have ironed out all the bugs." *No way.*

"Thank you. I will of course pay for it."

"I'm sure we will come to some arrangement, Olivier." *No chance.*

"I hope you are happy with your new look."

"It seems to meet my requirements as far as I can tell. As I have told you, I was really unhappy about the way I looked before."

"I must take pictures for the clinic, as a matter of course, in case there are complications." *Or legal cases.* He never ceased to be amazed by the changes people – more especially women - required, but business was business and his chateau would benefit.

"And I just want some for myself, not to sue you."

He managed to smile without any trace of humor.

*

Forty

They both carried cups of weak institutional coffee into the meeting room and sat down in front of 'C'.

"We have a fix on the location of Boromir. Baskerville has done it again."

"Are you sure Caspar?"

"Yes, 90% facial match to a passenger who landed in Rabat yesterday, on an Air Maroc flight from Riyadh."

"Riyadh? The bastard certainly gets about. Can we backtrack from there?"

"No, there was a technical problem with data from Riyadh – the passport system went down. Passengers were processed manually."

"Too bloody convenient!"

"Yes. He's traveling under the name of Belaid Hamrouche, on a genuine Saudi passport."

"The name doesn't sound Saudi, more like Algerian or Tunisian, maybe Lebanese, some French influence."

"No, it doesn't, I agree, but surely he's just picked the name out of a hat?"

"Maybe. How close are we?"

"The results are six hours old. Baskerville tried to link to the Moroccan Immigration Database to find out what address he's registered at on his visa, but it seems that Saudis are exempt from visas when entering Morocco. I've asked our Head of Rabat Station to put a watch on the *Arabian Princess.* The bastard may be cocky enough to go back there. But then, the yacht *is* owned by a Saudi Prince."

"I very much doubt that he'd go back there following that bloody communique. Still, we'd better keep all avenues open."

"We have to nab one or both of them and get to the truth. Or not. Nab Alice and terminate Boromir. Baldwin is right in the middle geographically and knows the targets. We'll have to use him. Where's Telion?"

"On leave, Sir."

"Get her back in and send her to wherever Baldwin is."

"He's in Gib, Sir."

"Let's do Boromir first and simplify the picture. As to Alice, the AstraTen group is getting restless – we've been bogged down for over six weeks and need to deliver something. The PM is not happy with us and they're winding him up."

*

The day after Baldwin and Stone had arrived from Olhão following the attack on Saluscent, they had been standing on the quay in Marina Bay, Gibraltar. Baldwin was in turmoil with the memories of Ellie, their time there together after they had sailed *Rubaiyat* back from Morocco with Liam and then completed the purchase of the boat. The memories were still painfully raw. And now Stone was leaving.

"I'll be gone all day, Steve. I need to buy a few things like decent clothes and new underwear for a start. I need to start feeling like a woman again, not a gypsy. I'll get lunch in town and pick up something for supper, maybe steak. How does that sound?"

"Fine. You go and enjoy yourself, you've got an early flight tomorrow."

"Okay, I'll aim for five pm. Maybe we can grab a drink in the bar before eating."

"Whatever suits."

"Why are you so bloody miserable, Steve?"

"You know, too many memories here." *Eight months, it feels like yesterday.*

"But they were good memories, right?"

"Right. Look, why don't we eat out tonight as it's your last night?"

"That sounds good. You know Gib. better than me so you decide where – maybe in town, not here in the marina."

"Okay."

"But please, not somewhere that brings back memories. Somewhere that's new for you and for me."

"Aye aye, skipper, whatever you say." He tried to smile with a mock salute. She leaned in and kissed him on the cheek, turned quickly away and sashayed down the quay towards town, her hips swaying with exaggeration. Baldwin watched and felt his sap rise. *Would that be so bad?*

"Hello Baldwin."

Baldwin hadn't recognized the man who stepped out from behind the building on the quay at Marina Bay, but he cursed as he recognized the type. "Who are you?"

"I'm a friend from London. The name's Barbary to you. We need to talk."

"Another Barbary ape! Fuck off back to London. I've nothing to say to you."

"I think you should hear me out. Come on, let me aboard."

"You're not coming aboard my yacht so piss off."

"Then can we go somewhere to talk in private?"

"Did you hear me at all?"

"Very well we'll do it here." Barbary looked around – there was nobody nearby. "Ben-Zhair is alive."

That certainly got Baldwin's attention.

"No way."

"He is, and there's proof – proof that you provided."

"How do I know you are Barbary?"

"A will, a house in Wentworth. Does that satisfy you?"

Barbary looked at Baldwin. This was not the Stevenson that Baldwin had previously known in Gibraltar as Barbary. The codename was the same, the man different. But he knew enough.

"Where's the other guy I knew as Barbary?"

"Promoted, out of the way."

"And what about Kovacs?"

"She's no longer our concern. Come on, get in my car. We need to talk or the BBC news item finally goes out and you're in a shitload of trouble. Personally, I don't want to see that."

"What BBC news item?"

"The one about you being hunted for killing your wife."

"That's old news, so fuck off. I did the deal and gave you guys what you wanted. Borthwick knows."

"There's new evidence."

"Bollocks there is. It was a set-up."

"The evidence relates to the man who killed your wife, whoever it was. Come on, get in the car and I'll explain."

Half an hour later they were standing overlooking the Strait of Gibraltar, high above the town, having driven in silence while Baldwin was digesting the little he'd been told and while Barbary was mentally rehearsing the gambit. A warm easterly wind was blasting through the Strait and the gulls were ridge-soaring in front of them, the sky cloudless except for a small wrap around Jebel Musa across the Strait in Morocco.

Behind them the huge World War 2 gun emplacement known as Spur Battery stood bare and forbidding, a place for lovers' trysts at night and secret discussions in the day. Even the place for occasional murder as Baldwin had cause to remember. And yet another place with memories of Ellie. His tension notched up while his mood notched down, way down blue.

"You have got to be shitting me! Morocco? I'm not going, right, whatever you do to me. I'm sick of being pushed from pillar to post, so fuck right off!"

Barbary looked at Baldwin's red face, the veins throbbing in his neck. He pushed on. "We need you Baldwin, your country needs you. We believe *you* are the best person for the mission. You are the best, because you will be the most motivated, and because you know the target."

"Just bugger off and do your worst. I don't fucking care any more."

Barbary paused, trying to manage the moment. Baldwin was close to breaking down, he thought. "Look Baldwin, those in the know do really understand how you felt about Ellie Williams – Mrs Baldwin as she was. *I* know you were set up."

The intensity in Baldwin's brown eyes deepened and focused. Barbary watched him tense more, coiling tighter like a spring. A Walther pistol appeared in Barbary's hand as he took a step backward. "Don't move, don't even think about it. Just hear me out. Your marriage was genuine enough, I know, and the threats about a murder charge and forged will were a clumsy exercise in my view. But we have to move forward and now we're giving you an opportunity to avenge your wife's death."

He continued to watch Baldwin carefully. He'd read some of his heavily redacted file and knew he was very dangerous, doubly so when his hackles were up. "Abu ben-Zhair is the man responsible. From your own de-brief he was the man who shot your wife. He was the head of the organization that designed and carried out the two nuclear atrocities. We want him dead. We know where he is and the US does not. We – you – are going to terminate him, in Morocco. And bring back DNA evidence. A ear will do."

Baldwin looked at Barbary and agonized. He didn't know why he'd originally given them the story that ben-Zhair had shot Ellie. He'd been there at the time on the hill near the University site at Sidi-bel-Abbès in Algeria, struggling with Maruška Pavkovic when her gun had gone off and Ellie had been hit, not fatally, but enough to lead to her death without medical attention – which he, Baldwin, had been unable to deliver.

He blamed himself and couldn't really deal with the reality of it, ashamed of having failed Ellie and ashamed of his inability to face up to it. He felt that he'd been bested by a woman – Pavkovic - and because of that Ellie was dead. The fact that Marûska Pavkovic had been one of the most formidable assassins in the world and that Baldwin had killed her moments later counted for absolutely nothing in his mind. *Beaten by a fucking woman.* His attitude was almost sexist in its naivety, the pain sharp like a sword in his guts, the bile rising in his stomach. Now he was hung up on his story – not that it changed much at all. Ellie was dead and he was serving a life sentence for it, a sentence imposed by Pavkovic.

"Well?" said Barbary.

"I handed over ben-Zhair to the US Seals team in Algeria. Then they burned Ellie's body. I flew with them to the US Navy base at Rota in Spain. He was drugged up with morphine, out of it completely, I know - I'd injected him myself. Then a few days later the US announced publicly that he had been killed by their Seals and his body buried at sea so that there would be no martyr's tomb for the nutters to pray at. You read the file. End of."

"You also handed over a hair sample to my predecessor, a sample taken from a shower drain."

"So what?"

"So what if it wasn't ben-Zhair you handed over to the Seals. But it was ben-Zhair's hair sample you picked up."

"Don't be stupid. The guy matched the picture I was given and the US wouldn't get something like that wrong! I chased the bastard out of his command bunker under the University buildings."

"The US don't know that it wasn't ben-Zhair you handed over. But HMG does – or at least a few of us do. And that few now includes *you*. And I assure you that if you say anything it will all be denied and you'll be made out to be a madman – or worse - on the BBC. We need to resolve the situation."

"If what you say is true then ben-Zhair would be out there now, shouting it from the rooftops, making the US Government look like idiots."

"It *is* true I assure you, and thanks to you we have the evidence. There is absolutely no doubt about it – we have a match to a DNA sample from Rome, from a café at Ostia Antica. You were there."

"Really? I don't remember that at all."

"So it seems. Apparently you lost your memory. Hasn't come back yet has it?" Barbary's expression was a mix of mild amusement and cynicism, his lips in a firm line but curling ever so lightly upward at the sides, shaking his head. "You pulled a good one over my predecessor and the doctors at that hospital. But I'm not that stupid. A lot of mistakes were made. I aim to correct them."

"I've got no idea what you're on about. Rome is a total blank to me."

"Perhaps so. Anyway, I'm sure ben-Zhair has good reasons for lying low. He's demonstrated that he's a supreme planner who delivers on his promises, however vile they are. If only *we* had some politicians like that, but that's by the by. He probably finds it very convenient to be under the radar, for now, no doubt preparing his next big surprise for us. And then the US would look *really* stupid, on top of all their recent political turmoil. Surely even you can see that we must nail ben-Zhair. And quickly."

"How do I know you're not just using me again?"

"You don't. But what have you got to lose? I'm clearly *not* threatening you – this pistol is just for self- defense in case you over-react. But I doubt that you will. In fact, here, take it."

Baldwin shook his head the proffered Walther.

"You might feel a whole lot better if you settle the score with ben-Zhair. It's the carrot approach if you like. The world would certainly be grateful – if they were ever told. And your own conscience might rest easier. Then you'd be able to sail off into the sunset on your boat."

Baldwin shook his head in resignation. He was trapped by his own lie about Ellie's death; maybe after all this was a way to put her memory to rest and give himself some peace.

"I still work for Borthwick. He owes me a wad of money."

"That will be sorted, don't worry. Anyway, your three month contract with *ScutumEst* has ended hasn't it?"

"Yes."

"So now you can sort out ben-Zhair."

Baldwin shrugged in resignation. "What the fuck, let's do it." *Maybe this will help erase the pain. Or me.*

"Good. I'm glad you've made the right decision. You'll get a much more detailed briefing in the next couple of days."

Indeed he would. Beyond the usual mission parameters, there was one more detail that Barbary had to address, but now was definitely not the time.

Stone would be on the mission with Baldwin. Six had to have somebody there who they could trust absolutely. Two men would be suspicious, though handholding between Arab men friends was not unusual or indicative of non-Islamic tendencies, but a mixed couple would lower the mission risk profile. Trust absolutely? He wasn't sure about that.

Morocco was a much more relaxed country than Algeria, and Barbary's own parents had met in a cave on the hippy trail to Marrakesh almost sixty years before, so Barbary did not think a marriage license would be necessary for cover in this case - that would have been a truly impossible ask. Then he smiled as he thought of his parents. Loving and well meaning, classical hippies, they were probably turning in their graves if they were watching him now, working for Six, the antithesis of what they believed in.

Barbary slipped the Walther back into its pancake holster and they drove down into town. *Tricky times ahead and history repeating itself?* He hoped not. He fought through the lunchtime traffic and dropped Baldwin outside the marina entrance after another tight-lipped car journey.

Barbary checked his watch and saw that he'd be a few minutes late for his lunch appointment. Never mind, she would wait as ordered.

*

Forty One

At his desk in the Aquarium in Moscow, Captain Andrei Stepanovich was reviewing the Vulture file. His access was limited and what he could read on his screen had been heavily redacted on the orders of General Vadim Mikhailov.

Ublyudok! Bastard! "How do they expect me to run this operation with my eyes closed?"

Newly promoted First Lieutenant Popov looked across the desk at Major Drozhdov's replacement. A good temper, he thought, and our sweep can be started again. No one expected GRU cyber specialists to be killed in the line of duty, but Drozhdon and Sokholov had been the first – and hopefully the last. Popov took a shot "They never give us the proper tools to do the job, Sir."

"Bloody right they don't. How the fuck are we supposed to find the woman?"

"Perhaps the SVR can help us, Sir." *Light the fuse.*

Stepanovich spluttered. "By all the holy saints I will not talk to those bastards. They would not tell me anything anyway."

"We should try, Sir, shouldn't we?" *Burning nicely.*

"No we fucking well shouldn't. Go back to your desk and get your useless fucking team to find this woman. She must have left a trail!"

Popov saluted smartly and left the Captain's office. The fuse burned for less than thirty seconds. That should be enough to win the pot this week. As he closed the office door he started to shout at his own team, beginning with newly promoted second Lieutenant Andreievich who bit back his grin.

In his Kremlin office, General Vadim Mikhailov was operating on the mushroom farm principle and the manure was trickling down. The SVR, the FSB and the GRU were now all competing to find Ponomarenko and the missing CryptoRubles. Indeed, the manure had started a short distance away above Mikhailov's own head, right in the primary seat of power in the Grand Kremlin Palace.

But it was the SVR that won when their London mole Skopa reported that Ponomarenko had been located in Paris two days previously, in a clinic.

There was no doubt in his mind that there was only one way to run the operation now, and that was to instruct the SVR to go ahead. After all, their mole had found her. The Vulture joint operation in Olhão had been an unmitigated disaster, but he could hardly blame the GRU for that, but he'd do so anyway.

The SVR had been the lead agency and now they were under the hammer. But for the moment he'd keep the GRU in the dark and let them work away at it, trying to locate the CryptoRubles with the threat of blame being a great motivator. They might, after all, come up with something interesting though he doubted that.

Finding the woman was one thing, getting back the CryptoRubles was another, as his supreme boss had reminded him about his responsibilities in no uncertain terms. He wanted both.

*

FSB Major Gregor Suslov was in his office in the complex known as 11 Kolpachny in the Yasenevo district of Moscow.

"Yes, the British have located him in Morocco."

"How did they do that when we haven't been able to?"

"Those details were not included in the report from our source."

"That is something we need to know very urgently. If they can do it why can't we? Our Technical and Scientific Directorate may be sleeping on the job."

"Perhaps the British have a source close to him?"

"Whether they do or not we need to know. I want ben-Zhair captured and his brain turned inside-out. He has huge funding from somewhere, and we know that the Iranians and North Koreans were involved at some time. He has threatened those heathen Chinese and the fucking Americans and he has threatened Mother Russia *herself* with economic catastrophe. We need to get a step ahead of the British. And we need that Ponomarenko bitch too – and the CryptoRubles."

"Are we then taking over the hunt for the CryptoRubles from the GRU?"

"No. Not yet. They are using the back door in the blockchain to track the CryptoRubles, but somehow that bitch has jammed the lock. It's just a matter of time they say. I will let you know when we need action from you on that matter. For now, focus on ben-Zhair. To capture him would really piss off the Americans."

Suslov set to work. Another team would be required, but where? Since receiving the information from Skopa in London, the *Arabian Princess* was being watched by agents from the Russian Embassy in Rabat. Until recently, Rabat had been a bit of a diplomatic backwater, but since Morocco had recognized Israel in December 2020 then the

FSB team at Rabat had been strengthened. Still, the agents there were not the pick of the crop.

*

Forty Two

Communique

ANNOUNCEMENT
Issued by Islamic Caliphate Operations Command
Dated: 24 Tammūz1442 A.H., 06:00 hours, Mecca time.

Operation Saker (Falcon)

The IC today advises the infidel states of the world that it has initiated a devastating economic attack on the major economies of the world to take place at a time of our choosing. Recent events are just the beginning.

We have a list of demands which we expect to be met unconditionally by the appropriate countries and organizations if further attacks are to be avoided. These demands must all be met by 1 Aylūl 1442 A.H. (1 September this year). There will be No negotiation, No agreement, No truce, No dialogue. All diplomatic channels – and backchannels - are closed.

Our demands are:

1 Formal recognition of the Islamic Caliphate in the Maghreb by the US, EU, China, Russian Federation and all other members of the G20.
2. IC Membership of the United Nations
3. Freeing of all IC prisoners worldwide
4. Withdrawal of all infidel forces from IC territories in the Levant and Maghreb
5. Abolition of the so-called State of Israel and transfer of the government to IC control

Our previous warnings were ignored and because of this many thousands of people died unnecessarily. We do not lie and we deliver on our promises.

Our Commander in Chief is alive and the USA is lying about his death.

You know that we have the capability to make our threats a reality and you ignore this communique at your peril.

Signed: Abu ben-Zhair
ICIM Operations Commander in Chief

End

There was worldwide pandemonium.

Market reaction was unprecedented. Investors knew that the IC threat of continued action was highly credible and commentators gave it a success probability of better than 95%.

They noted that what had previously called itself 'ICIM – Islamic Caliphate in the Maghreb' had now promoted itself to IC – Islamic Caliphate.

The Dow plunged 15%, followed quickly by all leading markets around the world. Oil prices rapidly climbed above $200 a barrel within 12 hours with no sign of slowing.

The political reaction was furious and the USA re-stated that there was incontrovertible DNA proof that Abu ben-Zhair had been killed by one of their Seals teams and buried at sea in the Atlantic.

However, the world's news media were not convinced, with screaming headlines typically of the form

'ANOTHER US GOVERNMENT LIE?'
'ABZ – No Body, No Proof!'

'EXPECT ANOTHER ATTACK ON WORLD FINANCIAL SYSTEMS'
'ABZ still alive'

'DOES ABZ HAVE ANOTHER NUCLEAR BOMB?
'The public must be told!

The USA responded by publishing the full DNA profile of the dead Abu ben-Zhair, and that of the 'confirmed' sample provided by the British Government - a perfect match. No other background information was provided.

Still, the markets plunged and cryptocurrency prices shot upwards along with those of oil, gold and precious metals.

To the market analysts a threat of economic disaster made by an Arab terrorist organization usually meant an attack on oil supplies, but this time there was a wide divergence of opinion among the analysts and pundits. History had shown that the ICIM could cause mayhem in many ways and at will.

Behind the scenes in Washington and London the action was frantic.

*

Ben-Zhair laughed as he surfed the news channels back on Prince Khalifa's yacht in Rabat. The Prince had not accompanied him, preferring to stay in his desert palace in Saudi Arabia for a few days more and mourn the loss of his Bitcoins. The *Arabian Princess* was scheduled to depart Rabat in 3 days time and head up to Malaga. Then she would head via Cannes and Monaco to Sardinia for the Rolex Maxi Cup yacht racing on the Costa Smeralda in Sardinia in early September.

Ben-Zhair was not planning to take the full cruise. He had a meeting to attend in Malaga.

He called the Prince.

"Have you seen the news your Highness?" and received the inevitable response.

"Have you recovered my Bitcoins yet? The price is climbing quickly. My losses are mounting!"

"Our teams are still working on it. We are getting closer but the perpetrators were fiendishly clever." *No chance*. "Allah is with us, we only have to threaten action now and the markets plunge and oil prices climb steeply."

"Oil? You told me that bitcoins were the future, not oil. It's the reverse."

"It is only temporary your Highness, while *Operation Saker* is under way."

"I'm running out patience!"

"The gold price is climbing too. I did advise you to buy forward before we issued the communique."

"I do not want gold, I have tons of gold. Get my Bitcoins back."

The call was cut abruptly and ben-Zhair barely restrained the urge to throw his smartphone into the harbor. *By Allah, the success has gone to his head. He is like a spoiled child. Maybe he should have an accident.*

He had not told the Prince about the problem with *Operation Saker*, about the digital passkey that had been embedded in the software by the dark web developers. His team in Dubai had foolishly outsourced the work on the dark web. Now *he* was being held to ransom and $45 million in bitcoin was not enough for them.

His Dubai software team leader had paid with his life, tortured by ben-Zhair's Head of Security, Ahmed Abdelghani. Ben-Zhair had learned the hard way that crooked people who operate in a crooked hidden dark web marketplace could not be trusted. Ahmed Abdelghani had cunningly used others from the dark web to uncover the principal of the software development operation which was trying to extort him, but unfortunately that principal had been murdered in a mugging Kiev before he could be reached.

Ben-Zhair had been at a standstill for two weeks seething with frustration, and then he had been contacted by the thieves. Did he still want the passkey? Certainly, but how could he be sure it was genuine? They had told him to be in Paris the following week. It had to be someone in the company.

One thing was sure, the plan had changed – someone else had initiated an attack on cryptocurrencies and he had been forced to issue the communique earlier than planned. $100 billion or so was in reality a small hit on the world financial system. It was simple to claim responsibility and everyone was listening to IC. But he still had to deliver the maelstrom that the communique had promised as there was no chance his terms would be met. There was always *Operation Thu'ban*. That had taken many years to prepare but the final pieces would not be in place for another year.

For now, *Operation Saker* had to work. He needed the passkey to deliver on that promise but there was no way that the Prince would provide any more funding for *Saker*.

Ben-Zhair smiled. *I wonder if that ton of gold is still in the hold below?*

He opened the secure Brave browser on his smartphone and discovered that there were 80 standard 400 ounce bars of gold in a ton, and they were worth, at the latest price set on the London gold market, US$80 million.

There might yet be a way forward but he'd be gambling with $90 million that the passkey would work. Still, it wasn't his $90 million. If he wasn't careful he could end up killing the golden goose.

*

At VX, 'C' looked across his desk at Conlon and Macsen. "What the hell is going on? We have irrefutable proof that Alice is responsible for the crypotheist – or at least I thought we did - and now ABZ says it's the IC! Well?"

'C' glared at them and Macsen finally broke the silence. "I'm convinced that Alice was the prime mover. That begs the question as to whether she is involved with Boromir. There is of course the possibility that Boromir is just claiming it, as Alice has not bothered to and there is no proven link. Terrorists frequently lay claim to events that they have no link to – they want the publicity. And criminals *never* claim responsibility – they just want the money."

Conlon interjected "That's not entirely correct - we have placed them both in Paris at the same time, without doubt."

"Yes, without doubt, but that could be coincidence. There's no proven link between them."

"What do you think the chances are of them both being in the same city at the same time, without there being a link?"

"The chances are non-zero, but that doesn't make it a hundred percent, or even fifty, as I said. No proven link."

They continued to debate the matter for a few more minutes, then 'C' summarized. "Very well, the facts are clear and we believe our own intelligence as far as it goes. We will proceed on the working assumption that there *is* a link between them. We cannot ignore the possibility. You two will have to work closely together on this."

Macsen was the quickest to ask the obvious question. "Which of us is the lead, Sir?"

"Neither. I'm taking direct operational control. We meet twice a day until further notice. And be clear that I want positive progress reports at *every* meeting. The first meeting will be at oh seven thirty tomorrow. Now get back to work."

*

This time it was tea at 4 pm. and before they had seated themselves 'C' opened the meeting without preamble.

"I'm very concerned by this report, Caspar."

"Yes sir, but our people did well to spot them. The agents are new to the Embassy in Rabat – we haven't seen their faces before. They must have come in just after Morocco normalized relations with Israel. They're clearly beefing up their Embassy."

"So, we think that Moscow has a bead on Boromir?"

"It looks that way."

"How in hell did Moscow find Boromir in Rabat?"

"I don't know, sir, but it's a major concern."

"He could be a tool of theirs, of course."

"That would link them to Rome and to the Canaries. I can't see Russia getting into nuclear terrorism."

"Nor can I. There's still doubt over the source of the tritium starter for those fusion devices. If they'd been fission or regular fusion bombs with a fission starter we'd have a much clearer idea from the radionucleatide traces. We did have intel that led to Iran and North Korea, although it wasn't strong enough for Washington to pick their targets."

"A leak – or worse – from the Cousins?"

"They don't know where he is, as far as we know, and we're definitely not sharing - yet."

The elephant in the room remained unmentioned. Two of the three people there wondered about it. But only one of them knew. The noose was tightening.

*

Forty Three

"Have you seen the alert, Josh?"

"Yes, Boss, just now."

"So the *Arabian Princess* is headed for Malaga?"

"That's what the clearance papers apparently say, according to GCHQ. If she's carrying members of the Saudi Royal Family they may turn off the ship's AIS tracker, but we'd pick them up going through the Strait of Gibraltar – apparently they have to have clearance to move through the traffic lanes."

"Would the family really be aboard – wouldn't they fly?"

"That's not explicit on the data that GCHQ obtained. They may be traveling on diplomatic passports. However, the declared crew list includes Ashraf Ibrahim."

*

After Stone left Gibraltar for the UK, Baldwin hit the whisky again. The Marina Bay dock was depressing him with too many memories of Ellie but he also realized that he was missing Stone, compounding his gloom and guilt. Liam, one of the marina security staff had again invited him out for beers, but Baldwin had declined. He'd tried to get a few maintenance tasks done on *Rubaiyat*, but lacked enthusiasm.

Then he ran out of whisky.

He'd finished the last bottle with a morning snifter in his tea and headed for the nearest liquor store shortly after 10 am. It was a fine morning, cloudless, with the air cooler than of late and he looked up at the summit of the Rock. There was just a hint of a small cloud trailing in its lee. He breathed in deeply and then coughed. And coughed again.

And then he started running.

It was over an hour and a half before he completed the Rock Run and reached the end of the road near the top of the Rock.

He was breathing hard, doubled over, exhausted. *You're not fit, son. Get a bloody grip!*

And he did.

He looked down at the Strait, gazed across to North Africa and the turned to face south east, Algeria, where Ellie had died. He knew

Ellie's last letter word for word and he re-read it in his mind. And then he finally understood what she had been telling him.

He jogged gently down the hill, struggling with his weak ankle, looking down at the long Gibraltar breakwater protecting a string of docks, expensive waterfront developments, and a marina. He knew it was Queensway Marina, a 'posh', relatively expensive marina. And he could see vacant berths.

An hour later he had arranged a month's berthing for *Rubaiyat* at Queensway. A new start.

He headed back along Queensway Road ignoring the liquor stores. He stopped in café for a double-shot espresso and a large glass of water and watched the tourists. *My grieving is over Ellie. I love you, but I will move on, as you asked.*

Liam was quite happy to help him move *Rubaiyat* to Queensway Marina, getting off shift at 4 pm. It took less than a couple of hours.

"Thanks for your help Liam. I'll buy you a beer tonight if you're free."

"That's be great Steve, thanks. I was getting really worried about you."

"Thanks for your concern, mate, but it's time to move on. The dock at Marina Bay was too noisy next to the airport."

"And I guess there were too many memories there for you?"

"Yeh. Yeh, I suppose that's the real truth of it."

"Well, I'll see you at seven then, at the dock gate here."

Two weeks later *Rubaiyat* was gleaming. Baldwin had gone through her, de-junking, cleaning and servicing. He'd removed her sails, had them checked, washed and repaired. She'd need a bottom scrub and some anti-fouling paint and he hadn't yet decided where to get that done. It was a Saturday afternoon as he sat in the cockpit with a mug of tea, crossing the final items off his maintenance checklist.

"Had a bit of trouble finding you, Baldwin. I see you've moved the boat."

The figure was standing in the sun. Baldwin squinted, but the voice was a giveaway.

"Fuck off Barbary. I wondered when you'd show up again. I'm not going to Morocco."

"You don't need to. You've seen the news?"

"If you mean about ABZ and the heist, yeh. So he *is* alive."

"That's what I told you a couple of weeks ago. Can I come aboard for a chat?"

"Anything you have to say, you can say from there."

Barbary glanced at the next boat, a Grand Banks trawler yacht, where one of the crew was hosing down the decks. "I don't think you'd like your neighbor to hear what I have to say."

"Then I'll walk along the dock with you, find somewhere suitable. You. Are. Not. Coming. Aboard. My. Boat. Final. You people always leave something unpleasant behind."

Baldwin locked up the cabin hatch and they headed out of the marina complex without speaking.

"Prince Khalifa of Saudi Arabia is on his motor yacht *Arabian Princess,* with ben-Zhair, aka Ashraf Ibrahim, our code name Boromir. He's listed on the crew roster as Entertainment Manager. They will be leaving Rabat tomorrow. Next port of call is declared as Malaga. So the job is on, but in Malaga. You and Stone."

"I think not. Things have changed. I'm moving on, so if that's all you've got to say then piss off."

Barbary glanced at his watch. "Stone left Gatwick just after noon and she's on her way to Gib, should be landing in the next hour, actually."

Baldwin realized that his heart missed a beat and wondered if Barbary had noticed anything in his eyes, or his color, which he knew was his tell.

"I'm not doing a wet job with Stone, even if it is for revenge, even if it is ben-Zhair, Ashraf wotsit or whatever else you call him."

"Boromir. And at the moment it's not a wet job so you can put your knickers back on about Stone. Or maybe take them off? Just remember to keep *your* trousers on - dropping them is not good for operational efficiency." There was the faintest questioning look in in Barbary's eyes, a raised eyebrow and what looked suspiciously like a smirk around his thin lips. Baldwin grasped his glass of beer tightly, lifted it, looked at it, looked at Barbary. "Not in here Baldwin. We'll take it outside if you like, although I wouldn't advise it."

Baldwin sipped the beer and put the glass down. "Fuck you Barbary, you're as bad as Stevenson and he was fucking useless, squared. If you're supposed to be my handler then you need to go back to spy school. You're a twat. Sorry, no, a twat is useful. You're not worth the energy – or the beer."

Barbary laughed. “You got a good line in insults, Baldwin” but his amusement was not reciprocated.

They were seated in a corner booth at the rear of the Premier Sports Bar on Line Wall Road. The English Premiership season was about to get underway and there were two pre-season friendlies showing on the Sky Sports screens. The bar was almost full of holidaymakers, many well-oiled even at afternoon tea time. The atmosphere was raucous and provided plenty of cover for the conversation.

Baldwin looked again into the pint of beer between his hands. It was properly cold and he watched the condensation dribble down the side. The air in the bar was comfortably cool, the AC struggling to with the heat generated by the crowd of football fans and the hot humid Mediterranean air which leaked in occasionally as the crowd increased through the doorways.

“Listen Baldwin, there’s much more to this. We’re back on the track of Sveta Kovacs – code name *Alice*, by the way. Use it. Remember her? She left Geneva two days ago on a flight to Madrid, complete with a new face and passport – or two - and then took a rental car. The rental agreement says car was to be dropped off in Alicante. That’s a convenient ferry port. Except she didn’t go there. She left the rental car in Malaga Airport early this morning. We’re pretty sure she didn’t enter the terminal.”

“Malaga? That’s a coincidence, has to be.”

“Even you know that’s too much to believe. We think Boromir is now using cryptocurrency to move funds for his operations. And crypto, incidentally, is Prince Khalifa’s latest hobby. Prince Khalifa is a member of the Saudi Royal Family and there’s half a suspicion that the Prince has funded all Boromir’s operations. That would be a huge diplomatic problem for HMG. We need to stop him. Now we have proof that Alice and Boromir were recently in Paris at the same time. And of course there is the fact that Alice’s demonstrated specialty is in cryptocurrency. Coincidence only goes so far. Kovacs is not professionally trained, other than for hacking and cybercrime. So tradecraft is not her strong point, and she’s left a trail, indistinct, but enough for us to follow. Overconfidence or ignorance we don’t know which, but clever people can be arrogant and overconfident. The very clever people recognize their limitations and work around them.”

“It’s stupid to put me there if there is anything in it. Both of them know me. But she *is* an arrogant bitch.”

"There you go - overconfidence in her own abilities. As far as she is concerned you don't know her with her new face. She would believe it was coincidence. And, from the debriefing you gave us we do not believe that Boromir knows you. After all you only met his stand-in, didn't you?"

"Maybe, but the jury's out on that. *Now* I'm OK here in Gib but I'd be going back *into* the EU. Are the Portuguese on my tail? The Spanish security services? Do your guys know?"

"No. You're off the hook on that score, they never were. Borthwick straightened that out." *But we may choose to put you back on as a motivator*. "All you and Stone have to do is find out what's going on, nothing wet is planned unless the op goes tits-up. You'll have technical backup. And I'll be at hand, just in case."

"Well that's fucking comforting. On hand to do what exactly?"

"Just nearby, as support."

"Why don't you just do it yourself?"

"Because she knows you. We want *reaction* so that she will know we can track her anywhere. Then she will be more compliant. We plan to give her a lift to a new life in England. And to lift her you will definitely need support. We want to confirm that she really is linked to Boromir because we can't find anything electronic between them. She's stolen a hundred billion plus dollars in Bitcoin that we know of, God knows what else, plus she cleaned out the Russian CryptoRubles fund."

"What? That much? She was behind that big scam in the papers? But ABZ claimed responsibility publicly. I saw the news."

"Yes. Interesting isn't it? One or the other, or both together. We need to find out. She had the set-up right under your noses in Portugal." Barbary watched carefully as Baldwin swung one way, then the other. Maybe Stone was a hook that Barbary should use dangle more obviously.

"Jesus! That much! Why doesn't she just retire then?"

"You said it earlier. Arrogance Plus, undoubtedly, technical challenge. And she's like a black widow. We know she terminated one of her partners in Kiev. They'd been pretty close once. The question is, what is she going to do next? That explosion in Portugal was caused by acetylene gas, who do you think arranged that?"

"Shit that's why…"

"What?"

"Nothing."

"And what about Boromir? He doesn't mess about either."

"What's he got, must be nearly ten thousand deaths to his name – Malta, Rome the Canary Islands, Florida, the Caribbean?"

"And revenge for Ellie of course. You'll be doing the world a big favor."

"Stone would be there with you as cover."

Baldwin looked skeptically at Barbary, sure that he was not being told the whole story – some things just did not add up and there were too many gaps. "So that's what the Russian assault on Saluscent was all about, the fact that she'd robbed their bank."

There was a huge roar and they looked up in surprise, starting to move, to prepare for assault.

But Manchester United had scored.

"Fucking football!"

They eased down into their seats.

"No, it started before that. They knew beforehand – or wanted her for something else. It was planned before she emptied their crypto-treasury and in fact took place as she did it. Now the stakes are much higher. It's likely that Moscow is still after her, but we're sure we're ahead of them."

"How sure?"

"Ten percent."

"That's hardly a racing certainty."

"I'm being straight with you, whatever London tells me. Come on, we'd better go meet Telion."

"Telion?"

"Stone to you, remember? Once we confirm the link with Boromir we'll let it run for a while and see what develops. We may change tack with him – it would be convenient to have some leverage on the Saudis through Prince Khalifa. Then you'll lift *Alice* and take her in your yacht to rendezvous with a ship offshore."

"Like fuck I will. My boat stays out of this. I've lost one already because of you lot. No way. And I'll not involve Stone either as I said."

"Stone is non-negotiable but we may have some flexibility about your boat. You can't have it all your own way."

"It's a bloody stupid plan. I don't care who nicked what. Things have changed. I'm not doing it. End of."

"Well then, the BBC story goes out tomorrow morning and you'll be a hunted man within twenty four hours. Gib's a small place. It's not my decision. I've got to meet Stone now, why don't you come with me and think it over. Don't forget that she'll be doing this Malaga job anyway, with or without you. You know each other, work well together. You could look out for her."

And Baldwin was hooked, caught by the BBC story as Barbary struck and Stone the barb made the hook immovable.

It was then that Baldwin knew he had really moved on. Things *had* changed.

*

Forty Four

It was just after dawn when Sveta fired up the script on her laptop in her 5th floor suite in the Mandarin Oriental. After leaving the Paris clinic she had booked in to the Georges V hotel for a few days while the bruising reduced and she learned more about the use of make-up – she'd never before been very interested in the more prosaic interests of her gender, but now it was a necessity. During her stay at the clinic she had resisted the temptation to do any online work and focused on her recovery and on setting her plans for the future. Now there was more to be done online – she had a vast portfolio to track – and she set about it with a will.

Then after her few days preparation in the Georges V she hired a car and drove leisurely from Paris to Geneva over a period of three days where she took a suite at the Mandarin Oriental on the quai Turrettini, leaving the car at Geneva Airport as arranged. The hotel suite overlooked the River Rhone. The next day, as the first rays of the August sun over the Alps slanted across the heavy drapes and into her room, she looked down at the barges on the river and had a vivid flashback to Kiev. It had been just over three years since Danylo had died at her hand, but it seemed like an age.

She turned back to her new laptop and watched the verbose dialogue as the script executed. The software proceeded to login and check through more than 500 credit card accounts that her software bots had opened six months before. It downloaded the balance details and updated a simple Excel spreadsheet. Everything seemed to be proceeding well and she ordered a room service breakfast of coffee and croissants.

An hour or so later the script closed down after notifying her that the task was complete. The script had been unable to open 39 of the online accounts for a variety of reasons ranging from bad connections to site maintenance. None of the errors was due to security problems – her script handled two factor authentication where sites required it, Captcha, and a variety of other security mechanisms using the opensource SciKit AI she had built in to the software.

The credit card accounts had been fed random deposits typically of $5,102.50 to $9,762.30 (never 'round amounts') from a range of Paypal, Stripe, Payoneer and 18 other payment systems and countries which accepted cryptocurrency deposits and which her software had transferred in from her many hundreds of cryptocurrency accounts. It was a huge automated money-funnelling operation. Now that Swiss banks were accepting Bitcoin there were other avenues open to her for laundering. And then there was the Cayman Islands – she'd visit there next winter – and maybe move on from there to Panama.

Finally this first tranche of her money was cleaned and laundered and tomorrow she would 'rinse and repeat' the process. For the present she had a little over $4 million of spending money, a drop in the ocean of her reserves. That would be further consolidated and washed over the coming weeks. There would be an electronic trail but it would take years to unravel, if ever. The trail was now becoming almost too complex even for her to understand, run by AI and executed by bots. All she needed were the encrypted account details and credentials. After all, she had so much money what was a few million here or there?

The night before, Sveta had dined at the Yakumanka Restaurant in the hotel. It had been a surreal experience, a Peruvian restaurant in an Oriental-themed hotel in the heart of a Swiss city. Her tastes were not adventurous so she had avoided the raw fish of the *tiraditos* as most of the fish she had eaten as child in Kiev had been of poor quality. Later she had found out that much of the fish in the Dnieper River had contained high concentrations of heavy metals.

The wok-sautéed fillet of beef in the Yakamuka had been melt-in-the-mouth excellent, accompanied by a robust Bordeaux which the waiter had recommended - although acquiring a real liking for rare beef might take her some time. Over the dessert of *mousse au chocolat peruvienne* she once again realized she had much to learn about the world but now had the money and time to enjoy the education. After she had emerged from the tight focus and intense research of her Ph.D., Danylo had taught her much about some of the finer things in the Ukraine that he knew about but there were still huge gaps in her knowledge and experience, and even Danylo's knowledge was limited.

After breakfast she planned to walk over to the Fedex office on the Rue des Ateliers to collect a package from Budapest and then after a leisurely lunch at a café beside Lake Geneva she would visit the UBS bank with her new passport and open an account. Dinner would be in one of the many riverside restaurants, perhaps outdoors in the late summer warmth. Then the next couple of days would all be very much the same - the crypto-laundry, a parcel from an Embassy, a private bank.

She smiled as she bit into another perfect croissant. All was going to plan, but there was just one test she had yet to complete.

And then there was Dmitri's scam. $45 million was small in comparison to her overall assets, a drop in the ocean, but she hated Muslims. She was in a new, exciting stage of her life. It was fun, winding the Arab up on Telegram, but soon it would be face to face, for a change. She wondered if she could do it, take the risk, look into his eyes. Then she remembered the night she had pushed the knife into her father's back. Yes, she knew she could do it. She was not backing off now.

*

Just before 11 am Sveta breezed out of the doors of the Mandarin. She was wearing the blue contact lenses which matched those in the pictures she had sent to Hungary. Her natural black hair was cut short and over that she wore a black wig cut rather severely in a bob. Unused to wearing much make-up since her days with Danylo, she had applied some mascara and a dark red lipstick. A black leather blouson worn over a light silk blouse was complemented by passé DKNY denims and black leather ankle boots with modest heels and faux gold buckles. Fashion was not her strong point but she thought her eye was good. She was happy with her appearance but still surprised every morning when she went to the bathroom and saw a stranger in the mirror, even stranger after she had put in the colored contact lenses.

She checked her smartphone for directions then headed across the river on the Rue de Coutance. A light wind was blowing down the Rhone and ruffling the surface. She paused briefly and looked at a family of ducks, this year's chicks well on the way to maturity as they paddled against the flow, then fussed to safety by their mother as a barge chugged past. After crossing the river a short stroll down the Rue Du Rhone led to the Piaget store.

This was to be a very quick test and she almost got caught up in the delight of choosing a luxury watch, over-running the time she had allowed herself as her eyes wandered over the fortune on display. *I could buy this shop many times over.*

One particular watch had caught her eye in a magazine she had read whilst in the clinic. She checked the picture she had stored on her phone and showed it to the salesman who soon located the model in a display cabinet and helped her try it on. "Ah yes, the 'Possession' model. A beautiful choice if I may say so, and well in keeping with your particular *mode.* Also the most inexpensive in our range." There was almost a sneer in the salesman's' voice as he used the word 'inexpensive'. "And your wrist is of the perfect size! We do not need to adjust the wristband I think. It is comfortable yes?"

"Perfect."

Her choice was modest – for a Piaget – with a tag of just 4,000 Swiss francs – about US$4,500.

"Can I interest you in some jewelry, a pendant perhaps, or a brooch?"

"No thank you, not today."

"Very well. And how would Madame like to pay?" asked Albert, the middle-aged, sharply dressed salesman with the condescending attitude and definite leer – not a good combination to attract a lady.

"PopID, please."

"Of course. If M'amselle would please look into the screen."

She stepped across to the payment desk and looked into the screen which he indicated. The device which looked much like large smartphone, did not capture and store pictures, only dimensions measured by the camera and erased immediately a transaction was confirmed. Sveta's stomach knotted and her heart raced with the apprehension. Albert pressed the button and 80 datapoints on her face were measured, encrypted, transmitted and analyzed, and Clarisse Beauchamp's e-wallet was $4,500 lighter within seconds.

They waited a few seconds.

Then the device beeped.

"Thank you Mademoiselle. That is all in order. Would you like your name on the receipt?"

So, the work she had done with the Paris surgeon in preparing the shape of her new face had been successful. Although the surgeon knew nothing of the fact that he had in his operations on her face altered 30 datapoints and 5 key ratios, her new face matched less than 60% of her previous *visage*.

"No, thank you" she said, her relief carefully hidden. "I prefer to remain anonymous and try to save the forests at the same time" Sveta smiled coquettishly.

"Yes of course, as do many of our clients. I hope that you enjoy your most excellent watch for many years to come. Would you like it gift-wrapped?"

"No, thank you. I intend to wear it now." Sveta slipped the band over her wrist and snapped the clasp.

"Yes, why not enjoy it straight away?"

"That's what I thought."

"*C'est si bon.* Now, can I be of service in some other way, Mademoiselle?" Albert smoothly enquired.

Sveta wondered of this was a come-on or just stiff Swiss courtesy and shook her head "No thank you, I have spent enough for today. But you can keep the packaging – I don't need it."

"Of course. Please do not hesitate to call again."

He escorted Sveta to the door and she stepped out into the Rue du Rhone with an almost audible sigh of relief as the lock clicked shut behind her. Her face had passed the test. Clarisse Beauchamp's identity was alive. Now, there were the other identities to activate if that pedophile in the Hungarian Ministry of the Interior had done his job.

*

"What have you got for me Josh?"

"We've heard from Budapest HOS. They've nailed the chap who was touting passports. Miksa Pulszky. We're calling him *Jorah.* He was – is - into pedophilia."

"They didn't expose him?"

"No, no. They'll keep him on the back burner for future use. Put too much pressure on these people and they top themselves."

"And?"

"Fifty eight names, with digital copies of the passports – we got the lot."

"That's a bloody good haul."

"Yes, He was doing all right at ten thousand euros a pop. But the milch cow is now dry. HOS is well chuffed. We'll get someone in GT to look at them, once we've had a full look at the females."

"Anyone promising?"

"Well, I picked out Borbola Goraya and Svetlana Goraya, so they are nailed, straight off, clearly Alice's image. We're scanning the other images now in case there are more passports with that face."

"But that only takes us to Paris."

"Quite. We have half a dozen other female passports within the same age group – and no face to match it to, if we ignore that of Putin."

Macsen laughed. "But Baskerville can check those passports?"

"Yes, but that will only work if she has crossed a Schengen border."

"Or she's recorded on some other video like a railway station or even a mall camera."

"That's a huge task."

"The PM has given AstraTen priority one. I didn't say that."

"Say what? Even so, it would tie up GCHQ for weeks, unless we got lucky."

"What about the new search bots – they're calling them the B-pups I think I heard someone say."

"Yes, Baskerville's offspring, out and roaming the deep web. They're still only trying them out as far as I know."

"Well, this could be a good test for them. I'll call Trenchard at GCHQ and give her a nudge."

"It's certainly worth a try. There is just one more thing. The list of duff Hungarian passports includes a Clarisse Beauchamp. The passport application says she was a French mature student at the University in Budapest who has started a consulting business there. She has, apparently passed the tests for Hungarian citizenship, including the language test – and that's no mean feat it seems – if true, of course. The legend looks solid but we obviously know it's a dodgy passport and then there's the name, Clarisse. We know that Alice's tradecraft has weaknesses…"

"…And the new face in Paris was given to a Clarisse Duval."

"Yes, but it's just a hunch. If it bears out then we've got a picture of Alice's new face. The facial recognition software gives it a 55% probability. Some of the key facial dimensions and ratios are way off."

"So, Clarisse Beauchamp and a face at 55%. Feed it to the hounds, let's see what they sniff out."

"At 55% we may get a lot of false positives."

Macsen shrugged. "We'll just have to spin the wheel. Let's give it twenty four hours."

*

Forty Five

The Monday 8 am prayers session was a general heads of desks sharing of weekend updates run by 'C' and constrained by 'need to know', so the agenda was fenced by the need to keep some high priority operations – such as Looking Glass and Bilbo – tightly compartmentalized. Then, following prayers, 'C' met individually with heads of desks to address their specific off-agenda operations. It was Macsen's turn at 9.00 am.

"Nothing at all, 'C'. We've drawn a blank on Beauchamp and the new face, at least within the Schengen area."

"She could have crossed a border illegally, outward. The south European Med countries are only worried about people trying to get in, not out. They don't stamp the passport of EU nationals heading out."

"That's certainly possible, but why risk an unstamped passport, or lack of visa if she tries to enter a non-EU country?"

"She's smart enough to have handled that if she can get her hands on genuine passports - and we know she can - but maybe we are being short-sighted. Why only Hungarian passports? Perhaps she's got others too."

"So maybe we should just work on matching the face and not look for face *and* name together. But that would increase the false positives and take a lot more resources to resolve them."

"Or maybe she just hasn't moved at all, in which case it's a waiting game – which we can't afford to play. I take it you checked car rentals?"

"Baskerville should have done that."

"Well, double check that he has. Intelligence – artificial or not – is not everything. And Baskerville doesn't get hunches yet!"

"I'm sure it'll come though. It's bloody frightening really."

"Yes, frightening - but useful."

24 hours later Josh was back with 'M'.

"A problem with the latest Baskerville AI update. Fucking stupid program fault! I set him off to look for face *and* name, Clarisse Beauchamp. Apparently the development team pared the AI code right down for faster execution of the latest version. Because car rental companies don't store facial images the bloody software is so smart that it didn't bother to search databases where no images are stored. Or should I say that the bloody programmers are so fucking stupid. Another day lost!"

"I take it you've got some good news then?"

The wry humor passed over Josh's head.

"Yes, a Clarisse Duval – French citizen - rented a Hertz car in Paris five days ago, to be dropped off at Geneva airport. Paid by card over the phone when booking. A new card and the address is that of a terminal care hospice in Paris."

"Bloody Norah!"

"The car was dropped off in Geneva as arranged, two days ago."

"Now that is *real* progress."

"Only so far. Baskerville is due a brain transplant right now and I hope the fucking programmer is looking for a new job. It'll be about three hours before Baskerville is back on the trail with the AI patch release, checking hotels in Geneva."

"Can't we get anyone else to do it the hard way?"

"GCHQ says they're at full stretch and anyway it would be quicker to wait the three hours for the AI update than to put a data delve team together here."

"What about using the current version of the AI, re-instruct it?"

"Impossible, they took it off line as soon as I pointed out their stupid error. I've been told it's something to do with the AI knowledge base and neural network, and they must apply a warm patch."

"Oh bugger! Hmm…on the bright side we're almost in real time now. I'll call HOS Geneva and tell him to prepare to mobilize for a hot lift team arriving overnight. Start the planning. I'll talk to 'C' and let you know which team we'll use."

Sveta was just closing her hotel room door when one of her phones chirped - the special chirp - a warning. It was a push notification from her credit card supervisory software. An enquiry had been made on one of her card accounts, Clarisse Beauchamp.

She swore. *That is impossible. No one can know. It must be a mistake.* She logged into her supervisor and drilled through the account, deep into the Mastercard database, deep into the heart of the logging system. She drilled even further, clicking on 'Merchant ID' to track the enquiry source and the response was 'No matching merchant ID found, database error, please report to Support'. *That was no error, that must have been the Russians. Or someone else?*

Clarisse – Sveta - threw her clothes into her walk-on case, retrieved her documents from the room safe and within ten minutes was out of the hotel. She found a café and ordered coffee while she used her private browser to search for accommodation.

Two hours later she had checked into a pension, a very old, well-established pension, typically Swiss and typically inflexible when it came to the law. Cash accepted, but “Non Ma’mselle, I am sorry, we have to retain the passport while you are here. This is the law in Switzerland, you are not in Hungary or the EU now.”

She glared at him, exasperated. “But the large hotels just retain a photocopy.”

“I’m sorry Ma’mselle. A photocopy is not permitted in our policy. As you can see we are a humble *pension* and not a large hotel. But we do offer things that a large hotel cannot offer.”

“Such as?”

“Well, I am the proprietor and owner, you get my personal service.”

Sveta bit her tongue.

“All right then. My plans might change, I might have to leave at short notice.”

“That is quite acceptable. The desk is open for checkout between 7 am. and 9 pm.”

“And outside those hours?”

“That is highly irregular, checkout is not possible, the desk is closed and passports are safely locked away as you will appreciate. However by special arrangement with me you may check out in advance. Please let me know before the office closes at 9 pm.”

“And how do you expect me to check out if an emergency occurs during the night?”

“If you leave your credit card details then that will be possible. Or pay cash in advance?”

“Very well, I will pay for three days in advance by cash.”

“I’m very sorry Ma’mselle, we are fully booked. Tonight is all I have available. Do you wish to pay and check out in advance now?”

“Yes, whatever.”

“Very well. Would you like me to let you know if we have a cancellation.”

“No. One night will definitely be enough here, if you have a good internet connection?”

“Of course. A fast one – my son is a software engineer.”

Well that’s fucking something.

*

Forty Six

Bill Johnson took the call in his cabin, just behind the bridge of *Auric Adventurer*. He had been Charles Tobin's skipper for seven years and was completely trusted by the owner. He'd gone through an attack on the vessel in Argostoli in the Ionian and the kidnapping of Tobin in Malta eighteen months previously. Johnson's career was unmatched in the superyacht industry and he had turned down many offers to move his seaman's bag to other superyachts – but only after Tobin had matched the offers.

It had been some months since he'd last seen Tobin and that was unusual. In the meantime he'd moved the *Adventurer* from port to port in the Mediterranean with visits to Tunisia and Morocco being a regular occurrence to avoid paying EU import duty on the vessel, which was registered in the Cayman Islands.

Johnson looked out over the sparking waters of Cala de Volpe on the north east coast of Sardinia. They were surrounded by superyachts, many bigger than the *Adventurer's* 1200 tons displacement. The 'boys toys' of jetskis, windsurfers and even helicopters were widely in evidence in and over the emerald waters – it was not called the Costa Smeralda for nothing – as well as 'A' list celebrities paying their $30,000 a week per head and upwards to be there and mix with the people who mattered. There were of course many politicians too, often on ships owned by oligarchs and others who operated on or over the edge of serious criminality, but the politicians rarely coughed up hard cash for their holidays. They traded favors.

"Bill, I want you to move the *Adventurer* to Malaga, as soon as possible. When do you think you can be there?"

"Well, Mr Tobin, we still have a charter party and they will not be leaving until the weekend. There's another booking next week but we can cancel that. It looks like there's a Mistral due early next week so I think it will be later in the week before we can cross the Gulf of Lyon. Malaga is over 700 miles from here."

"That's only forty eight hours steaming, maximum. I need you in Malaga before the end of next week."

"Understood, sir. We'll work our way west and see how the weather develops. We may be able to make La Palma in Majorca before it blows too hard."

Bloody typical, I don't see Tobin for months and then I've got to jump like a dog in a shit weather forecast.

"Good. And I don't want you paying harbor dues along the way. Three thousand Euros a day is not on given that we're losing that charter, so keep her at sea."

"Yes Mr Tobin, as long as the weather is not too bad."

"The ship's built for it – and I pay you enough money to keep her safe. There's plenty of shelter around the Balearics."

"Understood, Sir."

"There's a new charter party joining at Malaga. Special friends of mine, not through the agency. Bare boat terms. You'll do a two day handover and then you and the crew can take a couple of weeks off. Paid, of course."

"Are you sure these people are up to it, Mr Tobin? Two days isn't much time for a handover on a ship as sophisticated as *Adventurer*." *I don't want them fucking up my ship and leaving a load of problems for me to sort out.*

"These people are top-notch, they can handle warships, I have it on the highest authority, Bill."

Handy in bloody war with plenty of crew.

"Understood, Sir. I'll get her to Malaga asap."

"Great, I'm relying on you. I'll send you details of the charter party. Keep me posted on movements." The line dropped.

Johnson cursed as he called his First Officer to the bridge before he emailed the Charter Brokers the bad news about 'an engine problem'. An excuse maybe, but Tobin's tight fist on maintenance costs meant that Johnson really did not fancy powering west at full ahead in a Mistral - an 'engine problem' excuse might turn out to be much more than a ruse to cancel a contract. A pity, he'd looked forward to meeting Angelina Jolie and her implants.

At the other end of the dead line, Johnson's cursing was more than matched by Tobin.

The day before, Tobin had received a short notice invitation to dinner at The Ivy from the Cabinet Secretary. Such invitations from the higher reaches of power were rare since he had fallen from grace so publicly. He quickly cleared his private diary for the evening. The lady from Southampton would be spending the night elsewhere. Much to his chagrin the helicopter to London was chartered – he'd had to surrender the lease on his own a few months previously. Cash flow, the bane of visionary entrepreneurs. The helicopter collected him from his estate in Winchester and a hired limousine from Battersea heliport took him to the 8 pm engagement, arriving precisely on time. It was a foul unseasonable August evening and the helicopter ride had been turbulent, unsettling his usually cast-iron stomach. As he climbed out of the limousine the air was warm but the rain was heavy and falling in sheets along West Street, powered by a depression moving up the English Channel.

He entered the restaurant and was greeted by the maitre'd. "Good evening, Mr Tobin. It's a pleasure to see you again. Your private room is ready and your guest has already arrived. Please follow me." *My private room, my guest? What the fuck?*

The maitre'd led the way to the door near the rear, Tobin nodding at a couple of faces he recognized as he trod the plush carpet. He stared hard when he entered the private dining room. The man at the table did not match the pictures he'd checked on Wikipedia. He was clearly not the current UK Cabinet Secretary. The maitre'd moved away to arrange a waiter.

"Hello Mr. Tobin." The man rose and offered his hand. It was a dry, firm grip, matched with confident and challenging eye contact. He was a few inches shorter than Tobin, and stocky with a slight paunch. "Please take a seat. I'm very sorry, but the Cabinet Secretary was called away on some urgent business and couldn't make it this evening."

"Who the fuck are you? Why is this room in my name? I was *invited* here!"

"I work directly for the Prime Minister." *Dotted line only for now but good enough.* "Would you like an aperitif?"

Henry Brewell nodded to the approaching waiter. 'I'll have a Glenlivet on the rocks and my guest will have…" He turned to Tobin.

"Make it a Bloody Mary, double, Absolute. No Worcester sauce." The waiter nodded and left the obviously tense scene. "Who the fuck are *you*?" The volumes of their voices were several octaves apart. Tobin had to listen hard to hear the quite reply.

"You can call me Henry. You probably knew my predecessor, Lord Gore."

"Gore? MI fucking Six. I should have bloody known!"

Brewell shook his head. "Perhaps."

Some of the nearby diners outside the room had seen Brewell come in and knew differently. The identity of the Chief of the Secret Intelligence Service was public knowledge – a strange paradox - and many of the people who dined at The Ivy made it their business to recognize such people. Indeed, when he entered Brewell had noticed two foreign gentlemen in whom his agency was currently taking a particular interest over the export of sensitive technology to embargoed countries.

Tobin ranted as the maitre'd glanced across with some anxiety. "Why is this room in my name? I was invited by the Cabinet Secretary. I'm not paying for your bloody jolly."

"A little subterfuge was necessary to get the room – and to encourage you to come. They are fully booked tonight and we knew it was one of your favorite haunts. It seemed wise to make it a private room given the nature of our meeting. What would you like to eat, Charles. I may call you Charles, mightn't I?"

Tobin nodded. His evening went steadily downhill thereafter and his stomach did not recover. He did not enjoy his meal, even less the conversation which was stilted as they worked through sole meunière and rack of Welsh lamb. He noticed that Brewell seemed to be remarkably well informed about gold and cryptocurrencies, but was very cagey about UK politics and the Middle East - as might be expected.

Brewell sought Tobin's views on the recent cryptoheist and they touched loosely on cybercrime. Tobin avoided discussion of his own bitcoin loss.

"I heard that you recently visited a crypto mining farm in Morocco."

"Did you indeed?"

"Yes, there were some interesting people there at the same time, it seems."

"You are well informed, Henry."

"It's my business Charles. You are a person of interest to us. Will you tell me what the meeting was about?"

"No."

"Hmm. Well, we have a pretty good idea who you met with, and I warn you, Charles, you are mixing with the wrong people."

"Fuck you Brewell. I'll not have you telling me who I can and can't mix with."

They paused while a waiter poured them Prunier vintage cognac, then Henry Brewell got to the point. He leaned towards Tobin and spoke quietly.

"And I'll tell *you* Charles that there are still serious problems arising from your previous ventures in the Middle East and Malta, and that Her Majesty's Revenue and Customs are due to start another investigation, imminently. Tax evasion is the phrase I heard. Evasion *not* avoidance. You know what that means, don't you?"

Tobin remained silent, passive, his face and body betraying no reaction as befitted a world class poker player.

Brewell continued "One of my colleagues will be contacting you tomorrow. *Which one* will depend on your response to my next request."

"Which colleague? What's the request?" was the flat toneless, response.

"It could be someone from HMRC, or it could be someone erm… less visible, shall we say? He – or she – may make certain requests as to the availability of your yacht over the next few weeks. Can your yacht be made available?"

"Do I have a choice?" No emotion.

"One always has choices, Charles. In this case they may be rather limited in range. But yes, you do have choices – or, should I say – *a* choice."

"It could be possible. I would have to discuss it with my Captain. We may have commitments to other parties."

"I'm sure that Angelina Jolie would not want to spend time on a vessel with engine damage."

"There is no problem with her engines." Brewell permitted himself a smile, watching carefully as Tobin continued. "Hmm...Angelina Jolie. now that *is* a surprise to me. Our clients are given code names to keep the paparazzi at bay. Even I don't know who they are."

Brewell shrugged, with another thin smile on his lips, disbelieving. He was sure he was getting to Tobin, although the man had superb self control. "I'll take that as a yes, then, Charles. My colleague will introduce himself as Clarence when he calls tomorrow."

"And what do I get in return for helping you out?"

"I'll pick up the tab for tonight. And I'll have a quiet word with my colleague at HMRC."

"And they'll be off my back permanently?"

"I can't really speak for my colleague at HMRC, but I think that *permanently* would be rather too much to hope for given the nature of your erm… ongoing activities." Brewell stood and offered his hand across the table. Tobin stood, turned on his heel and strode out of room and out of The Ivy.

Brewell thought that the plan cooked up by Conlon and Macsen was creative. It was rarely the case that he could justify eating at the Ivy and having some operational involvement, but he had enjoyed the evening tremendously and it was not yet over. He selected some very ripe Stilton and a bottle of port for himself. What he didn't drink he'd take home. Penelope loved port.

*

The following morning Conlon called Tobin and introduced himself as Clarence.

Tobin was advised that he really should move the *Auric Adventurer* to Malaga within a week for a crew change. A new crew would be provided under bareboat charter terms for two weeks. The crew would be highly qualified and a two day handover was scheduled for orientation. Reasonable expenses would of course be met on submission of a valid invoice to a specific company in Jersey.

Tobin had been put over a barrel and he hated it. He knew that this was one situation where bluff and bluster would get him nowhere. Besides, he *did* have too much to hide. Much too much.

*

Conlon notified 'C' of the arrangements with Tobin and via the Directorate of Special Forces a troop of the Special Boat Service at Poole was assembled. Josh Packard and Aston Parke (the senior case officer in Conlon's Bilbo team) traveled down to Poole on the late train and briefing began the following day.

This was not a typical special forces deployment and it called for the more nuanced approach to running a superyacht as opposed to an armed assault on a pirate-infested ship. The new crew would not be expected to serve cocktails to film stars or prepare delicate *cordon bleu* meals for bon viveurs or oligarchs. That would be too much of a stretch. The special charter guests would be Samuel Becket and his friend Emma Freud, and they would be well looked after. Becket was apparently a millionaire who kept a very low profile, and his girlfriend was a practicing psychologist. Only Major Smith who was running the team thought this amusing.

Tobin had provided Clarence with up to date specifications and drawings of the *Auric Adventurer,* including details of access to the citadel – the highly secure safe room where the owner could lock himself away in case of pirate or terrorist attack. There was also access to a mini-sub for escape.

The new crew for the superyacht was readied to fly out to Malaga from Bournemouth Airport, prepped initially as a rugby club on a summer jolly with golf clubs but without wives. Two members of the team were specialized seaman officers – they had to be quite capable of skippering cruise ships and oil tankers in case of hijackings, even the occasional superyacht. Another officer was an engineer. Threats to superyachts were not unusual especially when UK government ministers were on vacation.

The tools of their trade would be drawn from the Royal Navy armory in Gibraltar. By special agreement Gibraltar was still part of the Schengen area after Brexit so the small cargo would simply be moved by van along the coast from Gibraltar to Malaga without hindrance.

*

Baldwin and Stone packed their bags and strolled across the border from Gibraltar into Spain just following the road which actually ran across the runway of Gibraltar airport. They picked up a hire car in La Linea and headed along the A381 towards Jerez. The day was clear and hot, with temperatures rising towards 40 C as they argued about who should drive before agreeing to split it. Baldwin took the wheel first, driving through the heart of sherry country.

"It's a pity we can't stop here for a real steak and a robust red wine."

"I agree. I could stop here for a week quite easily. I love it."

"Do you dance the flamenco?"

Steve glanced across at her and shook his head. "You and your bloody flamenco. No, I bloody don't! I've told you I'm not a dancer, but I enjoy the music. Come on, open the package and let's rehearse our legend. We shouldn't be going on a mission without a proper briefing."

Stone sighed and took out her phone. She removed the two passports from the lining of her travel bag and started reading. Then she giggled and that quickly turned into a fit of laughter.

"What's so funny?"

"They must be bloody kidding! Your passport is in the name of Sam Becket and mine is in the name of Emma Freud."

"So?"

"If you don't know then I'm certainly not explaining it." She dissolved into another fit of laughter. "Our flight from Jerez to Malaga is on a private jet. You are a low-key real-estate multi-millionaire."

"And you?"

"A practising psychologist."

"You, a head doctor! Jesus, these people have no imagination. It sounds like a Friday job, everyone in a hurry to go home and they come up with this crap. It could compromise us."

"No, we should be OK in Spain, I mean who will check? Anyway, these legends are off-the-shelf, prepared in advance. They just stick in photos and a bit more detail to match the personnel."

"So is that Becket with one 't' or two?"

"One. Why?"

"If you don't know I'm not explaining it. London can't do anything right." Their eyes met.

"Watch out!"

Baldwin swerved and just avoided the offside of a truck in the other lane. "Shit! This whole fucking escapade is shaping up to be a bloody disaster." *It's her eyes.*

They spent the next half hour going over their legend which Ellie read from an encrypted message on her Six phone.

"There will be clothes, cards, phones and the rest on the plane for us."

"If I'm to play my part I'll need a load of cash."

"Don't be stupid, your sort never carry cash."

"Then how do I tip people. My PA isn't with us, as far as I know."

"Good point. I'm sure there'll be cash on the plane. We have to leave our genuine passports on the plane at Malaga."

"That's probably for the best."

They stopped for a quick lunch at a taberna on the outskirts of Jerez and then headed for the airport. Three hours later Sam Becket and Emma Freud landed at Malaga airport and the small jet taxied to the VIP terminal. Freshly changed and equipped they were met by a limousine.

Baldwin looked carefully at the driver who winked at him and nodded. Yes, they'd been in the same troop of jollies on a mission in Yemen. "Taff, isn't it?" said Baldwin.

"Spot on, Baldy, or should I say Mr Becket?" The Welsh accent was broad and lilting. "I'm driving you to Dock Two at Malaga harbor. Apparently we're not supposed to speak to you as you're so bloody rich and important, Sir. But putting that to one side, it should be a fun mission, better than the Yemen. Sir."

"Cut the crap Taff, tell me about the team."

"Major Smith - Smithy – is running the show for us. He's now the ship's skipper and he's alright, for an officer. He knows ships."

Baldwin nodded. That was praise indeed coming from a Jolly, as Taff continued: "Our troop has been specially put together for this job – whatever it is it involves running the ship, which we joined a couple of days ago for a handover. The other lads seem to be a good lot, after all we're all Jollies aren't we, know boats and ships? What I will say though is that a couple of the other types aboard, spooks I reckon, seem to keep themselves away from us. One is a woman – we know her only as Sara. She's a looker. Smithy takes orders from a Mr Colville, arrogant sod."

"That'll be Barbary then."

"Probably. I've heard that word a couple of times. OK here we are. Just need to show the IDs to security at the dock gates."

*

Forty Seven

"Fucking hell!"

"What's wrong Samuel?"

Baldwin stood on the quay and looked at the superyacht.

"Everything! I'll tell you later."

The Captain was immaculately turned out in tropical whites when he met them on the quay and led them aboard the ship while the driver collected their copious matching luggage set from the limo. Stone looked at it with interest. She'd seen it unloaded from the plane and hoped the quartermaster or whoever had picked out some decent clothes for her as befitted her new station in life.

"Welcome aboard Mr Becket and Ms Freud. I'm Captain Peter Smith, please call me Peter. I am at your disposal for the duration of the voyage. Here, these are ship smartphones – they will guide you wherever you need to go on the ship. Voice activated. You can call up a layout diagram or you can call a steward with it, or request cabin service. It's very flexible. All the crew have one each for this cruise as you might expect. Dinner this evening may be ashore, depending on what we are advised is appropriate. I will let you know as soon as I have been informed. I'm sure you understand the need for flexibility in the circumstances. I will show you to your suite and then in an hour's time after you have unpacked I will give you a guided tour, followed by drinks on the aft lounge area, Deck Four."

Stone smiled as she spoke. "Don't the stewards unpack for us, Captain? I mean, there's so much of it isn't there?"

Smith smiled. "Usually our esteemed guests bring their own staff. You don't appear to have any with you for this voyage. My crew respect your privacy and we would prefer that you unpacked your own designer wardrobe, Ms Freud."

"I can't wait, Captain. I love surprises."

Baldwin laughed while Smith and Stone tried to keep straight faces.

"You'll receive the dinner invitation on your ship-phones, but please memorize as much of the layout as you can."

"I know it already."

Smith looked at Baldwin in surprise.

"I did two months on this ship in Greece, but I can't tell you more or I'd have to kill you."

Smith smiled without humor and then Baldwin continued “I know the Avocet line.” Mention of the Exeter to Exmouth railway line which passed near the Royal Marines training camp at Lympstone was enough to make Smith relax. Clearly, he’d received a very limited briefing about Baldwin. “I’ve served alongside Taff.”

“Enough said, Mr Becket, thank you. That makes me feel a whole lot better.”

“Sam, this is wonderful! I just can’t wait to soak in the Jacuzzi!”

“Jesus JC, this is Charles Tobin’s yacht. I saved the cunt’s life here. Barbary’s been feeding us bullshit again! What the fuck is going on?”

“I doubt that, Sam, and I’m Emma by the way. It’s need to know I think, so let’s preserve operational security, shall we?”

“Need to know? No, it’s FOWYFAS.”

“What does for wife ass mean?”

“Find out when you’re fucked. As usual.”

“Just the chance would be a fine thing, Sam. Do we have time?”

Baldwin rolled his eyes and turned away. “Get changed, we’ve got the tour to do.”

“But we’ve got to act like millionaires, that means all sorts of hanky panky.”

“I’m not snorting a line for anyone! Get yourself ready. And I’ll be sleeping on the couch, wherever that is.” *Not that I want to.*

An hour later the tour of *Auric Adventurer* was complete, but Baldwin could have conducted it himself. He’d asked Smith about the vacant helicopter deck and was told that there wasn’t a helicopter aboard – the owner did not have one at present as far as he knew. They didn’t visit the crew quarters where Baldwin had found a dead crew member during the attempted murder of Tobin in Kefalonia a couple of years before, but the memories of that night seemed very fresh. He’d killed one of the attackers and wounded Marůska Pavkovic. He winced at the thought – if he’d killed Pavkovic that night then Ellie would still be alive.

The Captain led them to the lounge on Deck Four and they sat at a large circular marble-topped table with seats for twelve.

“Ah, here is the steward to take your drinks order.”

Baldwin did a double-take and then his face clouded. Stone smiled.

“And what will Madam and Sir be drinking this evening?”

It was Barbary, dressed in steward's uniform. "Just a little fun, Mr Becket."

Baldwin's look was thunderous. "Well I'm not bloody amused you twat. I'll have a Heineken. Can you manage that, Manuel?"

"I'll have champagne, thanks. Do you have Cristal?"

"I'll have to check the wine cellar Madam. I'm sure we'll have something of that standard."

Smith laughed trying to break the tension. "And I don't drink on duty, thanks. Just water."

Barbary's tone was sharp. "I didn't ask you Captain Smith." That established the command structure for the operation. He turned away checking his ship-phone for directions to what would surely be a well-stocked cellar. But Cristal?

Smith shook his head "Fucking spooks."

"What does that make us, Captain?" Smith stared at Baldwin and did not reply.

Ten minutes later Barbary had changed clothes and actually looked like a guest – dressed by Marks and Spencer but a guest nonetheless.

A Cristal bottle was nestling in an ice bucket and Baldwin had a green Heineken bottle in front of him.

"Cheers!" They all joined Smith's toast and then Barbary spoke.

Stone looked at her flute. "This doesn't look like any kind of champagne to me."

"It wouldn't. It's all water, the bottles are for looks only in case we're being observed. The wine cellar is strictly off limits for this cruise, orders from London. Apparently the owner's cellar is worth a fortune and it is locked. End of." Barbary looked at the glum faces while Smith grinned, wondering how quickly his team would get in there - at the end of the mission, of course. And strictly against orders.

Barbary droned on. "First, orientation. Don't all look at once, but if you glance over there at the quay on the right you will see a super-yacht bigger even than this one. That's the *Arabian Princess*, owned by Prince Khalifa of Saudi Arabia. The Prince is aboard with some guests and we know that *Boromir* is aboard her this evening. He's on the ship's crew list as Entertainment Manager. *Alice* is also in town though they haven't met yet – it's all *very* coincidental so far, but as you know I don't believe in coincidences and neither does London. I'll give you a full briefing after we've eaten, which will be here aboard this evening."

Baldwin looked at his green bottle. The evening heat was oppressive, with not a breath of wind and he could still taste that last beer he'd had with Barbary in Gib. He could also taste the line of bullshit he'd been fed, yet again. He grimaced. "When is zero hour?"

"We're still working on that, but *Arabian Princess* has her berth booked here for a week. This is day two. No more business for now, let's just enjoy the pre-supper drinks shall we?"

It was Captain Smith's turn. "Now, about supper. My guys had a great time getting the provisions from the supermarket, they were ordered to get what they liked, budget ten euros a meal, so it's a choice of microwave chicken chow mein or madras beef curry. I'll be happy to take your orders."

Baldwin's eyes brightened. "Two lots of curry please."

Three decks below them, in the bowels of the super-yacht two of the SBS team were making some final modifications to the ship's citadel, reversing the security to ensure that the strong room was impossible to break out of, as opposed to its proper function of keeping pirates out and the owner safe, in case of attack. But as priority they'd already found out how to crack the wine cellar.

*

Forty Eight

Sveta Kovacs checked into the Gran-Hotel-Miramar in Malaga. She'd just picked the hotel online because she liked the picture that she'd found on the web. Built in 1926, it was an architectural masterpiece. The cost of just under €500 a night was immaterial to her, but sufficient to indicate that it was a hotel of some standing and therefore worthy of the patronage of a billionairess.

Within three hours of her checking in, Baskerville in Cheltenham was on her trail with real time monitoring of all major hotel registers in the greater Malaga area. It matched the name she'd used with one or the list obtained by MI6 from Budapest and then rooted into the hotels security to camera system to confirm a facial match.

Josh Packard messaged Macsen and headed to his office.

"We've got her – or rather Baskerville has. His 'brain transplant' warm patch has been brought online and seems to be doing well."

"Great, now we're getting ahead of her game. What monitoring are you setting up?"

"I'm setting up e-monitoring of all the hotel's systems including internal phones, hotel intra- and inter-nets. GCHQ is burrowing into all the nearby cellphone tower links and then cross linking them to Baskerville. We're deploying a six person watch team in three shifts of two watchers in readiness for *Alice's* anticipated movement. I'm not anticipating serious countersurveillance from her, so I think that will be enough – it's hard to get any more bodies as our local resources are heavily stretched on a drugs operation."

"Isn't drugs a police matter?"

"Normally, but there are links to a hot Moroccan terrorist cell unrelated to this operation."

"OK, then brief Barbary and finalize the details of 'Elevator'. We'll initiate once we're absolutely sure that *Alice* is tied in with *Boromir*. Otherwise we'll initiate 'Elevator Two'."

"Are we happy with Barbary being in operational control?"

"Sounds like you have doubts. Don't worry, he'll be under real-time direction from us here."

"My biggest concern is that we cannot decrypt the cellphone comms in real time if she is using Signal or WhatsApp."

"Yes but we have at least one of *Boromir's* cellphone numbers. We know her room number at the hotel?"

"Yes, Suite 96 at the Gran Miramar."

"Well GCHQ should be able to detect any cellphone number used from that physical location by triangulation. We just have to tie that to *Boromir's* location and phone and we can kick off 'Elevator'."

"It's a long shot."

"It's all we've got unless they arrange a physical meet."

"If."

"Yes, if."

It was time for his run, and like it or not he'd have to meet the man in the park. His bitcoin account had taken a hit with the raid by *Alice* although he had been relatively lucky – nothing stolen, just the drop in price. Obviously too small to be bothered with. Anyway, it was his policy never to keep all his nest eggs in one basket.

*

Baldwin did not sleep well. He'd seen better plans on the back of a cigarette packet.

Dinner had been a strange affair of wine and takeaways held in the main dining room on a table which had 20 places. Despite Barbary's orders one bottle of wine was poured, a Chateau Margaux. No questions were asked about its source. Sara Carmichael, the putative ship's 'chef' and hostess, was one of the first females to make the front line in the Royal Marines, but she was not SBS. She had the good sense not to serve the takeaways in their foil cartons but on the best tableware - Barbary was very conscious that they themselves could be under observation from *Arabian Princess* or any of the myriad super-yachts and shore-side establishments around the dock. A couple of the team kept a watch from the bridge, not unusual on a superyacht.

Only five of them sat at the table – Barbary, Baldwin, Stone, Captain Smith and his lieutenant, Hugh Shapter, as Sara served their suppers on Tobin's best dinnerware. The talk was about sport, Malaga, the weather and the ship in general terms. Baldwin avoided any tales about his experiences aboard in Kefalonia. Smith tried to keep the conversation moving along but however well he tried, it was a stilted experience and all were glad when it was over in less than an hour.

After dinner they moved up to the owner's study. It was an expansive cabin on the top deck next to the owner's personal suite. Equipped with full audio visual equipment it was obviously set up for business meetings both on the ship and remotely via satellite.

Barbary avoided anything electronic and the study – along with the rest of the vessel – had been swept by Smith's radio man and pronounced clean. The techie had been impressed by Tobin's electronic surveillance countermeasures, announcing that 'the owner must have had plenty to hide', at which Baldwin had bitten his tongue.

Barbary ran through the plan using a whiteboard. He wrote Operation Elevator at the top using a black marker and underlined it in red. He then wrote the operational objective in red.

TAKE ALICE INTO CUSTODY

"You should have been a teacher" Baldwin said,

"Shut up until I've finished. If you do have a question then put your hand up like a good boy and I may let you ask it." Baldwin shook his head as Barbary continued with the details.

Baldwin again raised his objections to the idea that both he and Stone should be put in the same location as *Alice*. "It's bloody stupid and an unnecessary risk. If that's the quality of the planning then we're already fucked. What in hell do you hope to gain by this?"

Smith fought hard to suppress a smile as Barbary responded "I happen to agree with you Baldwin, but it's an operational requirement specified by London. There may be other factors in play here that we do not need to know about."

"If she gets the wind up then the operation is blown out of the water."

"Not necessarily."

"So where is this all to happen?"

"We don't know precisely where yet, but it will obviously be at night because a daylight snatch is too risky. What we do know is that tonight she dined at an Italian restaurant, 'Sotto Voce'. We have a surveillance team on her. They'e codenamed Cleaners and the van is rigged as a Telfonica maintenance van. The plan is to take her tomorrow night wherever she dines. People in Spain eat late in the evening, so it'll be dark when she finishes her meal. She came out of Sotto Voce just after ten thirty tonight. We'll have to flexible and fast. You and Telion will dine in the restaurant."

"Great, so she will see us."

"And you will see her, but without showing recognition."

"She'll run."

"Perhaps. I will be in a people carrier waiting for the Go from you by text if she does a runner. I'll have two others there, should be enough to cope. Or, if she plays it cool then when she has paid her bill you both follow her outside the restaurant and confront her, say 'Hi Sveta why don't you come with us?' The people carrier will be waiting and we'll bundle her in."

"Oh yeah, that'll work, her screaming and all."

"There'll be plenty of shouting and screaming don't worry."

"How?"

"My two guys will get into a brawl outside the restaurant as a distraction so there will be plenty of commotion. Alice will get caught up in it and get pulled into the van."

"And you think that will not draw attention?"

Smith looked at Baldwin, intrigued by his approach to an op and his attitude to authority, almost as if he didn't want to be there, as if he was barely under Barbary's control. But it was important to uncover risks, challenge assumptions and improve the plan.

There was clearly some bad blood between them. It made him uncomfortable as the command line would be split during the op. He had no idea why Baldwin was on this op, it seemed a really bad decision. He, Smith, would have no control over Baldwin who appeared to be a potentially loose cannon. His opinion of Barbary was low, but he had to stay in line. Unlike Baldwin. What on earth did Barbary have on Baldwin?

Barbary continued. "The people carrier will head back here and we'll put her in the citadel down below. That's *Alice* taken care of. Phase two is a little more complex and that's where Captain Smith's people come in. *Boromir* is a much more dangerous animal. We are pretty sure that he is on the *Arabian Princess* tonight. So far, London has detected no contact between *Alice* and *Boromir* but they do not believe in coincidence. Neither do I. Here's what we're going to do."

When Barbary had finished outlining Phase 2, Baldwin pointed at the still empty whiteboard. "That's some plan we have there. It's just as well you're not a teacher. Do you think it will work?"

"It's London's strategy, the detailed plan is mine. Just do your bit."

As a former Royal Marine - and a good judge of character (at least in his own mind), Baldwin respected Smith and realized that Phase 2 was not going to be easy. After 90 minutes or so the briefing ended and Smith headed off with Shapter to refine the details of the plan and assign their team's individual responsibilities.

The master cabin was just a door away from the study and as Stone closed the door behind them Baldwin said "that's the worst fucking set of plans I've heard since Portsmouth's owners said they'd get to the Premier League."

"Yes, but Redknapp did it didn't he?"

"Wow, I didn't know you followed Pompey."

"There's a lot you don't know about me, but you *can* get to know me better."

"No way, let's keep it professional. You know how I feel about getting involved with you. And all this stupid business about me posing as a multi-millionaire, it's bloody ridiculous!"

"You're here as a filthy rich arsehole, so act like one. You can do the arsehole bit well, you just need to act filthy rich. And horny."

"Very funny!" And it was. Stone giggled and Baldwin dissolved into laughter.

"I couldn't resist it. Can we forget about all the crap for just this evening? Look, I do understand how you feel, I can see it in your eyes. Forget involvement, just let yourself go for once, with me. Just do the horny bit. For me."

She reached out for him, but he moved away, backing into an armchair and falling in to it. "No JC, it's just not going to happen and I'm sorry to disappoint you. Anyway a billionaire would probably have half a dozen Russian call girls getting all wet in the jacuzzi."

"Hey, you're only a multi-millionaire, not a billionaire, so don't overplay it!"

"I'm not." *But I am rich. Jesus.* "I'm sleeping on that settee over there. You go and enjoy the Jacuzzi. You should set it on cold. Very cold. Good night, JC." *Nothing new – everyone had heightened hormones before an op.*

*

Forty Nine

At VX, Josh met with Macsen. There had been no calls detected from *Alice's* number at the Gran Miramar hotel, and no cellphone activity from the *Arabian Princess.* Elevator Two was given the green light.

Plans rarely survive first contact with the enemy, but this plan didn't even get as far as contact.

Baldwin looked at the maitre d' and handed him a €50 note, his own. "Sorry, we've changed our plans."

"Out, now, Emma, quickly, no fuss, no arguments. We're compromised." Baldwin took Stone's elbow and turned her smoothly towards the door.

He hustled her out through the door of the restaurant. They turned to the right and Baldwin raised his right cuff and spoke.

"This is Mad Hatter. Elevator Two to Concierge, abort, I say again abort."

His earpiece crackled. "Mad Hatter, Concierge What's going on?"

Baldwin was almost shouting into the mike in the cuff of his smart tailored jacket, the top half of a white linen suit. By now they were crossing the road to a garden area, moving away from the restaurant José Carlos Garcia on the Paseo de la Farola. The road ran along the dock area in Malaga just a short distance from the *Adventurer*. Baldwin's earpiece crackled again.

"You're asking me? I'm aborting that's what's going on, per protocol. Do you guys know your arses from your fucking elbows?"

"Concierge here. Copy that Mad Hatter and watch your language. All Units, this is Concierge abort abort. I say Elevator Two to ground floor."

"Mad Hatter your car is coming, we'll debrief in ten minutes."

"Make it bloody quick!"

Thirty seconds later a green Bentley Flying Spur V8 whispered to a halt beside them. Before the driver could climb out Baldwin had opened the door for Stone and walked round to the other side. He climbed in and tried to slam the door quickly but the dampened mechanism only allowed the door to close with a gentle but solid, expensive-sounding clunk.

The car accelerated away soundlessly into the heavy evening traffic.

"Problem Sir?"

"This plan is a crock of shit if you really want to know, Taff. I'm dressed like I'm going to a pyjama party and we nearly got made by the targets."

"It might be a crock of shit, Sir, but I'm really enjoying driving these wheels."

Ten minutes later Baldwin looked at Barbary, his anger obvious, Smith beside him.

"Why did you call an abort, Baldwin?"

"Because you or London hadn't planned for the circumstances at all. Somebody fucked up big time, here, on the ground. We could have screwed everything. I'm beginning to wonder if London actually planned for this to go tits-up. It stinks to high heaven."

There was a stunned silence, finally ended only by 3 blasts of a ship's siren as it maneuvered in the docks.

Barbary looked at Baldwin. "Don't be bloody stupid! Where did you get that insane idea?"

"Sveta Kovacs was having dinner with ABZ or Boromir as you Boy Scouts call him."

"Impossible, Boromir is on the *Arabian Princess* right now."

Baldwin looked up at the ceiling of the owner's study and let out a long sigh. Then he shook his head. "No, he's bloody well not. I saw him as the maitre d' was checking our non-existent booking. It's bloody lucky neither of them saw us. They're probably on the bread and butter pudding now, or the brandies if they're in a hurry for whatever it is you didn't tell us."

"Are you sure it was him?"

"Of course I'm fucking sure. I chased the bastard halfway across Morocco last year."

Stone was scathing. "And now we've probably missed the opportunity to find out what in hell they're cooking up."

"Did *you* see Boromir?"

"Yes, with Alice at a corner table. We saw her go in. We went in five minutes later as planned. She had her back to us, but I could see him clearly. He glanced at me, but he's never seen me before."

Barbary looked at Baldwin. "How come he didn't he make you then?"

"He very nearly did. I'd already seen him and I turned my head away as I pointed to the reservations book ready to bribe the maitre d' for a table. - with my own cash, I might add. Then I turned Stone and we headed out."

"Maybe London can get CCTV from the street or the restaurant. It would at least prove or disprove who you saw."

"Whatever. I'm not sure that we can believe London anymore. I know who I saw. But what's more worrying is that he can get off the *Arabian Princess* seemingly at will. I thought you people had him under surveillance. And didn't you have watchers outside the restaurant?"

For the first time, Barbary looked unsure. "We do. We did."

Smith and Shapter looked at one another and then Smith coughed. "It seems to me that we need a new plan, Mr Colville, after a few details have been checked."

Barbary replied. "We can still take them when they leave. We have maybe one hour tops to re-plan. Captain, get your team ready to move."

It was Smith's turn. "That would be a bad move. We don't know what we're getting in to and we haven't planned for a double pickup – we'd need more people and it would be too obvious. The best you could do is follow them after they leave."

Barbary was reluctant to let it go, but Macsen intervened over the open link. "London here. Baldwin, stop talking all that crap about London. Barbary, put tails on the targets and we'll re-plan overnight. Make sure you find out how he got off that ship. We'll contact you at midnight after we've reviewed the intel. Understood?"

"Understood."

"London out."

Barbary closed the comms. "Let's meet again tomorrow at oh eight hundred".

"Come on JC, we're dressed for a night out. I'm hungry, let's go out on the town."

"No-one leaves this ship tonight."

"Fuck off MISTER COLVILLE."

"Stone, Baldwin, you're to stay aboard. That's a direct order. Captain Smith, stop them!"

Smith looked at Colville and didn't move as Baldwin and JC left the study. "Sorry Mr Colville, I didn't quite hear that. Say again."

"Stop them, they're confined to the bloody ship!"

"Ah. OK is that what you said. I say, it seems that they've already left. That's unfortunate. I think you might have lost the confidence of your team Mister Colville. We'll leave you to work out how to rectify the situation while I go and send my report to my CO. We'll see you at oh eight hundred. Come on Hugh, let's head to the radio shack."

"Wait, wait. We need to work this out here, not in London."

"Very well. That would seem to be an eminently sensible approach to the issue Mister Colville. Why don't you take some time with your own people from the consulate to find out how *Boromir* got past the watchers – if of course there were any – so that we can be sure it doesn't happen again - and so that all our people know *exactly* what they are going in to. That way we can maximize the probability of achieving the mission objectives with minimal risk to our people. When you have some answers then we can discuss our options. And you need to get London in line. Any time tonight, whenever you are ready. In the meantime I'll send an anodyne progress report to my CO. Hugh, let's go."

"Where would you go Taff?"

"For a good night out I'd head along the coast to Marbella, the Golden Mile. I was there a few years back on a package holiday with the wife. At least she was the wife then, before she…well you know how it is with this job. It's about fifty ks, should take us about ten minutes in this beauty."

"Ten minutes?"

"Just kidding. I have to watch the speed limit – operational security and all that. But not too much."

"We may be a few hours, what will you do?"

"I'll find a fish and chip shop, there are plenty here. Have a few beers as well, man. After that I'll look for an upmarket flop-house. That's my three hours sorted. Hmm, if only. You're a multimillionaire, billionaire, whatever, don't forget. Such people have bodyguards. That's me."

"We'll be fine, Taff. I can take care of myself."

"That's as maybe, but my orders are clear. I have to play my part – and you have to play yours. I'll be sticking with you, Sir."

"I'm not a bloody officer, no 'Sir' needed."

"Yes, Sir, but you are my very rich employer. And you tip me generously and regularly, don't you? Sir?"

Baldwin smiled. "Yes, if you say so, Taff, if you say so. But people like me don't carry cash. You'll have to ask my wife, she doubles up as my PA."

Taff laughed as he raised his wrist to his mouth. “Concierge, Porter One here. We’re heading up the coast. Mr Becket and Ms Freud are going out on the town.”

“Porter One, Concierge. Tell them to have fun.”

Stone just managed to suppress a laugh. *Wife? Maybe he is loosening up at last.*

In a hotel about two kilometers away from *Adventurer*, a member of the Russian consulate in Malaga was meeting some tourists, two men and two women who had flown in that afternoon from Madrid. The tourists were familiar with the area although their most recent mission had been in Portugal, in a town with the name of Olhão, a couple of months previously. This time they would be doing more than covert observation. The briefing took an hour.

They opened the bags that their controller had delivered and checked the contents. Yuri Grigorovich and Boris Ivanov then took the bags down to the camper van in the hotel car park and stowed them. Boris checked the fuel for the long drive to the private airfield. Camper vans had worked well for them but they would not be doing an overnight stop with a passenger aboard.

*

Fifty

It was Spanish dinner time, just after 9 pm and another hot late summer evening with twilight and a new moon just expiring. The street was busy with Porches, Ferraris and the toys of the rich and powerful as another night of their excesses got under way.

Baldwin looked around carefully while Stone checked out a brightly lit shop window. They were still a little jaded after the previous evening in Marbella as arm in arm he led her gently along the side-walk towards Bon Vivant, an exclusive high-ticket restaurant with French cuisine. There was now a new, simpler plan.

They were making a pretense of window shopping. Baldwin was not keen on the clothes Stone pointed out as suitable for him. Then they came to a lingerie shop. Stone stopped and pointed at a set of flimsies. “How do you think I’d look in those, Sam? Baldwin half smiled, half turned walking away. “Come on Emma, we’ll be late for dinner.” *Pretty good I think.*

Taff’s ‘thing’ was cars, and as he eased the Bentley slowly along, 50 meters or so behind his charges, he whistled in surprise as he saw a black Mercedes-Maybach S600 Pullman Guard glide by and slow down. It was a car that only the very rich and powerful – or very frightened - traveled in, a step above even the wheels he commanded that evening.

Cars might have been his thing, but he recognized this model because he had once been involved in the prep to kidnap the head of state of a rogue African country. The mission had been aborted at the last moment, but he still remembered that its 5 tons was powered by a 523 HP V12 engine and was as bombproof as a car could be. Strange, even here in Marbella.

“Concierge, Porter One”

“Porter One, Concierge, go ahead.”

“Just been passed by what I think could be a Cat A’s car, a Maybach Pullman. No plates. One lead car, one pursuit car, both black Mercedes. Tinted windows, no personnel count. Thought you should know in case there’s someone important in town.”

“We’re not aware of anyone to be concerned about beyond the usual mix. No plates you said?”

“Yes.”

“Not good, I’m checking our Embassy lists and we’re streaming footage from the Cleaners van. Analyzing it now.”

"They're slowing. looks like they're stopping. Shit. Right outside the restaurant."

Baldwin and Stone continued strolling apparently contently along the sidewalk towards the restaurant. Then he looked puzzled as he saw that the chairs had been tilted up against the pavement tables. There were no outside diners. They were about 50 yards away.

Stone caught the look. "What's wrong Sam?"

"Everything. Again."

He broke in to the radio chatter. "Concierge, Mad Hatter. There's a heavy duty team just getting out of the cars outside the target restaurant. Very heavy, I'm counting at least six guys, with, I think, just one VIP. What's going on?"

"Mad Hatter, join Porter One and abort immediately. London's orders. There is a Cat A VIP there. Acknowledge immediate abort."

"Abort acknowledged. Moving now."

"All Escalator units return to Ground Floor. Escalator Two abort."

A bad plan was one thing, but getting involved in anything off-color near a Cat A subject – possibly a Head of State - in public was beyond risky unless they had planned for it in advance.

"Cat A. So that's why we couldn't get a table tonight. And Alice is definitely in there?"

"Yes, and Boromir. Our Cleaners have footage of them entering, but separately. He's slipped off the ship again without us picking him up."

"If he ever was on the ship. Escalator Two is a total wash-out."

"Drop it. Get back to Ground Floor now. We're not going anywhere near a Cat A person unless we know what this is all about."

"For once you are bloody right."

"Concierge, Porter, turning around now."

There was a gap in the traffic approaching as Taff accelerated hard then hit the brakes, pulling the wheel hard to the left and holding the handbrake. The Bentley executed a perfect handbrake turn, tyres screeching across the road opposite the restaurant and started to head back towards Baldwin and Stone.

Then as Baldwin and Stone moved to the kerbside and watched it approach, less than 50 meters away, the front of the restaurant bulged out and split open. An orange explosion was funneled straight out by the solid old stone walls of the building, pushing restaurant tables, chairs, debris and bodies outward, driving the two guards and the woman in pieces against the Bentley, flipping it across the road onto the Cleaners' Telefonica van, flattening its roof.

The huge bang was followed by a roar of rushing air and debris crashing.

Then there was an eerie silence which seemed to stretch for an eternity, seemingly punctuated only by the tinkling of glass, the high frequency sounds. Flames licked greedily in the wreckage. Then the screaming started, audible even through the growing cacophony of car and building alarms.

*

Six hours later Malaga was in lockdown with a curfew in operation. The world news channels were screaming about the assassination of the King of Morocco on Spanish soil. Moroccan Armed Forces were on full alert as the King's seventeen year-old son Hassan assumed the Moroccan throne. His first act as King was to declare a state of emergency. Unrest was spreading across the country.

The next day the Polisario Front claimed responsibility for the assassination as sporadic bombings took place in Rabat and other major cities across Morocco and public tension ramped up. The US, UK and EU condemned the assassin and issued statements in support of the Moroccan monarchy and government.

Spain, the former colonial power, was formally bound by its membership of the EU and was politically unable to despatch troops to bolster the Moroccan government. But it did so anyway.

A further day later the *Auric Adventurer* cleared harbor, heading west, with three crew and two passengers still missing. There were no captives in the citadel deep down in the vessels hull, and Barbary was en-route to London.

*

Three days after the assassination, Emmet Macsen stood in front of Brewell's desk in Vauxhall Cross. 'C' looked at Macsen, disbelief on his face.

"She's what?"

"Active, Sir, or at least she was. GCHQ have just confirmed that Alice's cell phone was active fifteen minutes after the bomb went off. They triangulated that activity to her hotel room. She called a burner phone they think. A short data burst, that's all."

"Why didn't they tell us before?"

Macsen grimaced. "They did. In all the confusion after the explosion I missed the notification. It's in the log. They've now pulled hotel video footage which shows her returning, and then checking out fifteen minutes later. You can have my resignation. Here." He placed an envelope on Brewell's desk.

"Put that away until we work out what to do. Her fucking trail is stone cold now." *You're not the only one who missed that and didn't check the log.*

"Yes sir."

"What a bloody disaster. Thank God we're in the clear, at least for now. Stay on top of that, we can't let the CNI find out that some of the people were ours – or at least SBS."

"Of course Sir. It should be straightforward, all three were SBS people, but they were carrying solid legend IDs. They will hold water with the Centro Nacional de Inteligencia. The Bentley was a rental."

"But one of the Cleaners was in the observation van – it was rigged as a Telefonica maintenance van wasn't it? And it had our surveillance equipment in it?"

"Correct, but that shouldn't be a problem. We're clean in that sense. The gear was mostly off-the-shelf stuff, and the van burned out, nothing should be traceable back to us. We've put out some boilerplate rumors about drug gangs and involvement with the Polisario Front trafficking drugs to fund their activities."

"Good. And still no news of Telion and Mad Hatter?"

"Nothing Sir. Her phone is dead and we can hardly go asking the Guardia or CNI for information."

"Quite. But they could be alive?"

"Possibly. GCHQ have still not been able to find any CCTV footage from the area. It looks as if it was disabled around the time of the attack, so there's no footage of them. We don't yet have information on all the dead – the Spaniards had clamped down really tight. We have no information either way."

"All right. Let's move from the housekeeping back to the main operation. Now, if Alice is still in play then it might explain why the cryptocurrency markets have nose-dived even more over the past two days. She's up to something. And if *she's* not a victim then Boromir could have got out as well. I don't think that it was luck. No, they were part of a plan, the question is, whose plan? What the hell was going on there?"

"I doubt we'll ever know, Sir."

"Perhaps. But we'll have to let things quieten down in Malaga before we send anyone back there. I hear that the Guardia and CNI have got over fifty Russians under interrogation. That was a good bit of disinformation you sowed."

"I'm not sure that it was Sir. Moscow was all over Alice in Portugal. They could have picked up her trail again in Malaga. And we know they were watching Boromir in Rabat. He lost our people in Malaga, he would surely have lost them as well."

"Yes, but how?" 'C' watched Macsen carefully. "We've got too many unanswered questions here. Could there be a leak?"

Macsen didn't miss a beat. "It's always possible Sir."

*

Epilogue

"I've just been reviewing the file, though I doubt it will ever be closed. Telion and Mad Hatter are completely off our radar?"

"Yes. Not a trace since the Malaga explosion. We're fairly sure their bodies were not in with the dead or injured. Looks like it was planned well in advance. Baldwin had left his yacht's AIS unit hidden with a mate in Gib. in the security hut at the marina. He left a phone there as well. GCHQ were monitoring the AIS and phone but were fooled good and proper. It looked to them as if the yacht was still in the marina."

"No-one from the Commission thought to go and check with eyeball mark one?"

"Er, no. And as you know, Barbary is not there, and we haven't replaced him yet. Anyway Baldwin's yacht is not anywhere in Gibraltar. Customs and Immigration say that they cleared it to leave for Morocco with a skipper – duly authorized with a letter from the owner – by the name of Liam O'Neill. That was just after Baldwin and Telion traveled to Jerez to catch the jet to Malaga. We reckon Baldwin's pal sailed the yacht to Tangier and met him – or them – there. He and Telion could easily have taken a ferry across from Spain to Tangier."

"And what does Baldwin's pal Liam say?"

"He caught a ferry back from Tangier and he's now gone on holiday – to Brazil apparently, or so he told his employers. Said he'd be away a few months, so they terminated his employment."

"What a bloody mess. Can they be tracked with satellites?"

"In theory yes, but it's too small a vessel in such a large area of the Atlantic. But there's probably nothing we could do anyway. Besides which, they're hardly a priority are they, Sir. I reckon they are on their way to the Canaries."

"Yes, given that Boromir and Alice are still off our grid."

"And Baskerville hasn't had a sniff of them, couldn't pick up the trail from that single data call after the explosion. But at least he doesn't sleep – one of them is sure to show up sooner or later."

"I bloody well hope so, but we can't run this show based on hope, can we? Follow the money – that's the way, but this damned cryptocurrency is so hard to track. Is it linked to that QKD set-up that Alice had? We never did uncover it's relevance, did we?"

"No, Sir, but we certainly need to find out if someone else was linked in to it. The techies are still saying her set up could not have worked based on the little we do know, despite the Chinese advances in the satellite technology. There was bugger all left of the Saluscent site for us to look at, even if we could have got in. And the Portuguese Intelligence Service and their armed forces are being very cagey about it."

"Yes, there's been some blowback at the Foreign Secretary and he's dumping on me, but there's no real hard evidence. It's Borthwick who's under the microscope, not us directly. And the Russians too - our man in Lisbon is starting to hear whispers about clear proof of their involvement. No details yet, unfortunately."

"It would be good to nail something on those bastards."

"We do have the bits of that crashed drone that we can use, though the FO will probably not publicize it – you know how cautious those politicos are. And now, finally, operational personnel – I need to write up their performance reviews."

"Yes Sir. A mixed bag of reports, I should think."

"Definitely. I took a look at Packard's personnel file. There's something not quite right there, but I can't put my finger on it yet. What do you think?"

"He seems to be doing his work well, you'll have read my last review from a few months back."

"Yes, but it wasn't glowing was it?"

"Not really, but whose is? "

"Yes, and I'll need to update yours. The only one who's come out of this with any real credit is Baskerville. By the way, are you going for a run later?"

"Yes, with Packard, actually, Sir. Why do you ask?"

"Just wondering. It's been hectic the last few weeks and normal life has been suspended."

"Yes, Sir. Then I'd best get going then if there's nothing else."

"Go ahead. Meanwhile I'll start trying to cover all our arses. Oh, yes, I do need you to get hold of that Major Smith in Poole. Charles Tobin has been chasing me. Something about valuable vintage wine unaccounted for when the Jollies returned his super-yacht to him in Gibraltar. Get Tobin off my bloody back will you?"

*

At that moment, approximately 1180 miles away on a bearing of 196 degrees magnetic from Brewell's office in Vauxhall Cross, *Rubaiyat* was making a shade over 12 knots surfing down a wave. She was 48 hours out from Tangier and they were averaging just over 8 knots. The wind was blowing about 15 knots out of the east, the sky was clear and the air off Morocco was hot, the scents exotic. Cape Safi was about 100 miles to the east.

Baldwin passed a cold beer to Stone and she raised her bottle in a toast.

"Here's to the future."

"I can't argue with that, as long as it includes plenty of sleep in the next few days."

"Yes, it's been bloody hectic."

"If this weather holds we should be reach Mindelo in the Cape Verde Islands in six or seven days time. We can spend a couple of weeks there getting ready for the Atlantic."

"Why not the Canaries?"

"That's a bit too obvious, a bit too European for my tastes. And a bit too handy for Six, those bastards never let go. That was a good idea of yours to move some funds into Bitcoin and get us some independence. Should get us through the next few years." *Until Konstanz & Young have finished selling up Ellie's estate.*

"Seems like they're hard to trace and flexible to use."

"But they can still be stolen. Or so it seems."

"So, where are we headed after the Cape Verdes?"

"How long have you got?"

"A few years maybe."

"Then we'll go wherever you want to go – South America, Australia. Maybe start with the Gambia. Maybe even visit Liam in Brazil after that. What do you fancy?"

"I'll tell you what I fancy." And with one deft movement she slipped off her bikini top.

He looked at her, nodded and smiled.

"OK. That seems like a good plan. We've only got a few years you said, so we'd better get started. But first I need check for ships. This is a very busy shipping route."

"I've already checked. There's nothing within 30 miles."

She stood and slipped out of her bikini bottoms. "And nothing within these." He watched as she twirled them - and threw them.

Despite the breeze, her throw was good and the bikini panties landed squarely on his head.

He pulled them off and smiled again, pressed them briefly to his nose and threw them back at her. She thought that he was happier than she'd ever seen him. But how long would it last?

Then they heard a snort of air and turned to watch as a pod of dolphins raced across from their port side and began to weave around, under and across their bows.

"That's a good omen you know."

"I certainly hope so, skipper."

"Yes, there's fish about. I'd better get a fishing line rigged."

"There's plenty of time for that, but some things really can't wait any bloody longer. I'm giving the orders today. Come here you old goat. Now!"

*

Author's Notes

The original title of this book was going to be 'The Nonce Exploit'. By now you should know what that means in the context of this book. However, the word 'nonce' has an unpleasant slang usage in the UK where it refers to a sex offencer – usually a pedophile. I thank my sister for having pointed that out to me.

Explaining even simply how Blockchain technology works is beyond the scope of this book – and fully understanding it is now well beyond the scope of my brain. So, I have tried to strike the right balance between informing you, the reader, and burying you in turgid mathematical detail. I hope that I have succeeded.

The 51% and 34% attacks on Bitcoin really did take place, but in other aspects there is practically zero probability of a fraud taking place by hacking the blockchain system, at least of Bitcoin. There have been several high value cryptocurrency scams but these have operated mainly by cheating outside of the mathematical structure of the currencies, for example by Dr Ruja Ignatova (the OneCoin scam). State currencies such as the e-Yuan of China and the CryptoRuble undoubtedly have tracking built in by their sponsoring governments, and no doubt, other back doors as well. Unlike Bitcoin, the source code of their software is not open to public examination.

As to MI6 I have simplified the command and control structure (as I understand it) in the interests of readability. 'C' as he or she is known these days, holds largely a political and administrative role, which is of course why the name and face is publicly known and no longer secret. Day to day operational control is exercised at Deputy Chief levels and below, and the names of these post holders are secret to the UK public although I would bet that they are well known in Moscow or Beijing.

On 17th July 2014 a Malaysian Airlines scheduled passenger flight from Amsterdam to Kuala Lumpur was shot down by a Buk 9M83 surface-to-air missile while flying over eastern Ukraine. All 283 passengers and 15 crew on Flight 17 were killed. The responsibility for the launch authority is unknown. My story has parallels but is speculative fiction.

Any errors are entirely down to me, but I hope the book has given you a flavor of the cryptocurrency subject and some enjoyment reading it.

I don't know how the future of cryptocurrencies will pan out. In early 2021, Bitcoin prices peaked at just over US$60,000, then fell back by mid-year to about US$30,000.

During the writing of this book I did buy a small quantity of Bitcoin and Ethereum (the minimum, less than $500 in total) to understand how the trading and security processes worked. I bought when the Bitcoin price was $6,000 and sold again when it had gone up and then back down to $6,000 – that was a surprise! No profit. I never mined any and my wallets are empty!

The bitcoin mining industry worldwide consumes more power than many small countries. China has a huge bitcoin mining industry fueled in the main by coal fired power stations and there are signs that China is now starting to limit cryptocurrency mining.

And if I did know how the future would pan out then I'd bet on it. But not yet.

Thank you for reading the story.

James Marinero,
Bay of Islands, New Zealand,
2021

About the Author

James Marinero grew up in West Wales and has at various times been a chef, a milkman, maths lecturer and private tutor. Then he spent over 30 years in IT as a consultant and project manager and ran his own computer business for several years.

He has been passionately involved with boats and the sea for over fifty years and is now achieving a lifelong ambition to write novels and entertain readers. He spends much of his writing time on his boat, which he has sailed extensively in the Atlantic and as far as New Zealand (2020/2022 during the Covid crisis).

During his various careers he has worked in the Middle East, Russia, Scandinavia, the US, Kazakhstan and much of Europe. His educational background includes a bachelor's degree in Physics, a postgraduate degree in Oceanography and an MBA.

His personal interests, career, education and travel background have equipped him well to write adventure and techno-thriller novels.

When he is not on his boat he lives on the Hampshire coast.

Blockchain Exploit
Cause of All Causes
Sword of Allah
Sicilian Channel
Gate of Tears

Available for Kindle, iPad/iPhone, Kobo and all e-readers as well as paperback at your local bookstore.

You can follow James on Facebook Twitter @jamesmarinero . On Pinterest you will find many of my research photos from around the world. Check out his website where he occasionally has a free book on offer.

References and Further Reading

Bank Hacking:

https://thehackernews.com/2016/06/ukrainian-bank-swift-hack.html

African Cryptocurrency:

https://www.express.co.uk/finance/city/913853/africa-nurucoin-ethereum-Isaac-Muthui-Venezuelan-President-Nicolas-Maduro
https://www.nurucoin.com/

Technologies:

RSK
https://www.rsk.co/ **RSK** is the first open-source smart contract platform with a 2-way peg to Bitcoin that also rewards the Bitcoin miners via merge-mining, allowing them to actively participate in Smart Contracts

ANONYMITY MYTH – CRYPTOCURRENCIES

http://www.sciencemag.org/news/2016/03/why-criminals-cant-hide-behind-bitcoin

CRYPTOCURRENCIES

Russian CryptoRuble
https://futurism.com/vladimir-putin-develop-new-cryptocurrency-CryptoRuble/

Venezuelan Petro:
https://www.coindesk.com/venezuelas-petro-will-harm-legitimate-cryptocurrencies-says-brookings/

CYBERWARFARE

Russian attack on Ukrainian messaging app
http://fortune.com/2016/12/22/russia-ukraine-app/

QUANTUM CRYPTOGRAPHY

Quantum Key Distribution:
https://www.theregister.co.uk/2018/06/14/quantum_crypto_commercial_optical_network/

Chinese Quantum Entanglement Test Satellite
https://www.newscientist.com/article/2101071-china-launches-worlds-first-quantum-communications-satellite/

CRYPTO SCAMS

OneCoin
https://www.bbc.com/news/technology-50417908

Aircraft Shot Down Over Ukraine

https://en.wikipedia.org/wiki/Malaysia_Airlines_Flight_17

Limited offer: get your FREE thriller:

jamesmarinero.com/free-thriller-book/

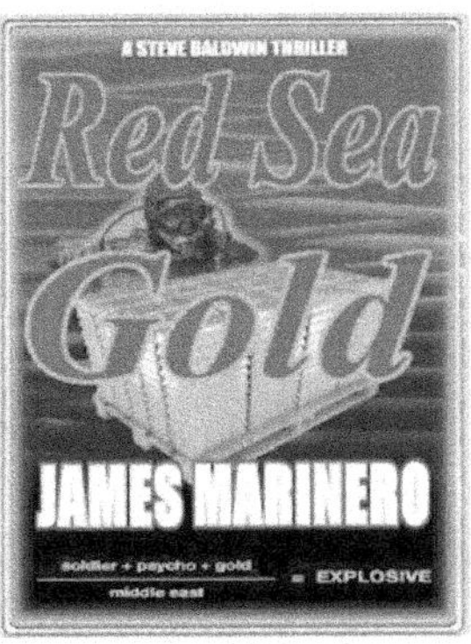

Steve Baldwin (an ex Royal-Marine) and Maruškas Pavkovic (a ruthless female Serbian psychopathic assassin) collide with a gold mining entrepreneur, espionage and Chinese expansionism. Baldwin is sent on a perilous mission to investigate secret Chinese missiles buried in a Yemeni bunker.

Meanwhile, Charles Tobin (a mining billionaire), is set to manipulate the world gold market with an audacious scam backed up by revolutionary gold-extraction technology. Gold from seawater? Yes, it can be done – and the Red Sea is the Key.

Duplicity is the name of the game at all levels and NATO naval forces line up to go head to head with the Navy of the People's Republic of China – all for the sake of gold. After all, gold is power…

Mix in political intrigue and the scene is set for savage and gritty action.

This action thriller is a special abridged promotional version of 'Gate of Tears'.

jamesmarinero.com/free-thriller-book/

www.ingramcontent.com/pod-product-compliance
Lightning Source LLC
Chambersburg PA
CBHW070155260626
47160CB00002B/355

* 9 7 8 0 9 9 5 6 4 1 0 8 2 *